TAKE
TWO

A That's Entertainment Novel

By Christine Harvey

That's Entertainment Series
Take Two
In Concert
Tasty Dish
Rising Stars: a Prequel Novella

TAKE TWO

A That's Entertainment Novel

Christine Harvey

Meadow View Press

Published in the United States by Meadow View Press

Copyright © 2015 by Christine Harvey

Second Edition 2020

ISBN: 978-0-9963152-3-4

Meadow View Press
www.meadowviewpress.com

DEDICATION

For Josh
My favorite second chance...

ACKNOWLEDGMENTS

To my critique partners, amazing people and writers: Wendy Young Howard, Tammy Kaehler, Cary Sparks, and Tracy Tandy. You are more than incomparable wordsmiths, you are friends. Not only are my books improved, but I am a better person for knowing all of you. Thank you for everything, and then some.

I learned so much about writing and completing a novel, along with critiquing other people's work, from Leslie Keenan and her classes, including the Wednesday night writing group.

My parents and family always had faith that I would be published someday. There's no way to express my profound gratitude for that.

Many thanks to my nephew Ian for the kamikaze burrito segment, even though at the time he had no idea he was inspiring a scene for a novel.

CHAPTER ONE

Distracted and worried about bumping into a certain someone whose career she ruined, Samantha Jamison almost stepped on the pink-dyed Chihuahua. And she knew she was truly back in Hollywood when its owner, a woman in a micro mini and stiletto heels breezed by, surrounded by paparazzi and a film crew.

"Where is my limo?" the woman shouted into a Swarovski-studded cell phone, hefting one arm so her crocodile Gadino Bag slid into the crook of her elbow. That bag went for $40,000, easy. Samantha thought she might be one of the Real Housewives, but couldn't be certain; they all ended up looking alike to her.

"Welcome to L.A.," she muttered. To regain her composure, she smoothed her hands over the sides of her chignon, then down the front of her tailored cream suit.

She'd been in Los Angeles fifty-three minutes—twenty-seven of those spent outside of arrivals at LAX waiting for her best friend, Liz Mendenhall—but the Housewife reminded her why she'd left L.A. five years ago and vowed never to come back.

Once known as tabloid TV reporter Sami Scandal, Samantha had traded in short, curly platinum hair for long, straight, honey blonde, understated rather than overpowering makeup, and had set her mind on keeping that sellout Sami at bay. And then her best friend called, asking for a favor.

Samantha had left the tabloid news show *Celebrity Live!* in disgrace and worked as continuity supervisor for the hit TV series *Honor Bound* in Wilmington, North Carolina, the East Coast's version of Hollywood. She re-made herself along the way, and a

1

secondary reason she'd agreed to Liz's job offer was to test her transformation. Her first reason? She would do anything for her friends. And besides, she *missed* them. And against all reason, she also missed Los Angeles, a feeling she thought would never recur.

She did worry about bumping into anyone who knew her from her stint on *Celebrity Live!*, or that certain someone whose career she'd ruined. But she was determined to succeed here now that she was back. And, really, what were the odds she'd run into *him*?

She straightened, hitching her shoulder bag higher, and her gaze moved down to her feet in taupe sling backs and the teal green luggage placed around them. She'd packed as if she weren't returning, but also wouldn't be staying, selling or giving away anything that wouldn't fit in her suitcases after confirming she had all of her supplies for the production. Where she would end up after filming wrapped wasn't on her agenda yet, but like Scarlett O'Hara, she would think about that tomorrow.

And it might just be tomorrow by the time Liz showed up, she thought, slipping a hand into a pocket of her shoulder bag meant for a cell phone, and pulling out a stop watch. To be successful, a continuity supervisor had to be blessed with three things: a great memory, a strong bladder and a completely silent stopwatch. A cell phone helped, but Samantha had a block against them, and had recently lost her third one in two years. She clicked a button on the side to show the date and time, and sighed. She had now been in L.A. for fifty-six minutes, and the dense Southern California heat mixed with exhaust from the cars, buses and taxis moving along outside the terminal had built up to a stifling level.

She'd forgotten how warm it could get here; January in Wilmington still had her wearing long sleeves. She unbuttoned her jacket and fanned at her face.

Liz had perfected being spectacularly late, so Samantha expected it, but with nothing to fill her time besides watching the shouting woman, and feeling antsy to get started with her new life, her irritation at her best friend's behavior spiked. She'd give Liz another ten minutes, and then she'd get a cab. She clicked the stopwatch feature, and watched the digital numbers flash by.

The micro mini and Chihuahua Housewife shouted that they'd be hearing from her people if they didn't get someone, in a white stretch limo, in front of her, right this instant, and that their man had better get her luggage and Trixie's carrier, and no one, absolutely *no one*, was getting a tip for this, and she'd expect twenty percent off the bill. The cameras and paparazzi captured her in all her wrathful glory.

Samantha rolled her eyes. That was it. She was out of here. She didn't need to see whether Trixie and the Housewife got their limo or not. She lifted the handle of her rolling suitcase, then bent down for the others and was just heading for the taxi line when a series of honks sounded behind her.

She glanced around and saw Liz pulling up in a black Ford Excursion, so close to the curb the tires rubbed against the edge with a screech of hubcaps. Liz leaned toward the passenger seat and hollered out the open window. "Where're you going, Lola? We've got a movie to make."

It took a moment for Samantha to realize Liz was referencing the movie *Run Lola Run*. To Liz and their friend Gary, everything in life had a film correlation and they regularly competed for the best allusions. Gary and Liz lived pop culture.

Samantha shook her head, suppressing a smile. She rolled her luggage to the imposing car and held her arms out from her sides. "You're late."

Liz pointed at her. "So are you. You should've been back here about four and a half years ago." Without waiting for a response, she climbed out of the driver's side, leaving her door open, and ran around the back on platform Mary Jane's. Arms out, she crashed into Samantha and her luggage.

"You're here. You're finally here." She took a step back and beamed. "Did you get taller?" She glanced at Samantha's feet. "Good God, did you wear that outfit on the plane? Why aren't you wrinkled? Aren't your feet about to fall off?" Still talking, she rolled a suitcase over the curb and to the back of the SUV. "You look amazing. Completely different. I mean, you'd sent me those pictures, and I saw you two years ago when I visited—God, has it really already been two years—but there's nothing like 3D, live and in person, to see how much someone has changed." She hefted the suitcase and tossed it inside.

Samantha winced, glad she hadn't packed anything fragile, and put the second suitcase in herself.

"The hair's great. Much more natural." Liz gestured to the passenger side door. "Time for the big getaway scene. Get in, Thelma. They're not taking us alive."

Samantha stepped onto the metal running board, then pulled herself inside using a bar above her head. Liz did the same, but had to use the steering wheel for the final boost up.

"Why did you get such a huge car?" Samantha asked, reaching for her seatbelt. She glanced at the back; her suitcases seemed miles away.

"I don't see you in years and those are your first words to me?"Samantha said, "You can take the girl out of New York…"

"But you can't take New York out of the girl," Liz finished for her, a routine established when they'd first met at UCLA film school nine years earlier. Liz waved a hand around at the people on the sidewalk, then started the car. "I finally pay this beast off and suddenly everyone's driving green. Electric cars everywhere and I'm too broke from financing this movie with all my credit cards to afford one. Besides Los Angelinos are crazy with their trends. Why'd I want to be one of them?" She grinned at Samantha.

Samantha gave her an easy smile back, noting that since she'd seen her last, Liz's black pixie cut hair had gotten a little longer, and her bangs spikier, but she still wore her signature dark clothing, today's outfit a charcoal gray skirt and top embroidered with tangled purple vines.

"If I recall," Samantha said, "your first words to me were 'you're late.'"

"No. I asked where you were going because we're making a movie. *My* movie. That *I* wrote, thankyouverymuch. But your response was not a good sign for someone who's hired to pay attention to the details." Liz eased between the cars parked at the curb, wound her way through the people putting their luggage in trunks and hugging each other hello, then floored it for about five seconds until Samantha guessed the SUV was about a millimeter away from the car in front of them.

"I'm great with details." Samantha pressed her feet against the floor, thinking of her stopwatch, meticulous notes, extensive supplies and marked up script tucked away in her bag. "I'm an amazing continuity supervisor. I'm the girl who makes sure everything matches, remember? And it's an amazing script."

Liz beamed at her. "Isn't it? I can see it in lights." She swept a hand in the air. "*Broken*, starring Kevin Madison. And the Oscar for original screenplay goes to…" Her voice drifted off into a dreamy sigh.

"I can't believe you got Kevin Madison for Jack."

"I know, right? Friend of a friend thing," Liz said. "We got lucky.

He's so brilliant. Edgy, charming, dangerous, all in one package. Gary's head almost popped off when we found out we got him. He's anxious to see you, by the way."

"Kevin Madison?"

"Ha! No, just our lowly director Gary, who believes you should've visited more often." She glanced at Samantha. "His words, not mine, but I wish I'd seen you more, too."

"You know why I didn't come here." Samantha crossed her arms over her chest and stared out the windshield. "I know Gary doesn't understand, and maybe I'll tell him everything someday. But for now," she added, then drew in a sharp breath and pushed her feet against the floor again as Liz whipped around a tiny red convertible. "I forgot about your driving," she said, pressing a hand to her chest.

Liz hit the horn when someone nearby honked. "Do you remember hearing at school when we first got here that people in L.A. know how to drive better than people in New York?"

"No. Are you telling me New Yorkers are better drivers?"

"Nope. We just have more fun with all of this room," she said with a whoop.

As they headed along Century Boulevard, Liz regaled Samantha with tales of her driving experiences, especially exciting for her since she'd traded in her Honda hatchback for the Excursion. Listening with one ear, but needing to distract herself from Liz's driving, Samantha mentally reviewed the contents of her supply bag as if it were a mantra: binders, correction tape, dividers and tabs, envelopes, flashlight, folders, folding chair, hole punch, paper clips, multicolored pencils, pens, Polaroid camera and film (she was old school in this, and hadn't switched to digital camera yet), rubber bands, ruler, scissors, stapler, staples, staple remover, stopwatch—on lanyard with built in book light—and three hole paper.

She had started on a mental list of her production reports—Story Sequence, Scene Count, Page Count, Continuity Summary—and had gotten to Wardrobe Outline when Liz turned onto La Cienega and bore down on a bright yellow Ferrari. At the last moment, she cut into the other lane and Samantha felt her heart find its way back down from her throat before it started beating again.

A phone rang to the tune of the *Addams Family* theme, and Samantha glanced around, trying to figure out where the sound was coming from.

Liz's hand plunged toward the purse she'd set on the console between them and she dug into it, her gaze moving from the road to the bag and back again. When she found the phone she held it up in triumph, then clutched it to her chest after a glance at Samantha.

Liz frowned at her. "No Bluetooth. I'll talk fast."

Samantha held her hand out.

Liz tried anyway. "It could be important."

Samantha wiggled her fingers. "A higher percentage of cell phone users get in accidents than any other drivers, even teenagers." Samantha didn't want to think about the disaster she'd caused with her own cell five years ago, one having nothing to do with driving.

Liz made a growling noise, then thrust the phone at her. Samantha flipped it open and put it to her ear; it sounded like someone was calling from underwater. She rolled her eyes, then said, "Liz Mendenhall's cell phone" in a loud, perky voice.

There was a pause, then, "Liz Mendenhall's cell phone isn't usually so sweet," came from far away on the other end.

"Gary?" Samantha smiled. "I'm so glad it's you."

Liz grumbled, "I told you it could be important. He's my *director*."

"Samantha? Smam? Why are you answering her phone?" Gary asked, then immediately said, "Ohh, she must be driving. Did you read her the riot act?"

"About her driving or about the phone?"

Liz growled at her again.

"I was just getting started on the driving part," Samantha added. "But my stomach was in my throat, so it was a little hard to talk."

"Why'd I invite you to L.A. again?" Liz asked.

Gary said something else, but his words were broken up by a garbled connection.

"What?" Samantha closed her eyes rather than witness more of Liz's Road Warrior-style driving. "I can barely hear you," she said, raising her voice. She put a hand over her other ear. "You what?"

Liz poked her in the arm. "What's going on? Is there a problem? Did he say there are problems? You need to give me the phone. I'll pull over."

Samantha eased away and made motions at Liz to leave her alone.

She heard Gary's voice raised at the other end, too. After a few more exchanges, with only bits and pieces getting through, she finally heard him say, "…her call me."

She shouted, "Okay!" into the phone, and hung up. She held the phone between her thumb and forefinger and dropped it into Liz's purse. "Call Gary," she said. "And you need a new phone."

"Can't afford it. I told you, I maxed my credit cards for this movie. Did Gary say what he wanted? Is there a problem? This film has been problematic from day one. Losing our script supervisor—"

"Continuity supervisor," Samantha corrected.

"–financing going nuts, production assistants wanting to do it, then not wanting to do it, the studio more involved than we wanted, a wardrobe designer who insists this outfit is better than that and who yells at the actors, not getting the locations we wanted, a quirky editor…"

"And you love every minute of it."

Liz banged at the huge steering wheel with one hand. "Of course I love it." She glanced down at her bag. "I just hate not being right in the middle of it." She looked at Samantha. "Did he tell you who we finally got for the female lead?"

"I'll buy you a new phone," Samantha said.

Liz waved a hand at her, and said, as if she hadn't heard, "Tracy Jennifer Lawson."

"Do you call her Tracy Jennifer?"

"She used to be *T.J.* Lawson."

"Really? Veronica from *My Favorite Neighbor*? I loved that show." Samantha remembered the character Tracy Jennifer played in a schoolgirl outfit with knee socks, all charm and bubbly personality. "I haven't seen her in anything for years."

"She went to public school after the show was cancelled, then decided she only wanted to do 'serious' films, but everyone saw her as Veronica, the girl next door, and we all know how hard it is to break out of stereotypes, especially if you're moving from TV to film. Some people have done it, of course. Will Smith. Tom Hanks. George Clooney. Johnny Depp, of course. Anthony Michael Hall—"

"He went from film to TV."

"Technicality. But he did three films in a row where he was a geek, and it took a lot of small roles and then him playing angry hotness in *Edward Scissorhands* before he could break out. Then there's Melissa Gilbert who will forever be Laura Ingalls, Richard Thomas as John Boy, and really, James Van Der Beek will always be Dawson—"

"So isn't T.J. Lawson a little young for the lead?" Samantha asked to break Liz's litany; this was a game better played with Gary.

"She's twenty."

"I was twenty once," Samantha said with a sigh. She had, in fact, been a twenty-year-old struggling actress when she'd been turned into Sami Scandal.

"We all were, honey." Liz hit the turn signal to pass another car. "She's a complete ditz, but she reads amazing. We did makeup and screen tests on her and she can look older for the part, too. And we got her just in time. She's in Quentin Tarantino's latest. Genius. He cast her as the girl next door, all right. The girl next door who's also an assassin. We approached her while she was filming that one—she decided to do it because of the spy angle in ours."

"I don't get it."

Liz shook her head. "Don't try. Tracy saw a connection, seems to think there's a similarity between assassins and spies, and agreed to read for us. She waffled for a while, but we finally got her. The Tarantino film's been out, and it's hitting big, so we can play off her success in that when we advertise ours, and it means we get her while her star's rising. It's a beautiful thing."

Samantha smiled at Liz's pleasure, and relaxed for the first time since Liz called asking for help. Despite her excitement, she'd still been nervous about coming back, and worried because she'd never worked a feature length movie before. But this film had two name actors, a great script, and Liz as a co-producer who wouldn't settle for less than perfect.

Samantha glanced out the window, looking toward Fairfax. She blinked at what she saw out there, turned around to look, and blinked again.

"Was that a giraffe?" she asked. It had been surrounded by a film crew, but still. A real, live giraffe in a parking lot.

"Huh?" Liz glanced around, but they'd already passed it. "Probably. You know L.A., baby. Never a dull moment." She grinned at Samantha, and Samantha couldn't help smiling back.

"Better get used to it," Liz added. "You're back in the middle of it."

Samantha shook her head, thinking about the Real Housewife with the Chihuahua at the airport. Liz was right. Hollywood was its own planet, and she would need to get used to that again. "I'm okay with seeing giraffes. Lions and tigers and bears are fine." She took a deep breath and leaned back in her seat, holding herself tight. "I'll be great, just as long as I don't see Evan Gallagher."

CHAPTER TWO

A slasher flick?"
Evan Gallagher stopped in mid-pace around his living room, cordless phone pressed to his ear, one hand resting on the back of a white club chair, his bare feet cushioned by thick, white carpeting. His best friend and agent had called asking if he wanted the good news or the bad news first. The slasher movie offer was supposed to be the good news. The bad? He'd just lost the fifth part in a row. To Kevin Bacon.

Evan leaned a hip against the side of the chair and looked at the white marble fireplace at the end of the room, but didn't really see it. All he saw was himself on screen, running from a machete-waving masked madman.

"It's Delaney Films," Paul was saying. "They're hot right now. Big studio backing. This could be a franchise like *Saw* and the *Friday the 13th* movies. It'll pay well…"

Paul's voice trailed off and Evan didn't try to hide his sigh. He ran a hand across his face. "Fine. I'll take it." He didn't want it, but he needed it. And, damn it, bloodbath movie or no, he missed the work.

He heard his son rattling around in his bedroom off the hallway, getting ready for a weekend with his mom, and realized Paul hadn't responded to his acceptance of the offer. In fact, he could hear him breathing on the other end. He and Paul had been best friends since fifth grade, but Paul was still a successful agent—and he'd perfected the art of appearing to never, ever breathe. It was too human, and humanity equaled vulnerability, something you never wanted to show in this business.

Evan's eyes narrowed and his grip on the phone tightened. "Paulie?"

"I've got a few more scripts here to look through. That's the good news…"

Evan waited.

"The bad is the guys at Delaney want you to audition. Do a screen test."

"What?"

"They want everyone to audition."

"It's a damn slasher flick." Evan started pacing again, veering around the glass coffee table and circling a matching end table before stopping at floor to ceiling windows to stare out at downtown Los Angeles in the distance. "For Scorsese, sure, but…"

He wanted to say, "I was Duncan Tanner, for Christ's sake," but held back, reminding himself that he hadn't played Duncan Tanner for six years now, and that Paul was already quite aware of that situation. The whole world knew he was Duncan Tanner—dubbed as Indiana Jones meets *Quantum Leap*—and the whole world saw when he fell, and took the Duncan Tanner franchise with him.

"So…what?" he asked. "They want to make sure I can look scared but determined as I go off alone to find out what the hell that noise was that the girl I was just screwing heard?" Paul snorted at that, and Evan would've smiled if this had been someone else's life.

"Big studio backing," Paul repeated after a pause. "Hot property. Lots of money available to them. They're a little…overzealous."

As the sun set, a light haze over the city started turning electric pink and orange, reflecting off the tall buildings of the Financial District. Evan no longer had a view from the top of Beverly Hills of cars winding their way along switchbacks and disappearing behind the lushness of well-tended shrubbery, but he still had trees, hills and a partial view of Silver Lake from the other side of the house. He also had a strained pocket book these days, having been out of work so long. He rested his head against the window and closed his eyes.

"Fine," he repeated. "I'll do it."

Paul breathed again. "I'll keep looking."

"I know."

"Once the Tom Hanks flick premieres with your cameo, they'll see you're serious about working again. They'll make more offers."

Neither one of them needed to define who "they" were: anyone who could cast him in a strong role again. He'd had offers in the past, great films like *Inception*, but he'd turned them down, too scared to leave Oliver alone for any period of time, and too proud to admit he'd screwed up and that there would be no more Duncan Tanner films.

"Yeah." He didn't know what else to say. The cool glass on his forehead felt soothing.

"Basketball soon?" Paul asked, and when Evan grunted a yes, Paul added, "Keep your chin up, buddy."

"Nah. Leaves my throat exposed for the knife," Evan added, and hung up.

He pushed away from the window and paced again, shaking his head, then running his fingers through his hair and tugging on sections at the back of his neck while trying to clear his head. Between Paul's news and waiting for his ex-wife to pick up their son for his first extended visit with her, Evan felt more restless than when he'd been waiting for Paul's call.

He went to the arched living room doorway. "Oliver!" he called down the hall. "You finished packing?"

"Almost!" came the reply.

Evan tilted his head toward the bedroom. He heard muted beeps and whistles as Oliver conquered the world in his latest video game. Oliver's delay would give Evan time to remind Zoey that her having visitation was on a trial basis, and she'd better not screw it up. She'd be mad at him, but she'd been mad at him for years now, even before the day of that stupid benefit five years ago when that tabloid show—

The doorbell rang, interrupting his thoughts.

"I'll get it!" Oliver hollered.

Evan had a clear view up the hall, of Oliver's bedroom doorway in the middle, and the front door straight ahead at the other end. Oliver raced out of his room up the bare wood of the hall, their sheepdog mutt Walker yipping at his ankles, and skidded to a stop. He pulled the door open so hard it banged against the opposite wall, causing Walker to drop to a crouch, tail in the air, and bark harder. When he caught sight of Zoey, his fuzzy gray ears drooped and he let out a low growl.

Oliver had a different reaction. He lunged at the short, curvy woman in the doorway. "Mom!" he yelled, throwing his arms around her neck and clinging to her, even though they were almost the same height.

She rocked him from side to side until his feet lifted off the floor. Evan smiled at Oliver's delight, but at the same time he felt like Walker. He wanted to drop down on all fours and growl at Zoey. Instead, he leaned against the wall, hands in the front pockets of his worn jeans and waited at the opposite end of the long hallway in the room she'd dubbed "the monochromatic marvel."

Color hadn't mattered to Evan when he and Oliver first moved to this house; he'd gone through a divorce, a long custody battle, and the death of his career, and he'd often sat in the room by himself, his back to the floor-to-ceiling windows, staring at all that white and letting the blandness of the room take over the tumult in his mind. He'd been thinking lately he'd like to change the room, add more color beyond his painting over the fireplace, but he wasn't going to admit that to Zoey. It was petty on his part, but he felt petty right now. Being reduced to auditioning for a splatter flick could do that to you.

"C'mon, Mom." Oliver grabbed her hand and pulled her down the hallway. "Come see my room. I just got some new posters."

"You finished packing, son?" Evan asked.

At the sound of Evan's voice, Zoey looked up at him. She wasn't as heavily made up as usual. No black lipstick or pink mascara today for the lead singer of the punk band The Anarchy Queens, but thick indigo blue lined her dark brown eyes, reminding him of the Egyptian exhibit he'd just taken Oliver to at the L.A. County Museum. She'd tucked black pants into Doc Marten boots and wore a vintage t-shirt onto which she'd hand-painted her own designs.

Thankfully, this one—New Kids on the Block—didn't have any strategic rips or suggestive words, although Donnie Wahlberg appeared to be sporting a pair of devil horns. Evan avoided looking at his latest oil painting stuck in the corner, not wanting to compare his frustrating efforts at self-expression with one of Zoey's slapdash, highly sought-after creations.

Still holding his mother's hand, Oliver stopped in his bedroom doorway. "I'm almost finished, Dad. I just want to show Mom—"

"Oliver," he said, as gently but firmly as possible, "you have a lot of time to show your mom things. I only have a few minutes with her." He glanced at Zoey, who had an unreadable expression on her face. When their eyes met, she brushed a lock of long black hair behind one ear. "I'd like to make sure she knows your schedule. Please go finish packing," he added, finally looking away from Zoey.

"And take Walker with you."

"Okay." Oliver let go of his mother's hand and headed into his room, patting his thigh and calling after the dog.

As soon as they were gone, Zoey took a few steps in, then stopped at the entryway to the living room, still looking at him. Her unblinking gaze had always unnerved him, but at least he no longer mistook it for lust.

"I got his schedule," she said. "You got it to me forever ago, Paul had it delivered to me, your publicist e-mailed it, her assistant faxed it, even though I don't got a fax…"

"Fine. I know." He pinched at the bridge of his nose. "Come in."

"No thanks." She made a sweeping gesture. "Don't wanna mess anything up."

"Zoe." He couldn't quite bring himself to say, "You wouldn't mess anything up," because she'd already done that, hadn't she?

Before he could respond, she said, "You remember that first night we met?"

He tried not to look surprised. Zoey liked to throw him off, but she rarely got sentimental. "Hard to forget," he admitted, but didn't say anything else.

He'd been twenty-one, and he and some friends had gone to see Anarchy Queens play, and then his friends had dared him to ask the lead singer out after the show. She'd blown cigarette smoke in his face, then said "Sure," with a shrug, and drove them to a dark spot on Mulholland Drive where they talked all night. He'd been so mesmerized that before he'd thought about trying to kiss her, she'd jumped over to his seat and ripped his shirt open so hard the buttons had popped off. She still had that battered '63 T-bird convertible. But they no longer had each other.

"You know, how we talked about everything," she continued, "and we—"

"Yeah," he interrupted her. He strode over and put an arm around her shoulders, easing her into the room even as he felt her stiffen against his side. He gestured behind them. "Big ears," he said in a low voice.

She relaxed against him, not moving away, but not looking at him either. "You said that night you believed in me. You'd always be there for me."

"I remember." He dropped his arm and stepped away from her. "Things change." They'd had similar conversations before, to no constructive conclusion, but they had ended when the divorce became final. Why was she bringing this up now? He looked over his shoulder, but Oliver was still in his room. He caught a glimpse of Zoey's T-bird through the open front door, pulled right up to the front steps in the circular driveway.

"We're going back on tour." She finally turned to face him. "Soon. I'd like to bring Oliver—"

"No," he said automatically.

Her eyes narrowed. "To practice," she said. "A couple times. Since I won't get to see him for awhile."

Realizing the implications of this, he took a few steps toward her. "Wait a minute. Why now? You just got visitation and you want to take off for months? Good thinking, Zoe." He tapped the side of his head with his forefinger. "Always thinking ahead."

"Nice." She pointed at his chest. "Always critical."

"That's not true. You know I—" He stopped, not wanting to get into another pointless argument with her. Yes, his intention had been to support her, but once they'd gotten to the point where they'd disappointed each other enough that neither wanted to fix it, he hadn't followed through. They both knew it. And they each blamed the other.

"Look," he said, running his hands through his hair, "we don't have time for this. Oliver's going to be ready soon. Let's talk about it later. In private." He began to pace, ticking things off his fingers as he spoke. "He's been trying to slide out of his math homework lately. He's decided milk isn't cool anymore, but try to get him to drink some anyway." He gestured at her. "Not by letting him eat cereal for dinner, though, right? Oh, and he's finally started eating broccoli, so don't let him make you think otherwise. And—"

"Evan."

He turned to face her. Her appearance was all hard edges as usual, but her voice had been soft. "Yeah?"

"I won't damage him…"

The word "again" hung in the air between them, but he held back from saying it or even suggesting it. Sober, she was a great mother to Oliver, and she'd been working hard on her sobriety, one of the reasons Evan had agreed Oliver could stay with her for a few days.

He was afraid he'd never completely trust her again, though, either with Oliver or himself. She'd broken both their hearts five years ago, but Evan could step back from her and not be emotionally involved anymore. Oliver didn't have that choice, and once Evan had overcome his initial anger, he realized Oliver wouldn't even want that choice. Zoey was his mother, and he wanted to be with her.

"I know," he finally said to her. "I know you won't damage him."

"You think you've got the market cornered on caring about him?" she asked, her voice still soft, her dark brown eyes on him.

"Of course not."

She reached a hand out, then let it drop. "You think you have the market cornered on feelings?" she asked.

"What?"

She stood in front of him now, looking into his eyes. "I think about that night on Mulholland," she said. "And other nights." She set her fingertips on his forearm. "We were good together—"

"Ready!" Oliver announced from down the hall. He ran toward them, backpack over one shoulder and Walker at his feet, and came skidding to a halt in the doorway in his stocking feet.

Evan started and turned away from Zoey, feeling the brush of her fingertips as she lowered her hand, his mind working furiously to deny her implication, and forced a smile for his son. "Yep," he said, glancing at Oliver's feet, "looks like you're ready to roll."

Oliver beamed up at him. "Got underwear, my toothbrush, Walker's snacks—"

"And shoes?" Evan interrupted, his smile now genuine.

Oliver tilted his head at him. "Walker doesn't need *shoes*," he said with a high-pitched giggle. As if to add to the point, Walker gave a sharp bark.

Evan wiggled his fingers in the direction of Oliver's feet. "No, but little boys do."

Oliver blinked at him. "I'm not little, Dad. I'm *eight*." Then he glanced at his feet, gave another giggle, and he and Walker bounded back up the hallway. "Don't go anywhere, Mom! We'll be right back."

Evan crossed his arms over his chest and watched them, as usual overwhelmed by how his feelings for his son healed the fractures in him on a regular basis.

"What'd he mean by that?" Zoey asked from behind him.

Evan turned to her. He could make some guesses, but it was another thing he didn't want to get into right now. "What were you going to say? Before Oliver came in."

She shrugged. "I don't remember."

"We were good together. That's what you said," he added, not wanting her to think he felt the same. The sex had been good, yes, but their relationship wavered from the beginning, two diverse people finding common ground only in youth, rebellion and artistic expression, which was not enough to build a future on.

Part of him sometimes wished for a show of vulnerability from her, an admission that everything that had happened between them hurt her as much as it hurt him. She'd lashed out, and blamed him, but she'd never cried in front of him over the loss of their relationship or apologized for her part in it. He didn't want that to come in the form of a suggestion that they get back together, for sex or otherwise.

"That's all," she said now with a shrug. "I think about it sometimes, don't you? And don't worry about Oliver," she added before he could reply, then brushed past him on her way to Oliver's room. "He'll be fine. Enjoy your freedom."

He nodded, even though she now had her back to him, then shoved his hands in his front pockets. Having Oliver spend time with Zoey wasn't freeing for him; in fact, thinking about it made his throat close up. And now he had the extra worry of wondering what Zoey had really been thinking. He walked up the hall behind them as Oliver danced around Zoey, peppering her with questions and suggestions for what they would do that weekend. He went through the door, bounced outside, stepped back in with a "Bye, Dad!" then raced out to the circular driveway with Walker right alongside him.

One hand on the knob, Zoey turned to look at Evan. "See you Tuesday."

He nodded, rocking back on his heels, not quite trusting himself to talk.

Zoey watched him a moment, head tilted up at him. "Thanks," she said, then closed the door before he could say anything.

He stood in the entryway, the tile cold on his bare feet, listening to the sounds of his son's chatter, doors closing, and finally the car starting up and pulling away, before he turned and walked back down the hall. He stood staring into that "monochromatic marvel" of a room for a few minutes before pulling his dark green t-shirt over his head and tossing it across one of the white couches. He gave a nod of satisfaction, then headed to the corner to retrieve his latest painting.

CHAPTER THREE

Liz started hitting the garage door opener a block from her house, dropping her hand in time to whip the SUV into the garage, and bang it into a plastic flexible garbage can before stopping with a jolt.

She hopped out, but Samantha sat rigid in the passenger seat, staring at the garage wall. "I'm getting a rental," she declared, intent on never again getting into a car that Liz drove. She found her way down to the ground and walked to the back where Liz was pulling luggage out and setting it on the ground.

"What was that?" Liz asked.

Samantha grabbed a couple bags. "Nothing," she said brightly, heading up the brick walk to the bungalow she had shared with Liz all those years ago after they'd met at UCLA.

Liz had been an intern at *Celebrity Live!* and was showing Samantha around when one of the producers saw her and insisted she would be a big star. "Honey, you were made to be in front of the camera." She, Liz and Gary had had plenty of laughs over her being "discovered," but none of them could have predicted how it would all turn out.

She shook her head to clear away those thoughts as she went inside the small living room that opened directly onto the kitchen. The house declared itself 1930s on the outside, but shouted 1950s inside with its boxy living room furniture, kidney shaped coffee table, and brightly colored vinyl dining chairs. In honor of Liz's favorite dark hero, a Batman cape hung on the wall across from the couch.

Samantha followed Liz into the office and guest bedroom down a hall to the right, which contained a small corner desk with Liz's laptop and a daybed, where they deposited the luggage, and headed back to the kitchen. Liz was saying something about how she'd wanted to paint the bathroom magenta, only Gary had talked her out of it, but Samantha found she couldn't concentrate.

It had sounded so simple when Liz called. Samantha's job on *Honor Bound* had ended, and Liz and Gary were adapting Liz's screenplay into a film and their continuity supervisor had been offered a job on the new Spielberg film. They all understood that no one could refuse Spielberg, so Samantha agreed to help. She wanted this to work, but some anxiety had started creeping in now that she was actually in Los Angeles.

"Hot damn, I'm glad you're here," Liz said, slamming two glasses of iced tea on the small Formica table in her dining nook, plunking herself down in a bright red vinyl chair, and beaming up at Samantha. "Sit," Liz added, waving a hand in Samantha's general direction, then leaning over for the purse she'd set on the floor. She pulled out a sack of mini candy bars and set it on the table.

Samantha looked down at her, thinking about all she still had to do. Maybe she should go review her notes.

Liz ripped the bag open and took out a Snickers. "Five years, right?" She cocked her head, and when Samantha nodded, she continued. "Five years, and we saw each other…twice. When *I* went out *there*. Would you please sit down?"

Samantha chewed on her lower lip and gripped the back of a purple chair. "Actually, I'm a little…"

"So that's five years, two visits, lots of phone calls, e-mails every day, some instant messaging. I knew you'd look different. I didn't know you'd be…"

Samantha waited, wondering what fascinating word Liz would come up with. When nothing came, she prompted, "What? I'd be what?"

"Well…prim or something."

Samantha fell heavily into the chair and pulled the candy bars closer.

"Don't get me wrong," Liz continued. "You look amazing. You're all pulled together, like a grown up or something." She grinned at Samantha. "It's just…" She waved the hand around again. "This is not the Samantha I remember." She grabbed her purse from where she'd dropped it back on the floor and began rummaging around again.

"Well, maybe I have grown up," Samantha said, smoothing at her skirt.

"Bo-ring," Liz announced, her head practically inside the purse.

"Sophisticated." Samantha reached over and tapped the table when Liz didn't respond. "What are you doing anyway?"

"I need a cigarette."

"Oh, no you don't." Samantha grabbed the purse from her, holding it to her chest after a pen, a tube of mascara and some change came flying out and clinked on the tile floor. "You quit."

"Well, I'm taking it back."

"You don't take back a commitment like that." She pointed at the bag. "Do you have cigarettes in here?"

"No." Liz pouted. "Maybe. Just an emergency one."

"An emergency one?"

"How about if I make a commitment to be a good, dedicated smoker."

"No." Samantha began looking for the rogue cigarette, glad for the distraction from the discussion of her primness.

"The old Samantha would've smoked it with me."

Samantha pointed at her, still searching. "I never smoked."

"No, but the old Samantha would've."

Samantha thumped the bag on the table, and Liz jumped. "The old Samantha wasn't perfect."

Liz put a hand on the leather handle, but didn't move it. "None of us are. But where's the girl who used to dance on tabletops and whistle at cute guys on the street? The girl who loved dressing funky and staying up late and having a little fun?" Liz pointed back at her. "The girl who had sex in the elevator with Billy Lamowsky in college."

Samantha crossed her arms over her chest. "That was you."

Liz grabbed a chocolate and popped it in her mouth. "Oh, yeah." She grinned, then chewed for a moment. "But you *wanted* to be the one to have sex with him in the elevator. So what happened?"

Samantha pressed her lips tightly together, fighting a habit she'd perfected over the last few years: gather up anything that hurts, shove it into a windowless room, and slam the door on it. She should've known it would be like this once she saw Liz in person; Liz knew all about dark spaces, and loved exposing them to the light.

And Samantha wouldn't have accepted this job if she hadn't

thought she was ready to open the door and start feeling again, even if it meant hurting. She just didn't think it would happen within the first couple of hours of her arrival.

Had she really done all of the things Liz said? She knew she had, but she couldn't fathom doing them now, or why she'd wanted to, then. Yet, remembering them, she also recalled laughing a lot. With Liz, at herself, with those boys she'd whistled at on the street and flirted with at the clubs. She looked down at her no-wrinkle skirt and the matching jacket, the one that had appeared cream in the store, but now looked beige. She hadn't flirted in years. Or been flirted with.

And she'd gotten beige.

She pressed her lips harder together because the bottom one had started to tremble. "I don't know what happened," she said, her voice shaky.

"No, no." Liz stood up and backed away, hands held in front of her. "No crying. There's no crying in my house."

"It's 'there's no crying in baseball,'" Samantha said. "And stop throwing movie references at me."

"Side effect of the business." Liz waved a hand around and paced back and forth by the table. "Anyway, whatever. No crying. I'm a New Yorker, we don't cry."

"Well, you don't have to cry, then," Samantha said, reaching for a napkin. "I'm from Iowa. We cry all the time." Liz gave her a look. "I really want to do this. But I'm nervous. I want it to be right," she added, ripping the napkin into little pieces.

"I know. You're a perfectionist."

The front door suddenly opened with a bang and Gary stood glaring at them from the doorway, wearing loafers, pressed chinos and a green shirt with an alligator stitched over the left breast. He clutched a cell phone in one hand and his dark blonde curly hair stood up in a few places as if he'd been pulling at it.

Liz spared him a small glance. "I keep telling you Izods went out when Duran Duran came in, Doogie Howser."

"You should be comatose, Norma Desmond." He stepped inside and slammed the door. "That would be the only excusable reason for you to not call me back."

He slapped the phone on the table in front of Liz and turned to Samantha with his arms out and a welcoming smile on his face.

"There's my girl. There's my Smam."

When Samantha had gotten the job at *Celebrity Live!*, they'd had a party to celebrate, and she'd had far too much champagne and gone around introducing herself as "Smammy Sandal," which had given Gary fits. It had been his nickname for her ever since.

She stood up and hugged him now, the tears threatening again. "Oh, Gary. It's so good to see you."

"You, too, my love. It's about time you came back." Still hugging Samantha, he turned to Liz. "The boys love Izod, by the way." He pressed his cheek to Samantha's. "How are you, sweetie?" He stepped back to look at her, holding her hands. "Good God, when did you become Margaret Thatcher?" He looked at Liz. "No, that's not right. Boring politician. Suit wearing actress. Who am I thinking of? I'm clearly having an off day."

Samantha let go of his hands and sat down hard. "I need a cigarette."

Liz laughed. "That's my girl."

Gary turned to Liz without skipping a beat. "If you had deigned to call me back, you would know by now that Tracy Jennifer is insisting on her own makeup person. And hairdresser. And stylist." He sucked in his upper lip and breathed out through his nose. "And having her personal assistant at all times. Paid." His nostrils flared. "By us."

Liz froze with a chocolate halfway to her mouth. "That would kill our budget."

"That would be correct," Gary said. "She's threatening to walk otherwise. She got mad when I told her I'd have to discuss it with my producer and get back to her." He pressed a hand to his chest. "We do not like Tracy Jennifer mad."

"I can't imagine that sweet little thing being angry," Samantha said.

Gary stared at her. "You've been away from Hollywood too long." He pulled up a yellow chair and sat close to her. "She threatened me with her *people*. She jumped up and down, she was so mad." He looked between Samantha and Liz. "Jumped. And her breasts don't move when she jumps." He put his elbows on the table and propped his head in his hands. "It was awful."

Samantha patted him on the shoulder.

Liz thumped a hand on the table. "I'm less concerned about her six million dollar breasts than I am about our barely six million dollar budget."

"We should give her makeup," Gary said.

"And hair," Liz said after a moment, but she didn't look happy about it.

"No stylist?" Gary asked.

"No stylist. And she pays for her own personal assistant."

"And if she walks?"

"We deal with it."

They looked at each other, nodding, and Samantha watched them, envious of the connection they still had, of being able to say so much with so few words.

"I'll get back to her," Gary said.

"You call me if you need me," Liz replied. "I need to be in the loop on this."

"Yes, my little control freak," Gary replied. Still pacing, he picked up his phone and dropped it into his front pants pocket.

"Because *we*," Liz said, turning to Samantha, "are going shopping tomorrow."

"We are?"

Gary stopped pacing and stared at Liz. "You are? You're taking a day off?"

"My best friend just got back in town after five years." She nodded, then took a deep breath. "I can handle taking a day off. We'll go to Melrose. You never know what you'll find down there."

CHAPTER FOUR

As Evan opened the tall wooden gate to the back enclosure of Melrose Fine Art, the gallery's owner, Corey Von Tilden, sailed toward him out the French doors. She had called the night before to tell him she'd displayed his latest work—the largest oil painting he'd ever done—but she couldn't know he'd be coming by to see it today, much less at what time, in order to make an entrance into the small courtyard to greet him.

He would never admit it, but Corey often unsettled him that way, like his fifth grade teacher, with an accent of unknown origin and eyes in the back of her head. But unlike Mrs. Jankowski, Corey had treated him very well the past few years when he felt he didn't deserve much of anything good, and he'd always be grateful.

Immaculate and all in white as usual, Corey held her arms out, the gauzy material of her duster sweeping behind her in perfect waves. "Darling," she called to him. The sun sparkled off the jewels in her rings and bracelets as she swooped in on him for her usual hug, one as light and airy as her clothing, but that always managed to leave her perfume on him for hours after.

"Corey," he said, as she wrapped her arms around his neck, then withdrew almost immediately. He barely had time to pat her on the back.

She tilted her head at him, then gave one section of his hair a gentle tug. "Being rough and rugged, darling?" She patted his arm, then headed back to the gallery, knowing he would follow. "I am fond of it."

He closed the door behind them, but before he could reply, she spoke again. "Come," she announced. "We shall be looking at your painting."

As Evan followed her to the front of the spacious, elegant room, she continued to talk, about the gallery, her morning, his work; his thoughts sprinted around as he listened with half an ear. Corey's speech always charmed him, but he felt restless this morning. He missed Oliver, and their routine together.

"I am bereft, as you know, at the loss of Gabrielle, to New York," Corey was saying, even as she made a sweeping gesture with one hand for Evan to come around and see the picture.

Evan smiled at Corey's turn of phrase, but kept quiet. Gabrielle, her assistant, had moved to New York to open her own gallery. Corey would rather blame the city than the girl for her loss.

"Bereft," she repeated, shaking her head. Her demeanor changed in a flash as she stood back for him to see the painting, arranged on an easel so it would be the first piece customers saw on entering. "It is dazzling," she said. "It will sell like the lightning."

He raised an eyebrow at that, but didn't say anything as he looked at the picture titled "Freedom," remembering what a struggle painting it had been after he'd finished so many pieces he hadn't liked. Although Corey had sold other paintings for him, he'd considered this one his first true success, and he'd completed it the day his divorce became final. He'd felt both melancholy and free that day, but not angry for the first time in a long time.

The picture showed a woman from the back as she stepped from the shore into a blue-green lake, her last piece of clothing dropping from her hand as she put one foot into the water. He'd painted it in wide brush strokes, with no minute details, the edges of the woman's body, the shore and the lake all blending into each other. It measured twenty-four by thirty-six inches and he remembered getting lost in it as he'd stood in front of the canvas, moving the brush in circles to make each element part of the other.

Corey patted his arm and said, "I have the paperwork to do." She brushed her fingertips along the edge of the frame, then headed for her office in the back corner. "You enjoy."

"Thank you," he called after her, and meant it. He'd been holding his breath up until then, unsure of his feelings. Now he pushed his hands into his front pockets and rocked back on his heels, finally letting out a breath and a genuine smile.

Corey Von Tilden, strange as she was, had faith in him. She believed in his work and not his name. His name alone would have sold this faster than "the lightning" six years ago, but when he brought his earlier pieces to her, she hadn't known who he was, and had agreed to sell them anyway.

"You were a name once?" she asked, and when he'd nodded, his face heating up, she'd snapped her fingers and said, "Darling, everyone is a name in Hollywood at this point or that." She'd leaned forward and smiled at him. "Names change. Art remains."

The bell over the door chimed, and Evan started, then turned to see Antoine rushing in, head down, books and folders balanced against his body with one arm. He wore an outfit reminiscent of Chinese pajamas, all black with a white mandarin collar and cuffs.

"Morning, Antoine," Evan said.

Antoine froze with a squeak, then pressed a hand to his chest. "You scared the socks off of me." He peered around Evan into the main room of the gallery. "Is she here?" he whispered.

"Yes," Evan whispered back. "She's in her office."

Antoine nodded. "Oh, good. Time to prepare."

Evan shook his head. "Prepare?"

This time, Antoine stood on tiptoe and peered over Evan's shoulder toward Corey's office, before looking back at Evan. "For *her*. She's bereft, you know."

Evan glanced in the direction of the office, too. "Ah."

"Exactly." Antoine gave him a look he couldn't read, then headed for a display of miniature vases in the middle of the gallery, his Chinese slippers whispering along the marble floor. He turned halfway there and looked back at Evan. "Bereft," he repeated.

Laughing to himself, Evan turned back to look at the painting when movement outside the front window caught his attention. Two women stood looking in at the display there. One was tiny and New York chic, in black and burgundy, her dark hair spiky, reminding him how much he missed the distinctive women in that city. But the other woman, easily taller than her friend by half a foot, her honey-colored hair pulled up into a twist, and her skirt and blouse casual but form fitting…well, this woman made him miss *women*.

He ran a hand through his hair as he watched them, suddenly jittery. Between living like a recluse and then all of the years focusing on Oliver, he hadn't been with a woman in—

"Damn," he muttered. Too long.

"What?" Antoine called.

"Nothing," Evan said, not taking his eyes off the blonde. When she headed for the door, he straightened and walked away from the front entry. "Except you have customers."

Antoine stepped from behind a statue, then brushed his hands down his outfit. "Are you leaving?"

"Actually—" Evan took a step behind the statue himself. The women had come inside and were studying his picture. Something dropped hard into his stomach. "I think I'll stick around. Talk to Corey." His gaze flickered again to the front of the gallery. "Or something."

Evan watched as Antoine meandered around the room, keeping an eye on the women, letting them know of his presence without being invasive. Evan was tempted to head over and start talking to them. He didn't necessarily want them to know who he was or even that he had painted the picture, but the idea of a conversation with a woman who didn't want something from him sounded restful.

He decided to wait while he considered the best approach and wandered away to look at a collection of landscapes on the back wall.

LIZ POINTED UP the street. "Hey, let's go in that gallery. I've heard there are some great pieces there."

Samantha peered in the window at a bust of a naked woman with a zebra head next to a sculpture of a man's groin, with giraffe legs. "I hope they're not all like that," she said, enjoying the memories that had surfaced as they'd walked along Melrose, most of them related to when she and Liz had been starving students, experiencing as much as they could of what Los Angeles had to offer. And she'd been amused to see everyone still checked everyone else out here as they passed by on the street.

"Hey, I kind of like the giraffe man. You think it would go in my sitting room?" Liz held the door open for her.

"What sitting room?"

"I could have a sitting room," Liz said.

Samantha grinned at Liz over her shoulder as she stepped into the gallery, only to stop a few feet from the entrance to stare at the painting directly in front of her. Her mouth shut with a snap.

"Wow," Liz said from behind her.

"It's beautiful."

"Amazing colors." Liz came to stand next to her.

"Now that could go in your sitting room," Samantha told her.

"I'd buy a house with a sitting room just so I could put that painting there and sit and stare at it."

Taller than it was wide, the painting depicted a woman stepping away from the observer into a lake, dropping her clothing, moving forward. Samantha felt like that woman, exposed, shedding the old, one toe in the new; this woman seemed confident of her journey, and Samantha wanted a taste of that. She glanced at the tag hanging below the painting.

"Freedom," she read, then turned her gaze back to the picture.

She was trying to think of a way to describe how the picture made her feel, and wondering if she could afford the hefty price, when Liz's phone rang. Liz swore and pulled it from her bag, stepping outside with a look of apology directed at Samantha.

Samantha didn't mind. She'd been in L.A. less than twenty-four hours and felt like she'd been caught in a whirlwind from the moment she stepped off the plane. Looking at this painting, she felt she could breathe for the first time and thought her move back to L.A. just might work. She let herself fall into it, like she often did when completely caught up watching a movie; everything else drifted away.

She started when the bell over the door rang violently and she turned to see Liz, face pale, push the door open with a slam of her palm and stand there with the cell phone clutched in her other hand. She shook it at Samantha.

"This...I...awful...just..." Breath wheezing, she bent forward at the waist.

Samantha held the swinging door back and eased Liz next to her. "What? What is it?"

"Gary," Liz breathed, still bent over.

"What? What's wrong with Gary?" Samantha put a hand on Liz's shoulder and Liz clutched at Sam's arm before straightening up.

The color in Liz's face rapidly went from gray to bright pink before she burst out, "Actors!"

Samantha let out the breath she'd been holding and staggered back from Liz's glare. "In general," she said, trying to lighten the moment, "or particular?"

"Our lead. Dropped out. Kevin. Madison. Dropped. Out."

"Oh, no."

"I'll say." Liz brandished the phone again. "We have rehearsals starting on Wednesday, two days from now—two days—and we start shooting next Monday. *Monday.* That's one week. I have to go, we have to go. No." She held a hand out. "I have to go, you should stay, finish shopping, get some giraffe legs. I have to meet Gary for an emergency meeting."

"Oh." Samantha glanced back at the picture. "That's okay. I can go with you."

"No." Liz put a hand on her arm, her coloring almost back to normal now. "Stay here and enjoy these. We'll be making a million phone calls, you'll be bored, me and Gary'll be arguing, we'll drive you crazy. I'll take a cab and Gary can drop me off. Enjoy some time for yourself, but let's meet back at my place for an early dinner, or I'll call you if we're delayed." She squinted at Samantha. "Oh. You lost your cell. I'll call you on my land line, or leave a message there if you're not back. Check the voicemail. The code's by the phone. But I'm sure it'll be fine and I'll be back in time for dinner, so I'll see you then." She dug into her bag and pulled out her keys, handing them to Samantha.

Samantha smiled at her. "Thanks. I'll wander around and get lost in things. Then maybe I'll spend a lot of money on some clothes I don't need. Are you sure you're okay?"

"Perfect. I'll see you back at the house." As Liz headed out the door, her cell rang again. "I know, I *know*," she said to it, flipping it open. "The world's coming to an end. Crashing down around our ears. What?" she barked into the phone as she headed down the sidewalk.

CHAPTER FIVE

Samantha felt guilty for letting Liz go alone, but then remembered her friend preferred her life this way: right in the middle of the chaos, and the more chaotic the better. Determined to relax for a while, Samantha turned back to the beautiful painting she'd admired earlier.

She meant to wander around the gallery, but her gaze kept returning to the picture. She wasn't the type to buy art from galleries, but she did have a chunk of money stashed away. Tabloid TV paid buckets of money, but it had come to represent guilt money to her. And she might not buy paintings, but she hadn't thought she'd get back into the business after leaving *Celebrity Live!*, either, and she certainly hadn't thought she'd ever come back to Los Angeles. Didn't she deserve some sort of reward for her bravery?

She nodded to herself, then took a deep breath, looking around for a salesperson.

"Good afternoon, miss," someone said from behind her. "I am Antoine. May I help you with anything? Answer any questions?"

She turned to find a beautiful man in gorgeous silk pajamas next to her, and smiled. "Yes, I have a question," she said. "Do you deliver?"

"We ship anywhere in the world and deliver within Los Angeles county," he said with a smile, tenting his fingers together under his chin and watching her.

She couldn't hold back a grin. "Then I would love to get this piece."

His formal façade slipped and he clapped his hands together.

"Fabulous." He bent down to retrieve the tag next to the painting. "Gorgeous, isn't it? It's one of Mr. Gallagher's newer pieces."

Samantha's stomach clenched and she suddenly found it difficult to breathe. "Mr. Gallagher?" she finally managed to squeak out.

Antoine straightened up. "Evan Gallagher. Fabulous actor," he whispered, leaning close. "Gorgeous man." He fanned himself with one hand. "Wondrous artist," he added in a slightly dreamy fashion as he studied the painting.

Samantha tried to swallow but couldn't for a moment; her throat had gone dry and she felt a little dizzy, as if she'd had one drink too many and stood up too fast. How had she missed his name on the tag? Despite her attempts to avoid it, she'd been all too aware of Evan Gallagher's name for years, so how could it have slipped by her now?

She knew he painted; she'd reported on one of his gallery openings in her segment, showing clips of celebrities slipping out of their limos, waving to the crowds and signing autographs or moving as quickly as possible up the sidewalk and inside. She'd quoted insiders who'd supposedly attended, and dished over who had spilled a drink on whom, who had canoodled behind a sculpture and exactly how many were wearing Prada and Versace with their Manolo Blahniks.

She hadn't actually paid attention to the art itself. Maybe if she had she would've recognized his work now. Or maybe not. When she left Hollywood, she'd tried to ignore anything having to do with the business. Other than hearing from Liz that Evan Gallagher had been cleared of the charges against him, she hadn't wanted to know anything else.

She knew she could never really forget him, but now she would have a reminder of him for the rest of her life. She tried to convince herself this was karmic restitution or something. She'd done Evan Gallagher wrong, but now she was paying for that—literally and figuratively—by buying this painting.

She raised her gaze to the ceiling a moment. Okay, she told herself. Buying a piece of his art would not make up for what she'd done, but it helped her feel a little better for a moment to think her purchase might help them both.

Samantha gave Antoine Liz's address, signed her name to the credit slip with a slight shake of the hand, then stood back with a mixture of pleasure and trepidation as she watched him reposition the painting's title card and affix a "sold" sticker to it. Antoine explained that since the "wondrous artist" did not have an official show here, the painting could be released right away, but would she be agreeable to them keeping it on display and delivering tomorrow?

"Of course." Samantha knew it looked good for a gallery to promote its successful sales. "Do you mind if I stare at it a little longer?" She really did like the picture, but she also needed a moment to slow down her breathing and get her heartbeat back to normal.

"Not at all," Antoine said. He held out his hand. "I hope you enjoy it."

She shook. "I will. I do. Thank you."

Antoine slipped away, and she pressed cool fingertips to her cheeks, hoping that this insane thing she'd just done would come to some good, that this would become a symbol of her new life.

She shook her head, her hands still to her face, and closed her eyes, letting out a loud sigh.

"It's not that bad, is it?" said a voice from nearby.

Samantha let out a squawk, dropping her hands, and opened her eyes to see a man standing in front of her. A tall man, at least six-two next to her five-eight, with auburn hair, a touch of sexy stubble, and a grin that had staggered many female moviegoers. She felt her eyes bugging out of her head.

Evan Gallagher.

Her cheeks heated up again and her heart thumped so hard in her chest she wanted to press a hand to it to keep it from bursting out. "Erk," she said, then pressed her lips together and stared at him, all rational thought having flown from her mind.

Evan held his hands out, palms facing her, a concerned look replacing the friendly expression on his face. "I'm sorry. I didn't mean to startle you."

Samantha blinked at him. "No." She cleared her throat and took a breath. "No, it's okay. Really," she said, hoping she didn't sound too horrified. She gestured at the door, unable to look him in the eye. "I was just leaving."

She managed to move her leaden feet and turned away, clutching her bag to her chest.

"Wait." He held out a hand. "Please. I wanted to thank you."

When she turned to face him, their eyes met, and she realized with a shock that during her time reporting, she hadn't paid attention to the details—of the planes of his face, how his wide mouth turned up a little at the corners, that his eyes were hazel. He had a genuine movie star jaw, strong and defined, and…and…she mentally shook her head. He'd said something…he'd said he wanted—

"To thank me?"

He gestured with his thumb. "The painting." He shoved his hands in his front pockets and dipped his head a little, so that a section of hair dropped over his forehead. "I'm honored," he added, and she noted a hint of color sneaking past the tan in his cheeks. "That you bought it."

She didn't know what to say. Floored didn't cover it. Flabbergasted, overwhelmed, touched. None of those words were good enough, but they all fit her emotions at the moment.

"I…" she began, then shut her mouth. To say nothing would be disrespectful, to tell him everything would be stupid, but anything in between felt insufficient. She finally decided on, "You're welcome," unable to quite look him in the eye, and staring at a point above his shoulder. Feeling rude, she dropped her gaze somewhere near the level of his crotch, felt her pulse quicken, and rapidly lowered her eyes down the length of his faded blue jeans to his feet. She gripped her bag closer to her chest.

She didn't think things could get any worse. Evan Gallagher not only had a great smile and long, lean legs, but he also wore fantasy-inducing motorcycle boots. She might as well curl up and die right now.

She made a little noise and realized she was still staring at his boots. And he was talking to her. She forced herself to look at him, wondering if the hot flush that had suffused her body would ever go away.

He was holding a hand out, gesturing around him. "So would you like a tour of the gallery? There's some wonderful work here."

Here Evan Gallagher stood in front of her, not visibly damaged, as she'd built him up in her mind. He obviously didn't recognize her, and she had to admit to a certain curiosity, despite her heart-fluttering panic. A part of her did wonder why he'd invite her to tour the gallery, but another part, the curious one, took over.

She nodded at him. "A tour would be nice." She let out a deep breath. The worst had happened—she'd run into him, face to face—and she hadn't been struck by lightning. She could handle this, she told herself. And if she could survive this, she could survive anything.

His smile broadened and he held a hand out as if to guide her by the small of her back. "There's a nice collection of landscapes at the back they just got in, then maybe…"

His voice drifted off when the front door opened with enough force to cause the delicate clusters of Japanese bells above it to smack against the wall. They flipped back down to hit the door with a loud clang, resounded for a bit, then stopped.

Samantha started and lost her balance, bumping into Evan's hand, and she would never, ever admit that Evan's fingers on her back gave her more of a jolt than the bells' chimes. As the two of them turned, he let his palm linger there until just after the new visitor came into view. Samantha's spine tingled.

One of the messiest and most beautiful women Samantha had ever seen stood in the doorway. Bo Derek cheekbones. Hair down to her shoulder blades and dyed so black it looked blue, sections of it twisted into dreadlocks while the rest went astray about her head and shoulders. Thick black liner outlined dark brown eyes and her outfit consisted of a black and white striped tank top, the hem ragged, and cropped black pants with a variety of silver chains hanging from the waist, pockets and even one cuff. Smaller versions of Evan's motorcycle boots completed the outfit. Samantha recognized her immediately.

Evan Gallagher's ex-wife, Zoey Highlander.

Zoey tilted her chin at Evan. "Hey." She glanced between them, at what Samantha noticed was a very small space separating her from Evan. Then Zoey turned her head slightly and looked at Samantha out of the corner of one eye but didn't say anything else.

Samantha thought this might be the punk rock version of the evil eye.

"Where's Oliver?" Evan asked.

Zoey gestured behind her with one thumb. "Getting something from the car. He'd better get inside soon, too. I don't want him playing in the street. Wouldn't want anyone to think I'm a bad mother or nothing."

Samantha cringed, looking sideways at Evan; his lips were pressed tightly together and a muscle jumped in his jaw. While he seemed to be working on not responding, Zoey shoved her hands in her pockets, looked around the gallery a moment with her lips pursed, stared at Samantha, glanced at Evan, then stared at Samantha again.

Samantha heard Evan shift next to her, take a step, then hesitate, and she realized with a start that she'd never told him her name. It had probably been self-preservation on her part, but it had led to a potentially awkward situation. When he cleared his throat and started to speak, Samantha forced herself forward, hand out, big smile on her face. "Hi. I'm Samantha Jamison." She realized with a slight sense of freedom that she could give her real name since she'd been Sami Scandal on *Celebrity Live!*

Evan stepped with her, and even without his hand on her back this time, that tingle zipped through her again. "Samantha," he said, "this is Zoey Highlander."

"I know you?" Zoey asked.

Feeling like a rabbit caught in a trap, Samantha moved closer to Evan, fully cognizant of the irony of him as the safer choice. The warmth of his shoulder near hers, and the outdoorsy scent he gave off led to a slight quiver that ran down to her toes and heated up areas in between that hadn't been warmed in far too long. "N-no. I mean, I know who you are. I like your band," she added lamely, feeling the blood rush to her cheeks and her heart start to pound hard again. Samantha had in fact interviewed Zoey five years ago, the day she'd also had the woman's husband, Evan himself, sent to jail.

"Huh." Zoey looked her up and down, but didn't say anything else.

"So what're you doing here, Zoe?" Evan asked.

Zoey gave Samantha another appraising look, then turned and hollered outside, "Oliver! Get in here!" A muffled response came from down the street, and she said, "We gotta get going!"

"Zoe—" Evan began, but stopped when she turned from the door and looked at him, her eyes narrowed.

"He forgot his homework," she said to him. "And the security code. You didn't answer your cell, Paul's assistant said you might be here. I don't got a lot of time. Practice."

Samantha had started edging to the door when a thin boy loped into the gallery, a heavy black knapsack hanging from one shoulder. A youthful combination of his parents, he had Evan's almond-shaped hazel eyes and wide mouth and his mother's compact body and unruly hair. He peeked at the picture behind Evan. "Hey, Mom, that's you!" he said, pointing.

"Oliver," Evan said in that parental warning tone known by all children, and then, as if this encounter couldn't get any more surreal for her, he introduced Samantha to his son.

"Hello," Oliver said with a smile, and shook her hand vigorously. "Do you have Rocket Raider Five?" he asked, holding up a portable video game player.

"Haven't been able to get that one yet," she said. "Is it good?"

As Oliver chattered about the advanced graphics and new evil aliens in his game, Samantha tried to take in what he'd said earlier. Was the model for her new painting really Zoey Highlander?

Evan leaned over and whispered, "You don't know what you're missing with the latest version."

His shoulder brushed hers and his breath tickled her ear, and when she looked up at him, he gave her that easy smile just as a lock of hair slipped over his forehead and brushed at his cheekbone.

"Guh," she said.

"And Raiding Rockets Six will be out by the time you finish telling us about Five," Zoey said to Oliver, her tone softer than it had been when addressing either Evan or Samantha.

"It's Rocket *Raider*, Mom," Oliver said, rolling his eyes, and turning his attention to the game.

Zoey had stepped away from the door, and Samantha saw her chance. "I won't take up any more of your time. It was a pleasure meeting you both," she said, directing it at Evan.

She groped behind her for the door's metal bar, found it and gripped its reassuring solidness, then looked into Evan's eyes. The expression on his face blocked out everything else—Oliver, Zoey, the gallery, that insanely expensive nude pin-up she'd just bought—and seemed sad and expectant at the same time, as if they weren't finished, that more needed to happen and to be said.

Then Zoey stepped in front of Evan and started talking to him, breaking the thin string that had held him to Samantha. She gave him a smile and slipped out the doorway, hurrying down the sidewalk, and wondering when her world had gone completely upside down.

CHAPTER SIX

Zoey cocked her head at Evan, then turned to glance at the doorway, where Samantha had stood a moment ago. Evan watched her focus on some watercolors on the wall by the door, as Oliver wandered away to look at other pieces. "Another drooling fan?" Zoey asked him over her shoulder.

"Don't."

Zoey turned back to him with a little, I-know-more-than-you-do smile playing on her lips. She flipped a long dreadlock over her shoulder. "She looked familiar."

He let out a sigh, running his fingers through his hair. Zoey's unexpected appearance had interrupted something promising, even if it was fleeting, and he resented the intrusion.

"Yeah? Well, she said she liked your music. Maybe she was at one of your concerts." He glanced out the window in the direction Samantha had gone.

Zoey snorted. "Can't see a priss like that at Spaceland."

Samantha hadn't seemed like a priss. He liked her chic sleekness, but he wasn't about to get into that with Zoey. "They get all kinds there." He flashed back to the times he'd gone to the club himself years ago. "I'll follow you up to the house to get Oliver's homework," he said. "He'll be late as it is."

He reached in his pocket for his keys, and had them jingling in his hand before realizing Zoey hadn't responded. She ran a finger over the SOLD sticker Antoine had placed at the edge of his painting's tag and dug a short black-lacquered fingernail into the edge of it until she'd scraped a section away. He held back from telling her to stop messing around with gallery property and said instead, "I'm just going to let Corey know I'm leaving," and turned to the office in the back.

Zoey kept peeling without looking up from the sticker, then said, "So, I'm screwing Dan."

Evan stopped with his back to her. He crossed his arms over his chest and looked up at the ceiling. Dan was a roadie for her band. They'd been flirting for years, and Evan wouldn't care who she slept with, except that anything having to do with Zoey also affected Oliver. He refrained from mentioning Dan's hyena laugh, sunken chest or fashion sense, which consisted of whatever pants and shirt from the pile didn't smell too bad. He counted to five and said, "And?" He turned to look at her.

She was watching him now. Waiting for a reaction? He didn't know.

She shrugged. "Just wanted you to know."

"Does Oliver know?"

"Yeah, he caught us—"

"Jesus, Zoe." He ran a hand through his hair and stepped closer, automatically glancing around to see that Oliver was out of earshot.

She flipped her hair back with a quick flick of her head and looked at him, her chin up. "Ease up. Dan kissed me the other night. Oliver saw. He's fine."

"Did you actually talk to him about it or did he just shrug at you and say, 'Okay'?"

She stared at him without blinking and he could tell from her silence that Oliver had shrugged it off and she hadn't talked to him. "He's eight, Zoe. He gets it. You need to talk to him."

"Or?" She put her hands on her hips. "Or else you'll sic his shrink on me? What?"

He pointed at her. "Stop making everything a drama. And don't screw around with his feelings. He's not going to hate you if you sit down and talk to him about your...love life."

"Love life," she said with some disdain, then turned her head and shouted for Oliver again, her voice booming around the gallery. Antoine was probably hiding under the desk. He usually made himself scarce if she came around; he'd confessed to Evan once that her hollering gave him an eye twitch.

Oliver loped over, backpack bouncing, and before he got to them, Zoey said to Evan, "Later. I'll talk to him. It's not all that serious anyway." She turned to Oliver and pressed her fist to the boy's shoulder in a mock punch. "So your dad's gonna follow us to open up the house."

Oliver ducked his head, grinning, and gave her a punch back. "Okay." He turned away, calling after them, "See you there, Dad!"

Evan put on what he hoped was a cheerful look. He also felt an urge to reach for his son and hold him really tight, but he knew Oliver would just squirm away from him and say, "Aww, Dad."

"We'll meet you there," Zoey said, heading out the door.

"Yeah," Evan said out loud to no one, going to the back door and the rear parking lot.

CHAPTER SEVEN

Evan read the last page of the script, rolled it up, then shook it at Paul, who leaned forward, elbows on his knees and fingertips pressed together. "It's good," Evan said, before tossing it onto the coffee table. "Damn good."

Paul nodded at him, then settled back into the thick white club chair. After Zoey and Oliver left, Paul had called him about a part that had just become available because the original lead dropped out, and he'd hand delivered the script that afternoon. Paul waited while Evan read it, studying a variety of scripts he'd brought along that might be suitable for his other clients.

"You interested?" he asked now.

"Definitely. It's—" Evan stood up, running his hands through his hair and wandering back and forth behind the couch. He'd been drawn right into the story—two brothers in love with the same woman—and all of its plot developments, and he already saw how he could play Jack, the former spy presumed dead, but actually in hiding to trap a terrorist. "It's smart, intriguing…" He rubbed his hands together, searching for inspiration.

"Tasty?" Paul offered.

Evan grinned at him. "Tasty," he said with a nod.

"You're okay with a filmed reading? Maybe tomorrow morning?"

"They asked, not demanded like the slasher idiots. I'm off that one, by the way." He stuck his thumbs through his belt loops and stared out at the city lights.

"You sure?"

"Completely," Evan said, without turning around. "Whether I get this one or not. Make the appointment."

Paul took out his cell and called his assistant, waiting while she phoned the director and made the arrangements. Since the original lead had dropped out so close to production, the director and producer were handling the auditions directly, bypassing a casting agent handling the first round for them.

Evan liked the idea of going straight to rehearsals and filming. No time to talk himself out of it, to wonder if he could do it. If he got the part of Jack, he'd be the lead.

He crossed his arms over his chest, barely hearing Paul's discussion. Could he carry a film again? He didn't know, and the thought scared the hell out of him. But this part was good, and he wanted it.

He turned around when he heard Paul ending the conversation.

"Ten thirty work for you?"

Evan nodded, unable to hold back a grin. "I have a feeling about this one, Paulie. You know the feeling?"

"Schwarzenegger terminating things kind of feeling, or Leo as king of the world kind of feeling?"

"Leo." Evan nodded. "Or close to. More like..." He shook his head, not quite getting the image he wanted. He loved movies but he didn't use them as reference points the way so many other people did. He wanted to pace again, only this time the restlessness felt good, because he had so much energy. "More like Dennis Quaid in the bike race in *Breaking Away*."

Paul grinned at him. "A little dated, but it works." He stood up and slapped Evan on the back. "I know you'll want to get to it, give it another read." When Evan nodded, he continued. "Break a leg tomorrow. Let me know about it. I'll let myself out."

Evan nodded again, barely hearing him as he reached for the script. He read it through twice, walking around his living room as he did so, saying some lines out loud, acting certain scenes out, until he felt he knew it well enough for the next day. Then he didn't know what to do with himself. Another read through would just reduce the story to words and he didn't want to lose the feel of it.

He stared down at the coffee table, hands in his pockets, then reached for the phone and dialed Zoey's number.

"Hey, it's me," he said. "Oliver around."

"He's playing that video game. You want to talk, or are you

checking up?"

"Just wanted to talk to my son." The phone clunked down and about thirty seconds later, Oliver came on the line.

"Hi, Dad!"

"Hey, buddy. How's it going? How was the rest of your day?"

"Good. We had mac and cheese for dinner. Mom thinks that lady today is an actress. So you remember in Episode One, when Anakin is in the pod race?"

It took a moment for Evan to switch gears from dinner to *Star Wars*, wondering if "the lady" in between was Samantha. "Sure."

"Well, at school the other day? Me and Brandon were playing pod race and he got his kamikaze warrior out and—"

"His kamikaze warrior? Was that in *Star Wars*?"

"No, it's from the TV show *Kamikaze Warriors*, but it was in our game at school. We needed another pod driver."

"Ah, of course."

"Anyway, so Brandon took his burrito and put the warrior on it and—"

"Wait. His burrito?"

Oliver let out a breath, then said patiently, "The burrito was his pod racer."

"Sure." Evan nodded as if he had no problem keeping up. "Go ahead."

Oliver continued on with the story of how he and Brandon had flown the warrior on a burrito pod racer to the far side of the gym or something, and Evan commented in all the right places, enjoying the sound of his son's cheerful voice.

When he hung up, he sat staring out the window, still missing his son, but more reassured about Oliver being at his mom's tonight. He wondered how Zoey had finally recognized Samantha, and what work she'd done. He could probably ask Paul about her...

If he could remember her last name. He ran his fingers through his hair, then dropped his face into his hands and laughed. He hadn't introduced himself to her, and he wouldn't have known her name at all if she hadn't stepped up and introduced herself to Zoey.

And things might have progressed nicely if Zoey hadn't interrupted.

But he didn't want to think about Zoey right now, wanted to push his focus of her to a lower level, but he knew that would be difficult, considering that in one way or another, she had been in the forefront for at least ten years. Too bad only a few of those had been good and that he'd had to become her bodyguard, watchdog, and parent instead of her lover, confidante and friend. He missed those last three, missed being able to adore someone, to spoil a woman just because he could, and not have to police her actions or question her motives.

And, hell, he missed sex. Steamy, sweaty sex. Tender, slow sex. And everything in between.

He pushed up off the couch and stood in front of the window, staring out without seeing. He turned, then went to stand in front of the fireplace. Shoving his hands in his pockets again, he sighed, and headed down the hallway into the kitchen. He looked in all of the cupboards, then stared into the refrigerator for a full minute before closing the door and wandering to the front of the house and out onto the top step. He stood, hands on hips, looking around at the perfectly landscaped yard, and sighed again.

Nope. Looked like he couldn't avoid the subject of sex anymore. Not if he stayed home anyway. He glanced around the yard, at the garage, then back through the door to the front entryway.

And wondered what Samantha was doing at that moment.

SAMANTHA STARED STEADILY into the refrigerator for two minutes before convincing herself that she wasn't hungry, she was just bored. And restless. She'd changed into khakis and a pressed white polo shirt when she got home, then listened to voicemail. Liz had left a message from her cell phone, sounding as if she'd just gone into a tunnel from the large number of fade outs: something about still being with Gary, putting out filmmaking fires, didn't know when she'd be home, so sorry. It was either that or Liz and Gary were being been firebombed by ferocious aliens. Samantha couldn't tell the difference from the sound.

She closed the fridge and walked to the living room, flopping onto the couch with a groan. She desperately needed to vent about her day, and had no one to call. She had some friends in Wilmington, but none too close. A cousin in Iowa, whose life was occupied with a new baby. A former roommate, Victoria, from her acting days who now lived in San Francisco, but whose hours were lost to reality TV production. Besides, none of them knew her history as Sami Scandal. In this world of blogs, tweets and Facebook posts, she'd managed to keep her true identity secret, mostly by living in solitude. Besides, she hadn't been the focus of the scandal five years earlier.

No, that focus had been the man she'd run into her second day back in Los Angeles: Evan Gallagher.

She pressed her palms to her face and tugged at her bangs with both hands. She could deal with this. He was just a person. A person whose path had crossed with hers. A person who'd done a nude painting of his wife. That she'd bought. A person who'd spent time in jail because of her—

No. Not going there. She took a deep breath, lowered her hands and closed her eyes. Okay, he was just a person. An actor, for heaven's sake. She let out a breath. That was better. Just an actor. Who could paint. And wear black boots and jeans slung low, but just tight enough to cling to his thighs and—

"No!" She sat up, staring into the room. Oh, this was wrong. Evan Gallagher was not attractive. He was...

Tall and lanky and—

"Oh, good grief."

She stood up, shuffled into her loafers, grabbed keys and purse and was out the door before she could talk herself out of it or finish her thought. She didn't know where to go or what to do, but she knew she couldn't stay in Liz's house, wondering at what point Evan Gallagher had become enticing.

Trying not to bump anything, Samantha maneuvered Liz's beast of a car along Hollywood Boulevard, passing tall, skinny palm trees in front of shops and restaurants interspersed with businesses offering a variety of cosmetic procedures. Samantha was laughing over the offer of a body wax during your lunch hour when she saw the silver Gateway Gazebo of the Hollywood Walk of Fame, and she remembered dragging Liz to Paul Newman's star years ago, the two of them crouched in front of it, and sighing dreamily.

Before she could prepare herself for it, more memories came rushing at her as she continued down the Boulevard, barely registering such famous sights as Grauman's Chinese Theatre, Ripley's Believe It or Not with the T-Rex eating a clock coming out of its roof, the black on yellow sign announcing the Hollywood Wax Museum, and the Musso & Frank Grill, a Hollywood institution where Raymond Chandler wrote *The Big Sleep*.

Samantha flashed back to nights on the Sunset Strip, hanging out with Gary and Liz at the Key Club or House of Blues, pancakes on Sundays at DuPar's, and wandering the flea market at Fairfax High School. The fun, the freedom, analyzing every detail of an audition, dreaming of her big break, and then she got that break, with unexpected results. She'd thought being Sami Scandal would open up her world, but it had closed it up instead, isolating her. She'd hurt people with her reports, all in the name of entertainment, and maybe Evan Gallagher hadn't recognized her, but Zoey Highlander seemed to. So who else might?

Her heart beating hard at the thought, she turned down Bronson, then pulled over at Sunset, parking with the tail end of the car slightly sticking out into the road. She got out and wandered to the sidewalk, then walked around the car and leaned against the back end, staring at the pavement. She missed so much about this area, but at the same time, her good memories were entwined with the bad. All of the streets back to Liz's house had past events connected to them: Hollywood, Sunset, Santa Monica, Melrose, Beverly. She'd wandered them all, in search of restaurants, clubs and shops at first, then on the hunt for celebrities and gossip, and had raced down Sunset at the very end to stop her final report. And just today she'd run into Evan Gallagher on Melrose.

Then she looked up and saw it: the Hollywood sign. The symbol of so many dreams.

She smiled as she got back inside. So she'd run into Evan Gallagher today. He'd seen her, the earth hadn't opened up, and it could only get better from here. She noticed some new businesses as she drove, but also some old favorites: boutiques like Beige, Liz's much loved furniture store, Carla, and the huge Beverly Center, where she and Liz had spent hours at the cinema, chatting over coffee, dissecting their lives along with their pizza, drowning any sorrows with ice cream, or dreaming over jewelry in Jennifer Kaufman, where they'd once spotted Courtney Cox browsing.

But those were her old memories, she thought. Now it was time to make new ones. So when she saw a large space in front of a shop advertising used cowboy boots she pulled in before she could talk herself out of it.

"Yeah," she said aloud as she opened the door and dropped to the ground. The new Samantha, she thought, reaching up to take the clips out of her hair and shake it loose. No longer scared and naïve, but strong and impetuous. She marched around the back of the car and headed for the first thing she saw: the tiny shop with a big neon cowboy boot in the window.

She stomped inside and stood in the doorway, feet spread wide, purse held tight in one hand. A woman sat on a stool behind a low counter with her booted feet up, loudly chewing gum and watching Samantha without a change in expression. Her thick auburn hair fell in waves past her shoulders and partially covered a face that could've been thirty or fifty, but appeared smooth and shrewd at the same time. Led Zepplin's "Kashmir" blared from speakers above her head.

Small stools were placed in the middle of the room, mirrors ran along the perimeter at foot level, and rows of shelves had been attached to every wall. Samantha had never seen this many cowboy boots in one place in her life—all colors, sizes, styles and conditions. Some looked as if real cowboys had worn them, some were shiny, glittery new. Before the woman at the counter could say anything, Samantha said, "I want some boots."

The woman blew a bubble, popped it, sucked the gum back in her mouth and said, "No shit."

"Excuse me?"

The woman dropped her feet onto the worn wooden floor with a thud and stood up. "You don't just *want* some boots." She stood in front of Samantha and looked her up and down. "You *need* some boots."

Samantha pointed at her as if the woman had just made the wisest statement in the world. "Yes," she said. "I *need* them."

The woman glanced at Samantha's well-worn loafers. "Size eight," she said, then turned away and began scanning one of the walls of boots.

"Seven," Samantha told her, watching as she ran a fingertip along the toes of the boots, skimming the shelves.

"Sure," the woman said, without turning around. The finger stopped at a pair of bright red boots, the toes faded, the heels worn down in the back, the stitching frayed in places. She held them out with one hand. "These." She handed them to Samantha.

"Red?"

"I been doing this fifteen years." She held the boots closer to

Samantha. "Red. Steel shank, fifteen inches, deep scallop, leather lining, Wellington toe, one and a half inch under-slung heel, better for walking" She jiggled the boots a little.

Samantha's jaw snapped shut so fast her teeth clicked. All she saw was a pair of tall boots with a dip in the front at the top, a slightly narrow toe and curved heel, clearly worn by someone else for a few years, but clean, and red. And red was...red was...

Different. Dangerous. Bold. Something the new Samantha would do, like buying a painting from Evan Gallagher.

Samantha shook her head, focused on the boots, then looked at the saleswoman. "What's your name?" she asked.

"Randy."

How could she not buy a pair of used, worn-in-the-heels red cowboy boots from a profane, gum-snapping woman named Randy?

"I'll take them."

Randy raised an eyebrow at her. "Size eight," she said.

Samantha nodded and let out a breath. "I know," she said, then smiled.

Randy smiled back. "Don't wanna try them on?"

"I trust you."

Randy let out a smoker's laugh. "Don't trust anyone in this town, honey." She gestured to a stool at the counter, opposite the one she'd been sitting on.

"Don't I know it," Samantha said, sitting at the counter and propping her chin in her hand.

"How you wanna pay for these?"

Samantha rummaged through her bag and pulled out a credit card, then handed it over.

Randy began to ring up the purchase. "So who was he? Producer? Director?"

Samantha shook her head.

Randy nodded. "Actor?"

"In a way."

"Ooh." Randy handed her the receipt and a pen. "C list actor? Yeah, been there."

"I've been gone five years," Samantha said, signing her name with a flourish, with more confidence than she had earlier when she'd bought that painting, then handed back the receipt. "He doesn't even remember me," she added.

Randy sucked in her breath and shook her head.

Samantha didn't know why she'd said that. Randy wasn't the cry-on-your-shoulder type, Randy wasn't even someone she knew, but there was something about having a sympathetic ear that made her want to embellish the pain a little—without actually having to tell the embarrassing parts.

"He still look good?" Randy asked, rummaging under the counter until she came up with a box.

Samantha thought of those eyes she'd never known were hazel, the hair she hadn't noticed was auburn, the man she hadn't realized was so tall. "Better."

"Shit."

"Yeah." Samantha dropped her credit card back into her bag.

Randy placed the boots into the box with great care, slipped the lid on, then eased the box across the counter toward Samantha. "You ask me, I bet you look better than you did back then, too. And with these boots? He'll eat his heart out."

Samantha picked up the box and held it to her chest. "Randy? You're an oasis in an endless desert."

"Fuckin' A."

CHAPTER EIGHT

Still in his front yard, Evan dug his keys out of his pocket. The Jeep's top was down, the weather was typical Los Angeles balmy, and maybe a drive in the night air would help distract him. As he wound his way down the hill, the lights of downtown spread out before him, he smelled warm concrete and jasmine, dry grass and earth.

With no specific destination in mind, he headed out of the Silver Lake area, which he now called home, and west on Santa Monica Boulevard in the direction of Beverly Hills, where he used to live. And where he'd once convinced himself that by being literally above the masses, he must be a more worthy person. Silver Lake suited him better now, not because he no longer had millions of dollars thrown at him, but because his career downfall had knocked some sense back into him and he remembered he enjoyed talking to his neighbors, attending local street fairs, and being one of the masses.

Still meandering, he took a left on Highland, then a right, and as he drove down Beverly, he smelled pastries from Susina Bakery, enchiladas at El Coyote, and good old-fashioned grease from Tony's Grill. People strolled in groups, talking and laughing, hemlines in style and not a hair out of place. As he crossed Robertson, a girl slid down from the driver's side of an Expedition. He watched her loosen her hair and shake it out, wild and sexy, as she stood there. Lost for a moment, Evan glanced ahead about a foot from hitting the car in front of him stopped at a red light. He slammed on the brakes. He swore, turning in his seat, but the girl was gone.

He looked up at the sky through the open Jeep. Girls weren't in the stars tonight. Not that he would've gone through the entire scenario of hitting on someone, and going home with her, but he wouldn't have minded a little companionship, some harmless flirting.

He hit his turn signal to go to Tony's Grill, which had a quiet bar to one side, shielded from the restaurant. No valet parking, no reserved tables, everyone treated the same, whether celebrity or grocery store clerk, and a loud but comfortable atmosphere.

A Lakers game played on the TV at one end of the bar and an outdoor adventure program showed on the other. Evan found a stool in the middle, easing between an older man in a business suit and a guy dressed as if he could be on the adventure show he and his friends were critiquing.

Evan ordered a beer and started to nurse it, leaning over with his elbows on the bar and listening to the hum of conversation around him. He wasn't having a rousing or intellectual conversation, but he felt more at ease than he had earlier in the day and thought he might be able to sleep once he got back home.

The businessman finished his drink and left, and a woman slipped onto the vacated seat before he'd completely gotten away from the bar. Evan glanced at her as she gestured to the bartender. Curly red hair, half pulled back in a butterfly-shaped clip, plump face with breasts to match and a yellow outfit he thought might be blinding in daylight.

"What can I get you?" the bartender asked her.

She wiggled a hand at him with long, red fingernails, then tapped one of the nails against her front tooth. Evan noticed a tiny diamond affixed to the tip. "Um…"

Evan handed the bartender some bills. "Whatever she'd like," he said, lifting his glass up to take the final swallow of beer and slide off the stool at the same time. He had one foot on the floor when she turned to him and grabbed his shirt sleeve.

"Aren't you sweet?" she began, then let out a little shriek when she saw his face, and clutched his shirt tighter, almost pulling him against those straining breasts. She held her free hand up, palm toward him, fingers out, as if to ward him off, then breathed, "Duncan. Tanner."

He tried to ease back, but she held him tight. "Actually, I'm not—"

She shook her head, her lips parted. "Duncan. Tanner," she repeated in awe. "Buying me a drink. I always knew you were a gentleman."

"I'm sorry, do we—"

"God, I love you." She patted his chest with the flat of her hand, pressing the chambray to his skin, then pulled back, staring at the spot she'd touched. "Just as hard as I thought you'd be."

What should a guy say to that? "Thank you" might be enough to encourage her, but keeping quiet didn't seem wise, either. He'd met women like her before, who thought he really was Duncan Tanner, and that everything about that character in the films translated into real life when they saw him on the street. Or, in this case, in a bar. He often wanted to say, "No, sorry, you must have the wrong guy. Wasn't Duncan Tanner in South America last time we saw him?" but his desire to please his fans usually won out and he just smiled and nodded until he could find a tactful way out. He wasn't sure tact would work in this case.

"I appreciate the…" He pulled away again, but she'd dug her nails into the fabric of his shirt again and they seemed to be permanently embedded there. He gave up and eased back onto the stool, trying to catch the bartender's eye for some help.

The woman beat him to it. "I'd like a screaming orgasm on the beach," she purred, then turned right back to Evan, one side of her mouth tilting up. He expected her to add, "And I'd like you to give it to me," but instead she leaned closer to him and said, "So what assignment are you on right now?"

"I'm not Duncan Tanner."

She waved her free hand at him. "Oh, sure, sure, I get it." She leaned forward, pushing her chest into his arm. "It's top secret, right?" she whispered, ignoring the bartender when he set down her drink.

Well, he'd wanted human interaction. This was interaction squared.

"I'm really not Duncan Tanner," he repeated.

She patted his arm. "You can trust me. I got a lotta secrets hidden away in here." She patted the top of her left breast. "The stuff I could tell you…" She grabbed his hand, and asked, "So, Duncan, what's going on with you and Amanda?"

"Amanda?"

"You were so off and on there. I was just wondering…" She ran a bright red fingernail along his palm. "Where you were at now?"

Oh, he thought. Right. Amanda Pierce, Duncan Tanner's

romantic interest in the films. Bianca Farentino, often mistaken for Catherine Zeta-Jones, played her but he wondered if anyone had ever talked to Bianca as if she really were Amanda. He could have a good laugh with Bianca over it if she weren't such a raving bitch.

Off, he wanted to say. Definitely off. He and Bianca had tried a little fling, but it had lasted all of five minutes after she began dictating exactly where he could touch her, when, for how long, and in what direction. He'd reminded her he wasn't another one of her paid playthings, and after she told him in exquisite detail exactly where he could shove his attitude, the only romance they developed after that was on film.

They should both have mantels full of Oscars.

Before he could answer her question, the woman shook her head and let out a little sigh, as if she understood all of his woes. "Off, is it? Such a shame." From the glint of incisor when she smiled, he didn't think she felt sorry at all.

He drew back a little, then said, "No, no. Actually, we're on. Very, very on." He lowered his gaze.

He slid his hand from hers and twisted his wrist as if to look at a watch. "And, actually, I'm late meeting her." He shook a finger at her. "And you know how Amanda is. She'll get that whip out if I'm late."

He shoved more bills across the bar and slid off the stool. Taking her hand, he held it to his lips for a moment. "A pleasure meeting you," he said, pressing her hand between his for a moment before making his grand exit.

It was the least Duncan Tanner could do.

Samantha pressed Speaker on the phone and dialed in the voicemail code before removing the top from the box and peering in at the boots. Red. Dangerous. A little naughty. She reached inside.

"Elizabeth!" a voice boomed out from the machine, and Samantha straightened up and dropped her hand as if she'd been caught doing something bad. "This is your mother," the voice added, as if Liz wouldn't know, then there was a pause so long Samantha thought the voicemail had cut her off. Then: "Your mother in New York. Why are you never home? You're never home when your old Ma needs you. Are you with that boy again? That Barry?"

"Gary," Samantha corrected automatically, just as Liz would've done. She looked into the box again, chewing on her lower lip, barely hearing Mrs. Mendenhall's rant. She knew enough from Liz's own rants about her mother that Mrs. M. didn't take Gary or their work seriously, and thought all Liz needed was "a nice boy" to settle down with. Back in New York.

Samantha gave the box a small shake. The heels of the boots seemed a little higher than she'd originally remembered. And the boots were…redder.

She reached in and pulled one out.

"That Barry isn't your type…"

"And she isn't his, Mother Mendenhall," Samantha said to the machine. "No woman is." She took in a deep breath, held the boot up with two hands, let her breath out with a whoosh, and pulled the boot on.

"He looks like he never eats and he never takes things seriously. He calls me Mothah Mendenhall like I'm eighty years old and says I tawk like buttah. He makes no sense. You need to find a nice boy. Janet Shorter's nephew just got out of college, and he's single…"

Samantha now had the other boot on and sat on the couch, staring down at her feet. These had to be the most uncomfortable-looking comfortable shoes she'd ever owned. Of course, she hadn't walked in them yet. She hadn't even stood up in them. But that almost didn't matter.

Randy was a genius.

She pushed up off the couch, bounced lightly on the balls of her feet, then walked around the living room and down the hall. Liz's mother finally signed off, the voicemail beeped, and Samantha heard some underwater whooshing noises and what sounded like Liz's voice. She bounded back into the living room, the desire to giggle bubbling up at how she felt about seven years old, a little girl playing cowgirl in the boots.

She hovered over the phone, straining to make out Liz's message as some words were dropped and long silences cut into others. "Cell phone again," she muttered.

"…late tonight…sorry…" Samantha squinted, as if that would make it easier to understand the message. "Hate…over the phone, but…so sorry…" Samantha restrained herself from throwing the phone against the wall as a few more words played that she couldn't form a complete sentence with no matter how hard she tried. Then the line cleared and Samantha let out a breath.

"So...we're having the readings tomorrow..." Liz's voice sounded tense. There was a pause, then she mentioned Underwood Studios, where she and Gary had office space. "I don't know if...I mean, maybe it's better..." More hissing and sputtering in the message, and Samantha did a little sputtering of her own and began walking around again, looking down at the boots. Liz sounded guilty. Maybe for leaving her at the gallery today? Meeting Evan Gallagher seemed far away, and right now, she felt pretty good. Must be the boots, she thought with a laugh.

"I'm really sorry," Liz's voice said again through the speaker. "We'll talk about it tomorrow, okay? If you're not okay, we'll make it better. Really. I mean it." Liz said goodbye, the phone beeped, and Samantha raised an eyebrow at it.

Liz had sounded really serious. Samantha stood looking at the phone a little longer, as if it would give her some answers, but when the next message started up and Liz's mother's voice boomed out again, asking why she wasn't home already, what kind of daughter was she to abandon her poor mother, Samantha hit the star key to go to the next message. Liz again, and more dropped words. Disgusted, Samantha hung up, then turned off the ringer for good measure. The girl needed to call from a real phone or not call her at all.

She went back to ambling around again. She appreciated Liz's concern, and maybe she'd razz her a little tomorrow about her cell phone, but then she'd reassure her that things were looking up. Maybe she'd even go into the audition, give Liz and Gary some moral support; it was good they'd found some actors to audition so quickly, but they were still going to have to make a fast decision. She might be able to give them an impartial viewpoint since they were so wrapped up in this production.

Then they could dissect her surreal encounter with Evan Gallagher, how she'd found an amazing new boot store with a fascinating owner, and help her rationalize how buying the painting karmically cleared her.

Samantha grinned. Who knew she'd feel this good being in L.A. after the first twenty-four hours had been so crazy?

She looked down at her feet. "I'm sleeping in these damn boots."

CHAPTER NINE

The next morning, Samantha sat at the small dining table, drinking juice and scanning the paper when she heard a shriek from Liz's room. She glanced at the clock, saw that it was eight twenty-five, and smiled. Typical Liz. When they first met, Samantha had tried to reform Liz, marveling how someone could live without any apparent order, always on the edge, but she eventually came to realize that Liz liked her life that way, and Samantha liked Liz that way.

Liz now stood in the doorway of the kitchen, red shirt untucked over a rumpled black skirt, one unbuckled platform Mary Jane on her foot, the other hanging from her hand, hair spiked out to there. "Do you know what time it is?"

"Eight twenty-six," Samantha said, and sipped her juice. She felt really good this morning. She'd found a skirt that actually hit above the knee, paired it with a crisp white top and had added the boots, having decided last night that sleeping in them might be a little much. Accustomed to sweeping her hair up in a French twist, she'd automatically done that after getting dressed, but figured the boots would balance out the beige.

"I can't believe I overslept." Liz plopped onto a chair and began struggling into the other shoe. "I can't believe you let me."

Samantha rolled her eyes, but Liz wasn't looking. "I tried about five times. You sleep like the dead, you know."

"Like Bill Compton, I know." Liz stood up, shoes still undone and let out another shriek as she stood there. "Omigod, did you get my messages?"

Samantha nodded, but before she could clarify that she'd really

54

only gotten bits and pieces of them, Liz continued. "And you're not mad?"

"Well, I'm a little annoyed, but—"

"Oh, God." Hand to her heart, Liz sat down again across from Samantha, watching her intently. "I'm so sorry. We were so screwed, losing Kevin that way, and if I could've avoided this, I really would have. Actually, it's really Gary's fault." She stood up suddenly and careened around the room. "If he'd just listened to me, this wouldn't have happened, but he never listens to me, does he? No. He just goes along his merry way and does what he wants. I said, 'Gary, you twit, this is a bad idea' and he looked at me like I had a screw loose and—"

Samantha stood up to block Liz's movements, then said in a stern tone, "Liz."

Liz looked up at her as if she'd completely forgotten Samantha was there. "Huh?"

"It's fine. And you're late."

"Oh, God." Liz raced to the living room and swiped at the papers on the sideboard until she found her keys. She swept her purse up and said over her shoulder, "So, I have to go. But you're okay. Right?"

"I'm okay. And actually I thought I'd come with you."

Liz blinked at her and the color drained from her face. Her fingers went slack, but she tightened them in time to keep her keys from dropping. "Really? Won't it be…ah, awkward?"

Samantha shrugged. "It'll be good for me. Get me more involved in the film. You and Gary have had a lot of pre-production time, I've only read the script and broken it down, gotten my notes together. I haven't had time for more."

"Sure. Right. Involved." Liz turned to the sideboard again as if searching for her keys. Samantha figured without her habitual morning cup of coffee, Liz's circuits were more loose than usual.

Samantha headed to the door and opened it. "They're in your hand," she said, smiling when Liz lifted the set of keys to her face. But the expression on Liz's face started making her a little nervous. "Maybe I should drive?"

Liz shook her head, marched outside, and pulled herself up into the SUV. "Get there faster if I drive."

"That's what I'm afraid of." Samantha hauled herself in and immediately reached for the seatbelt. She barely had it fastened before Liz roared out of the driveway, heading up their street to Doheny, the same route Samantha had taken the night before, only they'd be heading north to Burbank this morning.

Samantha held her bag against her chest for some comfort as they flew up the road, reminding herself she needed to get her own car. "Oh," she said, remembering, "Mothah Mendenhall called last night."

"Oh God. Oh God oh God oh God. That's some kind of a sign. It's always the final disaster in a series of three when she calls." Liz slammed the car to a stop at a red light, throwing them both against the seatbelts. She looked over at Samantha, her eyes wide. "You're really okay?"

"Yeah," Samantha said, "but maybe we should talk. Clear things up before the audition?"

Liz pressed a hand to her chest. "It wasn't my idea."

"You said that earlier. But I don't—" Samantha began, wanting to ask what idea Liz was talking about, but Liz cut her off.

"I didn't want it at *all*, but Gary insisted it would be fine. Oh hell, what does he know, anyway? He doesn't, really, you know?" She rummaged through the ashtray. "I wish I hadn't quit smoking. I miss my cigarettes. I need one right now." She let out a little moan, throwing her head back against the seat. She banged her palms on the steering wheel. "I'll just kill myself. That'll even things out in the universe."

Samantha gaped at her. "What are you—"

Liz pointed a finger at her. "I'll make it better. I swear I will." The light changed, the person behind them honked, and Liz shot off toward Highland and Cahuenga, which would take them to the studio. "I'll fix it. I'll make it better—"

Samantha couldn't stand it anymore. "Liz, stop. No more drama, please." She swept her bangs back and pressed cool fingers to her forehead.

Liz glanced at her. "But I asked you to come here, guilted you into it when maybe you weren't ready, and then it's all...it just..." She shook her head. "I feel terrible."

Samantha gave Liz's arm a gentle pat, finally understanding the source of Liz's drama: she thought she'd forced Samantha back to L.A. But Samantha had come here to help her friends and start fresh. Liz wasn't responsible for that. "I'm a big girl. I knew what I was getting into when I decided to come here." She waved a hand around. "So, okay, maybe I didn't know everything, but I'm…dealing with things as they happen. You haven't done any damage, I swear."

Liz let out a breath, and hit the signal to turn into the Underwood Studios lot. "You're amazing. And so much more mature than I'll ever be. God, if it were me…" She held a pass out to the guard at the gate, and made idle chatter with him while the gate went up. "Thanks, Ernie."

She waved and they continued down the road between large beige buildings that housed sound stages, studio executive's offices, and props for movies and television. Samantha peeked between the buildings to the permanent outdoor lots that, with a little film magic could be Main Street USA, a plucky single girl's new neighborhood or the dark city streets hiding a serial killer.

Liz pulled over and parked by a grouping of tan bungalows surrounded by a white picket fence; it looked like a small village. Samantha remembered hearing that Alfred Hitchcock pretty much lived in Bungalow 105 at Universal when he was filming.

Liz stared at the fence. "You ready?"

Samantha turned sideways, thinking they should get this cleared up before going inside. "Okay, I'll admit…" She brushed a palm along the edge of her seat, realizing some part of her had been angry at Liz at first for suggesting she come back to California, but that had been her fear of facing the past. And other than running into Evan Gallagher, things were turning out fine. "I was a little upset at first, but I've had time to think about it and it's really all for the best." She touched Liz's upper arm, but let her hand drop when Liz gave a start. "This is for your movie. This is a huge thing for you, and you need to do whatever it takes to make this the most amazing movie ever. And I want to help."

Liz stared at her. "You…" She shook her head. "You really are grown up. Is this what being in North Carolina does for a person?"

Samantha grinned at her. "North Carolina makes you just as crazy as L.A. You just don't flash as much cleavage there."

Liz grinned back. "At least not in public."

They got out of the car and went up the slate walkway to the office. Potted impatiens lined the sides, and a palm tree had been planted to the right, but the area was otherwise nondescript. "Gary is probably having fits," Liz said, swinging her purse over her shoulder and trotting toward the steps, the straps of her Mary Janes flapping as she went.

The front door opened onto a small reception area with a currently empty desk. Liz headed for the open inner door leading to the back room where Gary paced in front of a rectangular folding table with a video camera on a tripod at one end, three chairs behind it, and a lone chair facing everything else.

Samantha had been to quite a few auditions before, some at big round tables, some at small square ones, many with cameras, others without. And they all intimidated her, those continuous rounds of facing groups of people who had the power to say yes or no to a big part of your life, with the possibility of filming the entire reading so it could show up on a special edition release in the future. Giving that up had been a relief when she realized she would never make it as an actress.

When Gary saw them, he tossed down a clipboard he'd been holding and it dropped to the table with a bang. Liz kept walking into the room, but Samantha stopped with a jerk. From his loafers to his perfectly pressed khakis and bright red polo shirt, Gary's clothing was immaculate as always. But red spots stood out on his fair cheeks, and his curly hair stood up in wild corkscrews as if he'd been running and twisting his fingers through it.

He pointed at Liz. "You will be the death of me, Joan Crawford."

"Ease up, Charles in Charge," Liz said, sounding more calm than she had all morning. She pulled a brush out of her purse, and ran it through her hair. "I'm here, our first reader isn't even here—"

"And our leading lady isn't coming today."

Liz dropped her bag next to the clipboard. "What? Little Miss TV Star too good to read with her new leading man?" She stomped a foot and her buckles clattered against the floor. She let out a sigh and bent down to fasten them.

"I tried to call you and call you and call you." Gary ran a hand through his hair. "It rang and rang and rang at home, and your cell phone is off."

"My cell's never off." Liz straightened up and began rummaging through her bag. She held the phone up to her face and pressed a few buttons, shook it, then tossed it across the room. "Dead battery."

"I turned the ringer off at home." Samantha raised her hands up when the others turned in her direction. "I'm sorry. That message."

She dropped her hands to her sides. "I'm sorry," she repeated.

Liz was staring at her face, but Gary's gaze had drifted down to her feet. "Girl. Where did you get those amazing boots?"

Samantha couldn't hold back a smile, both at Gary's reaction and at his sudden shift in mood from the end of the world scenario to a fashion distraction.

Liz pointed at Samantha's feet. "What did you do?"

Samantha slid the toes of her boots together until they clicked, then spread her feet apart again. "Bought some boots." She tucked one foot behind the other, and added quickly, "So what are you guys going to do? About T.J. not showing up."

Liz and Gary looked at each other, then at Samantha, then back at each other.

"Harrison Ford did sides against other actors for *Star Wars* auditions," Gary said.

"He wasn't even supposed to get the part of Han Solo," Liz replied. "He was just doing a favor for Lucas."

Samantha stared at them. They often lost her when they started talking Hollywood trivia. But this was more weird than usual.

"She's not afraid of the camera," Gary continued. "And she knows the script inside and out."

"We know she looks good on film," Liz said to Gary.

Gary nodded. "She bought red boots."

"That's a girl who can't say no," Liz agreed.

They turned around at the same time and looked at Samantha, who had been listening to them with a feeling of dread creeping into the pit of her stomach. She looked back and forth between them. "What? What does Harrison Ford doing sides have to do with this?"

When they didn't say anything, only smiled at her, and it clicked that "sides" were lines from a script given to an auditioning actor, she shook her head and waved her hands back and forth at them. "No. Whatever you're thinking. No."

"You turned the ringer off," Liz said to her.

"I think there's a favor owed," Gary added.

"I'm not an actress," Samantha told them. *Anymore.*

"You're fabulous on camera, sweetie." Gary ran his hands over his hair now to smooth it down. "Very mini Uma Thurman meets Grace Kelly."

Not back then, Samantha thought. *More like a tarted up Meg*

Ryan. She growled at Gary, "I haven't been on camera in years. I'm behind the scenes now."

"But you've done auditions. You know how they work," Liz said.

"And it would really help us out," Gary added.

Liz and Gary stood side by side now, practically holding hands, preppie Hansel and goth Gretel, lost and trying to find their way out of the woods.

Samantha rubbed the heel of her hand against her forehead. "I'm going to regret this…"

Gary and Liz jumped up and down and hugged each other.

"Okay." Gary turned to Liz, going into director mode. "You prep her for the scene, I'll see if Steve has shown up and let him know we're running a little late and then I'll get the camera set up." He headed for the door, but paused and looked at them over his shoulder. "I haven't forgotten about you being late and giving me a heart attack over it," he told Liz, pointing a finger at her.

He went out and Liz shook her head, going to the table for the script. "If we survive this filming, we'll probably still end up killing each other."

Samantha held up two fingers when Liz turned back around. "You owe me twice now."

"I owe you huge for the first thing." She looked up through her bangs at Samantha. "I know it won't be easy. Yeah, you're a professional, yeah you're not afraid of the camera, you've had time to process this, you're all grown up, but this is…well, it's…"

Samantha held up a hand. "Would you rather do it, then?"

Liz's eyes got big. "Hell, no."

Samantha laughed, although she still felt nervous. She wiped her palms on her skirt before easing the script from Liz's fingers. "So what scene are we doing?"

Liz walked to the camera and began fiddling with the controls, her back to Samantha. "Page fifty-seven. Jack and Mattie. Having a confrontation."

Samantha scanned the page, her finger running down the words. She stopped at the bottom. She knew this scene well. "And kissing."

"And we're not having the actors mime their actions," Liz said, peeking over her shoulder at Samantha. "It's all real to save us time and get a feel for them. You don't mind, do you? Viggo Mortensen kissed Molly Ringwald for his Jake Ryan audition…"

Samantha slapped the script shut, cutting her off and not reminding her that Mortensen didn't get the part. "Of course I don't mind. I'm a professional. But this doubles the favors you owe me." She went to a corner and flopped into a chair, crossing her legs and bouncing one red cowboy boot to ease her nerves. She was tempted to jump up and race out of the room, but knew if she left now, it could compromise their choice of a lead and put them behind schedule. The actors could still audition, doing a monologue or reading against Liz, but she knew Liz and Gary wanted to see them react to another person on camera, that doing it this way would smooth and speed the selection process.

She sighed, opening the script. She knew all of the lines she'd be reading today, since she always memorized every script she broke down, but she needed something to distract herself.

Gary backed inside, holding a finger up toward the waiting room. "Just one minute and we'll be with you." He closed the door behind him and beamed into the room. "So, are we ready for Steve Connelly?"

CHAPTER TEN

Samantha stood up, boots thunking against the floor. She wanted to get this over with. "Let's go. Where's my marker?"

Gary led her to the middle of the room, positioning her this way and that according to Liz's direction while Liz looked at them through the camera's viewfinder. Samantha rolled her eyes when Liz directed her to the same position for the third time and finally declared it "just right."

Gary patted Samantha on the shoulder and gave her a pleading look that kept her quiet. She took a deep breath. They were making a movie here, and should take it seriously. She nodded to Gary and he turned to get Steve.

Tall, wearing pressed chinos, a white crewneck with sleeves pushed up to the elbows, and hair in a cut once called the Caesar but now best known as the Clooney—short-cropped and brushed toward the forehead—Steve Connelly bounded into the room in tasseled loafers. Samantha suppressed a grin.

"Steve," Gary said, "thank you for coming today and for being so patient while we figured out that technical problem."

"Sure thing." Steve made a sweeping gesture toward the camera, then beamed at all of them. "You get everything figured out?"

"We did, we did," Gary said.

"You cut your hair," Liz said. "It was longer in your head shot."

Steve ducked his head and ran a hand over the top of his hair, front to back. "Yeah. I figured Jack would have short hair. No nonsense."

Liz pressed her lips together. Samantha knew she'd been looking for a Jack with longer hair because Jack was a spy gone rogue, someone on the run. He would've had short hair when he was in service, but not at the point of the film. Samantha wondered where the chinos and tassels fit in.

"You read the script, Steve?" Liz asked, and Samantha held her breath. Steve could have taken the question as merely conversational, but knowing Liz was frustrated right now, Samantha saw it for the slap it was.

He lifted up the copy rolled in his hand. "Excellent script. Totally excellent."

"So Steve," Gary said, leading him forward by the elbow. "We appreciate you agreeing to read with Samantha today, who is standing in for Tracy Jennifer Lawson."

Steve looked Samantha up and down, and she couldn't read the expression on his face, but he didn't look quite as cheerful as before. "Sure," he said after a moment, bringing out the beaming smile again. "No problem."

Deciding to ignore his disappointment, Samantha stepped up and shook hands with him, flashing a big fake smile of her own, and hoping this would all be done soon.

"Tracy Jennifer's shorter than…" Steve gestured toward Samantha with the rolled up script.

"Samantha," Gary said, guiding Steve into position in front of the camera.

"Right." He gave Samantha an even broader, dental-enhanced smile.

"Yes, yes, yes," Gary said brightly. "Samantha is more willowy, elegant. But there is a quiet strength about her, too, just like the character Mattie."

Gary sat down behind the long table. "So, Steve, you know we're recording this today, and that's still acceptable to you?"

"Sure. Yeah. I signed the waiver." He did that hair flattening thing again.

Gary gestured to Liz, who turned the camera on. She made some final adjustments, announced the date and time and what the audition was for, then sat down next to Gary. "Why don't you tell us a little about how you see Jack, and then we'll go into the reading."

Steve slapped the script against his palm. "Jack's a rogue, right? A loner. Clint Eastwood as the pale rider, Bruce Willis in *Die Hard*.

Brando in *On the Waterfront*."

Samantha looked up at Steve out of the corner of her eye, shaking her head. They always brought up Brando. Then, remembering she was on camera, she changed her expression back to neutral.

Steve had begun to wax poetic on James Dean when Liz slapped her palms on the table, making them all jump.

"Fabulous," she told Steve in a flat voice. "Just…" She pressed her lips together for a moment. "Fabulous. Let's move forward, okay?" She gestured with her own script, which she had set on the table in front of her. "Page fifty-seven. Starting with the line 'I don't have long. They're on my trail.' And as I'm sure Gary mentioned to you, we're not miming any actions at this reading, although the slap won't be full force."

Steve nodded, turned to the right page, rolled the script in one hand, straightened his body, cleared his throat, and began.

"I don't have long," he said, leaning so close Samantha could tell he wore bright blue contacts and that he'd had something with onions for breakfast. She tried not to cringe as he breathed, "They're on my trail."

She lifted her copy of the script up between them, ostensibly to review her line. "You shouldn't even be here at all, Jack. This is too dangerous." She stared into Steve's eyes, trying to figure out if his original eye color was a dull brown or a blue he'd wanted to enhance. And were those plugs?

He stepped closer and she resisted the urge to press her script up against his mouth to ward off the onions. "I couldn't stay away, Mattie." He glanced at his lines, then at her breasts and back into her eyes. "You know that."

"I know what we were a long time ago, in another place, another world. We were other people. It's different now, and you know that." She knew she was rushing through her lines, but she didn't care if Jack and Mattie were tortured by their past and unsure of their present. Jack's breath smelled like yesterday's cabbage soup and Mattie needed some fresh air. And the shoe tassels had to go. When she got home she was giving every one of her pairs of loafers to charity.

"Not everything is different, Mattie." Steve brushed her bangs back from her forehead, his gaze hovering somewhere between her eyes and her mouth. He slid his fingers down the side of her face and she flinched as his rough skin caught on the edge of her ear. He paused and looked at his script again. "What we feel for each other..." Another glance at the page. "What we feel for each other hasn't changed. And it never will."

Samantha twisted away. "No, Jack. That won't work this time." She took in a big gulp of fresh air and turned back to Steve. "I won't let you do this to me again."

"And I won't let you make this sacrifice."

"You can't make demands on me anymore, Jack. You gave up that privilege when you left me. Thinking you had died." She positioned her body away from his again.

"You know what happened back then. I told you." He put a hand on her shoulder, and spun her around so fast to face him that her boots clattered against each other as her feet tried to keep up. "They'd caught me. I couldn't get away. If you could only know. If you only knew..." He glanced at the pages clutched in his hand. "If you only knew how bad it was there. How hard." He choked and dropped his head.

"Jack..."

He pulled her up against him so hard she squeaked, then turned her head, hoping it looked like she was shifting away from Jack's intensity and not Steve's breath. He grabbed her chin and lifted her face up, those faux blue eyes boring into hers. "Maybe I don't have the words. But I can show you another way," he said, then mashed his lips to hers, grinding them back and forth until their teeth clicked together.

She pulled away, gasping, then raised her hand up to slap him. In the script, Jack was supposed to block her hand, but Samantha didn't notice Steve surreptitiously scanning his script again for his next line.

Her palm struck his cheek with a small *thwat*, and the momentum carried her forward so that she bumped against him, throwing him off balance. He stumbled backward, one hand to his face.

Steve stared at her. "You hit me."

"I'm sorry. But you were supposed to stop me." She pushed away from him, brushing her hands against her skirt, then leaned down and picked up the wrinkled pages he'd dropped. "It's in the script," she said, waving it at him.

Gary stood up and clapped his hands together. "Okay, great," he said. "That was great. Good drama." He put a hand on Steve's arm.

"She hit me," Steve said, his hand still against his face.

"I know, buddy." Gary patted at him. "And your response was A number one. A great performance, really."

Steve lowered his hand. "Really?"

"Absolutely. Right, Liz?"

Liz gave him a flat smile and the thumbs up sign. "Quite a performance, Steve-o," she said. "Samantha's slap really brought out the tiger in you."

Steve broke into a grin. He gave Samantha a push on the bicep. "Thanks, Sam. A good actor is only so good as his leading lady."

Samantha duplicated Liz's thumbs up at him while Gary led Steve outside, showering him with reassurances.

"Does 'don't call us, we'll call you' ring any bells?" Liz leaned back in her seat, and put her hands over her face.

Too discouraged to attempt reassuring her, Samantha stood to switch off the camera, then sat back down with a sigh.

Gary came back in and slammed the door behind him, hands on hips, feet spread wide. "What was that? What *was* that? What, Thelma and Louise, was *that*?"

"Steve Connelly screwing up my great lines," Liz said. "Bruce Willis, my butt," she muttered. "Jack is nothing like John McClane in *Die Hard*."

"You're the one that was so excited to hear we'd gotten him."

"That's because—" Liz glanced at Samantha. "God, he was like one of those melodrama actors, practically twirling his mustache. If he were playing the female, he would've swooned. He's clearly not Jack."

Samantha stood up. "I'm going to get some coffee."

Liz and Gary stood glaring at each other.

"Are you joking?" Gary threw his arms out from his sides. "He won a Golden Globe—"

"For playing a deranged misfit," Liz cut in. "Everyone knows you win awards if you play mental."

"I found two name actors in a very short period of time that would be a credit to the film," Gary said through gritted teeth. "We're lucky we got even that. Steve Connelly is a known quantity and he's done good work in the past."

Enough drama, Samantha thought, easing along the wall and heading for the door.

"I don't need names, Gary, you know that," Liz told him.

"I know. You want the perfect Jack. You have this image in your head and you must know he doesn't exist in reality. It's one of the fallacies of Hollywood. Even getting close will be lucky. But you know the next reading's going to be better…"

The next reading. Samantha shook her head. She went out the front door, blinking against the bright sun and searching for a sign among the rows of industrial looking buildings to direct her to the commissary. Or a vending machine. She couldn't do another reading. She'd have to find a way to explain that to them. Liz could do it. See how she liked kissing someone with gorilla breath.

She rounded the corner of the office, and headed blindly toward a group of buildings set close together, head down and palm pressed to her forehead. "No," she said out loud. "No, no, can't do it."

Then she smacked right into someone.

Startled, she lost her balance, but felt hands take hold of her upper arms, keeping her from falling. The sun was behind him, blinding her for a moment and she couldn't see his face clearly.

"Are you sure you can't do it?" he asked.

Samantha blinked with dawning recognition. The hands on her arms prevented her from fleeing.

"Hello again," Evan Gallagher said, finally releasing her.

"It's you." What was he doing here, in front of her, for the second day in a row?

"And it's you." That voice. That strong, melodious voice that made women swoon. All it did was make her knees weak for another reason.

"What?" she squeaked. Had he recognized her? No. He was smiling. She had to remind herself that he hadn't recognized her yesterday, but she still felt like pressing a hand to her chest to keep her heart from bursting out.

"Samantha, right?"

She had to swallow before she could speak. "Right."

"Evan," he said, pointing to himself.

"Right," she said again, looking vaguely at a point above his left shoulder as she had at the gallery, terrified that if she looked directly at him, he'd look directly at her, and then he'd know.

He leaned into her line of vision. "I'm a little embarrassed about this, but I didn't get your last name yesterday."

"Oh." She swallowed again. Sami Scandal had never used her real name on air, but he could have discovered it somehow. She took a breath, wondering how fast she could run in the boots.

"It's-uh-Jamison," she said, running the words together. "Samanthajamison."

He held out his hand. "Nice to officially meet you, Samantha Jamison."

She let out her breath. Nothing, no sign of recognition. Relieved, she took his hand and shook. He held on a little longer than necessary. His palm felt toughened, maybe from working with his hands, but it did not feel rough like Steve Connelly's, and his fingers slid over hers in a little caress when he finally let go. "Yes," she said, her hand tingling. "Nice to meet you, too. You...um...have a lovely family," she added.

He laughed, his eyes crinkling up. "My son's at that stage where he wants to know about everything and then tell everyone else what he's learned, usually embellishing it and adding in some *Star Wars* references. And Zoey's..." He held her gaze. "My ex-wife."

"Oh." She'd known that, but wasn't sure how to respond, partly because she didn't know why he told her.

He glanced at his watch, and then toward the office. "I hate to cut this short, but I have an appointment and I'm almost late." He gestured at the building. "Would you happen to know where Don Scheimer's office is?"

"Don Scheimer?"

He nodded. "The producer. I'm..." He ducked his head, then looked up at her from the corner of one eye. He pulled a packet of papers from his back pocket and held them up. "I'm here for a reading."

Her heart thunked hard in her chest, once, then stopped. She was pretty sure it had stopped permanently. Liz and Gary were renting office space from Don Scheimer, a partner in Underwood Studios.

"I'm an actor, too," he said. "I didn't get a chance to tell you that yesterday."

"Uh." She pressed a hand to her chest. "Erk."

He leaned forward. "Are you all right?"

She nodded and wheezed out a breath. "It's a really small town," she squeaked.

Evan straightened up and smiled. "You don't work for him, do you?"

She had to laugh at that. "Not exactly." Although Don Scheimer had once pulled her onto his lap at a party. "I'm…I sort of work with Liz Mendenhall, who wrote the script." And I'm going to kill her as soon as I get the chance, she thought.

"You're…" Evan shook his head. "Are you one of the producers? I already talked to Gary on the phone."

"No, I'm…" Oh, this couldn't be happening. "I'm the continuity supervisor. And I'm helping them out today." She turned and headed back to the office on wobbly legs. "I can show you the way."

She reached for the door, but he came around and opened it first, gesturing with his other hand for her to go ahead of him. He stood so close, her arm brushed his as she forced herself over the threshold. She looked up at him before slipping inside and caught him watching her, his eyes on her face. "Thank you," she whispered, dropping her gaze as she walked in, her heart finally starting to beat again.

She couldn't believe this. She was going to have to read with Evan Gallagher.

CHAPTER ELEVEN

Without looking behind her, Samantha said, "I'll just, ah, check on whether they're ready for the...uh...and be...right back and all that and...." She slipped into the back room, shut the door behind her and leaned against it, as much to hold herself up as to have something solid to cling to. She needed both things right now.

Gary and Liz were still arguing, although it seemed less heated now, and Samantha stamped her foot to get their attention.

She took a deep breath, willing her heart to stop pounding so hard. In measured tones, she said, "Evan Gallagher is in the front room." She took a shaky breath. "Waiting to do a reading with you."

Gary's expression changed from strained to thrilled in an instant. "Oh, great," he said. "Liz, you set up the camera and I'll go get him."

He headed for the door and Samantha blocked him with her arm straight out like a traffic cop. "Oh great?" she repeated, her voice an octave higher than usual. "How is that great?"

Gary gave her a wary look. "Because he's here? He's a terrific actor?" He stopped when Samantha glared at him. "What?"

Samantha turned her attention to Liz, gesturing toward the front room. "Evan Gallagher," she repeated, watching Liz. "Is in that room." She stumbled away from the door, feeling light headed, and sat down hard in a chair. "How can this be happening?" She put her face in her hands.

"What?" she heard Gary say again.

Liz sat down next to her. "I thought you were okay with this."

Samantha straightened up. "When would I ever be okay with this?"

Liz gaped at her. "But today. This morning. At the house. In the car."

"What? I didn't say…" Samantha shook her head.

"You said you were a grown up and it was all for the best. I said I was sorry, and you were okay with it."

"I didn't know this is what you meant. How could you? After what happened with him?"

Gary sat down on Samantha's other side, leaning forward. "Ooh, what happened?"

"I don't want to talk about it," Samantha growled.

"But if—"

Samantha glared at Gary, then at Liz, then started pacing around the room.

"What was it, honey?" Gary asked her. "Did he break your heart?" He turned to Liz. "You held out on me about Evan Gallagher and Smammy."

Samantha stopped her circling and shook her finger at him. "Don't call me that." Her old nickname was just too close to her old stage name. She glanced at the door. "Not now. Please." Seeing Evan Gallagher once had been hard enough, but she'd managed. Seeing him again today made her realize she'd deluded herself. Bumping into him was one thing, but she couldn't imagine reading with him.

She heard Gary whisper to Liz again. "You held out on me."

Liz shushed him and went to Samantha. "Sam," she said. "You said you got the message. You said you were fine. You're not fine." She shot a quick look at Gary. "We'll send him home, tell him it's off."

Gary shot up from his chair. "We'll what?!"

Liz flapped a hand at him.

"Will you stop shushing me?" Gary said. "And someone tell me what the hell is going on?"

"I didn't get a *clear* message. It was like someone talking underwater. I didn't know it was…was…this." Samantha began looking around the room. "I can't do this," she said, spying her purse and heading toward it. "I can't, I just can't—"

She snatched up the purse and ducked her head to keep from looking at either Liz or Gary as she headed for the door. She threw it open and took two steps into the front room and—

Crap.

In all of the fuss over Evan Gallagher, she'd forgotten about Evan

Gallagher. There. Waiting to do a reading. With her.

He'd been looking out the window at the palm tree set in the courtyard, but turned when she opened the door. The expression on his face went from serious concentration to cheerfully expectant and something inside of her ached at his smile.

"All ready?" he asked.

She dropped her gaze, from that smile, those eyes, from the look on his face that she couldn't read, but that made it hard to breathe all of a sudden, and then she looked right down at his boots. Motorcycle boots.

She was in so much trouble.

And if he wasn't Jack, she didn't know who was. He had the long hair, five o'clock shadow, tight faded t-shirt, and jeans with a hole in the knee. He looked the part of the rebel loner, someone who'd been on his own far too long and didn't need a woman, but wouldn't mind having one in his bed for a while.

She pressed a shaky hand to her forehead and swallowed hard, but, still unable to speak, she merely nodded and backed into the room. She nodded grimly at Gary and Liz, and set her purse back on the chair. She heard Evan's boots thump in behind her, then his voice as he introduced himself to Gary and Liz.

She heard him say, "An exceptional script," to Liz and looked up in time to see Liz glance at her, then turn back to Evan and thank him.

Gary cleared his throat. "So, Evan, you know we'll be filming the reading." When Evan gave him a nod, Gary continued. "Tracy Jennifer couldn't make it today. She's sorry about that, but we have a great replacement in Samantha, who…" He glanced between the two of them. "I see you've met."

"Yesterday," Samantha offered, and Liz looked up from the table and stared at her. "I bought one of his beautiful paintings and he happened to be in the gallery at the time." She glanced at Liz, and saw that her face had gone pale. Good, she thought, but immediately regretted it and lowered her gaze.

"Oh," Gary said. "That's…fabulous. Small town."

"Indeed." Evan caught Samantha's eye when she looked up at him.

He smiled at her and she couldn't help smiling back, trying to convince herself that it was okay to notice that he was gorgeous and to have a response to that. You could ruin someone's life and still be attracted to them, right?

While she pondered this, Gary explained more about the audition to Evan and arranged them in front of the camera. Then Gary went back to sit behind the table and Liz asked Evan to tell them a little about how he saw Jack.

Samantha risked a glance at him as he gave the question some thought. "He's damaged," he finally said. He brushed a section of hair back from his face. "He's been on the run because of a situation he got caught up in, but had no control over. He felt he ruined Mattie's life, when all he wanted was to be with her. She started out with his brother, but he wanted her, and he was used to getting what he wanted. Even if it wasn't the right thing for her."

He glanced at Samantha, and she looked away, feeling as if he could read her thoughts, which were heading into dangerous territory. *I will not look at his boots*, she thought, *I will not look at his boots...*

"Now he has to face what he's done," Evan continued, "and realize that certain of his actions, while not intending to harm anyone, hurt the one person he wanted to protect. And it's almost too late when he realizes the effect all of this has had on his brother."

Samantha glanced at Liz, who looked like Christmas had just come early. Evan's evaluation of Jack had been dead on.

"Great." Gary cleared his throat and suggested they get started. He reminded Evan there was no miming for this reading, and to give it his all. He gave Liz a little nudge and she sat up straighter.

"Evan, we'll start with the line 'I don't have long. They're on my trail.'"

Evan nodded and turned to Samantha. She noticed he didn't have the script in his hand anymore and that he was looking directly into her eyes. He took a step closer until they stood barely a foot apart and he bent his head to her and said in a soft, but strained voice, "I don't have long." He glanced behind him, as if looking for his pursuers, then back to Samantha. "They're on my trail."

He stood so close Samantha had to lift her head to look at him. His gaze never wavered, and she almost forgot her line as she looked into his eyes. "Jack," she said, feeling her chest tighten. "You shouldn't be here. It's too dangerous."

A hint of a smile played at the corners of his mouth and he shook his head a little. "I couldn't stay away, Mattie." He reached up and brushed a stray lock of her hair behind her ear. "I could never stay away. You know that."

She blinked up at him, forgetting to breathe.

She barely heard Liz's stage whisper, reading her the beginning of the next line.

With a nod, she repeated: "I know what we were a long time ago, in another place, another world. We were other people." After she added, "It's different now, and you know that," she couldn't resist reaching up and running a fingertip along his jaw, a gesture reminiscent of his own, something an old lover would do, someone trying to let go, but who wasn't quite ready.

Evan caught her hand by the wrist, still looking into her eyes, and pressed his lips to her palm. "Not everything is different, Mattie. What we feel for each other hasn't changed. And it never will."

He closed his eyes, his eyelashes brushing against the side of her finger, and she thought she might pass out. She was pretty sure she swooned a little when Evan eased his cheek against her hand and held it there.

Samantha knew she should pull her hand back, that the script called for Mattie to be upset, to try to push Jack away, even though she didn't want to. So maybe Mattie would leave her hand there, she thought. That was the sign of someone conflicted, right?

"That won't work this time, Jack," she said, looking at Evan, his face peaceful, eyes still closed, as if in sleep. She had the desire to brush a hand across his brow, trace a finger along his temple and down his face to his lips.

She had to get the rest of the line from Liz again. "I won't let you do this to me again."

Evan opened his eyes and looked at her, then used the hand he was holding to pull her closer. "And I won't let you make this sacrifice."

Samantha gave an ineffective tug with her hand. "You can't make demands on me anymore, Jack. You gave up that privilege when you left me. Thinking you had died."

"I told you what happened back then. They'd caught me and I couldn't get away. If you only knew how bad it was. How hard."

"Jack…"

"Maybe I don't have the words," Evan said. He let her fingers go after giving them a squeeze, then raised both of his hands to her face, cupping it and tilting it up to him. "But I can show you another way."

He bent his head, holding her gaze. She watched in dismay and fascination until he lowered his lashes, then pressed his lips to hers in a kiss that was warm and sweet, and promising. She swayed at his touch, gripping his forearms to keep her balance. Later, she would try to figure out whether she was the one who pressed her lips more firmly to his, or if that particular delight was his doing, but at that moment she didn't care. She hadn't been properly, respectfully kissed in a long time, and she wouldn't give this up for anything.

His lips parted slightly and he slid the tips of his fingers into her hair, shifting his body closer as he did so. She responded by easing her hands up to his biceps and slipped her fingers under the sleeves of his shirt. His muscles tensed and jumped and she grasped him tighter. The tip of his tongue gently brushed over her upper lip and she was pretty sure she made a sound in the back of her throat as a shiver ran from the nape of her neck to the tip of her toes.

Her lips parted, his tongue brushed hers, and her entire body ignited.

Man, could Evan Gallagher kiss. And she didn't want him to stop. But he was supposed to. Because *she* was supposed to—

Her mind swirled around frantically, but nothing coherent came up. She was supposed to do…something…for some reason. Oh, who cared? This was better than chocolate, she thought, as she pressed against Evan and deepened the kiss.

Someone coughed, and Samantha staggered back, still gripping Evan's arms, and shook her head, trying to clear it.

They stood staring at each other, until he cleared his throat and whispered, "You're supposed to slap me."

She leaned toward him. "What?"

He grinned at her. "For kissing you."

She blinked at him, not able to comprehend for a moment why she should slap him for such an amazing kiss.

Gary's voice broke through her haze. Barely. "No, yeah. No. That was…great. We can forgo the slap, I think." He sounded just as dazed as Samantha felt.

Evan patted Samantha on the shoulder and stepped away from her. "Great reading," he said. "Thank you."

She glanced at her shoulder. Great reading? A little pat after an electric kiss that made all of her secret parts go zing? She looked up at him, but he had turned to Gary. She saw the red light on the camera. Oh, right. He was an actor. That was a little bit of a movie magic kiss was all, and she'd been suckered into it.

Damn it.

She didn't hear much after that, just slunk over to a chair behind Gary and Liz, their voices sounding a little to her like "blah blah, blah blah blah." Evan's rich voice demanded her attention, his lines spoken as Jack still reverberating through her head, but she refused to give him that. He didn't know it yet, but they were even. She'd crushed him and now he'd just crushed her. She refused to let her rational side remind her that she'd done more than crush him. But he had seduced her for a part, then patted her like a puppy and sent her away.

She crossed her arms under her breasts. Forget rationality. She was embarrassed and hurt, and felt like she'd been had, by everyone in the room.

"Samantha."

Startled out of her angry thoughts, she looked away from the window to see Evan standing over her, his hand out.

"Thank you for the reading."

She gave him a tight smile and a limp handshake. "Just doing my job," she said, and immediately wanted to take it back. She was about to add something a little more kind, but he straightened and left the room without another word.

She watched him go, regret coursing through her for what she'd said, but she wasn't going to let that stop her from making a grand exit and go hide under the covers for a few days.

Once she was sure Evan Gallagher had left the lot.

CHAPTER TWELVE

Samantha stood in Liz's guest bedroom staring at the red boots she'd set next to her old comfortable loafers. After catching a cab back to Liz's, she'd showered, changed into a long tan skirt and white top buttoned at the neck, then stood debating which shoes to wear since she didn't quite know what to do next.

Out of curiosity, she picked up one loafer and turned it over. Size seven. She wanted to say "Ha!" at Randy's insistence on her getting boots in size eight, but as she looked at the loafer, she realized how worn and stretched out it had become and she couldn't remember how long she'd had the pair. They were comfortable now, but had they been back then, when she'd had to cram her toes into them? Then she remembered Steve Connelly and his tassels. She dropped the shoe, disgusted.

The red boots had failed her, too—well, at the least, they'd gotten her into trouble. If she hadn't worn them to the audition, Gary wouldn't have pointed out that someone who wore boots like that would be the type of person to step in for a reading.

She toed the loafers. But then, the type of girl who'd wear tatty old loafers might not get kissed like that. And as mortified as she was by the entire episode, it had been an unforgettable kiss. The man deserved an Oscar.

Because his kiss set her on fire, and he'd acted like nothing had happened.

She picked up the boots with one hand, tossed them into the closet, slid the door closed, then went to sit on the bed. She sat ramrod straight, trying to pull in some bravado by appearing calm and poised.

But she didn't feel calm and poised. She felt the opposite, and looking proper wasn't going to change that.

She pushed herself up from the bed, chin lifted, and walked back to the mirrored closet, turning her back on Liz's desk and computer. Shirt buttoned up to here, khaki skirt to her ankles, belt tying it all together, hair swept up into a sleek French twist, nothing out of place.

She undid the belt, slid it out of the loops and dropped it onto the floor.

No, that wasn't it.

She undid a few buttons, then untucked the shirt, leaving it rucked up and wrinkled.

Better, but not quite. She slid her gaze in the mirror from bottom to top, stopping at the top. She reached up with one hand and slid it along the side of her head, smoothing back already smooth hair, then pulled at the clip and let it drop to the floor as well. She gave her head a little shake, the hair came loose, and drifted down her head to her shoulders and between her shoulder blades. She fluffed her hands through it, settling the waves so they flowed together.

Better.

A girl with bed head and a rucked up shirt could handle a liquefying kiss from Evan Gallagher. But a girl in loafers could not handle that sort of kiss if Evan Gallagher didn't mean it.

She had just kicked the loafers into the closet and retrieved the boots when Liz said from the doorway, "I called in for my messages. I see what you meant about the underwater thing. You were supposed to hear me apologizing because Gary had gotten an audition with Evan Gallagher."

Samantha had jumped when Liz first spoke, but now stood in front her, gripping the boots.

"We didn't find out he was reading until the last minute," Liz continued. "And you weren't home. I fought it, but couldn't tell Gary why. He was so happy, he thought Evan Gallagher was a big coup—"

"You didn't tell Gary what happened?"

Liz stared at her for a beat. "I promised you I'd never tell anyone. But I didn't know how to tell Gary I didn't want Evan Gallagher for Jack." She threw her hands out from her sides. "How could I not want Evan Gallagher for my movie?"

"Gary would've asked too many questions," Samantha said.

Liz nodded. "He asked about a million after you left."

"What'd you say?"

"I told him it was between the two of you." She smiled a little. "He thinks you had a torrid affair and he said he's never going to forgive us for not giving him all the details."

Samantha sat back on the bad. "If only that's what it'd been."

"Yeah. At least you would've gotten some sex out of it."

Not wanting to laugh, Samantha pressed her lips harder together and bowed her head. She snuck a peek at Liz, who was biting her lips, too. Samantha let out a sigh, as if she were making a hard decision. "Come on in."

Liz settled herself on the neatly made daybed, plumping the pillows up behind her. "I'm getting a new cell phone."

"Hallelujah," Samantha said. "No more fuzzy phone messages letting me know the world is on fire and I'd better get out now, only I can't understand what you're saying."

"That was pretty bad," Liz admitted, plucking at the bedspread. "But we're not hiring Evan. And I'm sorry. About all of this. Beyond sorry…"

"Evan Gallagher is Jack," Samantha said, not looking at Liz even after she saw out of the corner of her eye that Liz had turned toward her.

"I know," she said after a beat of silence, "but we're not hiring him. Gary was calling his agent when I left."

Samantha stood up, retrieving the boots she'd set by the bed, and pulled them on. Then she started scanning the room for her bag.

"What are you doing?" Liz asked.

"Making this better."

"What?"

"I don't know how, but I have to do something."

Liz trailed after her. "It's done. The word's out to casting to find more people to audition."

Hands on hips, Samantha stood looking into the closet. "That'll cost you more money."

Liz made a noise. "Better than hiring Steve Connelly."

Samantha went to the phone by the bed and lifted up the receiver. "You need Evan Gallagher in your movie. Call Gary and tell him to hire him."

"Not if it upsets you so much."

"I'll be okay if you hire him."

Liz raised an eyebrow at her. "I'm pretty sure pigs just started to fly somewhere," she said, but took the phone and dialed. When a muffled, "Hello," came through the receiver, she said, "Hey, Spielberg, you get hold of Evan's agent?" She smiled at Gary's response. "No? Well, when he calls you back, tell him Evan got the part."

Samantha let out a breath even as she heard Gary's voice squawking at Liz through the phone. Gary hadn't reached Evan Gallagher's agent. They still might be able to save this movie. That was great.

And it was awful. She'd see Evan Gallagher every day for about five weeks. How long would it take for him to figure out who she was?

"Listen, Urkel," Liz cut in, "some things have changed and if you'd pay attention, you'd find out the good news." She pulled the phone away from her ear, made a face, then held the receiver out to Samantha. "You tell him. He thinks I've lost it."

Samantha took the phone and said, "Evan Gallagher is Jack Dawson."

There was a pause at the other end. "I know?"

"Call his agent back and tell him he got the part."

"Samantha, what's going on? Are you going to tell me what happened between you and Evan Gallagher?"

Samantha looked over at Liz, letting out a sigh. "Let's meet for dinner," she said. "I'll tell you everything."

CHAPTER THIRTEEN

Evan drove up the long unpaved drive of J&B Ranch, took a right past the front of the house, and headed for a large barn in the near distance. The double doors of the barn had been pushed open, and three foals, their manes still bristly and tails short, romped around inside a paddock to the left. Evan parked the Jeep to the side, opened the door, and, his elbows resting on his knees, sat watching the colts.

One pranced toward the fence in his direction, head held high, and stood in place, watching him. The horse snorted, tossed his head, and raced around the paddock, followed by his companions.

Evan laughed, watching as they chased each other. He stepped down, shutting the door behind him, and looked up in time to see a man walking out from the shadows of the barn. Long and lean in blue jeans, legs slightly bowed from years of riding and his white hair almost covered by a battered brown cowboy hat, he reminded Evan of Paul Newman in *Hud*.

He had, in fact, done stunt work for Newman on that movie.

Evan greeted him with a grin and a handshake. "Jim."

The other man's grip was firm and his eyes warm. "What brings you by?"

"Need to get away for awhile."

"You want Shasta?" Jim inclined his head at the barn.

"I was thinking Rogue."

"Nothing like a good gallop to work some things out," Jim said, and turned toward the barn.

Evan held a hand up to stop him. "I can get him. I don't want to interrupt your work."

"Almost done anyway. Just getting some of the friskies out of the colts."

They both looked at the foals. "They look good."

"They do. You still interested in the bay?"

Evan nodded.

"Good. You bring Oliver out whenever."

Evan nodded again, and rubbed a hand along his jaw, still watching the bay colt. He took a moment, appreciating Jim's steadiness and generosity, then moved next to his friend and copied his pose.

He'd met Jim Barker on the set of the first Duncan Tanner movie, where Jim had been a horse wrangler, but Jim had made his name in the industry as a stuntman years earlier. Evan hadn't been on a horse in his life, and the script had called for him to be on horseback for a lot of the film. He told the director he could ride, and had stubbornly refused to confess that he couldn't.

Jim had recognized this inexperience right away, and instead of bringing it up and possibly embarrassing Evan—or losing him the role—he'd asked the director for additional "rehearsal" and prep with the horses during pre-production.

Jim hadn't had to say a thing as he watched Angus, the horse brought in for Evan, stop short, brush against a fence, and race for the barn when he heard the feed delivery truck. Evan had been unable to stop him and toppled off halfway through Angus' race. Aching, sweating, coughing from the dust, and swearing, Evan limped back to Jim and finally admitted he didn't know what he was doing.

Jim had worked with him, kept his secret, and they'd been men of few words and a strong friendship since.

"Lost that part I read for couple weeks ago," Evan said now.

Jim kept looking straight ahead. "Sorry to hear that."

"They gave it to Kevin Bacon."

"That boy's everywhere."

"Indeed." Evan let a few moments pass. "Got another audition. Horror movie."

Jim snorted.

Evan smiled, but it was fleeting. "Dropped that one for an indie I just read for this morning." He shook his head a little, before Jim could say anything, or ask him how it went, although the other man usually let him do most of the talking.

Jim straightened up and clapped Evan on the shoulder. "Take as long as you need with Rogue," he said. "Come in later for some of Brenda's cobbler if you want." His hand tightened until Evan gave a slight nod, then he turned away and ambled toward the house.

Evan went to his Jeep and traded the boots he'd chosen to get into the character of Jack for a pair of battered cowboy boots he kept stowed behind the seat. Tugging on one boot and pulling his pants leg over it, he remembered those red boots Samantha Jamison had been wearing, and shook his head, his hair falling into his eyes. He smiled, but it didn't erase how bad he felt.

He had been pulled right into the character of Jack during the reading, and then he'd been unprofessional by letting himself get drawn into the moment that way. And by kissing Samantha.

That way.

So she hadn't slapped him as it had been called for in the script, but her attitude toward him as he was leaving was payback enough. He didn't need a slap to understand her silent accusation that he'd overstepped his boundaries.

Gary and Liz had been kind, but he'd blown it, and he knew it. It wasn't Rule #1, but it had to be in the top ten that you didn't stick your tongue down the script supervisor's throat during an audition. Not without asking first, anyway.

He wasn't sure he believed in coincidence, but he didn't know what to make of their meeting at the gallery yesterday, then Samantha filling in for Tracy Jennifer at the reading, only to be followed by him screwing up. It had seemed like something positive, even if just to remind him there were other women out there, but why did she have to be associated with a job? A job he badly wanted.

And somehow he was going to have to explain all of this to Paul. As a friend, he'd understand Evan getting a little carried away; but as an agent he'd feel differently. And his agent wouldn't be thrilled by his actions.

He pulled on the other boot, and headed for the barn, taking out saddle, blanket, hackamore, brushes and hoof pick and setting them by the hitching post before going to Rogue's stall. The horse lived up to his name in spirit, but not in temperament, tossing his head in greeting, then pressing his nose against the side of Evan's face and blowing out warm breath that ruffled his hair.

Not the best kiss he'd had that day, but a good greeting, nonetheless.

He gave Rogue's neck a pat, then attached a lead rope to his halter and led him out, murmuring as he went. The soothing sounds were more for his benefit than the horse's, helping clear his mind as he went through the routine of checking hooves, brushing, setting the blanket and saddle on, cinching the latter loosely, then removing the halter before slipping the hackamore over Rogue's nose and behind his ears. Jim had taught Evan to direct horses using verbal commands and leg pressure rather than relying on bridles with bits, and while he'd ridden both ways, he preferred the silent communication of working with a horse over telling it what to do with tugs on the mouth.

With a pat on the rump, Evan left Rogue a moment to get a spare hat from the barn. He knew he'd never wear one with the ease of Jim, a born cowboy, but the hat and boots made him feel more the part.

He walked the horse down a well worn path and through a gate leading to the trails on Jim and Brenda's property. He knew he could ride for miles in these hills and canyons near Santa Barbara without seeing another person or a car, and wouldn't have to think beyond which direction to go next. He gave the saddle cinch a final adjustment, mounted up, and headed out, letting Rogue take the lead at first, crossing his hands at the wrist, and resting them on the pommel. As he watched the horse's head bobbing in time with his gait, Evan felt his shoulders lowering and his breathing came easier.

He took a trail that led uphill in a series of wide switchback turns; listening to the creak of leather and Rogue's gentle breaths, feeling the horse's body shift beneath him, he almost succeeded in forgetting about the audition. And Samantha. But the warm wind brushing his hair against his face seemed like a caress, reminding him of Samantha's lips against his. That soft inrush of breath when her lips parted, the way she'd pulled back just a little and then leaned into him, into the kiss. And how she'd held onto him, her fingers sliding up his arms and under the sleeves of his t-shirt. It had been so intimate and he'd been so caught up in it that he hadn't been able to resist running his tongue over her lips.

She should have slapped him.

Then he could concentrate on that instead of how her breasts had felt when she'd taken a small step toward him and he toward her, both of them off balance, yet moving in rhythm, supporting each other—until she'd pulled away.

He hadn't wanted to stop, hadn't wanted to let her go.

And maybe that was one of his problems, he thought, straightening in the saddle at the realization. Letting go.

"Yeah," he said aloud on a sigh. Rogue's ears twitched back, then ahead again. Evan patted the horse's flank, considering this revelation. He didn't like it much, it brought him too close to thinking about his relationship with Zoey, his failed career and all of the events leading up to his arrest. That had been the darkest hour, and he'd been able to push it all aside for months at a time, but had not been able to overcome the idea that he deserved that arrest, that as much as he wanted to blame Zoey for everything, he'd been just as guilty as she. He'd chosen parties and openings over spending time with his three-year-old son.

He'd chosen those things over his wife, too. But damn it, if she hadn't turned to drugs while he was making the first Duncan Tanner film, if he hadn't accepted her excuses and let her back...

He gave a command, stopping Rogue, and sat there letting out a few swear words. He didn't want to do this, to examine his life right now. What the hell use was looking at the past when it was done with? He needed to move forward, keeping his focus on his career and Oliver. That's what was important. And he was doing that. If he didn't get the part of Jack, he'd just go on the next audition, and the next, until he was back doing what he loved.

No psychoanalysis BS was going to do that for him. And neither was some honey-blonde woman in red cowboy boots that kissed him like she knew him.

"Oh hell," he growled, and encouraged Rogue into a teeth-rattling gallop sure to push all thoughts right from his mind.

CHAPTER FOURTEEN

I'm the one who broke the story on Evan Gallagher abandoning his son."

Ever since Samantha and Liz walked into Roscoe's House of Chicken & Waffles, Gary had looked expectant, and Samantha had been so nervous, she blurted it out as soon as she sat down. Then they all had to pause when the waitress came by and took their drink orders.

Now Gary just looked puzzled. "But you didn't...your show. Not you."

"Me," she confirmed. "I saw it happen. That was my voice. On the phone describing it—" She stopped, her throat suddenly tight.

"They used sound bites from her phone call on the show," Liz clarified. "They disguised her voice a little, didn't say it was..." She gave Samantha an apologetic look before adding, "Sami."

Gary's mouth fell open, and all he said was, "You..." before drifting off. He shook his head. "Not you," he repeated.

"I tried to stop it." All of the old bitterness started rising to the surface, the years defending herself—*to* herself—returning and beginning to roil around inside her. She let go of Liz's hand and grabbed for her water glass, almost knocking it over.

Gary righted it and slid it across the table to her. She picked it up and took a few long swallows too fast. She set the glass down hard, choking, and Liz pounded her on the back. She wiped at her eyes, sat back in the booth, and looked at Gary, feeling pathetic and speechless herself.

"Oh, honey," Gary said. "I was really hoping for a scorching affair. Not—"

"That I tarnished a hero," she finished for him. "I know."

"But, those things, that stuff…" Gary took a sip of his own water. "They weren't true. And it was—"

"I know. I know you know some of it. But I need to tell all of it." When Gary nodded, she continued. "Not all of it was true. But by the time the truth came out, it was too late." She pointed at him. "And I tried to get the truth out there. But the public doesn't like to hear the truth, especially if it exonerates someone and replaces their daily trash with some boring old reality."

They all paused and smiled politely as the waitress set their drinks in front of them and asked if they were ready to order. They hadn't even glanced at the menu, but Roscoe's was an old hangout, and they all knew what they wanted. Samantha didn't think she could eat much, so just ordered a salad, ignoring the stern look from the waitress and feeling as if she should apologize for not ordering something smothered in gravy.

Liz ordered a Lord Harvey—half a chicken with gravy, grits and a biscuit, with a waffle on the side and in response to Gary's look said, "What, Dr. Oz? I'm nervous."

When the waitress turned to him, Gary held up one hand, downed all of his beer, said, "Another of those, along with…" He waved a hand in Liz's direction without looking at her. "What she's having."

As soon as the waitress ambled away, Liz said, "Wow, Gidget, you're slipping."

"Listen, Cruella—"

"Stop." Samantha's voice was stern, even as she held back a smile. If they were calling each other names, things couldn't be too bad, but she knew they could go back and forth all night. "I really want to get this over with, Jan and Marcia."

Gary and Liz exchanged a look, and Samantha said, "No, I'm not going to tell you which of you is Jan, and which is Marcia."

"That's okay," Liz said, "because that was a good one."

Samantha found herself laughing despite the situation, and that helped her go on. "You both know how I got on the show. Discovered while Liz was an intern—"

"For a very short time," Liz grumbled. She'd left to work on a film shortly after Samantha started as Sami Scandal.

"Right. Joe—"

"The asshole producer," Liz interrupted.

"Insisting that I had a look people could trust." Samantha remembered Joe's words, his enthusiasm, the rush of those first few weeks: a screen test, signing a contract, fittings, coaching, promises of red carpet glory and money. Insane amounts of money. Of course, one of the stipulations of her contract was that she would never reveal who her alter ego was, which was ridiculous. How did people not recognize her as Sami Scandal when she was out and about as Samantha Jamison? But she quickly learned people saw what they wanted to see.

"I thought it was a dream at first," she said. "A way into the business, even if I was just reporting it." She sighed. "Then they permed my hair, dyed it platinum, put me in push up bras and low-cut bright tops, awful makeup and gave me the trashiest of the trash to report. It was like vomiting out the *Enquirer* on a daily basis."

She caught Gary's grimace. "Sorry. But that's what it felt like. Well, after the excitement and power wore off, anyway. It felt pretty good at first."

She paused while the waitress set down Gary's beer, remembering some of those awful reports she'd had to make, using terms like "fave celebs," and having to say things along the lines of "a certain actor speeding along on cruise control was up to a little risky business the other night…"

"I thought I'd make contacts, maybe get some auditions." She lowered her head, and added, "Ease my way into acting." It had been a long time since she'd talked about her acting ambitions, and she didn't want to go into them now; those days were gone. She'd discovered her real talent, and she loved script supervising; her job not only aided everyone on the set, but maybe helped make up for what she'd done. She wouldn't give up supervising for anything, but letting go of her original dream had been painful, especially considering the circumstances.

"The acting thing didn't happen." She cleared her throat. "But you guys know that. All I did was play Barbie Reports the Trash. And I let that be enough for awhile, let the money and meeting celebrities satisfy me."

It hadn't been enough, of course. And the shame of it, that she'd been so superficial, still burned inside of her. She took a sip of water. "I got it into my head that if I found an interesting story, I'd be taken seriously. I didn't choose Evan Gallagher for my serious story. He sort of found me." She let out a breath. "And then I didn't want him."

She had gone to interview celebrities at a benefit where they brought their children. *Celebrity Live!* had a clip somewhere of her interviewing Zoey Highlander. Or trying to. Zoey had been so wasted Samantha didn't think the other woman knew where she was. Samantha had gotten a few glimpses of Evan and Oliver, but hadn't been able to pin them down for an interview. It didn't occur to her until later that she hadn't seen Evan and Zoey together for the entire event.

Until it was over.

She'd gotten the clips she needed, her cameraman and producer had gone back to the studio for editing, and she'd edged her way out to the parking lot and was passing by an SUV so big she could have driven her MG inside of it when she heard two people arguing on the other side.

She froze, then peeked through the windows to the other side and saw Evan Gallagher and Zoey Highlander. She ducked down by the rear wheel and cocked her head toward their voices.

"You wanted her," Samantha heard Evan say. "It's not my problem."

"So sue me. It was a good idea at the time," Zoey replied. A pause. "She's really only there because of you. Admit it, you wanted her, too. You said it would be good for us."

"No way, Zoe," Evan said, his voice rising, "don't blame this on me. You need to take care of it."

"I don't know how to talk to her," Zoey yelled back, and Samantha heard a boot strike the cement. "She likes you better."

Samantha eased her purse from her shoulder to the ground, and slid her hand straight down inside, pulling her cell phone from its pocket. She hit the speed dial for Joe, her producer, and when he answered, whispered, "It's Sami. I've got something."

"I'm listening."

"Evan Gallagher and Zoey Highlander fighting. About another woman."

"For him or her?"

"Can't tell. Her, I think. Maybe both."

"Beautiful," Joe said, and she could practically see him rubbing his hands together. "Can you get it on tape?"

"Tom already left." And her cell phone was crap, no good for taking video.

"Damn."

Samantha searched in her bag for a portable recorder, a pad and pen, anything to note Evan and Zoey's argument. Joe was saying something to her when she realized the voices on the other side of the SUV were fading. "They're leaving," she hissed.

"Follow them," came Joe's command. "Give me a play by play."

Samantha put her bag back over her shoulder and peered around the car to see which direction they'd gone. For a moment she could only see Zoey and Oliver, winding their way among the cars in the lot. "What?" she asked.

"Follow," Joe repeated. "Play by play. I'll record you."

She wanted to say, "What?" again and ask if he was insane, but she realized two things at the same time: her producer, whose favorite phrase was, "Show me your tits!" was actually listening to her, and she had lost sight of Zoey. So instead she said, "I'm on it," and raced away on her toes to keep her heels from clacking on the cement.

She managed to find Zoey because her hair was in a bright pink Mohawk at the time, and she caught a glimpse of that tall hair being flattened into the passenger seat of another huge black SUV.

Squashing the phone between her cheek and shoulder, Samantha noted the SUV's location, searched for her keys and sprinted to her car a few aisles away. The convertible top was already down, so she tossed her bag and the phone onto the seat, yelling, "Hang on, Joe!" before starting the car and racing around parked cars in the general direction of the SUV. A motorcycle had pulled in ahead of her, but she caught up to Evan and Zoey as they pulled into traffic, then reached for the phone, tucking it against her shoulder again and asking Joe if he was still there.

Joe grunted and asked what was happening.

"I'm following them," she said, still trying to catch her breath. She could see Zoey's hair brushing against the roof of the car as she moved back and forth in the seat, gesturing toward Evan. "And they're still fighting."

She knew it was awful to hope that they keep fighting, but if this turned out to be nothing, she was afraid Joe would insist she show him her tits, then he'd show her the door. So she told him everything she saw, embellishing it, including words their writers had used in her segment—shocking, crazed, desperate—and forgetting that everything she said was being recorded.

The only thing she knew about tailing someone had come from movies and books but keeping a few car lengths behind, letting cars slip between them and going straight when they turned, then making fast, usually illegal U-turns seemed to be working.

She shouldn't have worried; they seemed more intent on arguing than wondering if anyone was following them. Both of them appeared to talk at the same time, and there were a lot of hand gestures, most of which Samantha was fluent in, having driven the L.A. freeways for a few years now. She didn't know what she would do when they stopped, but right then, she felt surges of power going through her that she enjoyed a little too much. She felt like she could do anything.

And then they pulled onto the freeway, and she lost them as the 110 merged into the 101 and Evan accelerated and got swallowed up in the sea of SUVs.

She pulled off at the next exit and to the side of the road, then slammed her hands against the steering wheel. She wasn't sure when she'd tossed the phone aside, but when it started squawking at her, she picked it up and held it to her ear. "Joe?"

"What the fuck happened? Where'd you go? That was great, so great, keep it going."

"I lost them," she mumbled.

"What? Well, then you find them, princess. Whatever it takes, because that was brilliant."

Brilliant. The word hung in her mind, sparkling and bright, sucking her toward it.

"Right," she said. "I need Evan Gallagher's address."

EVAN GALLAGHER LIVED in a sprawling Mediterranean wonder at the top of a T-shaped intersection on Summit Drive in Beverly Hills. Tall, hedge-like trees, their tops left brushy and hanging over the street, had been planted behind the fence surrounding the property. The sharp-looking branches seemed an effective deterrent, but the double black metal gate decorated with curlicues stood open, a paparazzo's dream. Security cameras were set around the perimeter, but Samantha could still see the curved front door, a five-car garage off to the left, and lights in all the windows as she drove by.

She backed up and took another look. Were the lights on because everyone was home, or for security reasons? The windows were uncovered and all of the garage doors were up, revealing a Maserati, Ducati motorcycle, beat up convertible and a BMW roadster. No SUV in sight. What was going on? Why would Evan Gallagher display all of his cars that way, and have every light burning in his mansion?

She sat in the idling car and tried to figure out what to do. She couldn't stay in front of his house. This street had few vehicles parked at the curb and hers would be noticed. She decided to follow the road to the right because it wound around a corner out of sight and she might find a better vantage spot from above. As she'd started up Summit on the way here, her phone connection had started fading, so she told Joe she'd call him back once she found a better signal and the action started up. She had to finish this. She wanted Joe to say she was brilliant again.

She put the MG in gear, and two more turns up the street, she saw cars lining the roadside; it looked as if someone was having a party nearby. She parked among the Bentleys, Mercedes and Ferraris and got out. Cursing her tight pants and heeled boots, she crept back down toward Evan's house, walking on the balls of her feet to be as quiet as possible, her keys in the waistband of her pants and her cell tucked down the front of her blouse since she had no pockets. She stopped at a house across the street near the corner that looked down at Evan's house and fancy open gate. This house had the same thorny-looking looking trees but she managed to squeeze between some of the branches, feeling more than a little ridiculous. Nancy Drew in slut shoes.

Evan and Zoey must be home, she thought, wincing as a branch scraped at her arm. They must have come in a back way after she'd lost them. Maybe they were so distracted and so used to being decadent that they left the gate open and merrily turned on all of the lights, not caring about the electricity bill.

But where was the car they'd been driving? A little voice in her head asked.

She was just pushing the branches aside to get a closer look when headlights flashed down the street on her left, coming up from

Summit. No way was she going to get caught coming out of the bushes, so she ducked down, inching back into the biting hedge, and watched as the SUV came up the street on her left, turned away from her, and stopped past the open gate with its back end to her. She tried to catch the back license plate number as the car turned, but the street was too dark, and the lights from the car didn't adequately illuminate it.

Still in her crouch and trying to keep the bushes from scraping her arms and face, she turned on her cell and checked the signal. Iffy. She moved the phone up and down, then side to side, then down lower. There. Perfect. She hit speed dial, and Joe picked up on the first ring.

"Talk," he said.

She described the scene for him. Oliver must have opened the back passenger side door while she was playing with the phone because it now stood open and the dome light had come on.

"Zoey Highlander has passed out in the front seat. Head rolled to the side…"

"Repeat that," came Joe's voice. "You're breaking up."

She swore and bent lower, tilting her head up to continue to watch the scene playing out down the street before her. She saw Evan lean back from the driver's seat, and gesture toward Oliver. She heard him say something, couldn't make out the words, but the tone sounded angry, insistent.

Oliver flinched and jumped to the curb, stumbling backward from the car.

Samantha started to stand up, hand clenched around her cell phone. What was going on?

Joe's voice squawked at her, but only a few words came through, including "breaking up."

She stopped paying attention to Joe. Evan had faced front, put the car in gear and driven off with the side door still open. It swung shut as he took a hard corner.

"Shit." Samantha hung up on Joe, dialed 911 and headed across the street toward Oliver, who had begun to cry loudly even as he stumbled toward the gate, clutching a teddy bear backpack.

Samantha was still quite a few feet away, in the shadows of a towering oak tree and talking to the emergency operator, when she heard the front door of Evan's house slam open and Evan himself came running down the walk toward Oliver.

He grabbed the boy up and collapsed onto the drive with him.

"You're okay," Samantha heard him say in the stillness of the night. "You're fine," he soothed. "You're okay." He sat there on the cement, rocking his son back and forth while Samantha stood frozen by the oak tree. What was going on? The man in the SUV wasn't Evan Gallagher, but he had been with Evan's wife and had left Evan's son on the sidewalk.

And she had just reported to the police that Evan Gallagher had abandoned his son.

"HOLY—" GARY TOOK a gulp of beer and set the glass on the table hard enough to make the utensils jump. "So you saw Evan and Zoey fighting in the parking lot, you lost sight of them…"

She nodded. "That must've been when they split up. Believe me, I've thought a lot about this, and I figure Zoey met the mystery man in the lot, and Evan was the guy on the motorcycle leaving the parking lot." She shrugged. "That's my best guess."

"Unbelievable." Gary shook his head, then straightened up and snapped his fingers. "So that's the real reason you hate cell phones, isn't it?"

"A good enough one, I think."

"A pretty spectacular one," Gary told her. "But there's more, isn't there?"

"A little," she said, taking a more sedate sip of water, then a deep breath. "But this is good. It's helping me figure out how to tell Evan."

Gary coughed and started choking. "What?" he asked when he finally caught his breath. He wiped at his eyes. "What?" he repeated.

"I have to tell him." Samantha looked from Gary to Liz. "I *have* to. I can't be around him. On the set. Knowing what I know."

Gary's eyes got big. "The movie…" His voice drifted off and he cleared his throat again. "You're going to tell him now? Before we start filming?" He looked at Liz, then shut his mouth, leaning back in the booth and crossing his arms over his chest

Samantha looked between them. "What? What's wrong with telling him?"

"Nothing," Liz said. "It's just going to be hard…"

"You think I don't know that?"

Both Liz and Gary had their heads down, and Samantha bit her lip. There was no doubt saying this to Evan would be difficult, but she couldn't work with the man, face him every day, with this secret between them.

She filled in the silence with the rest of the story.

"I didn't know what to do at that point. I couldn't move, watching this intense personal moment. Ironic, considering I announced celebrities' personal moments on television every day."

She let out a sigh and propped her chin in her hand, looking down at the table but not really seeing the remains of their dinner in front of her. She saw instead Evan Gallagher, sitting there in the driveway, his body curled toward his son's, one hand cupping his head and the other his legs, the trees above dappling them in moonlight and shadow.

She had lifted one foot and literally rocked back, then forward in indecision, just as headlights came up the hill again, and Evan's attention was diverted from his son to the car making its way toward them. He lifted Oliver up, she assumed to bring him inside, but he didn't move as the car came closer. She saw them there, Oliver's face pressed into his father's shoulder, his teddy bear backpack at Evan's feet, and she leaned slightly forward, not realizing she was waiting for the outcome.

The headlights illuminated the expectant look on Evan's face as well as the set of his jaw and his grip on Oliver, and then Samantha saw that the car was a police cruiser. Her heart thumped hard in her chest. How had they gotten there so fast after her call? Why was Evan just standing and waiting for them instead of taking Oliver inside? Something wrenched inside of her—she'd done this; it was her fault—and she pushed a hand against her breastbone in an attempt to hold herself together, then turned and ran, tearful and ashamed.

Wiping at her eyes with one hand, she reached for her keys with the other and realized she was still clutching her cell phone. Her hands shook so badly it took her a couple tries to turn on her phone and dial emergency again.

"Nine-one-one operator, what's the emergency?"

"It's the wrong guy," she blurted.

"Can you tell me what happened?" the operator asked in a calm voice.

Something about that voice only made Samantha feel worse, as if her stupidity had doubled and everyone else was calm and poised and made the right decisions. "Please," she said, her throat tight and the tears still falling. "I made a mistake. Evan Gallagher didn't do anything wrong."

"Ma'am, can you tell me your name?"

Samantha shook her head, as if the operator could see her. "I just called," she gulped. "To report Evan Gallagher abandoning his son. Please," she repeated, although she wasn't sure exactly what she was asking for.

"Did you give your information to the operator then, ma'am?"

She hadn't. She'd made an anonymous call, still feeling giddy over Joe calling her brilliant, but knowing she had to help Oliver. Nothing would have kept her from that. But she'd only made it worse. Not only had she called the police on Evan, but she'd given all of that information to the show.

She gasped and punched the END button, then hit speed dial for Joe's number. He'd recorded everything. *Everything.* Oh, God, what had she said? Her thoughts were spinning too rapidly. She couldn't remember.

Joe picked up, but the signal was worse here than down by Evan's house and the connection died before she could say anything. "No," she said, "oh, no, no." With the thought in her mind that this information couldn't get out, she had to stop Joe, she started her car and pulled out, circling around until she found a way down the hill that didn't go past Evan Gallagher's house, and ended up on Sunset. She'd call the police later, clear that up, give them her name, a signed statement, anything, but she had to stop Joe from releasing those tapes first.

She drove through the Sunset Strip with one hand, careening back and forth on the road as she hit speed dial over and over again, trying for a clear connection with Joe. She couldn't believe she hadn't gotten pulled over for reckless driving or hit anyone as she raced east on one of the busiest streets in the area; in her wretched state, she hadn't been able to think of another route to the studio.

She banged the phone against the passenger seat a few times out of frustration, but she and Joe only had exchanges like "Joe, you can't…" and "Sami, what the…" as they kept getting cut off.

A few blocks away from the studio, as she whipped right on

Ridgewood, she finally got hold of him. She kept repeating that he couldn't use the sound bites, she was wrong, it was wrong. She had raced down the hall toward his office, still on the phone, when he stepped out of the shadows, his own cell phone in his hand.

She practically skidded to a stop in front of him, then had to lean over to catch her breath. Somewhere in the back of her mind, she realized she was finally giving him his requested view of her breasts, but she didn't care. She'd flash him completely if it would make all of this better.

"Did you try that?" Gary asked now.

Samantha shook her head. "They had that special show that ran on Saturdays, catching up on the week's entertainment. My segment didn't run on Saturdays. They used Joe's recordings of my voice that night, saying they had a special correspondent who'd gotten some incredibly juicy—"

She pressed her lips together, then took a deep breath before continuing. "I tried to convince them to retract, apologize, something, but…You know the rest. They 'let me go,' gave me a huge severance to keep me quiet, replaced Sami's Scoop with Darlene's Dish, and did a great spin job on the entire situation. They spun me, too, asking me how would an entertainment reporter explain that she'd been stalking Evan Gallagher and his family? I was good for them when it suited their sound bites, but not if my actions reflected badly on them."

She took a drink of water, and said, "Liz knows this, but I finally went to the police. It's what I should've done first thing instead of trying to stop Joe. I thought if I just told everyone it was a mistake, it would all be okay. I can't believe how naïve I was."

"We all were," Gary said. "Now we're all so jaded we've forgotten how nice naiveté can be sometimes." He gestured at her with his glass. "What happened when you went to the police?"

She shrugged, but she didn't feel nonchalant about it; it was more a shrug of resignation. "The situation had already been taken care of. They'd found the guy. It was no longer a criminal investigation, it was now a personal matter and unless I was directly involved, thank you so much for your time and concern, Miss Jamison, and we'll call you if we need you."

"Did they know who you were?"

"I don't think so. I dressed down. No curls, no makeup,

conservative suit, that sort of thing." She looked down at her hands resting on the edge of the table. "So, long story short, the charges were dropped, but that part of the story was probably a small postscript somewhere. The damage was done to Evan Gallagher's career…"

Gary glanced at Liz. "I hear Tom Hanks had to offer some of his salary so the producers would give Evan a cameo in Hanks' latest. But I wouldn't say his career was ruined because of…your situation."

Samantha stared at him. She'd spent five years repeating to herself how she'd destroyed this man's career. Five years as a recluse, atoning for her sins. Gary had to be wrong. "But he didn't work. Hasn't worked all this time."

"Self-imposed exile," Gary said. "The work was out there. He didn't take it."

"How do you know that?"

"The work's always out there. I did hear he turned some things down, though. Big things. *The Descendants. Moneyball. The Town.*"

"Why didn't you tell me?" she cried.

"Honey, you left. Without any explanation beyond 'this business stinks.' You didn't want to talk to me or anyone else about Hollywood. *Some* people got to talk to you. The rest of us got postcard missives. You know 'the weather's great; wish you were here.' Speaking of which," Gary said, turning to Liz. "You knew all of this."

"Of course I knew. I couldn't tell you."

Gary pressed his fingertips to his chest. "I can't believe you lied to me, Mrs. Doubtfire."

They both stared at him. He paused. "First name that came to mind." He shrugged. "She did keep secrets, you know."

Liz added, "And for a good cause."

"See?" Gary said. "It fit."

"I hate it when you gang up on me," Samantha said, but the tension had been broken. She had confessed her worst and while she still felt the shame, and probably always would, she hadn't been struck by lightning for this, either. One confession down, one to go. "Why were you watching his career?" she asked Gary.

"I watch everyone's career. If I'd known he was the reason you left, I'd've watched closer. But you told me you left your job because you couldn't stand the lies anymore."

"That was true, just not the entire reason."

"But some of what they reported was true, right?"

"Sure. Or at least it couldn't be disproved."

"Then you know he was working his way to self-destruction," Gary said, his voice calm. "The parties, the money, the attitude."

Samantha shook her head. She didn't remember any of that, only what she'd seen: Evan and his son together in the driveway and finding out shortly after that his Duncan Tanner contract had been dropped. "I don't remember," she said now. "So if he's so awful why do you want him in your film?"

"The attitude's gone, I've heard. And he's a damn fine actor, even though he sometimes lives his characters a little too much. Anyway, it looks like you've been carrying around some guilt that you don't need. I just have two concerns now," Gary added.

"Okay..." Samantha waited, her mind reeling.

"How much was the severance and what'd you do with it?"

Samantha laughed despite herself. She may have done her best recently to withdraw from all of her friendships, but Liz and Gary hadn't let her do that, and for that she was grateful. She named a figure and Gary whistled. Samantha thought back to the other day, remembered her purchase. "You're going to like this one, Marcia." Gary and Liz exchanged a knowing look while Samantha continued. "I bought a really expensive painting by Evan Gallagher."

CHAPTER FIFTEEN

Evan opened the French doors wide and wandered onto his deck, punching in Paul's home number. While his body felt comfortably tired now after his long ride and a hot shower, his mind still spun, and he knew he couldn't delay hearing the results of the audition any longer.

"The disappearing man," Paul said.

Evan leaned back in a green Adirondack, resting his bare feet on the railing, and watched the first stars of the evening come out. "Sorry about that. I needed to get away."

"Jim and Brenda's?"

"Yeah." He ran a hand through still-damp hair.

"The audition that bad?"

"It was amazing," Evan said, before he realized he was going to say it. He'd been prepared to say it had been a failure, that he'd screwed it up, but he knew at the time it had been solid. His unprofessional behavior with Samantha didn't change that. He understood Jack, knew what it was like to be a loner and feel outcast.

Paul would wait until he'd analyzed the reading before telling him if he'd gotten the part or not, something that had irritated him early on in their working relationship, but that he appreciated now since seeing all sides of an audition could help in future jobs. But today, he didn't want to analyze, he wanted the bad news over with.

"I read damn well," he said, knowing how defensive it sounded, then held his breath.

"So I hear."

He let the breath out and dropped his feet to the floor. "What?"

"It's yours if you want it."

"What?" he repeated, standing up and starting to pace.

"When have you ever misunderstood me when I said you got a part?"

Evan went into the living room and sat back against the plump couch cushions, looking up at the ceiling, the phone clutched tight in his hand. "It's not misunderstanding, it's…disbelief."

"You said you read damn well."

"I did." He looked around the room now, but the objects there didn't register. He saw Samantha instead, looking up at him in that moment after the kiss, her cheeks flushed, her mouth open, that lower lip begging to be nibbled.

He'd be able to see her now and could apologize for his behavior. And he had a job. That realization loosened a few knots that had been tightly tied inside him for years.

He heard Paul breathing on the other end and asked, "Did you hear that Tracy Jennifer couldn't make the reading and they had someone stand in for her?"

"I did. The script supervisor, of all things."

Evan smiled, and rested an arm along the back of the couch. Based on Zoey's suspicion, he'd convinced himself she was an actress, and had been surprised when she told him her actual role in the production. She'd been competent, and knew all of her lines, but a good script supervisor would know the script forward and back. Thinking on it, he realized she'd seemed jumpy. That was understandable in light of her inexperience with being in front of the camera.

"They said you did a great job, despite reading against someone not an actor."

"That wasn't the problem," Evan said, "believe me." Before Paul could ask what the problem was, he added, "She was nervous, but read fine." He turned his head enough to look out the window behind him. "Did I mention there was a kiss in the scene we read?"

"You didn't."

"And that everything was acted out, not mimed?"

"Unusual, but not unprecedented," Paul said.

"And that she was beautiful?"

"Ah."

"Yeah."

"Catherine Zeta Jones beautiful, or Blake Lively beautiful?" In Paul's world, there were all types of beauty. He had no complaints about Emma Stone or Halle Berry, or anyone in between, but Evan knew it suited his purposes to use Catherine or Blake as benchmarks instead of throwing out a long list of women to compare against. Evan liked to say "Johnny Depp beautiful" sometimes when Paul asked this question.

"Neither," he said now.

"Emma Stone?"

"Mmm…same pale, glowing skin."

"Damn." He heard Paul shifting the phone around. "Legs?"

Evan was tempted to say, "Yes," and leave it at that, but he enjoyed contemplating Samantha too much to let it pass. "Haven't really seen 'em yet, just her knees. She's a little…prim." Even as he said it, it felt wrong.

"Schoolgirl prim or nun prim?"

Evan burst out laughing. "Jesus, Paulie. Just a little restrained, that's all," he said, feeling protective of her, of that shared moment. He thought about the kiss again, and remembered those red cowboy boots. The upswept hair. A little restrained at first, maybe, but Samantha Jamison kissed with heat and intensity, getting as consumed in it as he. Nothing prim about that.

"Attention to detail," Paul said. "One of your strong suits."

"She gets your attention," Evan said, almost to himself.

"Good. It's about time someone got your attention."

"Paul…" He stood up from the couch and paced, ready to argue that except for matters concerning Oliver, Zoey was now out of his life, that he didn't have to take care of her anymore because she was taking care of herself, but that didn't mean he was ready to move on with another woman. He felt the lock of hair between his fingers again as he pushed it behind Samantha's ear. Soft. Silky.

Hell, maybe he was ready.

"No lectures," Paul cut in. "Since you're starting late on the film, you'll have a lot to do this week. Sally's e-mailing a complete schedule over. You'll get a copy of the contract and we'll review it, but it's standard." He named a figure for Evan's payment, and Evan agreed to it. He heard Paul shuffling papers in the background. "Tracy Jennifer Lawson has requested a closed set for the love scenes, but has a moderate nudity clause. Discreet, tasteful, maybe a breast or two. They're not asking for anything out of the ordinary from you. You okay with a little skin? Chest, legs." More paper shuffling. "No butt shots."

"That's fine."

"Rehearsal tomorrow at nine a.m.," Paul continued. "At Underwood Studios. Stage 23. Map's included with the e-mail. Five weeks shooting time. Two weeks here, with a day in the desert, one week on location in Walterville, the rest back here and on soundstages…"

"All the usual," Evan murmured with a smile as Paul continued with the details. Even though he hadn't had one like it in years, the familiarity of this conversation felt good. He looked forward to shooting on location, and was glad things had shifted with Zoey so she could now watch Oliver while he was gone. He made a mental note to check her schedule with her.

Paul finished his litany and added, "I'm glad for you, Evan. It's a good start."

"Thanks, Paulie. I'll come by your office before the rehearsal to sign the contracts."

"Maybe you should ask that girl out," Paul said, and hung up just as Evan's doorbell rang. Startled, he glanced at his watch and knew it must be Zoey dropping off Oliver.

He set the phone in its cradle as the front door burst open and Oliver charged in followed by Walker. Evan met his son halfway, tossing him up over his shoulder and grinning at his son's giggles. Walker sat on his haunches, barking, then followed after Evan as he carried Oliver to the front door, where Zoey stood waiting, arms crossed, keys dangling from one hand and Oliver's backpack at her side.

"Come in," he said, "I've got news." He reached for the pack to set it inside, then headed back to the living room.

From his perch, Oliver said, "Did you get a part, Dad? Did uncle Paul finally get you something?"

"Well, I had a little something to do with it, but yeah, uncle Paul finally got me something."

"Yay!" Oliver kicked his feet against Evan's chest and beat small fists on his back in celebration. "Isn't that great, Mom?"

"Great," came the reply. "Congratulations."

Evan leaned over to plop a giggling Oliver onto the couch, then grabbed the boy's foot, wiggling it back and forth as he turned to Zoey. She stood in the doorway, again with her arms crossed. "I got the lead in an indie with studio backing. Just auditioned today."

"Fast work."

"Their initial lead backed out." He settled on the arm of the couch. "I've got a week on location. I'll get the dates from Paul tomorrow. We need to work something out for this little cretin." He made to tickle Oliver's foot, and even though Oliver still had shoes on, he shrieked and pulled away.

"He can stay with me."

"That okay with you?" Evan asked Oliver. "To stay with your mom for a week while I'm on location?"

Oliver pumped a fist in the air. "Yeah!"

"It won't get in the way of your tour?"

Zoey shook her head. "We won't be going out for a couple months. We got a gig at Spaceland next week, small, to stir things up. You can come if you're around. And Dan's taking me to dinner on Friday."

Oliver sat up. "Can I be excused? This sounds like grown up talk."

Zoey said, "Translation: you want to play that Spaceship game."

"Rocket Raider, Mom," Oliver said with great patience and a big grin as he got up from the couch. He gave Zoey a hug and said he'd call her and she told him to be good. He retrieved his backpack, then raced into his room with Walker following.

Zoey took a step back. "So, congratulations again," she said. "Call me when you want me to watch him. And if you wanna go to the Spaceland gig. If you're not too busy. I'll get you a pass."

"Thanks. I'll have to check the schedule," he said. "I'm glad for you, Zoe. The band going on tour." When she nodded, he added, "So you talked to Oliver about Dan?"

"Yeah." She gestured behind her to Oliver's room. "Didn't faze him. He might pay attention if I was hanging out with some Raider Rocket guy, but..." She shrugged.

"Or Obi-Wan Kenobi." He shoved his hands in his front pockets. "Thanks. For talking to him."

"He's my family," she said. "I'd do anything for him." She took a step into the room, watching him, and added, "It's weird. Not being a family anymore." She put her hands on his forearms. "Do you miss it? Do you miss us?"

CHAPTER SIXTEEN

The red boots made a cheerful tapping sound and the sun warmed Samantha's face as she bounded up the concrete steps to the doors of Sound Stage 23, the designated rehearsal space for the production of *Broken*. Liz had dropped her off at the rental car agency before picking up Gary, so Samantha arrived later than she would've liked, but she was still able to catch sight of a tour group in a tram wandering through endless alleys between the massive sound stages, a woman pushing a long rack with multicolored outfits hanging from it and a group of men loading fake palm trees into the back of a stake bed truck.

She and Liz had dealt with the aftermath of the audition, but Samantha still worried about Gary. At the end of her confession and their dinner at Roscoe's, he'd been subdued, and she didn't know if that had to do with her past actions, or the fact that she hadn't confided in him before, or both. She redoubled her vow to be completely honest in all of her dealings from now on, something that would be especially tricky considering her current circumstances.

Stage 23 was what Liz referred to as "Studio Chic," meaning her production company hadn't yet established itself with Underwood Studios, so they'd get free rehearsal space, but it would be in a sound stage past its prime converted to a warren of storage rooms. Their room had stacks of musty costumes pushed against one wall and crumpled, graying cardboard boxes filled with props against another. A third wall had been cleared away for long folding tables, covered with a bright red and white checkered vinyl cloth and a seemingly endless supply of bagels, cream cheese, scones, jams, croissants, granola, donuts, fruit, coffee, milk, juice and vitamins. They might have a shabby chic rehearsal space, but craft services—catering and more—were always top of the line.

The room smelled of used books and coffee, two reassuring scents that helped slow Samantha's heartbeat as she stepped inside. While she would observe today more than anything else, she would also meet more of the cast and crew, and planned to establish boundaries and guidelines with them. Variably, the continuity supervisor was treated as gopher, all-knowing, or invisible. The level of respect given her would depend on Gary's treatment and how she presented herself to everyone this morning. It was her least favorite time on a shoot, over in a short period, but crucial.

She caught a whiff of cinnamon roll and headed to the food table, noting three different groups of people in the room. Liz stood with three men, one who looked to be in his early fifties, and one of an indeterminate age, unlike anyone she'd ever seen: he stood about five-foot-three with bright orange hair, Austin Powers black frame glasses and green wader pants. The third man, in his twenties, studied the others with an intent expression.

Two men already seated at long tables in the middle of the room studied scripts that lay in front of them, not looking at each other. Having seen their headshots, Samantha knew both were actors, Carson Standish playing Jack's brother and Richard Maxwell playing their father.

The third group of people consisted of Evan, Gary, and a woman in black spandex shorts and a yellow cycling jersey with running shoes, holding a clipboard, her dark hair in intricate braids. She looked fit, relaxed, and gorgeous and Evan Gallagher had his arm slung casually over her shoulders as they both leaned toward Gary, who seemed to be directing the Philharmonic as he spoke, his hands flying around in the air.

Tracy Jennifer Lawson had yet to make her grand entrance.

The actors at the table would have to wait for an introduction from Gary, and Samantha wasn't prepared to interrupt him yet, so she grabbed a cinnamon roll and napkin and headed toward Liz's group.

"I like it," Liz was saying, "nice wide shots for Mattie's scenes with David, closer ones when she's with Jack, to delineate each of their relationships."

The young man clasped his hands together. "To show how Mattie and David are really distant, but she and Jack are close?" He nodded at all of them. "Man, I love symbolism."

"It's a little more technical than that," Liz said to him, "but okay." Her face lit up when she saw Samantha. "Hey. You made it." She grabbed Samantha's hand and pulled her to her side. "There's a...thing we have to talk about," she said with a little nod.

Samantha raised an eyebrow at her. "Okay."

Liz gestured to the three men. Up close, the younger one looked like a young Bill Gates and the older one reminded Samantha of Peter Coyote. "Samantha Jamison, I'd like you to meet Francis Wallace, our Production Assistant, and Lincoln Sharpe, one of the most talented cinematographers in the business. And this is Cooper Rangis, our...brilliant editor."

Samantha knew from the pause that this was the quirky editor Liz had mentioned. He studied her with a slight scowl and seemed about to speak, when Liz continued with her introductions.

"Samantha is our continuity supervisor for this shoot. She did amazing work on *Honor Bound* for three seasons."

Lincoln shook her hand and gave her a sweet smile, and Francis burst out with, "Whoa. *Honor Bound*? That's one of my favorite shows. The way they set it up so Logan is immortal until he releases the curse on his family, how he won't be whole until he does that, but once he does, he's no longer immortal, but in the meantime, he has all of these adventures, and they get to go through history showing them, and—"

"Yes," Liz said, "she's familiar with the premise." She dragged Samantha away.

"I didn't have anything to talk to you about," Liz muttered when they were out of earshot. "I just needed to get away from Francis. He's just so *eager*. Asking us all a million questions about lighting, framing, long shots, close-ups..." She rolled her eyes.

"I thought he was sweet," Samantha said, now glancing at Gary, Evan and the cyclist clipboard girl. Evan still had his arm around her. Was she a friend, a girlfriend, a—

Liz snorted. "Sweet. Sweet like a puppy that pees on you because it's so excited."

Samantha laughed, and Evan looked over, then gave her a brilliant smile. Her heart lurched in surprise, and she smiled back. He stepped away from Gary and the clipboard girl, and was heading in their direction when a voice, chiming out from the doorway, high and shrill, stopped him. "There he is. The handsome and mysterious Evan Gallagher."

As Samantha turned around to see who had spoken, Evan gave her a look she couldn't read, then changed his course. "The stunning and elegant Tracy Jennifer Lawson," he said.

He strode over to meet her, and Samantha stared. This was not the bubblegum sweet T.J. Lawson that Samantha remembered from a well-loved sitcom.

"You know, my people tried to call your people," Tracy Jennifer told Evan, gliding toward him in purple pointy-toed spike heels, skintight white capris and a black belly- and cleavage-revealing halter top. She had a pierced naval. "But, like, they could never get hold of them."

Evan put a hand to his chest. "Tracy J. I'm old school." He took her hand in both of his and held it. Probably to keep her in one spot for more than two seconds, Samantha thought. "I don't have people."

Tracy Jennifer, surrounded by seven men and women standing in a half circle behind her, all holding cell phones, bags or PDAs, and all looking terribly important, tilted her head at him. "How do you, like, get anything done?"

"I get great satisfaction from, like, being directly involved in my life."

Samantha smiled. Instead of sounding mocking by copying Tracy's speech pattern, Evan sounded like one of her contemporaries. More people trailed in behind them, but he kept his attention on Tracy. No wonder, Samantha thought, he must be dazzled by those brilliant teeth. Not to mention a few other brilliances that were hard to ignore.

"Amazing to look at, isn't she?" Gary said from behind her.

"Hmm." She turned toward Gary, who had a coffee cup in one hand, and a bagel in the other. The clipboard girl stood next to him.

"Dumb as a box of dirt," Gary continued in a complacent tone, between bites of bagel. "But one of those idiot savant actresses." He slung an arm around Samantha's shoulders; the cup dangled from his fingers next to her arm. "She's brilliant as Mattie. Can play both older and younger. She did this scene at her reading…" He shook his head.

"Makes you wonder at the universe. Even I, preferring broader shoulders, bigger biceps, and well, you know, men, really. Even I am drawn to her."

"So she's a freak of nature," Samantha said.

"Basically." Gary shrugged, lowering his arm from her shoulders. "That and a creation of L.A.'s finest surgical teams. But she'll be great for our film. Speaking of which, I'd like you to meet my right hand, Keesha Smith. Keesha, this is Samantha Jamison, our brilliant continuity supervisor."

Samantha and Keesha shook. By "right hand," Samantha knew Keesha was the First Assistant Director—the one who would keep them all on track and on time, among a million other things.

"Gary says you did work on *Honor Bound*. Sucks that it's ending. I love that show. You did good work. No major flubs."

"Thanks. I think. Does that mean you caught minor flubs?"

"Honey, there's always minor flubs." Keesha leaned close, confidential. "Doesn't mean they were your fault, though," she said with a grin.

Samantha grinned back. "We liked to blame it on the prop guys."

Keesha shook her head, linked her arm with Samantha's. "They never remember where stuff goes. Stopwatch?"

Samantha hooked a finger through the lanyard around her neck and raised it, revealing the digital stopwatch she'd tucked inside her blouse. "Triple display, backlit, can save a hundred readings, water resistant, dual timer, optional sound, time and calendar." She clicked the sound on and showed Keesha some of the options.

"We're gonna get on just fine," Keesha said, pulling at a similar lanyard and revealing a combination cell phone and compact PDA tucked into her cycling top. She held the clipboard out. "I only keep this to look official. And bonk PA's on the head when they're out of line," she added, with a pointed look at Francis, who now sat next to Carson Standish, the younger actor, and was pointing at the script and making dramatic gestures in the air.

Gary patted each of them on the shoulder. "I love my crew," he beamed. "Right." He clapped his hands together. "And we need to get this rehearsal started." He headed toward Evan and Tracy, clapping his hands again. "Okay, people," he called out. "Time to get things moving. Grab your favorite goodie, get that last blast of caffeine, and let's all sit down and take it from the top."

EVAN LED TRACY JENNIFER to the spot Gary indicated, holding her chair out for her. "Can I get you something?" he asked.

She lifted up a hand. "They'll do it."

Evan glanced at the coterie behind them.

"The usual," Tracy said, and one of the unit broke away and headed for the food table. "Did you want anything?" Tracy asked Evan. "They'll get it for you."

He shook his head, giving her shoulder a squeeze. "Not necessary. I can get my own." He watched the remainder of Tracy's group drift as one toward the back wall, then turned to the food and found himself walking behind Samantha Jamison.

He stood next to her and said, "Are you following me, or is it the other way around?"

She jumped, her fingers squeezing the thing she held in her hand, and it beeped frantically. She lost her grip on it and he saw it was a stopwatch hung from a lanyard around her neck.

"A true script supervisor," he said, as she fumbled with buttons to turn the sound off.

"What? Oh." She glanced at the watch before tucking it under her shirt. "Yeah, it's…" She faltered, then added brightly, "Can't live without it," before grabbing a donut and cup of coffee and turning away.

Confused, Evan watched her take her place next to Keesha, who sat at Gary's right. He smiled when he saw that Samantha would be sitting directly across from him, but realized from her reaction that he'd need to find a way to apologize to her for his behavior at the audition, and soon. The less tension on a set, the better, and he didn't want too much time to pass before he talked to her.

Besides, he thought, heading back to the rehearsal table with his drink, she intrigued him. He couldn't say the same for Zoey, who only frustrated him. He'd floundered a little the other night when she'd asked him if he missed being a family, being with her, but had finally said, "The good parts. But those are gone, Zoe." She'd stared daggers at him and left without another word. He knew he'd have to talk to her, to find out if she was thinking there was a chance they could get back together—which was impossible, for him—but he had to concentrate on this film right now, and on the rehearsal.

When he got to his chair, he pulled it out, turned it backward, and sat on it that way, propping his arms across the back, the cup dangling from the fingers of one hand. That's how Jack would do it. Jack wouldn't pay much attention to Gary's welcome speech, either, but Evan would, and he liked Gary, so he listened to Gary talk as Evan, while eyeballing Samantha as Jack.

Jack was rough around the edges, but respectful, so he wouldn't call her "hot" or a "babe." And she was more than beautiful. Samantha…simmered. There was fire under that creamy skin, waiting for someone to turn up the heat and release it.

And he could be the one to liberate it.

It would have to be a slow seduction; she reminded him of a skittish filly, fascinated and fearful at once, still finding her balance, and he wouldn't want to inhibit that. He'd want to encourage her, to bring out the playfulness and curiosity, to let her feel free to—

"And playing Jack is Evan Gallagher." Gary turned to him. "Evan?"

Evan cleared his throat, tried to look like he'd been paying attention.

Gary gestured at the way Evan was sitting. "Looks like you're already getting into character."

He then introduced Carson Standish, the actor playing Jack's younger brother, David, the man who marries Mattie after they think Jack has been killed. Evan recognized Carson from a couple of recently released independent films; he admired his work and would tell him so when they had a chance. It would be tricky to play tough against such a trusting face as Carson's, to find a way to keep the audience's sympathy on both of them, for different reasons.

Lincoln, the cinematographer, who sat next to Carson, gave everyone a little salute when Gary introduced him, and Francis, the production assistant, who'd been relegated to a spot at the foot of the table across from Gary, jittered around in his chair until Gary had gone on to the next person, Cooper Rangis, a brilliant editor, but eccentric man.

At first Evan wondered why Gary chose someone so green as Francis for a Production Assistant, but caught a glance at Keesha, who would be overseeing him, and stopped worrying. Keesha was known for wearing cycling outfits with her ornate braids, and for her ability to be both diplomatic and tough on set. She would kick Francis's ass up, down and sideways, but he'd learn everything he needed to know to make it in the business. She and Evan had worked together on the Duncan Tanner films, and she'd been just as tough then when she'd been the PA herself.

He gave her a wink and she leered at him while Gary continued around the table from Cooper, who didn't speak, to Richard Maxwell, a well-known actor from the '70s who had done only select films lately.

Evan nodded to himself, pleased with the solid crew. He took a sip of coffee, then set the cup on the table and watched Samantha, while Gary talked her up. She'd script supervised on *Honor Bound*, a popular show he and his son watched together, and had worked her way up doing some commercials and apprenticing on other shows filmed in North Carolina. Evan hadn't expected anything beyond her professional stats, but part of him had been hoping for more. How had she gone from North Carolina to Los Angeles, from a top rated show to an indie film?

He'd find out, and he'd find out as Evan, not Jack, although Jack could probably seduce it out of her in two minutes. He smiled at the thought and she caught him smiling. She gave him a shy smile back, then ducked her head, clutching at the stopwatch that she'd pulled out again. It gave a frenetic beep and she jabbed at it to shut it up, her cheeks going pink, then turned her focus to Liz.

Cooper spoke up for the first time. "Your notes will be meticulous."

"My notes are always meticulous," Samantha said, looking directly at Cooper as she addressed him. Evan noticed Cooper's gaze hovering somewhere in the direction of the catering table.

"I don't know about 'are,'" Cooper said. "Only will be. On this shoot."

Samantha straightened, but didn't look away from the editor. "My notes will be meticulous. Guaranteed. Please talk to me if there are any problems."

Cooper nodded, and Evan nodded himself, in approval of how Samantha had handled Cooper. Gary let out a breath and introduced Liz Mendenhall.

"Liz will be on set on a regular basis," Gary said, "not only as a reference for me as writer, but also as co-producer of this production. It should help keep us all on our toes."

Gary finally got to Keesha, making it clear to everyone that she was the boss if he was unavailable, but that didn't mean they got to harass her like a substitute teacher. Keesha's look had gone steely and Evan noticed Francis had stopped jittering and sat staring at her with his mouth open.

Gary continued. "I'd like to spend the rest of today talking about the script, discussing characters and theme, and doing a read. We'll start blocking tomorrow, and finish on Friday. I know some directors like to rehearse for weeks before shooting, some not at all. I like rehearsals, working out the kinks, but I don't want to lose spontaneity, so this will work perfectly." He looked around at all of them. "We'll take regular breaks, but the read will be non-stop. And while we're reading, don't hold back. I want to feel it," he said, holding up a clenched fist, then opening it. "I want you all to feel it. And I want us to listen to each other, to really listen, and not just wait for the next line."

He released all of them for a break at that point, and Tracy Jennifer began dialing a cell phone, getting up and heading toward her people before Evan could stand and hold her chair out. He shook his head. He knew she had an innate talent, but if his kid grew up and acted like Tracy had so far, he'd disown him.

He watched her stride toward the door in those fuck-me shoes as if she'd been born in them and resolved to get to know her as a person before any of their love scenes came up, which were thankfully all scheduled toward the end of the shoot. They would have two weeks shooting on location in and around Los Angeles, then a week in a remote area near Pioneertown, then back to Los Angeles for sound stage shots, including the love scenes. He knew a person existed behind all of the "people," and he'd find her so they could make their on-screen relationship look as realistic as possible.

He turned around and found Samantha watching him. When their eyes met, she turned quickly away, grabbing a script, and then Liz, and pulling her into a corner.

Samantha was another woman he wanted to get to know, for completely different reasons, ones more enjoyable than his interaction with Tracy J.

CHAPTER SEVENTEEN

Samantha watched as a team of people worked to make a red 1964 Polara convertible look like it had just made a cross country run. With small brushes and their bare hands, they applied materials to simulate dust and other road debris.

The first day's filming of *Broken* evolved around the scene when Mattie, having driven for days, is about to discover where Jack has been hiding out. Years before, Jack, a spy, asked his brother David to watch after Mattie if anything happened to him. After Jack is forced to fake his own death, David—secretly obsessed with Mattie for years—woos and marries her. Mattie has never gotten over Jack and when she discovers he may still be alive, she searches for him.

This was a sunrise shot, and the rest of the crew had been here, on the outskirts of Hesperia, since five a.m. It was now almost six and they were set to start filming in half an hour. According to Keesha and her detailed chart of sunrise and sunset times, the sun would rise today, February 7, at six forty-five. That attention to detail was one of the reasons Samantha knew this shoot would be a strong one, and that she and Keesha would work well together.

Shivering in the light sweater she'd brought, she held a cup of tea in both hands to warm them and wondered how she could have gotten used to the Los Angeles weather already. She'd been sweltering only a week before. Hesperia, seventy miles northeast of L.A. was high desert, and, again according to Keesha, the temperature was currently forty-eight degrees. Warmer than North Carolina and not as cold as the small Iowa town where she'd grown up, but definitely cold for Southern California.

She stood near the craft services trailer, and the tempting smells of coffee, donuts, scrambled eggs, bacon, potatoes, and pancakes with maple syrup drifted toward her as she watched the busy teams: along with the property crew at Mattie's car, electricians laid cable and set up lighting, the sound mixer worked at his board and the boom operator handed out earphones and Comtec units. Since they would be filming a traveling shot, Tracy Jennifer would have a mic under her clothes instead of an overhead microphone used to pick up sound. There was no dialogue in the script for this shot, but if Tracy decided to improvise something, Gary wanted it captured.

Samantha also hung out by the craft services trailer to hide from Francis, the eager Production Assistant, who, when he wasn't bombarding everyone else with questions, was asking her opinion on things like the terms script girl, script supervisor, and continuity supervisor and which one she preferred. Either that or he was expressing admiration for the amount of supplies she carried with her and asking if he could see her complete inventory, piece by piece, with a designation for each.

Francis currently followed at Lincoln's heels, interrogating him about types of camera filters, so Samantha had a reprieve from his attentions. Her supplies, including a set of binders, all sat in their designated pockets in the canvas bag she'd bought for herself after starting work on *Honor Bound*. One binder contained the current shooting script, another blank copies of all of her logs, and a third had numbered and dated copies of the script changes already made, different colored paper reflecting each change. The standard color rotation for script changes was blue, pink, yellow, green, goldenrod, and then back to white She had more binders waiting to be filled at Liz's house; she kept all the originals of her logs, but she also never knew how many changes might be made on any script or how many notes she would end up with. She'd already put her request in to both Keesha and Francis that once filming began, her revised pages not be in color, but to only have the word of the associated color—pink, yellow, green and so on—printed on the top in capital letters. She would have to copy her pages and send them along to Cooper, the editor, at the end of each film day, and colored paper often made messy copies.

A folding chair leaned against the trailer. She'd be out of it more than in, conferencing with the crew, taking notes and Polaroids, following the cameraman, but by the end of the day's shoot, she'd be grateful to have it.

The drivers directed their white vans, trucks and topkicks with attached trailers farther down the street, west of the crew, because they would be filming Mattie driving away from the sunrise and toward Jack. Other staff headed up and down the street to direct traffic. They were filming on a two-lane road without any close turn-offs, so they couldn't re-route anyone who came along, but vehicle travel was light here, especially at this time of day.

Samantha had already gotten her earphones and Comtec unit, but she needed to meet with Gary in a few minutes to find out if she'd be tucked down in the backseat of the Polara while filming or crowded somewhere in or on the insert car, which had the camera mounted to it and would move in synch with Tracy Jennifer's driving. Even with no scripted dialogue, Samantha would need to be able to note all of Tracy's movements for both she and Cooper to match up later. If she didn't get them during, she'd have to ask for video the next day or crowd around an extra monitor while they filmed, two options she preferred to avoid.

But for now, she could hang out here, greeting various workers, and enjoying the bustle. The crews worked toward a common goal—getting something on film—but each day, each shot, each team was different, and the changing energy always engrossed her.

Finishing her tea, Samantha pulled her binder and a notebook out, tucked a pencil behind one ear, hefted the bag onto her shoulder and headed up the dusty road away from the line of parked vans and trucks to meet with Gary.

She heard a door slam and footsteps behind her, and turned to see if the person wanted to join her on the walk up the set.

Evan Gallagher caught her eye, and smiled.

"Oh, crap," she said, then clapped a hand to her mouth and turned around. He wasn't supposed to be on set until later; after they filmed Tracy Jennifer in the car, they'd run through another moment, which occurred later in the film, of Jack and Mattie talking out in the desert.

Samantha took a deep breath. Evan was here now, though, hopefully not as eager as Francis, and he'd seen her. She was going to tell him everything when the time was right, but until then, she needed to stop acting like he'd just goosed her every time she saw him.

She let out her breath and turned back around. She caught a slightly confused look on his face before he smiled again, and she returned it, her heart beating hard. She clutched her papers tighter to her chest, trying to slow her heartbeat down. He lifted a hand in a brief wave.

"Hey," he said, stopping in front of her. Very, very close in front of her.

She held the binder up just a little higher. "Hi. How are you? I was just going to meet Gary."

He rubbed his hands together. "Great, I'll go with you." He looked around, grinning, as they walked up the road. "I'm early, but I couldn't stay away. It's so incredible out here."

Samantha squinted into the early morning gloom, but failed to find anything incredible about the dust, the cold, and what must surely be a landscape of tumbleweeds.

"It's mostly sage brush out here," Evan said, as if hearing her thoughts, "but even those are beautiful, with yellow flowers blooming in the summer and fall, and this brilliant system of watering themselves, drawing the water up at night and releasing it during the day."

They'd reached the area where the crew was just finishing up with the set and Samantha watched Evan as he continued to look out into the shadows of the desert. When he turned back, he stepped closer, still looking pleased to be surrounded by freezing tumbleweeds, and said in a conspiratorial tone, "But the most amazing thing is the mountain lilac. They won't be in bloom yet, but they create this circle of white among the silvery sage. Hard to capture in a painting," he added, almost to himself, as he turned to look back out at the landscape.

Samantha had been so shocked to see Evan at the gallery and audition, and so much had happened since then that she still hadn't processed those experiences. But this was an Evan Gallagher she couldn't have conceived of, someone that threw her completely off balance and fascinated her at the same time. Why did he have to be gorgeous, a great kisser *and* smart?

When he turned back to her, all she could think to say was, "Lilac? Really?"

As he shared a few more details about the area, she nodded in all the right places, heard what he was saying, but became transfixed by the play of light over him as the crew adjusted lighting equipment nearby. The teal of his shirt changed the shade of his hazel eyes and each time the beam flickered toward them, they glowed a deep green, and his irises contracted and expanded.

"Speaking of surprising things," he said, "I've wanted to ask you if we—"

She jumped. We? There was no we here. She'd be happily mesmerized by plant lore and his eyes, but she couldn't go beyond that. "Oh, you know? I have to meet with Gary right now. I'm sorry. I'll just…I need to…go."

Samantha backed away but one foot caught on the other in those stupid darn boots. She didn't fall, but she did trip, and her bag dropped, then her binder went flying, spilling papers in an arc between their bodies. He reached out, maybe to help steady her, but she popped down to start gathering her notes and pages of script, and he bent to help her instead.

She kept her head lowered, scooping up as much grass and dirt as papers in her haste to collect everything, embarrassed but also worried that she might not have enough time to get it all organized before the day's filming started. Then she would have to set up impromptu pages instead of using her well organized notes, and transfer everything tonight after shooting wrapped, making for a long day.

She glanced up at him. Head bent, he carefully collected her papers, put them in order, then tapped the sides together as he went. His hair fell into his eyes, but he didn't take the time to push it back, just kept gathering.

She clutched her own collection of documents, grass and dirt. "You're a very nice man," she said. "And I'm a terrible person."

He looked up at her, frozen in the act of reaching for one of her yellow note pages, his face close to hers. "I don't…"

"Back…" She gestured behind her, indicating the past. "What I did. It was disrespectful. I wish I could take it back."

"What are you—"

"I didn't plan it," she babbled, shocked at herself for saying anything at all, but incapable of keeping quiet in the face of his kindness. "It just sort of happened, but you were there, and you didn't deserve it, and I'm really sorry."

She couldn't seem to stop herself, even though the more she

talked, the more confused he looked. A part of her looked down on all of this with a sense of horror, asking the other part of her just what she thought she was doing, for heaven's sake, but he'd been nothing but kind to her from the beginning, and she was tired of holding in her guilt.

She lowered her head, unable to look in Evan's eyes anymore, and began grabbing up the rest of the papers on the ground. She added them to the pile, crumpling them in her haste, then reached for the handle of her bag.

"So, really, I was only doing what I was asked, what I thought I should, even though it wasn't right, but then I tried to make it right, and it was too late," she told the ground. "I can't believe what I did, and I'm really—"

She shut up when he reached out and put his fingers under her chin, easing her face up, gentle but insistent. The feel of the tips of his fingers on the tender flesh of her neck stopped her in mid sentence, not because she felt threatened, but because she'd avoided physical contact of any kind for so long, and now Evan touched her as if he knew her.

He tilted her head so it was level with his, and she raised her eyes until she caught his gaze, her breath stopping for a moment at the proximity of their faces. If she slanted her head and leaned a tiny bit closer, her lips could be pressed against his and they could finish what they'd started at the audition.

And then she remembered that it had been a staged kiss, at least on his part. But before she could turn away, to gather her papers and her pride and get up and walk away, he spoke.

"You shouldn't be apologizing." He shook his head when she started to protest. "I was the ass at the audition, not you."

She opened her mouth to ask him what he meant, but then closed it when she realized they were talking about different things. *The audition.* He thought she was apologizing for how she'd acted there. She had a flashback to her misunderstanding with Liz over that same audition, and wondered if she'd ever be able to explain herself clearly to anyone. Now what was she going to do with this situation?

She felt Evan's thumb brush against her jaw line, just a little. Just enough. A shiver shimmied down her back and when his thumb stopped moving and pressed slightly into her skin, she knew he'd felt it, too.

"I was out of line, and I'm sorry," he continued.

"You didn't do anything wrong," she said, shaking her head. Something inside her added, "Oh, yes, you did, buddy. You snuck a great kiss in there and didn't mean it," but she knew what she'd done was far worse. Sneaking a kiss was nothing when comparing sins.

"The kiss was inappropriate." He ducked his head, smiling a little. "Well, actually, the kiss was in the script and Gary said no miming. I just shouldn't have been so…It was a little too…" He raised his head, and even though his cheeks had flushed, he looked at her and said, "It was inappropriate, and I'm sorry for that." He leaned toward her and whispered, "But I'm not sorry I enjoyed it so much."

It was her turn to go pink, but she couldn't help smiling a little at the admission, even though his nearness made her short of breath and just a little too shaky for her own comfort.

Still. Her smile widened. He'd liked it.

"So you forgive me my roguish ways?"

She laughed, shaking her head because she liked this side of him, but he took it the wrong way and gave her a little frown.

"An apology wasn't enough. I can see that now." He put his papers on top of hers and then his hands encircled her upper arms and he helped her to stand. He gestured toward the catering truck down the road, its tables loaded with coffee, donuts, bagels, fruit, cups, plates and utensils. "Looks like I'll have to buy you a cup of coffee."

"Oh, no, I—" She stopped when he reached out and took the papers from her, and set them on a nearby chair.

"First things first," he said, shrugging out of his flannel shirt. "You're shivering."

She was, but having him near her wearing only a tight t-shirt was not going to help matters whether she had his flannel or a full down suit. She held up her hands. "Really, I'm fine. I couldn't."

He draped the shirt around her shoulders, then reached for her hands one by one to ease her arms through the sleeves, his face a study in concentration as he rolled up each sleeve. For too long, no man had given her his shirt to keep her warm, changed the tire when she ran over a nail, or even tucked her hair behind her ear when it fell into her face. She hadn't let them, and she realized now she'd been punishing herself for her failings.

And even though Evan Gallagher had been the one she'd tried to atone to with her independence, his kindness felt so good right now she didn't want to stop him. The irony didn't escape her, however, so tried not to enjoy too much the feel of his hands or his warm breath on her neck as he tucked her in to the shirt.

"So can I buy you a cup of coffee to make up for it?"

Her head shot up and her dazed mind cleared a little. She'd been entranced by his hands, pulling the shirt close around her, just missing the tops of her breasts. His hands still rested there, holding the front of the shirt together, and she tried not to stare down at them as she focused on what he'd just said.

Had she been inhaling, trying to take in long, lovely breaths of his scent? He smelled like a man, a real man, and she hadn't been drawn to someone like this in ages. Evan Gallagher smelled something like pine needles and air by a riverbank, warm sheets and warmer skin after sex—

She took a deep breath and held it, staring at him and trying not to let her eyes bug out.

No more smelling Evan Gallagher. She had to stop that right now. She shook her head.

Evan, thankfully, hadn't seemed to notice her sensory inventory. "Coffee won't make up for my faux pas? That's too bad. Sounds like I'll have to do something bigger then." He let go of the shirt and held his arms out from his sides, giving her a little shrug. Then he picked up her papers, put them back in her arms and said, "I'll have to make you dinner."

"Oh, I—"

Before she could finish, a door slammed nearby, and they both looked toward Tracy Jennifer's trailer, which had been set back from all of the other structures, far away from the food, as specified in her contract, but still close to the set so she wouldn't have to walk too far. As Liz had explained it to her, T.J. Lawson was as big a name as Evan Gallagher, but with a different reputation.

"A better reputation, you mean?" Samantha had said.

"Think of it this way," Liz had told her. "T.J.'s the girl next door and Evan's the bad boy and everyone's going to want to see what the bad boy does and how the good girl handles it. Or vice versa. Both on film and off."

Samantha watched Tracy for a moment; she was still far enough away that she wouldn't be able to hear them, so Samantha might have time to gracefully decline Evan's dinner invitation. Evan stood next to her as if they were any two people having any sort of regular conversation. Before she could speak, however, he leaned forward. He was close enough that she could smell the pine needles and warm sheets again, and he whispered, "Have dinner with me tonight. Seven p.m. I'll get you directions. Then we can talk easier." He suddenly grinned and took a few steps ahead, not looking at her. "Hey, Tracy J. Looking lovely this morning."

Tracy's face changed from intense concentration to beaming pleasure, and Samantha couldn't tell if she was acting or if it was real. It had happened so fast that Samantha could almost believe Tracy's happiness was genuine. As she watched, Gary, Francis and Keesha walked toward Evan, and Keesha held up one hand. Without interrupting his conversation with Tracy, Evan gave Keesha a high five and Francis a pat on the shoulder as they passed, while Gary beamed at Evan before breaking away to talk to Lincoln. Maybe Tracy was being genuine; everyone seemed to glow around Evan.

She watched Tracy put a hand on Evan's arm, leaning into him and laughing at something he'd said, then replying with more animation than Samantha had ever seen from her. Evan responded, gesturing with his free hand, then set it over hers, holding it against his bicep, his attention never wavering.

Samantha jumped, trying to mask her expression, when Keesha touched her arm.

"You ready, script supervising queen?"

Samantha looked down at her jumbled, dusty papers. "Not really."

"Had a little distraction, did we?" Keesha asked, glancing quickly in Evan's direction, and then back to Samantha with a smile. "I mean, a little mishap? We've got a few minutes to put it in order." She led Samantha to a table and helped her sort out the pages. Samantha kept her head down, relieved that Keesha didn't ask her any questions.

It was only six-fifteen in the morning and the day had already been eventful. She had no idea the rest of it would include a suggestive note and a cryptic talk with Liz along with the filming.

CHAPTER EIGHTEEN

I have to do this." Samantha straightened up at Liz's red Formica dining table. Since filming started so early that day, they'd been able to wrap early. Samantha had finished her daily logs and gotten her pages to Cooper before meeting Liz back at home. She'd told Liz all about fumbling part of a confession and Evan thinking she'd been talking about the audition, then asking her to dinner.

"But at his house?"

She could hear the edge in Liz's voice, but wouldn't let it sway her. She really did need to do this, and it had been a long time coming. "I should have him take me out to dinner, spend money on me, then tell him in a public place that I'm the one who broke that story and messed up his career?"

With a rare sigh in her voice, Liz said, "Maybe Gary was right about his career already starting to get off track back then."

Samantha shook her head. "They cancelled his contract for the third Duncan Tanner movie right after my...the report. Besides, even if Gary's right, Evan needs to hear my part in everything."

"You're sure."

"I'm sure."

"So what about at a neutral place?" Liz asked.

Samantha didn't answer right away, instead staring out the window, her hands wrapped around a mug of peppermint tea. "I thought about that," she said. "Doing it at a restaurant and going through all of the niceties of a date is insult to injury, if you ask me. And being in public is just begging for paparazzi and gossip columns. So it's at his house, or your house. Do you think his producer's house would be appropriate?"

Liz shook her head, but didn't say anything.

"I got pushed into a corner with this dinner, and maybe it's better that way. Now I'm forced to tell him, be done with it." When Liz still didn't say anything, Samantha added, "And how could I resist such a sweet request?"

She looked down at the table where she'd set the note to show Liz. She'd been captivated by it, she couldn't deny that. She'd spent the morning in the insert car as it followed alongside Tracy Jennifer for a few takes, then took notes while the crew adjusted the camera position, and hopped in again to film the Polara from head on, capturing Tracy as Mattie, heading toward her rendezvous with Jack. After a few more takes with a stationary camera filming the car moving past and turning onto the road that would lead to Jack's cabin, it was time for lunch, more notes, and then onto the next shot, a short one where Jack and Mattie talk outside.

After Keesha announced they were wrapped for the day, Evan and Tracy left and while the crew broke down the set, Samantha stayed to mark the shots in the script, noting where they should be included during the final edit. When she closed the binder, there had been a folded piece of paper with her name on it clipped to the front. She looked around, wondering who could have put it there, since the binder had been with her or right next to her all day.

She reached out now and brushed at the edge of the note, straightening it on the table so she could read it again. Or, rather, look at it. At the top Evan had drawn a grandfather clock, the hands set at seven, and next to that a little car, with an arrow pointing down to a map with directions to his house. Under that, he'd sketched pictures of steaming dishes of what looked like quite an array of food.

And one line below that, he'd drawn a shirt that looked remarkably like the one he'd loaned to her, only it was shown as if it had slipped from her shoulders onto the floor. Right next to it sat a pair of cowboy boots, one on its side. She didn't know what he meant by this, but it was suggestive to her. Especially considering what he'd written below the drawings.

"I would be honored by your presence. Wear those boots. And the shirt. Or not."

When Samantha brought the note out at Liz's house to show to her, Liz had studied it for a moment, then nodded. "If that's not a play, I don't know what is."

"But what does he mean about the shirt and boots?"

Liz gave her a look that made her feel about twelve years old again. "It means wear the shirt and boots…or take them off in his presence." She looked at the paper again. "Or maybe it means wear *just* the shirt and boots, and nothing else. In his presence."

They'd laughed over that, Samantha a little nervously, and had spent some more time speculating on the note's mysterious meaning. Liz's laughter had ceased when Samantha announced she was actually going to Evan's house to tell him everything. In fact, Liz had gone uncharacteristically quiet and now she pushed away from the table and began to empty the dishwasher, setting the glasses next to each other in the cabinets with high-pitched clinks. Samantha watched her for awhile, uncomfortable with Liz's silence.

"It's not a date, you know."

Liz opened the utensil drawer and dropped in flatware. "I know."

"I mean, if things were a little different, maybe…"

Liz gave her a sharp look.

"Well, he is attractive," Samantha said, feeling defensive but not sure why.

Liz stared at her, forks clutched in one hand. "You're not thinking…"

"Noo. No. That would be crazy."

"Crazy," Liz agreed, and went back to the dishes.

"So I'll just tell him right away." She looked at the note again. "Before I even step in the door. Tell him, get it over with, let him verbally abuse me, then get the hell out of there."

She looked up in time to see Liz staring at her again. When Liz still didn't say anything, Samantha asked, "So, what do you think?"

"Do…whatever you think is right," Liz said in a tight voice.

Samantha hadn't expected that. Where were Liz's strong opinions, heated debates, righteous indignation? "He needs to know. Right?"

"Eventually," Liz said after a moment, then turned away again and closed the dishwasher. She brushed her hands together, then said, "So do you want a snack or something?"

Samantha barely heard what she said. Something in Liz's voice still sounded off, but she couldn't stop looking at the note, wondering what it meant, and a small part of her enjoyed thinking about what it might be like if the situation were different and she could attend this dinner for real. As a real date.

Evan Gallagher seemed like a lovely man, and anyone who could have that much fun with an invitation had to be interesting on a date. She brushed the tips of her fingers over the shirt, which she'd draped over the back of the chair next to her. Flannel, soft from many washings, and she wanted to bury her face in it. She liked this man, was attracted to him, for heaven's sake.

Under normal circumstances, bringing up a painful past experience was difficult. But they barely knew each other, and Evan was an actor, a person who made his living keeping his emotions close to the surface. Having to face him and tell him her secret terrified her.

Gripping the shirt, she pulled it to her chest, then caught Liz watching her. "How big is this?" she asked.

"The shirt?"

Samantha gave a little laugh. "Not the shirt. The situation. Me. Evan Gallagher..."

"The two of you thrown together by ironic circumstances? I don't know. Depends on how big he's made it in his head." Liz rolled a mug back and forth between her palms. "Do you need to do this tonight? I mean, it doesn't have to be right away or all at once, does it? Maybe in pieces, or later, or easing into it with him, or trying to find out how big it is and then figuring out a way to let him know using that. Maybe you could just beg off tonight," she added.

Samantha let out a breath. "I don't exactly...want to."

"Got to you, did he?" Liz asked, her tone understanding.

Samantha nodded, but didn't say anything.

Liz nodded back. "He's hot."

Samantha nodded again, and this time she felt a little smile emerging. "Definitely hot." She brushed her fingertips against the note, easing it gently back and forth. "And really sweet. And smart. And talented. And kind. But that doesn't change things." Or at least it shouldn't, she thought. "This isn't a date, and I can't let myself think it's one."

"So what are you going to do?"

"I'm going over there tonight. And I'm going to tell him. And I'm going to wear old ratty undies so that I won't be tempted at *all* to remove any pieces of clothing while I'm there."

CHAPTER NINETEEN

As soon as Evan opened the door, Samantha secretly thrilled that she had changed her mind and worn the nice, lacy panties after all. He had on a soft white dress shirt, the collar lying casually open at the neck, the top two buttons undone, the sleeves rolled back to just below his elbows. The shirt was tucked into worn blue jeans, just beginning to fray at the pockets and cuffs, and his feet were bare. The shirt could be lazily unbuttoned, but was stylish enough to dress up the jeans, the jeans would slip right over his hips and—

She felt her eyes bugging out of her head.

She bit her bottom lip, commanding herself to just stop those thoughts, and returned his smile of greeting while running her practiced confession through her head. He held a hand out to draw her inside, his fingers light on her elbow, and as she passed him, he said, "Nice outfit. I appreciate the effort."

She pulled her gaze up from his feet. "What? Oh." She smoothed her hands down the front of the flannel shirt. "Gets chilly up in these hills, you know?" She looked down at her feet. "No boots, though," she said. "Didn't go with the shirt."

His gaze swept her from bottom to top, appraising. She wore a burgundy dress with a sweetheart neckline, spaghetti straps, and a wide black lace band accentuating the waist, and low silver sandals borrowed from Liz. She worried the neckline dipped too low and the sandals seemed overly fancy, but Liz had declared the outfit demure by Hollywood standards. "And just perfect for a faux date," she said, then immediately apologized. "I didn't mean it that way. You look really nice."

"Really nice" was okay; devastating was preferable, but Samantha didn't think that was appropriate for this occasion. Not that she really knew what was appropriate in a situation like this. She took another mental step back now, suspecting that Evan might have a different definition of "really nice" than Liz did.

"Lovely invitation, by the way," she said, trying to break the spell she seemed to fall under whenever she got within ten feet of him.

"I'm glad you liked it." He gestured toward her. "May I take your…shirt?"

She hesitated, having already gotten attached to it.

He must have sensed her reluctance, for he said, "Or you can keep it. I have others." Again that up and down appraisal. "Besides, it goes well with your outfit."

She looked down at the shirt covering her cleavage. "Right. No, it's fine." She eased out of it and handed it to him with something akin to regret.

He draped it over a bench in the front hall. "In case you get chilly later," he said, and she shivered just from the tone in his voice. He might as well have said, "In case you get naked later."

He gestured around him at the three wide arched entryways leading off the tiled foyer. "To the left is the master suite, to the right, the kitchen and stairs down to a big family room and my office. Down the hall straight ahead are Oliver's room, a bathroom and a guest bedroom. The living room and dining room are at the end." Evan put the tips of his fingers lightly against the small of her back, as he almost had that day in the gallery, guiding her forward.

Samantha took a step, then remembered it wasn't supposed to go this far. She was supposed to thank him for the invitation, then give him the speech she'd been rehearsing all afternoon. She started to say, "Actually, I wanted to…" but her words drifted off as he slipped around in front of her, cupped her face and pressed his lips to hers. He didn't go any farther than that, just held her face, the tips of his fingers brushing the delicate skin of her earlobes, and kept his lips there, letting her feel them, taste them, crave more of them.

He pulled back, his warm hands on her, and those intense hazel eyes observing every nuance. His thumbs moved across the tops of her cheekbones and his hands seemed to be the only thing holding her up right now. Otherwise, she'd slide into a puddle at his feet. Those lovely, bare feet.

He leaned close and when he spoke, his breath whispered against her face. "I should apologize, but I wanted to do that all day. I had to get it out of the way so I could have a conversation without wondering what it'd be like to kiss you again."

She stared up at him, dazed. When he leaned close again, she mentally shook herself. "So, did it help?"

He stopped, his head tilted. "What?"

"Kissing me. Did it help to get it out of the way?"

He reached up and brushed a thumb across the arch of her eyebrow. "No," he said simply, then slid his fingers along the side of her face and down her arm, where he took hold of her hand and led her up the hall.

He walked in ahead of her, but she halted in the wide arched entranceway when she saw the room.

It had been decorated entirely in white. White carpet, thick white couches, a white mantelpiece, white walls, and glass tables with white legs. The only color came from a gorgeous landscape to the left over the fireplace that she recognized as Evan's work, showing the sun setting behind an African acacia tree with vibrant shades of yellow, green, indigo blue and burnt orange.

The far right of the room was the dining area. The lights were off, but two lit candles sat on the table and strings of Christmas icicle lights had been hung around the entire perimeter of the room, just below the ceiling.

The effect of the darkened room, white furnishings and strings of lights lured her in with its combination of drama and romance, narrowing her sensations until she was aware only of the sparkling lights both in the room and dotted on the hills outside, and of Evan's hand in hers as he stopped and looked back at her.

"What a beautiful room," she said. "It's very…"

"White. I know." He looked around. "I've been thinking about changing it. I needed it this way for awhile. No…distractions." He looked at her.

"And distractions are okay now?"

"Distractions are welcome." He eased her forward. "Come in," he said, resting his hand on her back again.

She felt its warmth through her dress and wanted to lean back into it, into him. But that wasn't right. She couldn't let this continue. This room was set up for a date, for seduction if one was willing, and that wasn't her purpose here.

Isn't it? a little voice in her mind asked.

She pushed that voice away, then did a quick turn to face Evan and tell him everything once and for all. She could see from the look on his face that her move caught him by surprise, and suddenly his hand was pressed to her belly instead of her back. He dropped it, and the spot where it had been felt cool now, exposed, despite the lace and cotton there.

"Evan..."

He nodded as if he knew where this was going. "Too much too soon?"

"No, it's lovely." She looked into his face, at the shadows and planes created by the darkened hallway behind him and the twinkling lights above. "But it's not right." She started to speak again, to finally get to her speech, when he held a hand up.

"Before you say anything, let me get a couple things out. Then you can tell me if it's right or not." He reached out and took her hand, holding it lightly by the fingers, then cupping it with both of his. "First, I apologize for having you over to my house when a restaurant might've been more appropriate. I admit, I wanted you alone, but my publicist is on me to..." He gave her hand a little squeeze. "She's got a plan, and I'm trusting her with it, but that means no public dinners for now. Second, I'm well aware it's a bad idea to get involved with a co-worker. But I like you, and I'd like to get to know you better. I also know we had a weird start. First you meet my ex-wife and son, and then I get to kiss you, which seems out of sequence, but the kiss was...unprofessional. I've wanted to apologize for that for a while now. So consider this my apology, and you can leave if that's all you need or want from tonight."

Samantha's head spun. His hand warmed hers, his gaze never wavered, and he'd said all of the right things.

"Oh, and one other thing," he added. "If you're worried about dating a co-worker, too, I should remind you this shoot is fairly short and should go fast. So we won't be co-workers for long."

She looked up at him, at his eyes dark against the candlelight, at those high cheekbones, the lock of hair that never seemed to behave and slipped down against the side of his face, and that smile. That sweet, charming smile. He still held onto her hand. "I...I don't..." She faltered, and so did Evan's smile, although he only looked dispirited, not angry.

"Do you want to leave?"

"No," she said, and it was the truth. "But there's something…"

"Something…" he prompted.

"You should know."

"Ah."

She took a deep breath. "I did something terrible."

To his credit, his expression didn't change as he asked, "Is this 'are you sitting down' terrible? Or 'I need a drink' terrible?"

"I could use a little of both." That hadn't been the beginning of her practiced speech, but what the hell. It was a start.

"All right." Evan led her to a white couch with overstuffed chairs on either end that faced each other and a glass coffee table in front of it. The fireplace was to her right, the dining area to her left, and a large white shelving unit with a stereo, books and knickknacks faced her. Behind her were the big windows, French doors, a deck that ran the length of the house, and what was probably a spectacular view.

"What would you like to drink?" Evan asked as soon as she'd settled herself in a corner of the couch.

She had expected to feel jittery, with her heart pounding hard enough to leap from her chest, but she felt strangely calm, which was disconcerting. Jumpy made more sense. "Do you have red wine?" she asked, actually wanting something stronger that she could slug back for some courage, but thought that might not be such a good idea. It wasn't time for getting sloppy drunk and confessing sins.

He gestured behind him. "At the dining table." He got two glasses, handed one to her, then sat down in the chair to her left. He didn't drink his, just held it in both hands resting between his knees and watched her.

She took a sip before setting her glass down, then stared at it. He hadn't been gone long enough for her to collect her thoughts, to figure out how to go on from where she'd started. And now he was staring at her. Waiting.

Evan helped her out. "So you did something," he began, as if starting a conversation about what she'd bought at the mall earlier.

She nodded, willed herself to look at him. "I did something…a few years ago…that hurt someone."

He set his own glass down, then leaned back and crossed his arms. "All right."

"They didn't know I'd done this thing. Only now I have the

chance to make it better by letting them know it was me and that I was sorry and didn't do it on purpose. And that I've changed. Completely. And would never do something like it again."

Evan studied her a moment. "Is letting them know going to make it better for you, or for the person you hurt?"

That stopped her. She'd always believed she just needed to confess all, to get everything out in the open, but when he put it that way, she realized she'd also thought it would be cleansing for *her* to make the confession. But what about him? She felt he needed to know, but why? And would it make him feel worse to hear it, even as it helped her?

"I think it's more for me," she admitted, "but it's also one of those things that shouldn't be a secret anymore." Gary's face flashed in her mind, the sad look he'd given her as he left Roscoe's the night she'd told him everything. She'd not only kept it from Evan, but from Gary, her friend. He'd insisted Evan's downfall wasn't her fault, and he'd been surprised she was going to tell him. That afternoon, Liz had gotten unnaturally quiet, and at dinner, Gary had given a different picture of Evan's career. Then she remembered what else Gary had said.

"The movie…"

And it all clicked for her. She'd thought telling Evan would be best for everyone concerned, but his question made her realize it might not be, including for Gary and Liz and their movie. If she told Evan now, they'd all have to get through the rest of the filming together. And she had no idea how Evan would react. Would his response ruin the film, make it difficult to work with him?

"So this person doesn't know about it?" Evan asked.

"No," Samantha told him, still reeling from her revelation. "And there's another part to it. Telling him right now might also affect some other people's lives."

"Him."

Oops. "Not a boyfriend or anything," she rushed to clarify.

He nodded, as if considering that. "All right."

"And I'm not in trouble with the law."

"Good to know."

"It's just…weighing on me."

"I can tell."

She shifted, looking away from him. He must think she was a

complete nut. Here he'd gone to all of this trouble, kissed her, was patiently sitting through this with her, and she was talking like a madwoman, building up some mystery.

Evan leaned back. "Why are you telling me this, Samantha?"

She licked her lips. "Well…" she began, not sure what to say now that she'd realized her revelation could have an effect on the film.

"Are you married?" he asked.

"No."

"Have a third foot coming out your back?"

She smiled at that. "No."

He waved a hand in her direction. "So no big demons in the closet?"

She shook her head. "Well…no." Sort of.

"Let's see…" He looked up at the ceiling as if considering his words. "Are you needy, clinging, have control issues, in terrible debt?" He lowered his head to look at her. "Am I forgetting any?"

She smiled a little. "Emotionally stunted? Passive-aggressive? Unable to commit?"

He leaned closer. "If it eases your mind, I'm none of those things. How about you?"

She shook her head, but couldn't speak.

"So why are you telling me about this mystery?" he repeated, almost in a whisper.

"Because I've screwed up too many good things and I don't want to do it again."

He gave her a little shrug. "So don't."

She tilted her head at him. "You make it sound so easy."

"I spent a lot of time making things difficult when they didn't need to be." He stood up. "Sometimes…" He reached out to take her hand and eased her to her feet. "You just need to…" He led her to the middle of the room and stood facing her with his hands on her waist, watching her. "Relax and let it happen."

For a moment, she completely forgot what they'd been talking about.

"Do you want to leave now?" he asked.

She hadn't told him everything, but she still felt as if she'd taken a big step toward atoning for her actions. It was a start and had helped calm the panicky butterflies in her stomach that had shown up right around the time she bumped into him in the gallery. "No. I'd like to stay."

"Good. How about dinner?"

She told herself she was doing this for the movie, for Liz and Gary, so she wouldn't screw up any more people's lives, and that was all true, but she was also staying because she liked Evan Gallagher and she mentally sighed in relief that she could be around him now and not feel like a terrible person.

He led her to the table, held her chair for her, retrieved their wine, then served up chicken, wild rice and asparagus, describing the food as he went and treating her as if she hadn't just conveyed to him that while she didn't have a third foot coming out of her back, she had some sort of secret, and it could affect their future.

He sat down across from her and raised his wine glass. "To...a great shoot?"

She smiled and raised her own glass. "To a great film."

"To no rained out days."

"To perfect takes each time," she said.

"To an Oscar?" he asked with a grin.

"To multiple Oscars."

He tilted his glass toward hers. "To big box office."

"To the highest opening ever," she said.

"Oh, hell," he replied. "To everything."

Their glasses clinked. "To everything," she agreed and drank.

They ate in silence for a while and she felt warm and relaxed. And amazed at all that had happened since her return to L.A. not that long ago. This dinner, starting the movie, the audition, and meeting Evan at the gallery.

Remembering that, she gestured toward the painting over the fireplace. "Is that yours?"

He nodded. "My latest. I rotate them to see what they look like in an ordinary setting, before letting them out into the world." He shrugged. "An ordinary, all white setting anyway."

She smiled, and took a sip of wine. "That's a nice idea," she said. "How long have you been painting?"

He paused, his fork hanging above his plate. "Since my mother rolled out a sheet of butcher paper in the garage and plopped some finger paints in front of me. She said it was the first time I had been still in six months. I think I still have some of that paint in my ears."

She laughed. "How old were you?"

"About three." He glanced at the painting. "My son says I should put some zebras and tigers in there."

She followed his gaze. "At the very least, some monkeys hanging from the tree." When he turned back, she asked, "Does your son want to follow in your footsteps?"

He studied her a moment. "With art, or acting?"

"Either."

He leaned back in his chair, crossing his arms over his chest, his eyes softening as he seemed to ponder the answer to her question. "He sketches well, both people and animals. He has a notebook full of pictures of Walker."

"Walker?"

"Our dog."

"You have a dog?" She looked around the pristine room, thinking it must not be allowed in there. "Where is it?"

"With Oliver, who's with his mom. She thought you were an actress, by the way," he added.

Her heart gave a little lurch. "Really? That's…funny." Funny like a heart attack. She took a breath. "So you were telling me about Oliver's art?"

Evan took a sip of wine. "He doesn't want to paint, but he's shown some interest in photography, and I might get him a camera." He took a bite of rice, then continued. "He was too young to think about acting when I did the Duncan Tanner movies, but he's paying more attention to it now, especially since he sees me involved with *Broken*. I'd like to bring him to the set, but this film…" He shook his head.

"Too intense?"

"I think so." He sat back again, twirling his wine glass between his hands. "I want him to know the process, to understand what I do…" He drank some wine, then set the glass down. "But I want him to have as much magic as he can while he's young, and not worry about…"

"Grown up things?" she asked, when he seemed unable to finish his thought.

He reached across the table and took her hand. "And grown up things can be hard enough for both kids and adults, right?"

She nodded, feeling the warmth of his skin on hers as he massaged her fingers, and wondering what he might be referencing. Her near confession? His own difficulties? Would she always be so focused on what she'd done to him that she would associate it with any vague reference he made? She hoped not.

Evan looked down, indicated their empty plates with his free hand. "We got through small talk, dinner. Dessert could be next, if you'd like. Or do you want to leave now?"

"Depends on what you have for dessert," she said, enjoying it when he laughed.

"Well, I got sorbet for dessert." He stood and started stacking the dishes, and she got up to help him. "But I don't think that's appropriate now."

"Appropriate?" She stood waiting for him to go into the kitchen, holding her plate and a wine glass.

"Here." He gestured for her to set her plate on his. "Wait here," he added, heading toward the kitchen. "I have an idea."

She stood by the table, watching him, holding her wineglass up as if about to make a toast. An idea? Evan was known for coming up with interesting, spontaneous ideas on set, but she could only imagine the ideas he had for his personal life.

And what would make sorbet for dessert inappropriate?

Eating it someplace where it might melt?

She slammed the brakes on that thought, and gulped some wine. She was setting the glass down when Evan came back into the room, hands behind his back, and the corners of his eyes crinkled from his smile. "I'd like to show you something," he said, "and you may need the shirt." He gestured with his elbow for her to go ahead of him up the hall.

"Now who's the mysterious one?" she asked. She draped the shirt over her shoulders, and opened the front door at his request. She waited until he had come out, still hiding whatever he held behind his back, then shut the door.

They stood on the front porch, looking at each other a moment, taking no notice of the view of Silver Lake spread out before them down the hill.

"So where are we going?" she asked.

"See that path?" Evan lifted his chin at a series of stepping stones that led to one side of the house, then ran along the curved the driveway before moving alongside the detached garage and disappearing at the back.

"We're going behind the garage? You sure know how to impress the ladies." She grinned at him. She couldn't help it. She was having fun, she felt a sense of relief over their talk, and she loved this silly and mysterious side of him. And she wanted to know what he hid behind his back.

She tapped along the path toward the garage, blinking when her movement triggered a spotlight hung at one corner. It better illuminated the area, and she followed it along the side of the garage and to the back to a set of stairs, where she waited for Evan to catch up to her. The yard on the other side of the path consisted of low maintenance landscaping, what her father would call rocks and sticks, but to her had been so artfully arranged, she wondered if Evan had designed it. Geometric patterns fit together in a kaleidoscope of earth-toned stones and redwood bark running all the way up to the house. Eucalyptus trees high enough to block the view to and by the next door neighbors and more below bordered a fence that surrounded the property.

"After you," Evan said, and Samantha climbed up the wide wooden steps.

When she could finally see the roof, she stopped. The top of the garage had been walled off on three sides, and a desert sunset mural had been painted along each wall, one corner blending into the next section in deep violet, orange and russet shades.

Samantha gripped the railing, staring at the picture. It was muted because the lighting along the garage didn't quite reach up here, but its beauty was clear. Large jute rugs had been laid out on the floor, and two chaise lounges sat in the center, a small round table between them. When Evan reached her side, she asked, "Did you paint this?"

"Oliver and I did. Last summer."

She could hear the pride in his voice, and turned to look at him. His eyes roamed the length of the mural, and she wondered if he was remembering the time he and his son had spent together painting it. His gaze stopped at her. "It's beautiful."

He stood a step below her, his eyes level with hers, and nodded his thanks. "So are you."

She blinked at him, and felt her cheeks grow warm. "Thank you," she said back, thinking how much she would like to kiss him right then.

He rattled whatever it was he held behind his back. "Pick a hand."

"What?"

"Pick one," he said with a grin.

Flustered, she looked from the left to the right, then pointed at his right hand. "That one."

His smile broadened, and he held out a yellow rose, the edges of the petals a dark orange shade, the color of a California sunset. She took it and breathed its scent deeply. "Thank you," she repeated, holding it close. She pointed to his left hand. "So what was in the other one?"

He held up two bags of candy, shaking them so they rattled again. "Gummi worms and chocolate bars." He shrugged. "Couldn't decide which."

She shook her head, laughing, and continued up the stairs to the top.

Evan set the candy on the table, then moved it behind the chairs and eased those closer together. Samantha stood watching him, brushing a fingertip along one silken rose petal. She pressed a hand to her front, feeling a bit like the Grinch when his heart got too big for his chest.

"Have a seat," Evan said. "The stars put on a good show up here."

Samantha draped the shirt over the headrest, sat on the edge of the chaise to his left, and looked up at the sky. The walls cut off the surrounding light, and the trees across from them at the edge of the property blocked any illumination from that side, emphasizing the brilliance of the stars.

"Wow," she breathed. "I feel like I'm in the country."

Evan leaned against the headrest and looked up. "This is one of my favorite places."

Samantha followed suit, relaxing into the chair. "I can see why." She took a deep breath and let out it. "I wonder why the stars are always so fascinating."

"The possibilities," Evan said, without hesitation. "The mystery. We've explored every inch of the globe, mapped it out, made sure some one or some thing had a claim to it. But this..." He swept his hand in an arc across the sky. "No one owns it. It belongs to everyone and no one, and the possibilities are infinite."

Samantha sighed again. Just keep talking to me like that, she thought, studying his profile. He caught her watching, then reached out and took hold of her hand, squeezing her fingers and giving her a small smile before looking up at the sky again. The tightening in her chest eased.

"So do you know the constellations?" she asked.

"Just a few," he said. "Mostly I make up my own," he added, and she wasn't surprised. He pointed down and to the right. "There's Orion's belt."

"That's about the only one I can ever remember."

"Just down from that, see the really bright one?" He looked over his shoulder at her until she nodded. "That's Sirius. The dog star." He looked around a bit, as if searching for something. "And right there," he said, pointing now to the left. "See that upside down W?"

She squinted, trying to follow his line of sight. "No."

He slipped off the chaise and crouched in front of her. Taking her right hand in his left one, he lined her arm up next to his and wrapped his fingers around her hand, leaving his index finger free to point.

"Straight up." He lifted their arms together, then arched to the left. "Then just over there." He traced the outline of the W.

"I see it," she said, now the one to move their arms together, tracing it in wonder. This was better than Russell Crowe trying to impress Jennifer Connelly in *A Beautiful Mind*. "So what is it?"

"Cassiopeia." Still holding her hand and crouched by the chair, Evan added, "Cassiopeia and Cepheus had a daughter, Andromeda. Perseus saved her from a sea monster and cut off Medusa's head, creating Pegasus from the foam that dropped into the sea. They're all up there."

"Busy guy," she murmured, studying the constellation and feeling Evan's warm skin against hers. "I've seen this one before, but never knew what it was."

"Now you know."

"Now I know," she agreed, looking at him. The thought crossed her mind that they always found themselves very close to each other, but his nearness often kept the neurons in her brain from firing properly.

He leaned toward her, and she blurted, "Gummi worm?"

He stopped, his lips parted. "Sorry?"

She gestured behind her with her free hand. "I think this is the portion of our program where we break out the Gummi worms."

"Oh. Indeed." He had to let go of her hand to reach behind him for the bags he'd set on the table. "It was rude of me not to offer my guest dessert."

She sat up, holding her cupped hands out as he poured the candy into them. "I can't imagine you ever being rude." She popped a worm into her mouth and chewed, then gestured toward the bag. "Aren't you going to have any?"

He took one from the tangled stack in her hand. "Thanks."

Now they both watched the other eat and while she felt like squirming in her seat under his gaze, he looked calm and reflective. She didn't know any other man who could do that while crouching in front of her on a garage rooftop under the stars in Los Angeles, eating Gummi worms.

"I've had a lovely evening," she said.

He took another worm, let it dangle between them. "It sounds like you're concluding it."

She paused before answering. "I think the time is right. I don't want to go now, but I should."

He nodded. "I'm glad you stayed as long as you did." He took the rest of the worms from her and dropped them back in the bag, then, still crouched by her chair, took both of her hands and gently brushed the sugar from her palms and fingers. "Can I see you again?" he asked, waiting a moment after he'd asked the question before looking up at her.

She was very aware that he still held onto her hands, that he was again very close, and that she liked him very much. Underlying that, the thing that never seemed to leave, was the reality of their relationship to each other, even if he wasn't aware of all of it. "I think…" She took a breath, and tried again. "I would like that very much, but the time isn't right…for that."

He nodded again, giving her a quick smile. "I may not like that, but I respect it." He rose, bringing her up with him. "It's going to get chilly later. You should take the shirt."

She glanced at the shirt draped on the back of the chair. "Oh. No…" Oh, but she wanted to. She lifted it up and held it close. "Are you sure?"

"Yes." He took the rose and tucked it in with the shirt. "Positive."

He led her down the stairs, retrieved her purse from the house, then walked her to her rental car, both of them silent. She wanted to ask him what he was thinking, but was afraid to hear the answer. She knew she'd done the right thing by telling him it was the wrong time, but she realized that under normal circumstances, they'd be making plans for their next date.

But these weren't normal circumstances, and she'd be seeing him at work the next day, so it was better to keep things professional. She set her things in the car, and turned to him, prepared to say goodnight, see you on the set, thank you for everything, but just friends—

When he wrapped his arms around her, pulled her against him and kissed her hard. So hard and hot that she felt her spine go liquid and had to grab his hips to keep from sliding away. His tongue slipped into her mouth and her fingers slipped into his belt loops, pulling him closer even as he pushed her up against the car, easing between her legs and smoothing his hands down the sides of her face, caressing the curves of her breasts and hips, grabbing her the way she'd grabbed him, each of them trying to get closer even though no space existed between them.

She forgot everything in the heat of him, the rush of senses as his tongue brushed hers, the scent of him filled her, and his full weight pressed against the length of her body. His fingers brushed along the lace of her dress and tickled up and down her sides, making her squirm against him.

And just as quickly as he'd pulled her into his embrace, he stepped away, breathing hard. He swallowed audibly, then reached around her to open the door. "Maybe someday...the time will be right," he said, leaning into her. He brushed a lock of hair back from her face, his hand lingering as he pressed a kiss to her temple, then helped her into the car. "I'll wait until you're out the gate."

She nodded up at him, unsure how she'd gotten from practically having sex up against the car, to sitting inside the car, automatically fastening her seatbelt and putting the key in the ignition. Evan tucked in her skirt, then closed the door.

Looking up at him through the window, she realized he was going to stand there until she left. So she started the car, her head buzzing, her heart pounding, and headed down the driveway.

And just as she turned onto the street, she caught a glimpse of him in her rearview mirror, shirt rumpled, feet bare, one hand in his front pocket, the other raised in a wave.

She was very, very tempted to turn around.

CHAPTER TWENTY

Paul took one look at Evan, bounced on the balls of his feet, and said, "She a good kisser?"

Evan spun the basketball he held in his hand on one finger. They'd met for their weekly game, this time on the private indoor court in Beverly Hills that Paul reserved for them. Evan didn't say anything, just looked at the ball, but he couldn't hold back a smile.

Paul watched until the ball spun off Evan's finger. "Julia Roberts good or Sandra Bullock good?"

Both had guest starred in a Duncan Tanner movie, and Evan had had the good fortune to be able to kiss them onscreen, nice experiences, but not in the least as romantic as they looked. He bounced the ball to Paul. "Johnny Depp good," he said, laughing, as Paul missed the ball completely.

Paul pointed at him. "Cheap shot."

"You know I don't kiss and tell." It had taken a tremendous effort for him to pull back from that kiss and appear casual as he said goodbye to Samantha; he wasn't sure he could convey that to Paul, or that he even wanted to. He liked the idea of keeping that kiss to himself.

He jogged to the end of the court, retrieved the ball and tossed it in to his friend. They played for a while, the only sounds their grunts of effort and the squeak of their sneakers, until Paul, panting, called for a time out.

"Why do you insist on this barbarous game?" Paul asked, taking a towel from his gym bag and wiping sweat from his forehead. He got two bottles of water and opened one, drinking half of it.

Evan stood at the free throw line and tossed the ball through the basket with a swoosh. "Because it's good exercise, and it makes you talk like a dandy."

Paul retrieved the ball and bounced it to Evan. "A nice round of golf at Riviera could do the same."

Evan made another free throw shot. "Golf's for sissies."

Paul ignored the basketball this time, letting it roll away into the corner. "Golf requires skill, patience, timing and accuracy."

Evan backed off, wiping the sweat from his forehead with his shirt sleeve. "So maybe it's not basketball but golf that makes you talk like a dandy. That's why basketball's better."

This banter was also part of their weekly ritual. Paul preferred golf, so that's what they played when it was his choice. Evan usually beat him at that, too, but that didn't stop their teasing.

Evan got the ball and jogged back to his friend. He set it at Paul's feet, then grabbed a fresh towel and took the extra water bottle. "We could do something else. Like sword fighting." He raised the bottle to his forehead in salute, then held it out like a rapier. "Guard. Turn. Parry. Dodge. Spin. Thrust, ha-ha!" he said in a Daffy Duck voice.

"Yoicks and away!" Paul said, raising his own water bottle.

Both of them then started in on the song Daffy sings in the Robin Hood cartoon, "Oh join up with me, so joyous and free…" before Paul had to stop because he was laughing so hard.

Pretend sword raised and fisted hand on hip, Evan struck a pose before breaking into laughter himself, both at Paul's response and his memories of them copying the Daffy Duck cartoon in their childhood. This was another reason they got a private court.

They collapsed next to each other, wiping sweat and tears of laughter from their faces.

Paul laid back on the floor and put his hands under his head, as if studying the stars. "How's the movie going?"

"Great. Good first week, great crew, overly eager PA, but that's not unusual. Keesha'll keep him in line. No complaints, really."

Paul nodded. "Glad to hear it. I got the *Variety* with the news you're replacing Kevin Madison in this film. Got a couple phone calls about it. A few interview requests. I sent them Nancy's way."

Evan couldn't help smiling. "I tell you I got photographed going into Urth Café the other day?"

"And you're happy about this?"

"Last time that happened, I'd just spent the night at some party, could barely keep my eyes open, hadn't talked to Zoey for twenty-four hours or something, and even then, we'd had a fight. I was hung over, kept forgetting my lines during the shoot, and that morning at the café, I took it out on the poor kid at the counter who recognized me..."

"Again, you're happy about this?"

Evan sat up and drank some water, then swiped the towel across his face. "It's all different now, Paulie. I went in there this time followed by paparazzi, and I didn't care. Different kid recognized me, and he said he hoped I did well with this movie. We talked about the screenplay he was writing. It's all just so damn good." He paused.

"But?"

"Zoey's acting weird." He glanced at Paul. He knew exactly how his friend felt about Zoey, even though Paul had always done his best to be diplomatic. "Weirder than usual. Like she's putting out feelers to see if I want to get back together."

Paul sat up straight. "And your response to her has been?"

"Hell, no." He waited until Paul settled back down again. "Still...it's not like her. I'm going to have to talk to her." He rested his hands on his knees, letting the water bottle dangle. "I've got too much to do right now, too much else to focus on."

There was a pause, and then Paul asked, "You going to tell me about the date?"

Evan looked toward the end of the court. "Not sure."

"You like her?"

"I do," Evan said. He lay back, staring at the ceiling. "But she's got a mystery."

"All women are a mystery, my friend."

"No. She's *got* a mystery."

Paul turned to look at him. "What kind of mystery?"

Evan shrugged, but he didn't feel casual. "Something in her past, maybe. Something that's still resonating."

Paul was quiet for a few beats. "Resonating? Or happening?"

Evan took his own time answering. "Happening."

"Oh, man."

Evan looked up at the lights, remembered showing the stars to Samantha. "Yeah."

"Run fast," Paul advised. "In the other direction." He sat up, brushing his hands together. "You do not want a woman with a past. Especially when it's in her present."

When Evan didn't reply, Paul turned to look down at him and Evan saw the concern on his face and knew he wouldn't be able to reassure him.

"Too late?" Paul asked.

Evan met his gaze. "Pretty much."

"Shit." Paul pinched at the bridge of his nose. "Evan. The timing—"

Evan sat up. "No lectures. Don't be my agent right now. Be my friend." He stood, then held out his hand to help bring Paul to his feet. "She's backed off anyway."

"Because of the mystery, or because you scared her off?" Paul asked with a grin. "Made her watch Daffy Duck cartoons or something?"

Evan clapped him on the back. "Nah. Showed her my etchings." He tucked the basketball under his arm. As he headed back, he spun it on his head, let it slip down to bounce off one arm to the other, and back again, before flipping it to Paul with a twist of his upper arm.

Paul made a fumbling grab, caught it, then glared at Evan.

Evan made an elegant bow, then grinned at Paul. "Saw that in a movie once."

Paul snorted. "Actors," he said, before dropping the ball, then charging at Evan and wrestling him to the floor.

"SO HE SHOWED you the stars. And kissed like a dream." Liz sighed and reached for her glass of iced tea.

They'd set chairs on the grass of Liz's postage stamp back yard near a palm tree, enjoying the February sun. Trying to catch up on her tan, Samantha wore white shorts and a pink top, and new flip-flops graced her feet along with the sparkly pink polish of a pedicure. Liz always insisted her own natural olive skin tone meant she didn't have to tan, but they both knew she just liked to wear dark, dramatic clothing on a regular basis, including today's long black crinkled skirt and matching gypsy top. In honor of the occasion—finally having time for Samantha to give full details about the date instead of just bits and pieces—Liz had also painted her toenails pink.

"Don't forget the Gummi worms." Samantha picked up the bag of mini chocolates Liz had set on a small table between them and peered into it, searching for a Milky Way.

"Of course. Better than the kiss, I'm sure," Liz said. "And quite unique."

Samantha closed the bag and set it down without taking anything from it. "He's unique."

"I think we knew that already."

"We did know that. We didn't appreciate it." She changed her mind and poured some chocolates out on the table and took one.

Liz looked at her over her sunglasses. "Oh, wait. Now, wait a minute. You're appreciating him now?"

"No." Samantha crossed her arms over her chest until she saw Liz's eyes narrow. "Okay, I am. But how can I not? He's perfect. Except for that one thing. But that thing doesn't have anything to do with him as a person. As a person he's..." She stopped. "Don't you raise your eyebrow at me. What?" she asked, when Liz continued to stare at her.

"Well, I'm wondering if you've thought this through at all. I mean, maybe we need to do a chart or something, because this is such an unusual situation, keeping track of all of the oddities. And let's not forget you don't exactly have the greatest track record with men. Do you remember Brad? Stuart? David?"

Samantha gave her a look. She hadn't forgotten any of her messy, failed relationships, which was a big reason she hadn't had one in a long time.

"Exactly," Liz said. "All nice guys except for one thing. There's was always one thing."

"Cheating, already having a girlfriend, and being a petty criminal don't count," Samantha said, crossing her arms over her chest and looking away.

"Because they were great otherwise?"

"I mean, they're not the same. It's different with Evan, the situation, him, us," she said. "He's different. He's not a criminal, I know he doesn't have a girlfriend, and he doesn't seem like a cheater."

Liz shook the bag at her and Samantha took out three bars, grumbling, "It really is different."

"You've got it bad, don't you?"

"No," she said sullenly. They were quiet for a while, eating, and then Samantha mumbled, "Shit" around a mouthful of candy bar. "Yeah, I do."

"But you didn't tell him…"

Still chewing, Samantha shook her head.

"Started to, didn't finish," Liz said, recounting what Samantha had already told her. "He was understanding of your plight." She flapped a hand when Samantha rolled her eyes. "He fed you, he was charming, at some point you realized if you told him now, it might make things miserable for the shoot. Thanks, by the way…"

"Mmm." Samantha waited for the punch line.

"You're still determined to tell him, just waiting for the end of the shoot."

"Right."

"So have you figured out what else you'll be doing after we wrap?"

Samantha shot her a look. "What do you mean?"

Liz waved a hand around. "Part of our contract with Underwood is that they get first look on our next script. I don't *have* a script yet. Hey, I'm mulling," she said when Samantha raised an eyebrow at her. "Anyway, I'd love to have some help. Your help. Writing it."

"I'm not a writer."

"But you've seen a bazillion scripts. You know how a good one works structurally. And this is really my sort of blatant attempt to get you to stay in Los Angeles and to distract you from the Evan Gallagher thing and hope that if something happens between you two, or doesn't happen between you two, or whatever, that you'll still be here, with a job, and friends, and something to occupy you."

"I want to stay in L.A. But I'm not sure about anything right now. Ask me again closer to the end of filming." When Liz nodded, she added, "I'm going to be distracted no matter what, considering I'll see him every day."

"Hmm. Well, look at it this way. Would Dear Abby recommend a relationship, considering this situation?"

Samantha laughed. "No." She pointed toward a pot of browning geraniums on the edge of the deck. "You ever water those?"

"No." Liz picked up the candy bars. "Nice try at distracting me, but it won't work. If you find yourself tempted, just remember one thing."

"What's that?" Samantha asked, knowing that despite Liz's quirky personality and rambling chatter, she had a sharp mind.

"He's an actor," Liz said. "Actors are nuts. If they aren't needy or egotistical, they're both. Their days are spent having their every wish granted that it becomes so automatic, they expect things to come to them, and they forget what life is like for the rest of us schmoes."

Before Samantha could say, "But he's different," Liz continued.

"Their lives are skewed to the extreme, and they like it. Any time they bitch about it, it's to the press, and it's done in such a way to let the little people think they're just like everyone else, just like us little people, and they do it to keep the general public from hating them. And speaking of the press, actors don't forgive bad press easily, especially when someone in the media screws up their comfy little lives and lets the world know their heroes have done something monstrous."

When Samantha opened her mouth to protest, Liz added, "Even if it's not true."

Samantha looked up at the sky. "So I'm screwed."

"You'd be screwed even if you didn't have this monumental thing between you."

Samantha turned to her. "Why?"

"Did I not just give you the 'actors are crazy' speech?" Liz upended the bag onto the table. "You are far gone, aren't you?"

Samantha slumped in her chair, pulling her knees up to her chest. "I need more chocolate."

CHAPTER TWENTY-ONE

Y ou're the script girl, right?"
A tall young woman who looked like a combination of Gwyneth Paltrow and Pamela Anderson—sleek, platinum hair, trim body, chic outfit, and humongous, shelf-like breasts—towered over Samantha in four-inch Lucite platforms.

"Continuity supervisor," she said as politely as possible. "And my name's Samantha."

"Tracy Jennifer Lawson would like you to read lines with her."

Whenever anyone in Tracy's entourage referred to her, they always used all three names. She was never Tracy, Tracy Jennifer or Ms. Lawson. Most of the crew used one of these or the other; Evan was the only one who could get away with calling her Tracy J.

Samantha glanced at her watch, then her call sheet for the day to see when she would be needed on the set, even though she already knew it by heart. She was only stalling for time. Keesha, who'd taken a rare moment to sit with her while she prepared her logs for the day, gave her a sympathetic look and a pat on the shoulder as she got up from her chair. "I'm pretty sure I've got something I should be doing," she said as she wandered off. When it came to who enjoyed working with Tracy, Evan again seemed to be the exception.

Samantha gathered her things and followed the girl across the lawn and up the stairs of the house they'd rented for three days in Pasadena. It would serve as Jack and David's family home, and later in the film, the house where David and Mattie live as a married couple. The house was empty except for the rooms being used for the movie, and the property master and her team, along with the carpenters and electricians, were prepping these.

Driving along the 110 the first day of filming here, Samantha had remembered going to the Rose Bowl and the Cherry Blossom Festival in Victory Park with Liz, but the memories hadn't been as overwhelming as those on her first day back, when she took Liz's SUV along Hollywood Boulevard. She'd been in Los Angeles nineteen days now, and with each day she felt more at home here again, more comfortable and settled.

"The city gets into your bones," Liz had told her when Samantha mentioned this. "And she's a sneaky wench."

No matter the reason, Samantha had thought Pasadena a beautiful city five years earlier, and she felt the same now. As the big white vans containing all of the film crew's gear had shown up at the Victorian on Markham Place, clumps of neighbors and passersby had gathered to watch the cast and crew. With the exception of Tracy Jennifer, each of the actors had come out during a break and chatted with the onlookers, taking pictures and signing autographs.

The unused rooms had been designated for wardrobe, hair and makeup, and the actors. Tracy Jennifer had ensconced herself in the third floor master suite, and as Samantha and her guide reached the top of the stairs, Sam saw that Tracy had also made herself quite at home. She sat propped against the headboard of a massive bed that looked like it came from the property department, talking on the phone via a Bluetooth earpiece, getting a pedicure, looking through a magazine, and petting a Pug dog that sat in her lap and gave Samantha an inquisitive look.

The Gwyneth-Pamela look alike glided over to Tracy, bent down to whisper in her ear, then went to rejoin the rest of the helpers. Samantha didn't even question why one of them couldn't read lines with Tracy; they were all clearly Very Important People with Very Important Things to do. Liz had told her that Tracy Jennifer once admitted she only surrounded herself with beautiful people because she could in no way be associated with anything ugly.

Without looking at Samantha, Tracy waved toward a high backed chair next to the bed and said, "Sit," and continued her telephone conversation. Resisting the urge to pant like a dog being told what to do, Samantha headed toward the chair, and the Pug gave her a grin as if he knew how she felt.

"Oh, I know," Tracy was saying. She was already in full makeup and costume, with tissue around her collar to keep the makeup from staining her clothes. Samantha wondered if she could get Mary, the head of wardrobe, to come upstairs and see one of her creations being crumpled. Mary was one of the few people fearless about hollering at the actors.

"I know," Tracy said. "Uh huh. No, yeah, that's it exactly." A pause while she nodded, then adjusted the earpiece. "Right...right...yeah, right. Right. Oh, I know. No, I know." More nodding. "I know, right?"

Samantha cleared her throat.

"No, I know, that's right. Nuh uh. Oh, well, yeah, of course..."

Samantha barked and the dog stood up and wagged its rear end, grinning at her. Well, at least someone was paying attention to her; and if getting Tracy Jennifer's notice without making her angry meant bonding with her dog, then that's what she'd do. Samantha had perfected diplomacy on the set, but she'd never claim to enjoy it, so if she could have some fun with a dog at the same time, she'd indulge a little.

"No, yeah, I have to go. I have to read lines or whatever," she said, as if Samantha were making her do this. "Yeah, I know. *Exactly*." Tracy clicked her phone off and said, "Such an important call."

"I'm *sure*." Thank goodness for the dog, because otherwise Samantha would've been tempted to strangle the actress. "So you wanted someone to read lines with you?"

"Yeah, I've got speeches and shit. Big dialogue scene, whatever."

Samantha pulled out her script, deciding to ignore that. "So where did you want to start?"

Tracy rifled through a pile of papers next to her, tossing some aside until she came to what she wanted. "Page twenty-three. Where I'm all in love with Jack, but think his brother's gone weird on me."

While Samantha read the parts of Jack, David and their father, Tracy spoke her lines with a grumbling monotone, trying not to look at her copy of the script as they went through the scene. If Samantha hadn't seen otherwise, she would've thought Tracy Jennifer Lawson a terrible actress. Tracy saved her energy for the camera, bored and dull during rehearsals, but when Gary called, "Action!" she became heartbreakingly good as Mattie, the girl who'd turned to one brother for comfort after she thought the one she truly loved was dead.

After a mind-numbing hour, Christopher, the Second A.D. came running up the stairs and said, "Ms. Lawson, they're ready for you on the set." Samantha gave the Pug one last wiggle, then grabbed her things and followed Christopher down the stairs.

Evan, Carson and Richard were already heading for the dining room when Keesha announced, "Put us on a bell!" The sound mixer played a noise like a bell, which rang throughout the house and signaled that everyone involved in the scene needed to gather around the camera. Samantha joined Gary, Keesha, the set decorator, the property master, the boom operator, the head electrician, and the key grip to discuss how best to run through the master shot for this scene. They all waited to see what information Gary might impart that would affect their particular responsibilities.

"Okay, this is a table scene," he began. "Dinner, passing bowls and dishes while talking, a continuity nightmare." He smiled at Samantha. "It's also a light moment on the outside, but David has brought Mattie home to meet his family, that girl is going to end up falling in love with Jack instead of David, and we just begin to see David's..." He paused, clearly looking for the right word.

"Ickiness?" Carson suggested, and everyone laughed.

"Ickiness works," said Gary. "So we're going to want to convey all of that with looks, motions, David's affection for Mattie, his...pride, if you will, at having done something better than his brother for once. He's the good soon, always obeys the rules, while Jack's been a rebel all along, and yet he gets the accolades, especially from their father. Now he's brought home a nice girl, and Jack has gotten into some kind of trouble he won't talk about, so David thinks things are finally going his way."

As Gary continued to give an overview of what he looked for in the scene, Samantha took a peek at Evan. Hair, makeup and wardrobe had provided the appearance of Jack, but Evan took it the rest of the way, one arm slung around Carson's shoulders, as Jack would do with his little brother, David, listening to Gary, but also scanning the room, not leaving his back open or his mind unaware of potential risk.

He glanced at the dining room table set up, and when he looked around again, his gaze settled on Samantha. He gave her an Evan smile, not a Jack one, and that was just fine. She'd done her best to avoid lengthy conversations with Evan since their "date" and her talk with Liz, but life on a movie set meant being in almost constant contact and to keep morale up and encourage cooperation during long shooting days, the crew worked just as hard at being diplomats as they did at their respective jobs. It could be a challenge, and Samantha felt emotionally worn out from being pleasant but distant to Evan, and then dodging him if it looked like he might want to talk about anything other than the shoot. That hadn't stopped her from researching local tree names—Blue Oak, Oracle Oak, Mountain Mahogany—in case native flora came up in a conversation.

She smiled back, and he gave her a wink.

She felt her cheeks go pink, but she was saved by Gary asking the actors to take their places, and could turn her attention to Lincoln looking through his viewfinder to figure out depth of field for the shot, and conferring with the electricians for proper lighting. As the actors went through a rehearsal, including making all of the movements they would do during actual filming, Samantha timed everything and took notes, and Lincoln decided he wanted to use two stationary cameras for this scene.

Lincoln continued to refine the shot with each subsequent rehearsal, while the microphone operator discussed with the sound mixer where best to place the recorder panel. The property master, Rita, and her crew moved a few set pieces around under Gary's direction, and Samantha got into the flow of the set up. As Gary gave more instructions while the shot was being refined—"I want a close up of Jack as he notes David reaching for Mattie's hand under the table, and Mattie pulling away; and a close up of the hands"—Samantha wrote down everything.

Once the scene was blocked, Keesha said, "Mark 'em" and Lincoln's First Assistant measured the distance between the actors' noses as they sat in place to keep proper camera position. Once this was done, all of the actors stood and left the set while their stand-ins came in for the final lighting adjustments.

Samantha took this time to review the next shot while answering questions for some of the crew: what time of day is it in the dining room scene, what was the timing on the rehearsal, was Mattie's bracelet on the right wrist or the left in the last shot? She also peeked forward to the other shots they'd film at this rented house. *Interior*: Jack on the phone. *Exterior*: Jack and David on the front lawn; Jack, knowing someone is after him, asks David to take care of Mattie if something happens to him. *Interior* and *Exterior*: later, after Jack is thought dead and David and Mattie are married, Jack watches them through the window. Both of those moments would have to be filmed separately, Jack seeing what he thinks is a loving exchange between his brother and former girlfriend, and the real situation, with David quietly threatening Mattie that if she tries to leave, he'll kill her.

When Samantha finally raised her head, Evan Gallagher stood in front of her, script in hand. Today, wardrobe had dressed him in black jeans and boots, and a tight red t-shirt with the sleeves rolled up; his slicked back hair enhanced his eyes and cheekbones.

"I didn't want to interrupt," he said.

"That's all right," she replied, the answer automatic, even as her heart beat faster. Everyone got equal attention when she was on the job, but no one else on the crew elicited that particular result from her.

"Would you mind reading lines with me?" When she nodded, he said, "It's the next shot, when I'm talking to David outside. Can't quite get it right."

He moved a chair around to face her, so close the side of his leg rested against hers, and told her what page and line to start at.

As David, Samantha read, "So what's really going on, big brother?"

Evan paused. "Dad looks a little tired, don't you think?"

"C'mon, Jack. You've been gone for weeks, no word, then all this stuff in the news. Those kidnappings, the bombings. We know you're involved…"

Evan let out a sigh. "You know I can't talk about it."

"So you did help them escape," Samantha said. "You did see who was behind it."

"Is Dad okay?"

Evan's leg brushed against hers and Samantha glanced up from the script. She couldn't read the look in his eyes, wasn't sure if he was watching her as Jack or as Evan at that point, but she couldn't look away from him in either case. "He's worried about you," she said.

"I feel the same about him."

"Don't. He went to the doc. He's fine. Strong as a bull moose, like he always says."

Evan laughed, but it didn't reach his eyes. "One less thing to worry about."

"What else is there?"

"Mattie," Evan breathed, still watching Samantha.

Samantha knew there was a pause in the script here and let it happen now, her gaze still locked with Evan's, his leg warm against hers. "Mattie," she repeated.

"Promise…you'll take care of her if something happens to me," Evan said.

"Hey, don't talk like that."

Evan reached out and grabbed her shoulder, as she knew Jack would do to David. "Her safety and happiness are more important to me than my life," he said. "Promise me."

"I promise," said Samantha.

Evan let go and leaned back, then gave her a smile. "That's not in the script."

Samantha shook her head. "What?"

"David doesn't promise right away. Not like that."

Samantha glanced down at the script, but didn't really see the words. He was right, of course. She knew the script by heart, but Evan's insistence and his hand on her shoulder had something inside her head saying, "Anything he wants! Promise him!" She gave him a shaky smile. "Sorry about that," she said, and before he could reply she bent her head to the script again and read the correct next line. "What are you talking about? You're sounding crazy."

"I'm looking forward to going on location next week," Evan said.

Samantha's head shot up. Evan smiled at her—all Evan, no Jack. "That's not in the script," she told him.

"Improvise," he said, leaning close to her.

"I'm looking forward to it, too," she said. "It's supposed to be beautiful out there."

"Lots of good stargazing."

She flashed back to their date, how he'd twined their arms together and showed her the constellations. Fed her Gummi worms and kissed her to a fever pitch. All of it wonderful, and none of it hers for the taking again. She cast about for a more neutral subject. "So where's your son staying while you're gone?"

Evan straightened, studying her. "With his mom. Her band's getting ready to go on tour and it'll be good for them to spend some time together."

"You'll miss him," she said, before she could stop herself. She'd seen something in his eyes that spoke of sadness even as his words said his son would be happy.

"I will. We haven't been apart this long for…years." He grasped her knee, shook it a little, then seemed to shake himself out of potential melancholy. "But we'll be so busy, it'll go so fast we'll hardly remember it."

He stood up suddenly, said, "Then we'll only have two more weeks on the shoot," gave her a wink, and sauntered away.

"ROLL SOUND," KEESHA said, after calling for quiet on the set.

"Scene 43, take one," Samantha announced.

"Speed," came from Tony once the sound recorder had come up to the correct speed.

Shelly held the slate up, then waited for Aaron, the camera operator, to say, "Mark it," before snapping the slate and sprinting out of the way.

"Rolling," said Aaron.

Gary waited a moment, called, "Action," and Evan turned to Carson, who began stalking up the church aisle toward him in a dark suit and trench coat and said, "You don't look surprised to see me dead." Evan squeezed his eyes shut a second and held up a hand. "Sorry, sorry."

"Cut."

Evan bowed his head; he hated screwing up a first line. As Carson returned to his starting point, Evan took a few deep, quiet breaths. It was Friday and their last day filming in Los Angeles before going on location for a week. Oliver would be with his mom, practically bouncing every time it was mentioned, and Evan was glad Zoey was in good enough shape to take him, but he'd miss his son.

Samantha reminded Carson that he needed to run his hands over his hair after Evan's line, then announced it was "Scene 43, take two." Evan raised his head, getting back into character, and waited for his cue.

This time, as Carson strode toward him, boots thudding, Evan said, "You don't look surprised to see me alive."

Carson ran his hands over his naturally wavy hair, slicked back for today's shoot. "Mattie told me."

Evan repeated her name, clenched his fists. "Where is she?"

Carson shrugged, looked away as if he didn't care, as if he hadn't betrayed both his brother and his wife. "Gone. Left me." He stared at Evan, held the look for a beat, and added, "Again."

Evan held up a hand as if to reach out to Carson, but dropped it when the other man flinched, made as if to step back. "I never wanted to hurt you, David," Evan whispered.

Carson ignored this, and going back to Evan's question about where Mattie was, said, "This time, though, she's not running to you. Not after what you did, betraying her like that, betraying all of us like that."

"You know why I had to do it," Evan said. "You know damn well they would've killed you and Mattie both. Maybe even gone after Dad."

"Not me," Carson said. "They wouldn't have touched me."

"Why not?"

On her cue, Tracy stepped out of the shadows, a gun drawn and pointed at Carson's back. Evan saw her first, and tried not to react, not to set off his brother.

"Because you're working for them," Tracy said and raised the pistol higher. "You set us up."

Without turning around, Carson sneered, "Well, if it isn't my darling wife."

"You had me kidnapped," Tracy said. "You set it up so Jack thought he had to go into hiding to protect me." Carson finally turned around and Tracy said to his face, "What I really needed was protection from *you*, you bastard."

Just as Tracy eased back the hammer, Gary called, "Cut. And print that." He jumped out of his chair. "Beautiful. Thanks, everyone."

Keesha said, "Let's start setting up for the cover shots. Tracy's close-ups first."

Tracy lowered her arm, then handed the fake pistol over and headed out to her trailer, which was parked in the church lot. Evan clapped a hand on Carson's shoulder. "Nice work. You had me wanting to hit you."

Carson smiled. "I wanted you to. David's such a shit. But what a great character," he added with a grin.

"Indeed," Evan told him as they walked to the front of the church where craft services had set up. "It can be great to play the bad guy. Gets rid of a lot of demons."

"Yeah." Carson handed Evan a cup of coffee, then got one for himself. "And I tell you, the girls dig it."

Evan gave him another slap on the shoulder and a smile, but refrained from comment. He took a sip of coffee and wrapped his hands around the cup; the old church in Culver City that they were shooting in was beautiful, but dim and chilly, any warmth created by the portable heaters escaping toward the high ceilings.

Carson looked around, then said, "So what do you think of Tracy Jennifer?"

"I think she's a terrific actress," Evan said without hesitation. He wouldn't add that he also saw her as spoiled and abrasive. "She gets more involved in her character than a lot of other people I've worked with."

Carson leaned against the sanctuary wall. "And she's got amazing tits."

Evan blew on his coffee and made a noncommittal noise.

"She invited me to some party at a club this weekend, for a friend's birthday. She said her friend's got a crush on me. I wonder if it's the tall one who looks like Pamela Anderson..."

As Carson continued to talk, about girls and their assets, and then about what else he'd be doing that weekend—jumping out of an airplane, going to a concert—Evan realized he was glad to not be that young anymore, and past the point in his life of needing constant stimulation. He peeked at Samantha over the rim of his coffee cup to where she stood with Gary, Keesha, Lincoln and Rita, the property master. Since they had a prop gun on the set, the Firearms Safety Handler hired for the day also joined the group.

Samantha held the ever-present binder to her chest, watching Lincoln intently, and nodding at something he said. She made a note on a legal pad propped on the binder, then pushed a stray lock of hair behind her ear. He itched to take her hair down and run his fingers through it. She wore a long dark blue skirt and those boots with a long-sleeved top that had frills on the bottom and cuffs. He saw himself running his hands along those frills before teasing the shirt down her shoulders.

He'd been flirting with her off and on, giving her hints about the end of the shoot, reminding her they wouldn't be co-workers soon, but trying not to push. He just hoped that whatever made her nervous wasn't him. His friendliness with the cast and crew on set would have extended to her, no matter how he felt about her personally, but their interactions had a sharpness to them, something that kept him on edge, in anticipation. He hadn't enjoyed that sort of tension in a long time and he wanted to see her more often after the shoot, easing her apprehension away, and in the meantime enjoying the buildup.

And when the release of that tension came, Samantha Jamison should be one relaxed woman.

CHAPTER TWENTY-TWO

Samantha, Gary and Liz stood in a row in the middle of the main street of Walterville, arms crossed, surveying what would be their home for the next week. Located about an hour north of Pioneertown, which had originally been built in the 1940s as a movie set for Westerns, Walterville looked like the setting for a hometown the hero needed to leave. The crew of *Broken* would be filming there for five days outside the town's limits in the surrounding hills.

The cast and crew would be staying at the Sleep Rite Motel, which sat to their left in its faded green and pink splendor, its side parking lot already crowded with the crew's ubiquitous white trucks. The General Store next to it included a soda fountain, and a combination video rental and pizza place. Down the way were the post office, and pharmacy and across the street were a market, the Fill-Er-Up gas station and a feed store. Farther down, small houses had been built parallel to the main street on narrow roads.

Mountains rose behind the motel, overshadowing the town and the rest of what Liz called the "prairie" around it. Other than the buildings and mountains, there didn't seem to be anything taller than themselves for as far as they could see. In fact, the area appeared to consist of scrub, dry grass and struggling weeds.

Standing on the dusty blacktop, all three took in the view to the left and the right.

"So we couldn't film here last week because it was their annual Founding Fathers Rodeo Days and the town was booked solid?" Samantha asked.

Gary nodded. "Yep. Place fills right up. But it's also cheap to film here."

Liz turned in a half circle, then came back around. "I assume Walter was one of the founders. So Rodeo Days must bring in twenty, thirty people then, instead of the usual five?"

"And it's usually cool and crisp this time of year?" Samantha asked, wiping away a line of sweat that had begun to drift down her temple.

"Yep," Gary said again, and let out a sigh. "Never gets hot here in February, the mayor told me. Ever."

Liz stared at him as she flapped the bottom of her shirt back and forth trying make a breeze. "They have a mayor?"

Gary looked up at the bright blue sky. "They have a film commission. The mayor happens to be part of it."

"Is he the sheriff, innkeeper and barkeep, too?"

"No, but he owns the market."

Samantha and Liz leaned forward, past Gary between them, to look at one another. They each raised an eyebrow at the other, then straightened up again.

"It was so pretty and cool here when we scouted it," Liz said. "This is a nightmare. So is Tracy Jennifer going to kill you for this?"

Gary let out a breath. "Probably. She's already holed up in her room, blasting her air conditioner and swearing at me because we wouldn't pay for her entourage to come here."

Samantha and Liz nodded, crossing their arms again to look out over the blacktop that trailed away in the distance as heat waves shimmered above it.

At the bang of a door, they turned in unison to see Evan trot down the steps of the motel office dressed in a white t-shirt, cargo shorts and brown and white Pumas, whistling as he headed across the street. He gave them a grin as he came over, clapped Gary on the shoulder, and said, "Great out here, isn't?"

He continued past and they turned once again in a group to watch him go by. He spread his arms out, said, "Wide open spaces," then turned to them, walking backwards. "Can I get you anything from the market?"

They shook their heads.

He raised a hand to them, turned back around, and bounded up the stairs.

They watched a few moments more, until he was out of sight, then shook their heads again. "Actors," Gary said, and led them back toward the motel.

CHAPTER TWENTY-THREE

Samantha pressed a dampened washcloth to her forehead, and edged closer to Keesha under the umbrella, currently one of the few objects in the area providing any shade. Francis had been sent back to town with two of the electricians to buy any available umbrellas, fans, ice, and coolers and to hopefully find another generator, since one of theirs had burned out.

Keesha held up her PDA, waited a moment, then said, "Yep. Hundred and three."

Samantha waved script pages, alternately fanning herself and Keesha, and moved the cloth to the back of her neck. "You've got to be kidding."

"Nope."

"I'm even too hot to be impressed that your James Bond gadget reads the temperature." Samantha plucked her blouse from her chest and fanned down her front, sighing in relief at the small breeze she created. She thought Keesha might have the right idea with her cycling shorts and cropped top meant to pull moisture away from your body, but she didn't think she could get away with a similar outfit.

"Sends out death rays, too," Keesha said, flipping the PDA closed. "Mostly at annoying PAs."

They grinned at each other. Francis had done everything he was asked as Production Assistant, never complaining, but he and Keesha would clearly never bond. "Boy's never going to make it past PA status," she'd told Samantha earlier in the shoot. "Too eager to please."

Samantha looked out over the location they'd chosen to film Jack's hideout. It definitely looked remote, slightly rolling plains, a few Joshua Trees poking up, and lots of those tumbleweed things that Evan had known the real name of in Hesperia but that she couldn't remember for the life of her. She didn't see any of those pretty flowers he'd talked about that first day of filming. It was dry, dusty and unbearably hot.

Crew members hung out in the stingy shade of the building that Marcus and his carpenters had built for Jack's cabin, the awning of the crafts services trailer, and the trucks and trailers that had carried equipment and crew out to the site. The usual bustle that occurred at any film site had been reduced to a slow shuffle, but Samantha knew the crew, including herself and Keesha, would move into high gear no matter the temperature as soon as they got the word to start up again.

Tracy Jennifer had had one of her people bring up an air conditioned RV at her own expense, something Gary paid for with pieces of his hide every time he had to deal with her off camera. She continued to give a stellar performance, but whenever she encountered Gary, he got a diatribe on some made up problem or another.

"You think we'll have to cancel today?" Samantha asked now.

"Would kill our schedule," Keesha said as she pulled her braids back and secured them with an elastic band. "Hurt the budget. Might kill Gary if he has to stay on location any longer with Miss Indulgence. She'll make it even harder for him if we have to stay here longer than planned."

"He could send Francis to give her the good news."

Keesha gave a little whoop. "Gary could hide in a trailer and give Francis all of his directions for the rest of the film through a Comtec."

They laughed, but not too much. Even that small exertion made them hotter.

"This is crazy," Keesha said. "Let's sit." She led Samantha to their director's chairs, which they dragged to one side of the cabin in a slice of shade, and propped the umbrella up after they sat. "Not counting today, this has been a fun shoot."

"Yeah?" Samantha waved the damp washcloth around to cool it off, then settled it around the back of her neck again.

"Yeah. Nasty little script, veteran crew, strong cast, not too many problems."

By "nasty," Samantha knew Keesha meant good, with teeth, and despite what they were dealing with today, and the myriad other issues they'd handled, it really had been a low stress shoot. She tried to sound casual as she asked, "You worked with Evan Gallagher on the Duncan Tanner films, didn't you?"

Keesha shot her a look. "I did. He was good then. Better now, all around."

"What do you mean?"

"Better actor. Better man. Sometimes a little adversity is good for the soul." Her phone rang before Samantha could ask her to elaborate on that. "Hey, Francis." She raised her eyebrows at Samantha, then pulled out a copy of the list she'd given him when he went into town, checking things off as she nodded and said, "Uh huh, uh huh. Good. Great." She paused, listening. "No extras in this scene, Francis. Jack's alone out here, no people, that's the point. Hang on a sec." She covered the mouthpiece and looked at Samantha. "Boy found a local who wants to loan us two RVs with air conditioning and generators if he can be in the movie." She rolled her eyes. "I swear. But I can't pass this one up. Francis," she said into the phone. "Tell them yes, but they won't be in this scene with Jack. Get him to sign a waiver. We'll figure something out." She hung up, laughing. "Shoot's back on."

THE REST OF the day had gone well, with the extra fans and motor homes to help cool everyone off, and while Gary had pushed them to make up for the lost time, they'd wrapped at five since they would be losing light after that and Samantha rushed through her daily logs to get back to town. The townspeople had graciously offered to keep many of their stores open longer than usual for the crew, and Samantha only had one thought on her mind right now as she walked up the steps of the General Store: ice cream.

Most of the crew either rested in their rooms or hung out at the pool. Liz and Gary were meeting in the conference room to go over some details, so Samantha had a little time to herself.

When she pushed open the front door, a bell tinkled overhead, and a woman fairly bursting out of her pink shorts and matching halter, tinted hair piled high on her head, gave her a warm smile from behind the counter.

"Hey, darlin', you from that movie outfit?" Her name tag read: Judy.

"I am, and we're all grateful to you for keeping your doors open longer for us. It makes a difference."

"Oh, pish, it's no problem. So hot right now none of us could sleep anyway, and it isn't never hot here in February, so we're all out of rhythm. And I swear, old Earl's just beside himself to be able to be in a real movie."

"I think Earl saved the day for us. We were melting out there."

She beamed and a little dimple formed in her left cheek. "He'll be glad to hear it. Now what is it I can do for you this evening?"

"Well, I hear you have the best ice cream around."

Now Judy had matching dimples. "We sure do." She headed to the side of the store where they'd installed a soda fountain, a counter with stools, and tall tables that looked out the window. The rest of the store seemed to be packed with anything you might need: kitchen items, clothing, books, camping gear, jewelry, furniture, rugs, bathroom accessories, sports equipment, even gardening supplies.

Samantha followed Judy to the ice cream counter and stared in wonder at all of the flavors: chocolate, vanilla, and strawberry competed with butter pecan, Neapolitan, cookies and cream, cherry, coffee, rocky road, mint chocolate chip, coconut, pistachio, cheesecake, banana and bubblegum.

"Wow. I'll never be able to decide."

"Then don't pick just one." Judy pointed to a sign behind her. The ice cream special of the week was a triple for the price of a double. "In honor of your movie, but also because it's so darned hot. And if you'd like, we've got a nice porch out back with a swing, just perfect to sit and cool off and watch the moon rise."

Samantha indulged and got a triple with scoops of chocolate, coconut and cherry. She didn't take Judy up on the offer of the porch swing because her ice cream started to melt as soon as she stepped outside, despite the fact that the sun had set. She went back to her room, finished up the cone and lay on the bed in a stupor for a few minutes, wondering if it would be overindulgence to go back and just get a single scoop of that coconut.

She opted for a shower and trying to get some sleep instead, but only tossed and turned on the coverlet, her mind busily going over the day, checking and re-checking her work—had she gotten everything right?—and pondering Keesha's comment about adversity being good for the soul. More than one person had suggested that while Evan Gallagher had always been a good actor, he was now a better person. She didn't know what to make of the idea that Evan's problems had led to him…improving in some way. She hardly thought he'd thank her for her part in things, for her report pushing him over the edge so that he could crawl his way back a better person.

Oh, who was she kidding? There was no justification for what she'd done, she knew that, but the more she got to know Evan, and the more she liked him, the less she was able to connect what she'd done with the man she knew. Or thought she knew. The reality of him overshadowed her imaginings until she couldn't quite recall them as clearly as she'd once done.

She sat up in bed. This was getting her nowhere. She didn't know what to do with these thoughts, and if she wasn't going to be able to sleep, she didn't want all of this on her mind. She got up and opened the door, peeking outside. People still hung out by the pool, but maybe it had cooled off a little. She glanced toward the General Store, but it was blocked from sight by two of the film crew's trailers in the parking lot. It might be cooler and quieter over there.

Restless, she put on white shorts and a filmy white top that buttoned up the front, and decided to check out that porch.

CHAPTER TWENTY-FOUR

Isn't never hot here," Samantha said aloud as she climbed up the wide back stairs, pulling her hair back from her face; she wished she'd put it up. "No, never."

She made a hmphing sound, her head down, and moved toward the big porch swing on her right. Something "hmphed" back at her and she yelped, her head coming up. She pressed her fingers to her mouth and backed away as someone rose up from the swing, causing it to squeak in protest and begin to sway.

"You take another step you'll go tumbling backwards," Evan said.

Samantha dropped her hands and took a quick look behind her. He was right. Her heel was poised over the top step. She inched it ahead until it rested on the decking, then took hold of the pillar to steady the rest of her.

"What are you doing here?" she asked.

Evan set his feet on the floor and turned his face to her. She caught his profile, the flash of his teeth as he talked, but the rest of his face was still in shadow. "Same as you, I expect. Trying to find a cool place to sleep."

She noticed he sounded a little like the town residents and a little like his character Jack. "You were sleeping out here?"

She heard a little huff of breath, his version of a chuckle, she'd learned. "Jack would've slept outside." He lifted his arm and gestured toward the mountains. "I was headed out there, actually, but Gary caught me and made me promise not to go too far."

"I guess he's learned about your acting methods."

He cocked his head and it was her turn to chuckle. "So it's true that you slept in your costume out in the jungle when they were making the second Duncan Tanner movie? It's a film legend, you know."

She saw one shoulder in a white t-shirt lift up, then fall, outlined by the indigo haze of the sky beyond him. "Duncan was stuck out there. It's what he would've done."

He slid to one end of the swing and she let go of the pillar and sat next to him. "I think that's taking method acting to the extreme," she said. She could see his face now in the moonlight, his cheekbones more pronounced, his smile still bright.

He tilted his body toward hers, rested his elbows on his thighs and leaned close. "I don't do anything halfway."

"No," she said, having witnessed that for herself, "I don't believe you do."

He straightened, laughing. "Neither do you."

She stared at him, but he stayed resting against the back of the swing, head slightly tilted up as if he were studying the stars past the porch awning. "Why do you say that?" she finally asked.

"I've been watching you work," he told her. "Continuity's a tough job. Takes a lot of energy and concentration on details." He kicked his feet up and rested them against the porch railing. The swing swayed a couple times, but he stopped it by crossing one bare foot over the other and pushing back with his legs.

"Thanks." A pleasant shiver swept up her spine at his praise, and he nodded. He seemed content to sit in silence after that, so she decided to do likewise, leaning back, head tilted up toward the stars just making their appearance, and her feet on the porch railing. She had to slink farther down to make her feet reach.

More stars appeared, the moon rose on their left, and as she'd hoped, a breeze made its way along the porch, ruffling her hair against her face. She closed her eyes, enjoying its cool glide over her hot skin.

She let out a happy sigh, and felt Evan rest his hand over hers. She automatically twined her fingers with his, and turned to look at him. He was watching her, and she wondered how long he'd been doing it. He smiled at her and squeezed her fingers and she found herself responding in kind to both. Still smiling, he leaned back again.

"Are you Jack right now?" she asked in a whisper, not wanting to break the mood, but at the same time curious why he wasn't talking.

His booming laugh startled her. He didn't let go of her hand, but his feet dropped to the deck, causing the swing to lurch, and her feet to drop. He leaned over his thighs. "No," he said, shaking his head. "No," he repeated, his voice softer as he looked at her. "Jack couldn't sit quiet with a woman." He gestured toward the sparse patch of grass past the faded, beat up railing in front of them. "He'd have you down there, out of your clothes, before you could say 'good evening'."

She looked at the grass, remembering it from the daylight as stunted and yellowing, the dirt it attempted to grow in a reddish brown, and shuddered.

Evan squeezed her fingers again. "He'd have been charming about it, at least. Made you think it was your idea."

"Sure. That's reassuring," she said, but smiled as she spoke.

She turned to him to add something else, and he bent and kissed her. She leaned into him, feeling his warm lips, his hair tickling her cheek.

He raised their clasped hands and pressed them to his chest, flattening her hand until she felt his heart beating under her palm. He covered her hand with his a moment, then slid his fingers up her bare arms to cup her neck, brushing the sides of her face with his thumbs.

His lips parted and she slipped her tongue inside his mouth, brushing it against his. She wanted to kiss him all over, to run her tongue along the back of his neck and down his spine, to taste the salt on his skin and press herself naked against the length of him.

The kiss deepened and she took his hand and placed the palm over her heart, just as he had done with her. She wanted him to feel her heartbeat, to know the strength of it, to understand his effect on her. She might not be able to express her feelings in words, to tell him everything, but her body didn't lie.

He wrapped his other arm around her and pulled her tightly to him, and she found herself firmly seated on his lap, facing him. She could feel his heart against her chest now; she slipped her hand around his back and eased it under his shirt to press her palm against the hot skin there.

She traced the curve of his spine even as he caressed the side of her breast, then gripped her waist, squeezing hard. Before she realized what had happened, he'd pulled away. She opened her eyes and saw him watching her. "What's wrong?" she asked, trying to catch her breath, to disconnect from the feel of his skin under her fingers, and failing.

He brushed her hair back from her face with both hands, looking into her eyes. Gripping her hair into a ponytail at the back of her neck with one hand, he brushed his thumb along her cheekbone with the other. "I want you," he whispered.

She nodded. She wanted him, too, naked, over her, whether they were in the hideous crab grass or not.

He shook his head. "I can't have you."

She didn't want to ask it, willed herself not to ask it, but curiosity won. "Why not?"

"A few reasons…" He let go of her hair and leaned back with a sigh, looking out at the mountains again, and absently running a hand along her thigh. "There's that caveat about not getting involved with a co-worker," he said. "You know that reason, though. Another is that I like you too much."

"Is that like respecting me too much to throw me down on this swing and take me here and now?" Her thighs felt warm against his as he shifted under her.

He looked at her out of the corner of his eye, then turned to face her, one side of his mouth quirking up. "A little bit."

"I don't understand."

"You remember the Gummi worms on our date?"

She smiled at the memory. "Yes."

He brushed a lock of hair behind her ear before whispering into it, "You have a secret."

Her mouth went dry. It was a statement, not a question, but something she felt deserved a response. "Yes." She couldn't look away from him, but wanted to when she saw his mouth set in a firm line. There was nothing and everything to be added to that word, but she waited to see what he said next.

And the wait seemed endless, especially when he didn't move, just watched her.

"Is this a secret you can't tell me now?" he finally asked. "Or ever?"

"Just now," she said with regret. *Get off his lap and off this porch, Samantha*, she told herself, *and march yourself back to your room before this gets trickier than it already is.*

"So someday? After we've taken the time to get to know each other? When you can trust me?"

She shook her head, answering his question at the same time she told her rational side to shut up. "I trust you now. It's…complicated."

"Most secrets are."

"I promise I'll tell you everything. Soon," she added, but she kept coming around to the same question: would he feel the same way, would he look at her with such passion, after she told him?

He lifted her hand again, then kissed her fingertips. He looked into her eyes, and said, "And that's why I want you, but can't have you." He wrapped his arms around her, pulling her close until her head rested on his shoulder. He let a section of hair fall through his fingers before picking it up and doing it again. He kept playing with her hair as he talked, his chin brushing the top of her head. "Besides, if I threw you down and ravaged you on the swing, that's all we'd think about, isn't it?"

His tone was light enough that she allowed herself a giggle, and she relaxed against the soothing stroking of her hair. "Depends on how it went, I think."

He laughed, his chest expanding, and held her tighter. "Good or bad, we'd focus on that, and not on watching the stars appear or knowing that we both love cherry ice cream."

She raised her head to look at him. "You love cherry ice cream?"

"Judy told me all about that sweet girl that got a triple-decker and she seemed surprised those were my favorites, too. We must've just missed each other."

"But now we've found each other." And she found him gentle, charming and sexy.

Looking into his eyes, studying his face, she didn't want to think, only to feel, to breathe him in, so she pressed her fingertips to his cheeks and ran her thumbs across his lower lip, then bowed her head and rested her forehead to his.

"I thought I said something about waiting," he murmured, "but maybe it was a dream."

"No," she whispered back, feeling his breath warm on her neck and down her chest. "This is the dream."

He raised his head, forcing her to lift hers and look at him. "Then it's a good dream."

She ran her thumbs back now along his cheeks and up to the corners of his eyes. "Indeed," she said, using one of his pet words, before pressing her lips firmly to his.

"I don't want to wait," he murmured against her mouth.

"I don't, either," she said, surprised that she would admit it, but not surprised at her feelings.

He took her face in his hands, kept her close. "I don't want to hurt you," he whispered.

"I feel the same way."

"So what now?" he asked, pressing his lips to her cheekbone.

Her eyelids fluttered and her head tilted back a little, even as he held her face, moved his lips down to her neck. "I...oh. I don't...know. Maybe we can...ahh," she sighed, when his tongue caressed her collarbone. "Just...sleep together."

"Okay," he breathed.

"No strings," she added, shivering, as he pressed a kiss against the base of her throat.

"Okay," he said again, easing the neckline of her shirt off to one side. Then his lips froze against the flesh of her bare shoulder, and he lifted his head to look at her. "What did you say?"

She straightened slowly, blinking at him. "What?" she asked through a haze.

"No strings?"

"I—"

"Is that what you want?"

"I want you," she said.

"But you don't want anything else."

His body had stilled. His hands rested on her hips, she sat on his lap, but it was as if he had pushed her off and walked to the other end of the porch.

"No, that's not it." She wanted *everything* else, she thought, but she couldn't say that to him, couldn't ask it of him, considering the circumstances. "But I'm scared," she admitted. "I'm not ready for more."

He sat still and silent for so long, she thought she should just get up and leave, but then he said, "Neither am I," on a sigh, and she released the breath she'd been holding.

"I have a bit of a past," he said, giving her a quick smile.

She pressed a palm to his heart. "Don't we all. But I believe in second chances. I just don't..." She took a breath. "I don't want you to pay for my mistakes."

He tilted his head. "I'm not sure what you—"

"So sex without a relationship," she said brightly, not letting him finish the thought or delve too deeply into what she'd just said. "Perfect solution, right?"

"I'd be an idiot if I said no."

"You're definitely not an idiot, Evan Gallagher."

"I'm more of an old fashioned guy, though. This is a little…"

"Different?" she finished for him.

"New," he said. "For me."

"But acceptable?"

He ran a hand along her jaw, down her neck, brushing his thumb on the edge of her ear. "Evan Gallagher is not an idiot…" he repeated.

She shivered at his touch, a little dazed, pretty sure she'd just agreed to something wildly insane, but really great. "So no relationship," she said. "No big scary emotional stuff. Just sex."

"No relationship."

She felt giddy. Sex without a relationship meant pleasure without sharing secrets. She could do that. "Promise?"

He crossed a finger over his heart. "Only the sex."

Giddiness turned into a little whimper of apprehension combined with the thought, "Yes, please, that sounds good" running through her head.

"So…" he began, and let the word trail off, watching her.

She felt him waiting, felt him shift underneath her, felt something…

Her eyes widened, and riveted on his. "Oh. You mean…" Her voice dropped into a whisper, as if they were talking in class and might be overhead. "Right now?"

He raised an eyebrow at her, then grinned. It looked wolfish in the moonlight. But then, she supposed it probably would have looked wolfish in bright daylight. "I promise not to throw you into the crab grass."

"That would be appreciated," she said primly. She smoothed at a fold in her shorts, then pleated the material together. "So, no relationship doesn't mean no responsibility, right?"

"You can be responsible and still have fun."

"Of course you can." She waved her hands around, trying to find the words, wondering how she could be such an independent woman on the job, and feel so ineffective when it came to relationships. "I just meant—"

He caught her flailing hands, wrapped both of his around them. She felt them wanting to escape, to flutter like wild birds, as her heart was fluttering, but the warmth of him, his skin rough against hers, his fingers gentle, calmed her.

"I know what you meant," he said, his voice as reassuring as his hands. "I have a condom."

She blinked. "Should I be pleased or offended that you have one with you?"

"You should be grateful," he said, and when her mouth dropped open, he laughed.

His laughter drew her in, and she found herself laughing with him. Her heart beating fast, she leaned close enough to kiss, to feel his breath on her face. "You're the one who's going to be grateful in a little while."

He spread his arms out. "I'm all yours."

She smiled at him, but at the same time, she hesitated. *Don't say that*, a little part of her cried. *Don't say you're all mine.*

And why not? Another part asked. *It's what you want, isn't it?*

"No," she said out loud, trying to push the thought back, not wanting to delve into the idea that that was, indeed, what she wanted.

"No?" Evan repeated. His hands settled on her waist, the tips of his fingers slipping under her shirt and brushing against her skin. "Need me to make the first move, then?"

"No, I—" She shut her mouth with a little snap of teeth. Shut everything out, including those subversive little thoughts that wanted to ruin this moment. She pressed her cheek to his, her lips to the edge of his jaw, felt his hands tighten on her, begin to move up her back. "Just touch me," she whispered into his ear.

In response, he angled his head and found her lips, kissing her hard and wrapping his arms around her tight enough to push the air out of her lungs, but she didn't care. Oh no, she didn't care, because this felt so good. Kissing someone again, kissing him with the abandon of a teenager, but the intensity of an adult that knows what the final result will be from such a wild ride, wanting to savor it while in the next heartbeat wanting to be devoured by it.

And she wanted to be devoured. To be so thoroughly paid attention to that there would be room for nothing else in her mind, no questions, no guilt, no fear.

And as Evan eased her back onto the swing, his lips trailing warm kisses down her neck, she knew she was getting her wish. Coherent thought gave way to pure, physical desire when Evan teased one finger down her collarbone and his lips followed. He traced the curve of her breast with a palm, swirled the tip of his tongue below the neck of her shirt, and then smoothed it across her nipple.

Arching up, she moaned, wanting him to keep doing that forever, craving more. She ran her hands through his hair and down his back, feeling the bunched muscles in his shoulders, then ran her hands down his arms and rested them over his. She squeezed the hand that cupped her breast, and he raised his head long enough to look into her eyes, to see her desire, her impatience, her willingness.

He sat back, pulling her with him so they faced each other, then traced one fingertip along her brow, then toward her hair, lifting it out from the sides of her face, letting it run through his fingers, watching it settle back in place.

"So beautiful," he murmured, brushing the backs of his hands across her cheeks.

She closed her eyes, just listening to him, feeling him.

"I don't want to rush this," he said.

"Me, either." She opened her eyes. Feeling him was one thing, seeing him another. He looked eternal in the moonlight, and she knew the moment would freeze in time for her. She didn't want to spoil it by going too fast. Then his thumb traced the bottom of her earlobe, sending shivers through her body.

"Oh, screw that," she said, slipping off the swing onto the porch and pulling him down with her.

They landed with a thud, but she didn't let it slow her down. She pulled his shirt from his pants, then slipped it up his back. He yanked it over his head to finish the job for her and tossed it somewhere past their heads, then bent down to kiss her again.

Free to touch more of him now, more bare skin, she ran her hands up and down his back, alternately using her fingernails and the tips of her fingers. She didn't want to miss any of it, wanted to make sure she covered every inch. She felt the line of his shoulders, the curve of a shoulder blade, the dip of his lower back, his skin warm and smooth. She slipped her fingers under the waistband of his pants, then in between their bodies and undid the button of his shorts. When she reached for the zipper, his fingers closed over hers.

"Wait," he said, his voice husky.

"What?"

"Not too fast." He smiled down at her.

"But I—"

He stopped her with a kiss, then whispered in her ear, "No underwear."

"Oh." She dropped her hand and let him ease the zipper down, then laughed.

"Hey," he said, slipping off his shorts, but still smiling. "It was hot out."

She put her hand over her mouth, still giggling. "I'm not wearing any, either."

He leaned over her, naked now, and she stopped giggling. He exceeded all of her expectations, and she wanted to slide her hands over every part of him, from the solid planes of his chest down the muscled indentations on his stomach to his hips and beyond, but she paused in her inventory when Evan flipped up the tab of her zipper, holding it between thumb and forefinger.

"I'll be very..." He slid it down a few notches, and the sound was loud in the night. "Very..." A few more notches. "Careful," he breathed, and brought it down to the end.

He rested his palm over her and she felt his fingers curl there for a moment. Heat shot down her body with such force she was sure his fingers would scorch, but he only smiled at her, then reached up to undo the buttons on her top. She closed her eyes and tilted her head back with a groan. Good God, all he had to do was rest his hand there and she felt electrified. Imagine what his—

"Oh." Her eyes shot open and she instinctively grabbed hold of him as he traced her nipple with his tongue. Heat shot back up to her chest, and she moaned, tightening her hands on his back, tilting her hips up to him.

He pressed kisses along the underside of her breast, then down to her stomach, where he circled it, warm and wet, then trailed more kisses down. His tongue flicked out and she curved up to meet it, clutching at him.

He eased her shorts down and she wriggled out of them, alternately sighing and moaning as he kissed his way back up her shin, knee, inner thigh, to the sensitive, tender flesh there, and higher up to press a kiss between her legs. He shifted his mouth to her navel and circled it while his fingers dipped down, pressing, circling, teasing. She pushed her feet against the porch, tightened her legs against his waist, the wood rough against her bare skin, and she didn't care, because she felt that deep, sweet pressure beginning to build and all she wanted was to give in, to let him release it.

Somewhere in the back of her mind, she sensed Evan reaching out, heard him dragging his shorts toward them, knew he was getting the condom and thanked the heavens that he was both responsible and talented.

One finger slipped inside her and she moaned. Her hands tightened on his shoulders, then she pressed into him, urging him on, moving with him until the pressure broke in waves, and she fell back against the deck, gasping. Evan held her hips and rested his head on her stomach as she caught her breath.

Peering through one eye, she saw his head moving up and down with her breathing and reached for him, easing him toward her. He lifted his head, smiling down at her. "You're not going anywhere, are you?" she asked.

He shook his head, balancing over her. She felt him press between her legs, but not go any farther and raised her eyes to find him watching her. "Are you sure?" he asked.

She nodded, unsure if she could speak right then, but sure about him, and reached down to squeeze his hips for emphasis, pulling him toward her. Their eyes still on each other in the glow of the moonlight, he slid into her then held still a moment. Holding her gaze, he began to move slowly until they found a rhythm together, then faster as the heat grew between them.

She pressed her hands to his face, then slid them down his arms, pulling him down to her, closer; she couldn't get enough of him. Lost in the connection of their bodies, the feel of his flesh against hers, his eyes as he watched her, the rightness of this moment, of them together, released something inside Samantha and she gave herself fully to him.

"Yes," she breathed, and it was all he needed.

He wrapped his arms around her shoulders, held her tightly to him and they rocked together, faster. He brought her to the peak again, then followed soon after, both of them tumbling over the edge. Pressing his face to her shoulder, he murmured her name, then kissed her tenderly before collapsing onto the deck with her.

They lay together, catching their breath, and she felt a cool breeze brush over her body, making her shiver. He pulled her close to him, holding her against his side with one arm and tracing his free hand along her hip, dipping down to the small of her back and up to her shoulders. Samantha thought she could fall asleep there, could stay on that ugly, rough porch forever.

"Are you warm enough?" Evan asked.

"Mmm hmm." She pressed her face to his chest, breathing him in. "You?"

"Mmm..." He lifted her hand up and kissed the palm, then pressed their clasped hands to his chest. "Here I thought I came out here to cool off."

"And you got hotter instead?"

"Much." He leaned over her. "Too bad I only had one condom."

She raised an eyebrow at him. "About that..."

He raised an eyebrow back. "Do you really want to know?"

She thought she'd like to know it was for her, that he'd wanted to be prepared just in case, that he'd hoped an opportunity would come up for them to be together. But if that wasn't the case, she should know that, too. She nodded.

"You can hope as much as you want, but if you're not ready for the dream when it shows up, well..." He gave a little shrug, then brushed her hair from her face, watching her. "Then I'd be an idiot," he added.

"And Evan Gallagher is not an idiot," she said, remembering his words when she proposed they have sex.

He laughed, then bent down to kiss her forehead. "Thank you."

"You're welcome," she said. "But what for?"

He kissed her, firm and sweet. "For everything."

Before she could respond to that, he'd pulled her close, tucked her head against his shoulder, and rested his own head on hers. She wanted to spend the rest of the night talking to him, listening to his voice, finding out more about his life, but as she felt him relax against her, she realized she would have to content herself with listening to his breathing.

And that sounded just fine.

CHAPTER TWENTY-FIVE

I had sex with Evan last night."

Liz had been mid-yawn, and she now choked and coughed for a couple seconds before staring at Samantha. Stumbling out of her chair, she said, "Wait!" and held her hands out in front of her. "Wait." Then she pointed to the chairs they'd set up side by side. "Move those out of earshot. And don't you dare go anywhere. Just…just wait."

It was rare to be out of anyone's earshot on a movie set, even at an outside location, but Samantha dragged everything farther back from the crew, cables and equipment. They were at Jack's cabin, and would be filming close-ups today, always trickier for Samantha than a master shot, because every detail of the close-ups had to match what occurred in the master. Samantha had barely gotten two hours of sleep the night before, but she felt both alert and calm as she sat watching Liz get a few items from craft services. She marched back, handed Samantha a muffin, and plopped down next to her.

Samantha opened her mouth to share her story, but Liz held up a hand, took a sip of coffee, then another, and a third. "Okay," she said, taking one more drink of coffee. "I might be able to handle this now. Maybe. I think." She rubbed the tips of her fingers along the bridge of her nose, looking around before whispering, "You slept with him."

"Yes." Samantha took a bite of cranberry orange muffin. It was the best muffin she'd ever eaten in her life. And it didn't even have chocolate in it. "On the porch of the general store." She smiled at Keesha who walked by with a phone to her ear and a clipboard in hand. Keesha gave a distracted wave, and continued walking.

When she had moved out of sight, Liz said, "Well, I'm stumped."

"We agreed there were no strings, though." Samantha looked toward the horizon, and the rising sun. She closed her eyes. It would be hot again today, but for now, a cool breeze brushed at her cheeks and ruffled through her hair. She would have to pin it up later, but having it down right now reminded her of last night, how Evan had lifted her hair up from around her face, let it fall through his fingers—

Liz reached over and pinched Samantha's arm.

"Ow! What was that for?"

"Just checking," Liz said. "To make sure I'm not dreaming."

"Then you should've asked me to pinch *you*." Samantha rubbed at her arm.

"What do you mean you agreed there were no strings? How does that...how in the world could that...I don't get how..." She spluttered a few seconds longer. Took a sip of coffee. Glared at Francis who happened to be passing by. He scuttled away with a glance at her over his shoulder. "And...whose idea was this?" Liz asked when the area around them was again clear.

Samantha looked away, chewed at her lower lip. "Well...umm...mine?" She glanced at Liz, then away again. "I think."

"You think?"

"Yeah, I'm pretty sure." She gripped the arms of her chair and turned toward Liz, hoping to explain in a way that Liz would understand. She knew Liz would understand the sex part, the doing it on a porch part, but she might have trouble with the Evan Gallagher part. How could Samantha explain how things had changed, he wasn't the Evan Gallagher she thought she'd known, that she knew him as a man now, not as an actor or tabloid fodder, much less the man whose life she thought she'd messed up.

"Did we not have the 'actors are crazy' talk?" Liz said, before Samantha could start to explain. "Did we not agree that this way lies madness?"

Samantha squirmed in her chair. "Things...shifted."

"Shifted. I see. So did the earth move before or after?"

"It was just sex," Samantha told her, knowing it was a lie. "Like I said. Nothing more."

"So you're just going to sleep together, but not talk to each other?"

"No, we talk. Just not about…the big things."

"But you're still going to tell him everything?"

The muffin stuck in Samantha's throat and she coughed. "Yes."

"After production?" Liz asked.

Samantha nodded. "After."

When Liz didn't say anything, Samantha looked at her. "What?"

"Messy," Liz finally said, but Samantha knew she wanted to add much more. Liz rarely said just one word without following it with a slew of others.

Liz was right, though, and the more Samantha talked about it, the more uncomfortable she felt about the arrangement. It had looked so good last night, but not so great right now. How could she have gotten so lost in the moment?

And how could she not?

"Crap," she said and pressed her forehead into her palm.

Liz raised an eyebrow at her when she finally looked up. "Does that mean it wasn't good?"

Samantha laughed. "No. No, it was amazing. Staggering. Ethereal. Transcendent."

Liz put her hands over her ears. "Oh God, stop. Stop. I haven't had sex in ages, much less transcendent sex."

"Oh." Samantha sat back, took another bite of her muffin. "Sorry."

They were silent, sipping and eating while watching the crew in the distance. Keesha brandished a clipboard at Francis and he scampered away. One of Marcus's construction assistants held a ladder steady on the rocky ground so they could patch a hole in the roof of Jack's cabin. Lincoln stood next to Gary, framing the scene with his hands.

Liz sighed. "So it was transcendent, huh?"

Samantha gripped Liz's arm. "Romance novel sex."

Liz gripped her coffee cup. "Damn." Then she sat up and pointed at Samantha. "But that's not the point here. The point is…" She looked around again, then leaned over and said in a whisper, "You slept with Evan Gallagher. And came up with some agreement that there would be no commitment. I know you like him, I know you're attracted to him, and you say he's different, but…Sam…"

"What?" Samantha stared at her. "Sam, what?"

"I don't want you to get hurt," Liz said after a pause.

"And?"

Liz took another sip of coffee. "And nothing. That's all it comes down to."

Samantha slumped in her chair. "Well, I won't get hurt, that's all. I just won't."

"Of course you won't."

Samantha crumpled up her napkin and stared down at it, balled in her hands. Head bowed, she said, "Yes, I will."

"Of course you will." Liz stood up and paced in front of Samantha. "God. How can you not? What're you doing here? You nuts? You lost it? What about all that happened? What about what you said, that first day of filming? It would be crazy to get involved with him. It *is* crazy to get involved with him. Do you even remember the role you play in his past?"

"I never forget that," Samantha said, beginning to protest, but stopped when she realized that wasn't completely it. "It's more like I want to forget it. But like I said, things shifted. I don't know how to explain it, but we've gone past what happened, somehow." She paused again. That sounded like such an excuse. They couldn't have gone past it, because Evan still didn't know her side of the situation. Despite their shared time together, she had been progressing alone. "If that thing wasn't there between us—"

"But it is there." Liz's gentle tone had more of an effect than if she had shouted. "And now you've added another element."

"When did you get to be the voice of reason," Samantha grumbled, but knew that again, Liz was right. But she couldn't take back what happened last night. She didn't want to take it back. It had seemed like the perfect solution for everyone involved, but now her "without strings" reasoning only seemed like justification for her to have sex. She pressed a palm to her forehead.

Liz patted her on the arm and whispered, "Heads up. Here comes your string-less guy now."

When Samantha looked up at her, she saw that Liz had a smile on her face, but her eyes looked sad. Concerned. "I have to go meet with Gary," she said. "We'll talk later?"

Samantha nodded. "Yes. Of course."

She watched Liz head away, greeting Evan, and appreciated how Evan stopped and took a moment to say more than hello. His cheerful smile matched the look in his eyes, and she couldn't help but smile back as he strode toward her dressed in his outfit for the day's shoot: jeans worn so thin she knew they'd feel soft under her fingers, black boots and a faded blue t-shirt with the sleeves rolled tight around his biceps.

She had to grip the chair arms tightly to keep from touching him as he stood in front of her. "Keesha said you had the day's changes." He leaned close and added in a whisper, "You look beautiful this morning. I like your hair down."

She felt her cheeks flush, and bent her head to look for the packet Keesha had given her and she'd tucked in her bag. She wore plain khaki shorts and a white t-shirt this morning, and he thought she looked beautiful. "Thank you," she whispered back, as she handed him the changes. "Here you go. She couldn't track you down this morning."

His fingertips brushed against her knee as he moved to sit in the empty chair, flipping through the script pages. "I went for a walk." He glanced at her. "Couldn't sleep."

"Oh?" They'd slept for awhile on the porch, then he'd walked her back to her room, kissing her lightly on her lips, her cheek, her eyelids, before stepping away with a look she couldn't decipher, and heading toward his room.

"Too wired." He grinned at her, then bent his head to study the pages in his lap. Without looking up from them, he murmured, "I want to kiss you."

She uncapped her highlighter and ran it across a section of her own script that might be troublesome during shooting. "I want to throw you onto the crab grass and rip your clothes off," she murmured back.

He laughed out loud, crunching the pages he held together, then slipped a hand around her neck, pulled her close, and kissed her, fast. Then he jumped down from the chair and said, "You make me feel dangerous."

They both glanced around, but everyone seemed engrossed in their work, and Samantha let out a breath. "That seems to be going around," she said, feeling naughty.

"We'll have to see what we can do about that." He lifted the papers up. "Thanks for the changes." He lowered his voice again. "Can I see you later?"

"I'd like that." And that was true, despite the misgivings that had come up when she talked to Liz. "I may have to meet with Gary and Liz."

He nodded. "Maybe tomorrow then." He started backing away, smiling at her. "I should get some sleep anyway."

Right, she thought. Sleep. How could she ever sleep again, with so many daydreams to have? About his smile, his voice, how he held her afterward, all they talked about.

As he headed away, she wanted to call him back, to tell him she could cancel her meeting, postpone it, but she knew that would be a mistake. And she desperately wanted to avoid making any more mistakes.

He gave her a little wave and she returned it, watching him until he'd gone around the corner and out of sight.

HE'D BEEN SO nervous last night. But when she'd breathed in his ear, given him permission, asked him to touch her, it had been like getting the green light at the races, and there was no stopping him.

And apparently he was still ready to go, because he wanted to head right back around the trailer, lift her out of that chair and carry her off to some place where they could be alone all day.

And talk about this arrangement they'd come up with. When Samantha had made her suggestion about sex without strings, he'd jumped on it because, as he'd said, he wasn't stupid—he'd wanted her, and wouldn't deny that—but it wasn't in him to have a fling without being involved in some way.

Keesha called his name, and when he turned, she jogged up to him, holding out his cell phone; he'd asked her to watch it for him, in case Oliver called. "Your PR lady," she said. He took the phone with a word of thanks, and Keesha trotted back to the set.

"Hey, Nancy."

"Evan. Sorry to call you on set. I tried at the motel, but they said you'd left there already."

"Early call this morning," he said.

"You have time now?"

"I'm on my way to makeup. You've got me until then."

"I'll be fast, then. First, I heard from Corey Von Tilden. The woman's a scream to talk to, but she thinks it would be a good time to do a show of your work. Great timing for our PR blitz."

Evan smiled. "I like the idea. Can we all meet when I get back into town?" He raised a hand in greeting to two electricians as they passed.

"Good enough. Second, I've got interviews for you. I'll text the details over to Keesha. I've also got you on escort detail, a great opportunity, good press, lots of that positive we've been looking for."

"Escort?"

"It's the thing now. You know that." Before he could respond, she continued. "I know. We think this went out with the '50s and the Golden Era. But having a gorgeous person at your side has never gone out of style, and a good photo op can't be bought."

He pinched at the bridge of his nose, trying to hold back a sigh. "Who would it be?" he finally said, conjuring an image of Samantha in a fiery red dress, her hair up, feet in strappy sandals. It took him a moment to replace that image with the person Nancy mentioned.

"Rita Wilson asked for you special, since Tom's on a shoot. He could make it back in time for the premiere, but if not, she said she'd be thrilled to go with you."

To go with him. Not be her escort, but be her equal. He'd reached the makeup trailer and stopped to lean against it. He lifted his chin in hello at Christopher, the Second Assistant Director.

He heard Nancy shuffling through some papers on the other end. "Then there's Tiffany Lynn Stearling. She's seen the Duncan Tanner movies. Thinks you're hot for an old guy, but don't take that personal—"

"No eighteen-year-olds," he cut in.

"Evan," she began, now using her schoolteacher tone, which only came up when she knew her point was right and only needed to convince him. "We've got three opportunities in front of us: the premiere with Rita, the Hanks premiere, then your opening of *Broken* in a few months. Go with Rita and the focus is on her, but we'll script you for any *Access Hollywood* or *Entertainment Tonight* interviews. All positive, life is great, moving forward. The same for Hanks. By the time you show up for *Broken*'s premiere, they'll all be moving forward with you. Hollywood loves a comeback. We go for that angle."

"You sound so damn reasonable," he muttered, shoving his free hand in his pocket, and she laughed. "Rita," he added. "Not Tiffany."

"And if Tom shows up to escort Rita?"

He hesitated.

"Think about it," Nancy told him. "Call me in the next few days."

He didn't have to think about it. He knew she was right, and he agreed to the premiere, which would be a necessary evil on two levels: to promote *Broken* and to focus everyone on Evan Gallagher's positive future instead of his negative past.

As he reached for the trailer's doorknob, he glanced back to where Samantha now stood in a circle with Gary, Keesha and Tony, their sound man. She'd put her hair up again. He wanted to press his lips to the tender warm spot at the base of her neck, to feel her hair brush against his face.

With Oliver happy and secure again and this film starting, he'd thought he had all he needed. He hadn't discounted women but hadn't spent much time considering the idea of a relationship, in part because he didn't think he'd have the time for it, but also because he'd been so burned by his relationship with Zoey. He'd told Samantha the truth last night when he said he wasn't ready for more. What he hadn't told her was that he thought that with her, he could be.

He pulled the door open and stepped from the bright outdoor light into the dim of the trailer, letting his eyes adjust as he headed toward Alice, who stood at the table arranging jars, tubes and brushes. She looked up when he came in and smiled at him.

"There's my rock star," she said, lifting the cap off a container of loose powder.

He slid into the chair in front of her mirror with its outline of bright bulbs, and grinned. "How'd you know my secret fantasy?"

She brushed his hair back from his face to study his eyebrows— one of her big obsessions—and said, "I know everything, honey. They think I'm in the background, patting on the powder, so away they yammer to their entourage." She straightened up and tapped the side of her head. "I hear it all, I file it away, and I keep my mouth shut." She cocked an ample hip. "Some say that makes the perfect woman," she said with a grin before reaching for a jar of foundation.

"Alice, as my granddaddy used to say, 'You are a caution.'"

She laughed, switching more lights on before turning to him. "That's my sign, sweetheart," she said, brushing the liquid over his face with a makeup wedge. "Another hot one today. I'll have to use some of my top secret techniques to keep the makeup from running."

Alice had been doing film makeup for thirty years, and he knew there were few who could do better. He had faith that what she applied today could get him through the hardest and hottest day of filming.

"My face is in your hands," he said, leaning back and closing his eyes.

"Words any woman'd love to hear from you, sugar."

He smiled at that, eyes still closed, but didn't respond. Partly because he knew this was Alice's usual patter—she flattered and flirted with everyone—but also because he didn't know what to say. Her words had affected him in a way she'd never know. He didn't care about just any woman. He cared about Samantha.

He'd like to believe he couldn't stop thinking about her and that those thoughts made his heart beat faster because she was the first woman he'd been with in a long while. But the truth was, he'd been with her because he thought the two of them could have something together, and that felt pretty damn great.

"Stop smiling so much," Alice warned. "You'll make creases."

He couldn't stop; he'd just thought of a great way to surprise Samantha.

CHAPTER TWENTY-SIX

When Evan heard Samantha's footsteps on the dry grass, his heart beat a little faster, and he stood up from the porch swing.

He'd dared to request a few minutes with her on set earlier in the day to ask if she'd meet him that night. She'd looked pleased, and had said she'd get away as soon as possible, but might have to meet with Gary.

She stood at the bottom of the stairs now, one hand on the railing, watching him. She'd left her hair down, and wore a pair of dark shorts with white Keds and a cropped top with buttons down the front that he itched to undo. Slowly. When she didn't move, he went to her, down the steps. Before she could speak, he cupped her face, studied her a moment, then pressed his lips to hers in a hungry kiss.

When she hung limp and ready to collapse, and he felt a little shaky in the knees himself, he pulled away and said, "Hi."

"Hi," she breathed.

"I've been wanting to do that all day."

"Mmm, me, too," she said. "I needed to get it out of the way so I could talk without wondering what it would be like to kiss you again."

She smiled up at him and he remembered saying something like that on their date at his house, when he'd stopped her in the hallway with a kiss. He took her hand. "Did it work?"

"Not really," she said with a grin as he led her away from the porch. "So where are we going?"

"It's a surprise," he said. "Do you like surprises?"

"Only if they result in chocolate."

"Then you'll like this one." Hand in hand, they walked along the path that ran behind the buildings parallel to the main road. "When we get back to L.A.," he added, "I'll have to take you horseback riding."

"I used to love riding when I was little. I was going to be a cowgirl when I grew up."

He looked down at her, but she had ducked her head. The moon glinted on her hair. He nudged her with one hip. "I was going to be a rock star."

Her head came up and she laughed, nudging him back. "So what happened?"

He shrugged. "Couldn't sing. So I did the next best thing. Didn't have to hold a note, but I still got to wear tight pants and get a lot of attention."

She smiled, but didn't laugh this time. He figured maybe he shouldn't have brought up the tight pants when she switched back to the previous subject and said, "So, I didn't know you had horses. Where do you keep them?"

"They're not mine," he told her. "My good friends Jim and Brenda have a ranch near Santa Barbara and they let me borrow their horses when I need to get out and ride." They walked parallel to a row of cottages that he knew from daylight inspection had been painted in storybook shades of blue, yellow, pink and green. A line of junipers had been planted to shield them from the backside of the Main Street's buildings, but he could still get glimpses of the houses as they went along the path. "Jim does horse rescue and has some colts I'm looking at, so they might be mine one day."

"Does Oliver ride, too?"

"Oh yeah. He wanted to be a cowboy when he grew up, too."

"Wanted? What happened?"

"He discovered video games." He let go of her hand and looped an arm around her shoulders, bringing her closer, but she didn't move to touch him. Yet. "He's a rare one, though. He loves books, too."

"It sounds like he's pretty well-rounded."

"He is. He's smart and funny, energetic, generous, and the biggest *Star Wars* fan ever."

"Oh, I don't know," she said. "He might have to fight me for the title on that one."

He felt her arm go around his waist finally. Whether it was their conversation or the *Star Wars* reference, he didn't care. He was just glad she seemed to be relaxing. "Yes, but have you watched Episode One on DVD three times in a row every day for months?"

"I think he's got me there. But quantity doesn't necessarily equal the degree of fanaticism."

"Tell that to my son," he said, and they both laughed.

The path had gone past the row of houses now and into the surrounding countryside, but small trees grew here and there and he now led her to a thicket of them that had formed around a grouping of boulders.

He stopped at a clearing where he'd set out a large blanket. A picnic hamper sat on a rock just above, along with a cooler and six fat candles. He walked ahead of her to the hamper and cooler and opened both. "I've got sandwiches, potato salad, macaroni salad, strawberries, crackers, brie, champagne, and..." He reached in and lifted out a well-wrapped package. "Chocolate chip cookies, brownies and peanut butter bars with chocolate frosting. Is that good enough for the chocolate portion of the evening?"

She hadn't moved from where he'd left her. She stood just off the path, her arms across her chest, and didn't say anything. He set the dessert down and went to stand in front of her. "Too much chocolate?" When she still didn't speak, just stared at him with her eyes wide in the moonlight, he said, "Not enough?"

She laughed at that, although it sounded a little sad, too. "When did you do all of this?" she asked.

"Tonight after we wrapped. I have to confess, Judy helped me, from the General Store. I didn't say who it was for, but she told me it was guaranteed to make a woman swoon." He rubbed his hands up and down her arms. "Am I going to have to ask for my money back?"

She shook her head. "No. No, I'm swooning, really. I just can't believe..." Her eyes darted up to his, then to the picnic behind him. "There's so much," she added, then stepped around him and went to the blanket, settling herself on it. She cleared her throat. "I mean, how are we going to eat all of it?"

He sat down next to her, watched her until she turned to him. He wished he could read her expression better, but the trees filtered out some of the moonlight. "Maybe we'd better start with the dessert, then."

She grinned, reaching for the bag of cookies. "You *always* start with the dessert, didn't you know that?"

He took a peanut butter bar, and while they ate, he set the candles in the dirt and lit them. He lay the food out on the blanket, along with utensils, cups and napkins.

Samantha leaned against a rock and said, "It's pretty out here." She looked around. "And something smells good. Not just the food."

Evan gestured behind them at the trees. "New Mexican Locust. Usually blooms later in the year, but the heat must've brought it out. The blooms are pretty during the day. They remind me of lilacs." He handed her a sandwich, which she took and laid in her lap. She stared at him. "What?" he asked.

"How do you know so much about…" She waved in the direction of the grove. "So much."

"About plants, you mean?" When she nodded, he said, "Natural curiosity, I guess. I know I'm going somewhere, I study up on it. I see something that interests me, I want to learn more about it. I see something…beautiful, I want it in my life."

She'd started unwrapping her sandwich, but stopped as he spoke. She tilted her head and said, "Are you flirting with me, Mr. Gallagher?"

"I believe I am, Ms. Jamison." He gave her a light kiss on the lips, just enough to feel them, firm against his, to smell her, to want more. "Is that all right?"

"Better than the chocolate," she breathed.

"Good." He gestured toward the food. "Now eat."

She took a few bites and leaned back against the rocks again. "Mmm. Judy is a genius."

"I'll be sure to thank her." Evan poured them each some champagne, and handed her a plastic flute. "Congratulations on surviving half of the shoot."

She had just taken a sip and looked startled at that. "I can't believe we're halfway through."

"A pretty tight shoot," he said. "But I did warn you it would go fast."

"You did," she said. "I think I prefer…if things go a little slower. At first anyway."

He got her meaning. Okay, he could go slow. "So how did you get into continuity supervising, Ms. Jamison?"

Samantha didn't answer right away. He watched her eat some more of the sandwich, wondering why that might be a tricky question. She was one of the best script supervisors he'd ever seen, able to keep a large number of details in her head, along with taking copious notes, and she'd caught a lot of potential matching errors on the shoot. Maybe her entrance into the trade hadn't been all that exciting or worth noting; he was curious just the same, so he waited.

"Sort of fell into it," she finally said, then took a long drink of champagne. Evan topped off her glass. "I'd been working at one of the studios in Wilmington, just some secretarial work, and I met a woman named Diana. We got to be friends, and I went to watch her work one day. She'd been doing supervising for years, and she'd told me a little about it, so I knew she'd developed a lot of instincts for it, but as I watched her, I was fascinated. She seemed to get so absorbed by it, lost in it, but at the same time, she was retaining everything. The job seemed to require her to be involved in all aspects of filmmaking, and I'd always loved the idea of being part of making a movie. I thought, 'I could do that.' So I asked if I could apprentice with her."

"And how'd that go?"

"I was awful." Samantha laughed and took a bite of her sandwich. After swallowing, she said, "I'd had no idea how good Diana was, how hard the job. But I loved the details, the knowledge, the intensity of it. Pretty soon, I was getting absorbed in it, too. I did some small things first, commercials, then second unit for a television crew, and then I heard the supervisor for *Honor Bound* was leaving, so I applied for it and got it."

"Was it a good crew?"

She thought the answer to this one over, too, taking a few more bites of sandwich, sipping champagne, and taking a couple of strawberries from the plate he'd set out. Finally, she said, "It was a good learning experience."

Evan laughed, then ate a strawberry himself. "That sounds like a diplomatic response if I've ever heard one."

She gave him a sheepish look, then admitted, "Okay, they were a spoiled crew with a really spoiled lead actor. We worked eighteen hour days, often on location, had constant script changes, and nonstop cancellation threats the second season." She shrugged. "I know. Everyone is enamored of the show now, but when it first started, it almost bombed. We didn't know if we should be happy or upset when the ratings jumped after we started adding guest stars and they renewed for a third season."

"Sounds brutal."

"I've heard of worse." She spooned some macaroni salad on a plate. "But it was definitely tough."

"So did you grow up in North Carolina?" Evan asked. "I only detect a touch of an accent on certain words, as if you either picked it up or you're trying to get rid of it."

She ate a couple spoonfuls of salad, washed it down with some champagne, then said, "Moved there five years ago." More champagne, then she held her glass out to be refilled. "I actually grew up in a tiny town in Iowa. West Branch, population two thousand or so."

"Herbert Hoover's birthplace," Evan said, nodding.

Samantha waved her spoon at him, laughing. "You've got to stop doing that."

"What?"

"Knowing so much." She looked at her plate. "It's…unnerving."

Evan set his own plate down, reached out and gently took hers before setting it on the ground, then took her hands in his. He felt her wanting to fidget, but held on. "I want to feed you, make you smile, make love to you and surprise you, but I never want to unnerve you."

"Oh, damn," she said. "But you just did."

He gave her hands a squeeze before letting them go, then he lay on his back, propped his head on his arms and looked up at the sky. "Okay, go ahead and ask me a question. I'll try not to be too unnerving."

"Okay." He heard her taking a breath. "How did you get into acting?"

"Oh, that one's easy. Twelve."

"Twelve?"

"Yep. That's how old I was when my parents divorced and I could go out on my own for longer periods of time. Let's just say my parents were so focused on other things, I could do what I wanted most of the time. My friends were at camp, I was bored one day, nothing to do, so I went to the local theater and saw *Jurassic Park*. I went back the next day and saw it again." He crossed his feet at the ankles, still looking at the stars. "That got me interested in adventure films. After that, I went to the movies whenever I could, sneaking in if it was R-rated. I saw *The Fugitive, Cliffhanger, Schindler's List*— took me awhile to recover from that one—*Sleepless in Seattle, Mrs. Doubtfire, Point of No Return*. That one sparked my first thoughts of—"

"Becoming a female assassin?" she asked.

He tilted his head and looked at her as she giggled with a hand over her mouth. "Acting," he said precisely, raising an eyebrow at her. But he was grinning, too. "Didn't hurt that Bridget Fonda was so mesmerizing.

"So when I started high school, I disappointed everyone who wanted me to go out for football, and took drama instead. Did *Our Town, Oklahoma, West Side Story*, all the standards. Still couldn't sing, but I loved it too much to care. I pleased a few people by going out for sports, but then I'd revert back to my mutinous self, and start painting or acting again. Came out to Hollywood from my own small town with a friend, did some small films, and got a pretty quick lucky break with the Duncan Tanner movies."

He stopped, not really wanting to go farther in his acting history than that right now.

"So what made you fall into it?" she asked. "What do you love about it?"

He cleared his throat and said, "I like being someone else for a little while, meeting new people. I love what I learn from the films I do, from each character, each crew. I like…" He shifted a little, not embarrassed exactly, but because he'd never admitted this to another person. "I like the magic of it."

"You're magic," he heard her whisper from behind him.

He sat up, turning to her. He took her hand and pressed it between his, then laid it on his chest for her to feel his heart beating. "No," he said. "Just a mere mortal."

"But…" she began.

Before she could finish, he pulled her to him and kissed her. She tasted faintly of strawberries and champagne and warm skin, and she leaned into him as the kiss deepened. He ran his hands down her body, brushing against the sides of her breasts, along her hips, and then swept them under her legs and shoulders, scooping her up to lie next to him on the blanket. He stretched his body along the length of hers, tangling their feet together, and kissed her without reservation.

It turned out they hadn't had dessert first, after all.

CHAPTER TWENTY-SEVEN

"I have to watch Evan have sex with Tracy Jennifer today," Samantha told Liz, who sat next to her while they had their morning coffee and watched the crew set up. Samantha had a binder in her lap and was making notes, but her concentration was shot. "And it's all your fault."

"And you know I wrote that scene with this particular scenario in mind," Liz replied. "Script supervisor sleeping with leading man who plays someone who throws his long-lost girlfriend—who's played by a beautiful spoiled brat—up against the wall of his hideout, and everyone except the brat has a past."

"And because the script supervisor has to pay attention to everything, she gets to see it up close and personal."

Liz gestured toward her with a bagel slathered in strawberry cream cheese. "Oh, right. I forgot about that part." She leaned toward Samantha and whispered, "But the actual sex scene isn't today. And you know it's not real, right? The little people on the screen are just acting? Oh, and speaking of body parts," Liz added, "*A Midsummer Night's Dream* is going to be at The Ivy Substation in Culver City next month. You want to see it when we get home?"

"Sure. Oh, that reminds me." Samantha waved her pen around. "Keesha told me about this great film noir exhibit at the Hollywood Museum. You interested?" she asked, but missed Liz's answer when she caught sight of Evan and Gary walking over.

The area near her chair had become designated as the preferred spot for Gary to talk "privately" on set because most people stayed away from the continuity supervisor. "Too observant," Gary had said, as if she'd report anything she heard back to him.

"You had some concerns about this shot?" Samantha heard Evan say.

The first filmed shot of the day would be Mattie finding Jack's cabin, which would be matched with the first scene they'd filmed that cold morning in Hesperia of Mattie driving toward Jack's hideaway.

"I don't need to tell you what a pivotal scene this is," Samantha heard Gary say to Evan. "You've been hiding too long, you want to get back into the world, but you've got to clear your name first. You're this close to doing that, but you're not there yet."

Samantha glanced over and saw Gary with his thumb and forefinger almost touching, Evan leaning a little over him, his eyes never leaving Gary's face. Samantha abandoned her notes for the moment and watched them.

Evan nodded and Gary continued. "So you're making a choice when you open that cabin door. You're letting Mattie back into your life and your heart. But you're also exposing her to this great risk…"

"And exposing myself," Evan said.

Gary snapped his fingers. "Exactly."

"It's also showing that I want to trust," Evan added. "I didn't before and it's important she knows I've changed, even though I'm torn about having her know I'm alive."

Gary practically swooned at that. Samantha knew he loved it when actors "got" a character or a moment in the script. She shared a smile with Liz as Gary continued. "Couldn't have said it better myself." He patted Evan on the arm. "I'll be talking to Tracy now, then I'll want to talk to both of you. Make sure we're both clear on the sex."

Gary walked away and Evan caught Samantha watching him. He had his arms crossed over his chest, and lifted one hand at her, one side of his mouth turning up. She smiled back at him, flashing on the night before as he made to love her under the stars, covering her naked body with the blanket and wrapping himself around her afterward, pressing kisses to her bare shoulder…

Liz cleared her throat, then excused herself and slipped away, her long chiffon skirt whispering as she went. Samantha barely heard it as Evan moved close to her, so close she felt his breath warm on her face.

"So you clear on the sex?" she blurted.

He gave her a smile she couldn't interpret, then held a section of her hair up, watching it drift across his fingers, before looking at her again. "When it matters."

Somewhere in the back of her mind, she knew she should worry about someone seeing them, but everything else drifted away when he looked at her so intently, and she wished she were somewhere else, somewhere she could have him translate that look into action

She managed a small squeaking noise, then a deep breath, and nodded as if all they were discussing was his golf game or a grocery list. She looked away, breaking their eye contact. "Good. That's good."

He gave a gentle tug on her hair and she looked at him again. "You clear on it?"

"With the right person."

His smile stopped her heart and when he reached out and stroked a hand down the length of her hair from the top of her head to her shoulder, she wanted to start purring. "Good," he said, "that's good," then headed over to meet with Gary and Tracy Jennifer.

This scene was going to kill her.

SAMANTHA STOOD NEXT to Aaron as he made a final adjustment to the shoulder brace attaching the Steadicam to his body, both of them waiting alongside the path Tracy would take on her way to Jack. Evan was positioned out of sight in the cabin to their left and Gary stood with Tracy by the open door of the convertible to their right, giving her what looked to be some final words of encouragement. She nodded and he patted her arm and strode back to Aaron.

"We're doing this one straight through, people," he reminded them.

Keesha called for quiet on the set, each crew member went through his or her routine, then Gary called "Action."

Crying Jack's name, Tracy raced away from the car, leaving the door open and one tire tilted up on a mound of small stones. *Entering CR,* camera right, Samantha noted. Tracy's boots kicked up pieces of rock and Samantha could hear the thud of each step like a heartbeat. As she got closer to the cabin, Tracy lifted the hem of her skirt so she could run faster.

"Jack!" she called, and stumbled, her heel caught in a depression in the uneven ground. She made a noise in the back of her throat, and everyone leaned forward as she lost her balance and fell, still calling out for Jack. Her hair fell in her face as she stayed on her hands and knees a moment, sobbing.

The medic moved toward her, even as Aaron tilted the camera down to follow, but Gary held him back with a gesture. Samantha could see Tracy was still in character, and to stop the take now would shatter her concentration. As callous as it seemed, Samantha knew they might not get as good a take next time. And Tracy probably wouldn't want to do the fall again on purpose.

Tracy lifted her head and brushed her hair back from her face, effectively clearing the view of her profile for the camera. "Jack," she whispered, the word catching in her throat. She got one leg under her, then the other, and made a limping run to the cabin door, the camera rolling.

She tried to turn the knob, but it was locked. She pounded on the wood of the door and the frame, peering into the window, crying his name over and over. "You're here," she whimpered. "I know you're here." She pressed her forehead to the door, then lifted her head. "You have to be here."

"Jack, don't hide from me anymore. *Please.*" She hit the door with the flats of both hands, repeating his name with each beat. Her voice got weaker and she turned to lean her back against the door. "Don't take this from me, Jack. It was you. Always you." She slammed a fist into the doorframe, but it was as if the last of her energy had faded after that one action.

She sobbed. "Always you," she said, her voice barely audible now.

Samantha knew the final edit would show Jack's face peering out of the window at this point, his expression tortured. Then cut to Mattie again, her face also a mirror of her pain, of what this trip—and realizing Jack wasn't at the cabin—was costing her.

Tracy had just begun to slide down, her hands now covering her face when Christopher gave Evan his cue via Comtec to open the door. Tracy's slide stopped and she leaned inward, turning and falling into Evan's arms in one smooth motion, as if she was meant to be there, as if they were one. He embraced her so tightly she made a noise, but he still held onto her, lifting her off her feet and moving onto the small porch, then setting her gently down.

They pulled away enough to see each other's faces, and she pressed her palms to his cheeks as if he were a precious object of art.

Evan's expression showed his joy at holding her in his arms again, but with the knowledge of what he'd done—faked his own death, and now exposed her to a new danger—his face showed anguish, too.

"Mattie," Evan began, but she shook her head, still holding his face.

"You're alive," she sighed, and a tear slid down her cheek. She traced every part of his face with her fingers, from forehead to chin, and back again. When she reached his eyes, he shut them and she caressed the lids with her thumbs.

When he opened his eyes again, she said, "I always knew you were." She suddenly slammed a fist against his shoulder. "What you put me through. I died with you. Oh, God, Jack," she said, and fell against him even as he pulled her closer.

"Mattie," he tried again, but this time he was touching her, too, proving to himself that she was really there. Their hands roamed over each other's bodies, and finally their lips met, and when they did, it was fierce, possessive.

Gary moved in a crouch with Aaron at the camera, watching the action as if transfixed. Following both men, Samantha continued to take frantic notes, hoping she'd be able to read her shorthand later, because for now she could barely look away from Evan and Tracy.

From *Jack* and *Mattie*, she corrected, because that's who they were right now.

Jack and Mattie, torn apart by circumstance, brought together by love, desperate in their passion, and—at least for the moment—determined not to let each other go.

Samantha knew they were all witnessing the miracle that made a film magical, the indefinable "something" on the top of every filmmaker's wish list, with no guarantees of getting it into the final product.

She could tell from this one master scene that it would look beautiful on film, and her fears about watching Evan with Tracy, and her conflicted feelings over her own situation with Evan, receded into the background, if just for now. She was too busy to worry about anything but her job, and she kept writing: *Both of Jack's hands cupping Mattie's face, Jack's head tilted to the left, Mattie's hair flowing over her left arm, almost covering her face—*

Gary moved next to Samantha and gripped her shoulder as she

continued to take notes. She saw his lips moving, whether in prayer or thanks, she didn't know. She spared him a glance, but his gaze remained on Evan and Tracy, Evan's arms tightly around Tracy now, lifting her off the ground and pressing her against the outside wall.

Evan pushed Tracy hard against the wall, but from Samantha's angle, she could see Evan cushion her with one arm, and with his free hand, he pulled the bottom of her blouse from her skirt.

As Evan's hand slipped under Tracy's blouse, Gary called, "Cut!" and Samantha staggered back, automatically clicking her stopwatch off and writing "print" in her notes seconds after Gary said it. The crew burst into spontaneous applause.

Samantha moved up to snap some quick Polaroids, and heard Gary, still reciting a litany, the words clearer now that they'd stopped filming. "Please, God, don't ruin the film," he whispered. "Don't let the processing go bad. Don't let the film courier's car crash…"

Samantha stepped back and gave them the all clear. Evan pulled away from Tracy, but kept an arm around her, giving her a squeeze. Samantha heard him tell Tracy she'd done a great job, and Tracy beamed at him. Evan pulled his shirt over his head and held it against Tracy's knee as Gary headed to them, gesturing for the medic, and blocking Samantha's view.

Keesha walked by, fanning herself with that day's script pages. "Hot, baby, *hot*," she announced to no one in particular. As she passed Samantha, she fanned the pages at Sam's face. "You're looking a little flushed yourself, girl," she said.

CHAPTER TWENTY-EIGHT

"So I've got an idea for my new script," Liz said.

Samantha popped a spicy shrimp in her mouth, and leaned back in a lounge chair.

They'd wrapped filming for the day, and for their shots in Walterville, and the cast and crew decided to hold an impromptu poolside party at the motel. Evan had yet to show up.

"That's great," Samantha said. "What's it about?"

"Another twisted family tale," Liz said with a grin, crossing her legs at the ankles, and taking a crab puff from the selection of appetizers on the table in between them. "Mmm, we should always have craft services cater our parties." She wiped her hands, then said, "So I was hoping you'd help me."

"With what?"

"The script. Write it with me, like I asked when you first got here. You weren't ready then, but I'm hoping you're ready now, that you'll stay and do this. And hopefully be our script supervisor when it gets made into a movie."

Samantha smiled at her. She realized, for the first time in a long time, not only was she happy, but she could really see herself staying in Los Angeles permanently. "Looks like pigs are flying again somewhere. Can you stand me underfoot for awhile longer?" She held out her hand.

"Wouldn't have it any other way," Liz said, and shook.

They were still grinning at each other when Keesha walked up between their lounge chairs and sat on the edge of Samantha's. "You two look like the cats who ate the canaries."

"Samantha and I are going to write a script together," Liz told her.

Keesha patted Liz on the knee. "Well, that's great news, honey." She looked around. Samantha followed her gaze and noticed that almost everyone was in or around the pool. Keesha leaned toward her and whispered, "She know about you and Duncan Tanner?"

Samantha's jaw dropped, but she nodded.

"What's wrong?" Liz asked.

"There's some talk," Keesha said, still whispering, but now looking between the two of them.

"About…" Samantha prompted.

"You know what happens on the set stays there," Keesha said. "For now. But something could get passed along that you don't want. To people you don't want. And some of the crew are noticing how…friendly you and that boy are. How close."

Samantha crossed her arms over her chest. "Close."

Keesha nodded. "No judgment, from me or anyone else. And it's just talk now. They've seen on-set romances before—"

"It's not a romance," Samantha told her.

Keesha patted her on the shoulder this time. "You call it what you want, honey. Just thought you might want to know."

"Thanks," Liz told her.

Arms still crossed, Samantha nodded. "Yeah." She didn't know why she felt so angry, why it should bother her to know people were talking. She'd been one of those crew members who'd seen sparks between people on set, but she'd never spread the gossip herself, and she felt uncomfortable to be the topic of such talk now.

More than uncomfortable. Embarrassed.

She forced a smile for Keesha, who was, after all, trying to help her. "Thanks, Kee. I appreciate it. I'm just…" she said vaguely, then waved a hand around in the air. "I need to be alone for awhile," she added and got up to head to her room, her realization that she'd be staying in Los Angeles and felt happy about it replaced with Keesha's information.

The tables had been turned on her, and she didn't like it. And she didn't miss the irony, either. But she felt protective of her personal life and her relationship with Evan, and she didn't want anything to intrude on that. She hated the thought of people gossiping about her and Evan, no matter their feelings for each other.

She felt bad for leaving Keesha and Liz so suddenly, but she needed time to think. To get away from everything, pack, and have a long bath or get lost in a good novel or something. She took hold of the railing to head upstairs, the sounds of the party by the pool drifting away behind her.

She had a lot to think about, she realized, as she dug into her shorts pocket for her key. Staying with Liz or finding her own place, having people gossip about her, and getting a job until Liz finished her second script and it went into production. And, of course, Evan, and what she wanted from him. Did she want more than what they currently had? Did she want it to continue after they left Walterville and got back to Los Angeles? Would it be better to say goodbye to the romanticism of being on location and not worry about getting too emotionally involved, which could just lead to more problems later?

She didn't know. But when she thought about going back to L.A. and not seeing him anymore, she felt like she'd be losing something she hadn't realized she'd had in the first place.

Damn, what was she going to do, she thought, as she opened the door.

The first thing she saw was the candles, set on every available surface and casting a warm glow throughout the otherwise dark and plain room. The second thing to hit her senses was the music, something soft and instrumental.

But the man lying in the middle of her bed in faded blue jeans and nothing else, hands behind his head and grinning at her, really got her attention.

She blinked a few times.

Yep, he was still there.

"Hi," she said, standing in the doorway, one hand still on the knob. "I figured you weren't going to the party."

"I was going down there if you didn't show up soon."

"How did you get in here?" She gripped the doorknob.

Evan sat up, the bed cover rustling under him, and set his bare feet on the floor. She caught sight of the planes of his chest, remembered running her hands over them the night before when they'd met outside, the smooth skin, the small scar just below his left nipple, which she'd kissed and run her tongue over as he lay back on the blanket. His jeans had a small tear in the left leg and with a little more wear, that knee would be peeking out, would be accessible to—

"Samantha?"

"Huh?" Her head shot up and she looked into his eyes. "Sorry. I was just…" She stepped in and shut the door, then leaned against it, feeling that if she moved away from it, she would no longer have anything to hold her up.

Evan stood and walked toward her, watching her the whole time. "I wanted to surprise you," he said, smoothing the bangs out of her eyes. "Looks like I did."

She nodded, then couldn't help smiling at him. "I'm glad you did."

He cupped her face. "Yeah?"

She nodded again, feeling warm and safe as he stood close, stroking her skin. "Yeah."

"Good." He tilted her head up and pressed his lips to hers. When he finally pulled away, he said, "It's our last night here."

"I know."

"Two more weeks of filming, we'll be back home, my son's going to visit the set one or two days in the next couple weeks."

"Oh, that's—"

He didn't let her finish. "I wanted this time with you."

"I'm glad." She ran her fingertips along his jaw.

"But?" He captured her hand and kissed the fingertips.

"No but," she said, letting him lead her to the bed.

At her look, he said, "I figured this was a sitting down thing. Whatever it is you look ready to tell me."

She shook her head. "Keesha just told me some people are talking. About us." She peeked at him, but he was looking at the floor.

"I'm surprised they didn't earlier." He squeezed her hand, met her gaze. "Looks like we're being dangerous, then, baby, being in the same room together."

She gave him a fleeting smile. "It doesn't bother you?"

He straightened up, shrugging. "Sure. But some risks are worth it."

"Oh, damn," she said.

Instead of replying, Evan kissed her.

When she could breathe again, Samantha said, "Danger must be my middle name these days," then gave his shoulders a push. They fell backward together, kissing and tugging at each other's clothing. Tank top, shorts, jeans, bra and underwear all fluttered onto the floor and then he was touching her all over, stroking and kissing, bringing her to orgasm before sliding into her with a moan while she arched up and clung to him.

He moved slowly, watching her, and she couldn't look away even as the pressure built again, and her thighs quivered with it. When he moved faster and his breathing quickened, she held his face between her hands and said, "Yes," before letting her head fall back and closing her eyes, letting the waves of pleasure wash over her. She felt Evan drop his head to her shoulder, shuddering, then collapsed on top of her.

They lay in silence together for a few minutes until their breathing had evened out, matching the other. Evan pressed a kiss to her shoulder, then lifted his head. "What were you saying yes to?" he asked in a throaty voice.

She brushed the hair from his face. Looking into his eyes, she thought she knew, but didn't know how to express it. "To everything, I think," she said with a smile.

He rolled to his side, pulling her against him. "To everything."

CHAPTER TWENTY-NINE

Samantha thought she'd be relieved to have a day on the set without Evan, but she found herself looking for him throughout the morning, thinking she heard his voice at the other end of the studio or around a corner, hoping to see him so she could tell him about buying a Honda over the weekend and how she'd taken a different route to work this morning and saw a new bookstore along the way. They had spent so much time together in Walterville, it had seemed like more than a week, and she'd gotten used to having him around.

In general, this felt like a good thing. When she tried to analyze it, it made her head hurt.

Now that they were back in Los Angeles, they would spend the next two weeks on sound stages at Underwood Studios, filming shots for the inside of Jack's cabin, Mattie and David's house, a terrorist hideout, a prison holding cell, and Jack and Mattie's apartment, among other things. Today, they were in Stage 12, one of the smaller stages at 8,000 square feet and thirty-five feet to the overhead lighting. A catwalk ran the perimeter above, and sheets of plywood, ladders, grip stands, cables, carts, nail guns and a dolly track surrounded the crew below. Without the supplies, workers and equipment, the sound stage looked like a plain, well-lit room with concrete walls and a bare wood floor.

The first shot of this morning would be one side of a telephone conversation that Mattie has with David after they marry. On the outside, it seemed like an ordinary conversation between husband and wife, but the viewer would see the beginnings of David's obsession here. They would be filming David's side of the conversation on a different soundstage tomorrow, and Cooper would edit the pieces together into one scene for the final cut.

The rest of the day's shots had only Tracy Jennifer, Carson Standish and Richard Maxwell, who played Jack and David's father, on set. Evan had the day off and on their last night in Walterville, he'd told Samantha he'd be spending the time taking care of some things at the gallery, meeting with his publicist, then hanging out with Oliver when he got home from school.

Evan had teased her about the painting she'd bought, and she told him she was still living with Liz but they'd given it a place of honor next to the Batman cape. He'd asked if she'd forgotten her meds, she'd tickled him, and they'd ended up making love again.

She sighed, staring at Marcus and his crew as they put the finishing touches on the morning's set, working around the lighting technicians, but she really saw herself lying on that awful bed with the dip in the middle at the Sleep Rite Motel, Evan's arms wrapped tightly around her.

"You're either in love or have digestive issues that I don't wanna get into," Keesha said, leaning against the wall next to Samantha, and crossing one tennis shoe over the other as she watched the crew herself.

Samantha felt her cheeks heat up. "I knew you didn't buy that 'it's not a romance' thing."

"Are you happy?" Keesha asked.

Samantha looked at her and nodded.

"I don't really have to ask this, because I know the man, but is he good to you?"

Samantha nodded again, then thumped the back of her head against the wall.

"Then screw the gossip hounds. There's plenty of 'em in this town that'll do what they can to tear you apart, even if you're a saint. Don't let 'em rule your life," she added, then patted Samantha on the shoulder and trotted off at Gary's summons. Having been a gossip hound herself, Samantha knew Keesha was right, and none of that information helped in the least.

She went through the rest of the morning by rote, having spent enough time with this cast to know their habits by now. She timed, she took notes, read lines with Richard Maxwell, and watched

Aaron's assistant, Shelly, read David's lines off camera while they filmed Tracy Jennifer's telephone conversation.

But in the back of her mind the whole time was what Keesha had said that morning and what Liz had said the day Evan invited her to dinner: maybe she could let Evan know her side of things in pieces, easing him into it, or possibly trying to find out how big it was for him, then using that information to figure out how best to tell him. She hadn't known Evan Gallagher long enough to be in love with him, but she definitely didn't have any digestive complaints, so if she hadn't fallen, she was at least on her way.

So much for sex without strings.

After lunch, she asked Keesha to watch her things, and went outside for a quick walk. It was the last day of February, the weather in the 70s and the Los Angeles sky looked clear and blue; recent rains had cleared out the smog and the Santa Ana winds seemed to have quit early this year. She took a deep breath, enjoying the fresh air, circled a few sound stages, then headed back to Stage 12, enjoying being in love with this crazy town again. Was it the job, Evan, being back with Liz and Gary, or all three? She wasn't sure, but found that she didn't care about the reason, just the result.

The red light wasn't on over the door, so she let herself in and got her bag for a quick review of the rest of today's shots. She plopped her script binder onto a small table to one side of the room and stared down at it.

A white envelope with her first name on it had been clipped to the front of the binder.

She looked around the room, but everyone was either busy finishing lunch or prepping for the next task. She picked the envelope up, slipped a thumb under the flap, and pulled a single sheet of paper out. Unfolding it onto the desk in front of her, she gave a delighted laugh.

Four blocks had been drawn across the page, and inside of each block was a picture. The first was an eye, the second a pine tree, the third the number four, and the last a disgruntled-looking, but fluffy sheep. At the bottom of the page, Evan had scrawled, "primitive, but heartfelt." She took another look around, but didn't see him anywhere. He must have snuck in while she'd been on her walk; she was sorry she'd missed him.

Catching sight of Liz peeking through the door, Samantha waved her over. When Liz reached the table, Samantha held the paper up for her review, beaming like a proud parent.

Or girlfriend.

Liz pulled a chair up and sat next to her, then took the paper and studied it for a minute. "I tree for sheep?"

Samantha rolled her eyes at her. "Did no one ever write cryptic messages in your yearbook?" She flipped a page over in her binder and wrote:

2Good
2Be
4Gotten

"I must've missed that social amusement," Liz said, handing the paper back.

Samantha rested it on the table and smoothed a hand over it. "It's 'I pine for you.' Probably easier than figuring out a picture for 'miss.' You know, I miss you."

"Huh." She looked at Samantha. "So he pines for you, huh?"

"Well, it's not a digestive disorder," Samantha said cheerfully.

CHAPTER THIRTY

Samantha timed Evan and Tracy as they ran through a line reading of scene #47, the love scene inside Jack's cabin, after Mattie finds him. He and Tracy only rehearsed the lines, because Tracy Jennifer's contract contained a variety of stipulations in regard to love scenes, including that they be on a closed set and that she not rehearse actions.

Samantha took a quick peek at her production schedule, noting that she'd been back in L.A. over a month and they were now on day nineteen of the shoot; they had six working days left. She and Evan had only been able to have short, impersonal conversations since he'd snuck her the note three days before, although she did get a chance to thank him for it, and he had stolen a kiss behind a moveable wall the other day.

Today, the sound stage had been turned into the inside of Jack's cabin, where he'd been hiding from his enemies, from Mattie, even from himself. This was more than a love scene. It was going to show that Jack was letting Mattie back into his life, and also that he was inviting danger closer to both of them.

The carpenters had built a small bed in one corner, with a battered nightstand next to it. On the opposite wall a long, narrow table held a water pitcher and basin and a rough towel. Across from the foot of the bed sat a scarred dresser with one small, framed picture on top of it and nothing else. At one point, the film would show a close-up of the picture, which was of Mattie. The cabin also contained a small pot-bellied stove in a corner, a rocking chair and a weathered duffel, with all of Jack's possessions inside of it.

There were windows on three sides, two of which were meant to look out the front and toward the road, while the others gave views so Jack could see if someone tried to sneak up on the cabin. Oilcloth covered all of the windows, saving the art department having to find photographs or paintings to put outside of the windows to represent the outdoors.

Evan and Tracy stood just outside the doorway, which was where they'd ended the filming of this moment on location, right after they had started kissing. Cooper would edit the scene together so that the film would cut from them outside kissing, to them moving through the doorway and making their way inside.

"And we'd stop there," Gary said, his voice breaking into Samantha's thoughts. She clicked her stop watch.

"Then we'll set up the next shot, move the cameras around so we're right in the cabin with the two of you." Gary looked from Evan to Tracy. "You'll go through your dialogue with the master shot, and Tracy you'll pull Evan to the bed with you. You both want this, but it's scary. For different reasons for each of you. Tracy, you'll want reassurance that he's really alive, and that he still loves you. Yes, you see him here in front of you, but you want to touch him, to feel him, to make love to him."

Samantha closed her eyes. That was pretty much how she felt every day.

Gary turned to Evan now. "It's the same thing for you, you want reassurance that she's really here in front of you, but there's more. You need her to know that you've accepted her back into your life, allowed her to know you're still alive. And that means you're both in danger, and that you're willing to do anything to protect her, but that right now, right this instant, all you want is to touch her and be with her. There's a moment of hesitation where these things go through your mind. At one moment, you want to let her know of the danger and that you may die protecting her, and in the next, all you want is to love her and not think about anything else.

"But the danger is there, always there with you and in your life, so the sex is going to reflect that. Not to scare her, but to express that it's inside you, a part of you, and she needs to understand that."

Gary turned back to Tracy. "Mattie is going to embrace that. She might not understand it in words, but her body will recognize it. Jack will express it and she'll receive it, and there will be an understanding between the two of you. All right?"

Both Evan and Tracy nodded, and Samantha heard Evan ask Tracy Jennifer if he could speak to her alone for a few minutes, to make sure they were clear on everything and that she was comfortable with it. "All right, Gary?" Evan asked.

Gary nodded, and Samantha thought he looked pleased.

Samantha took the opportunity to take a bathroom break, and walk quickly around outside the soundstage. She took a deep breath, let it out, automatically checked to see if the red light was on above the studio door, noted it wasn't, then went inside, letting the breath out in a long whoosh.

Evan and Tracy went to makeup, and when they got back, Evan was wearing the outfit he'd worn the day of the shooting on location, and Tracy showed up complete with a light dusting of dirt on her cheek and a made up cut on her knee to match the real one she'd gotten when she fell that day.

Samantha nodded, impressed that the makeup people had matched her Polaroid of the cut so well.

Gary called to Samantha. "Which way were they facing at the end of the last scene outside the cabin?"

"Mattie was up against the wall, to the right of the door, Jack facing her."

"And their hands?" Gary asked.

She pressed her lips together. "His right hand up her shirt, both of her arms around his neck," she said, as she began flipping through her binder for the Polaroids.

She dropped down from her chair and brought them over for everyone to study. She could feel Evan leaning over her and he took hold of the corner of one of the photographs she was holding to steady it. She kept her head down, not really looking at the picture, as his breath warmed a spot on her shoulder. She wanted to lean back into him. All it would take was just one little move. Close her eyes, and she'd be pressed up against that warm, broad chest.

"Okay, everyone got the positions?" Gary asked. When they nodded, he said, "Let's get into place. Samantha, stay close with those. We'll need them to verify."

She nodded and stepped back, watching as Evan and Tracy positioned themselves just to the right of the doorway, Evan with his hands up Tracy's shirt again and she with her arms around his neck.

Evan watched Gary, nodding at his directions, while Tracy looked bored.

And she was chewing gum. Samantha rolled her eyes and stepped forward with her hand out, palm up.

Tracy stared at her as if she'd just landed there from Mars. "Gum," Samantha said, and Tracy spit it into her palm without a word. Samantha took the piece of paper Keesha handed her and wrapped the gum in it, then handed it off to the Second PA.

Samantha couldn't help smiling a little. If only people really knew about the truly glamorous world of filmmaking.

Gary leaned toward Samantha again and she automatically held up the photographs. He eased Evan and Tracy a little closer together, adjusted Tracy's hair, then stepped back. "Perfect," he said. "Okay, we're going to shoot this one with Jack moving Mattie into the cabin, then set up for the next shot, which is them pulling at each other's clothes, then right after that, we'll start shooting with them on the bed."

He walked back behind the cameras and Samantha followed, glancing at Evan, who had a hand up Tracy's shirt, just under her left breast. Tracy still looked bored. Samantha couldn't tell what was on Evan's mind, but he was looking down at his feet.

Shelly slated the scene and Gary called action.

Evan leaned toward Tracy and put his lips on hers and she came alive, mashing herself against him and making noises in the back of her throat. She broke away and Evan trailed kisses down the side of her neck. She threw her head back as he eased her through the cabin doorway.

"Oh, Jack," she said, her voice sounding five years and a pack a day older than normal.

Evan bowed over her, enveloping her, and she seemed to collapse under him, an action not in the script. Samantha swore under her breath and began taking notes, glancing rapidly between her script pages and the scene in front of her.

Samantha saw Tracy go limp and she wondered if she'd fainted under Evan's caresses.

She bit at the corner of her bottom lip to hold back a grin. This was something she could understand. She'd felt a little faint at Evan's touch herself.

Evan slipped his arms around Tracy's back and under her knees and brought her to the bed, setting her gently on it.

"Cut!" Gary said, his voice so high pitched Samantha looked over at him. His cheeks had spots of red on them, but he didn't seem to notice as he clapped his hands together once.

"Brilliant," he said. "Great. Print that."

He walked over to Evan and Tracy, who had kept their positions, while makeup and hair people waited in the sidelines. "Okay, that was great. Tracy, great swooning. Mattie's overcome, she collapses in his arms, he brings her to the bed. Perfect."

"Since you won't be removing each other's clothes as you're walking across the floor with each other, let's have Tracy Jennifer on her knees on the bed with Evan in front of her, removing each other's clothing that way."

He gestured behind him. "Samantha, you're getting this?"

"Yep," she called out, writing it down, even as she slipped from her chair and looped the camera from the back of her neck to the front. "Keep your places, please, everyone," she commanded, and snapped a few pictures.

"So let's note that the scene following them going into the cabin has been adjusted and for this one...call it the undressing scene. We'll film that one next, do a master shot, then move on for them actually on the bed, making love."

Taking notes, Samantha headed back to her chair to mark the pictures and make the changes on her copy of the script while the crew set up for the next shot.

When they were ready, Gary gave Evan and Tracy instructions on how to tear each other's clothes off.

"We're frantic," he was saying. "We're desperate, we're scared, we're passionate. All of those things rolled into one. It's hard to say who's feeling more of which feeling at each given moment, but all of them are rotating around for both of you. Let's get down to Evan's shirt completely off, his pants undone, and Evan slipping Tracy's shirt over her head, and we'll stop there. All right?"

Everyone nodded, and took their places. Evan looked at his feet again. Tracy looked like she wished she had her gum back. When Gary called action, the pair reanimated, going at each other's clothing just as directed, conveying passion and intensity Samantha knew neither of them felt. Tracy slid her hands up under Evan's shirt, her fingers spread, lifting it, and he finished the job by pulling it over his head and dropping it on the floor behind him. While he did that, Tracy unbuttoned his pants, and he put his hands in her hair, kissed the top of her head. When she looked up at him, he reached for her shirt and started lifting it up by the hem.

"Cut!" Gary called. Evan and Tracy froze.

Samantha rushed over with her camera and took a few shots, then gave them the all clear. They stepped away while everyone moved in for the next set up, and while Samantha went back to her chair and made some final notes in her book before slumping back.

She couldn't imagine what the actors felt, but she was exhausted. There were so many more details involved in filming a love scene. If they were getting into it, improvising, and it looked and seemed to feel good, no one wanted to stop them or slow them down. It took a lot more work getting everything to match up, sometimes taking longer to set up the lighting and making sure nothing got missed or bungled as they did the close-ups, but all of the crew knew how difficult love scenes could be, and wanted to make them as easy for the actors as possible.

A good love scene looked amazingly sexy in the final product, but could be boring torture to film. On *Honor Bound*, since the main character was immortal, he met a new woman practically every week, so the star got to have a love scene almost each episode, and the crew had gotten experienced at letting the actors do what they needed to be comfortable and get through the scene while making it look as sexy as they could.

Samantha stood up and wandered around a little, waiting for the camera and lighting crews to get set up for the shot of Evan and Tracy lying on the bed—the actual sex. She took a few deep breaths, swinging her arms around to loosen her tight muscles and try to distract herself. It was simulated, everything was properly covered up so that no one had any naughty bits touching, but still…

His hand would be on Tracy Jennifer's body, just as it had been on hers. He would be kissing her—a staged kiss, yes, but she knew that Evan had already talked to Tracy Jennifer and had the "tongue talk." Tracy had given quite a speech: "Sure, whatever, you want tongue, I'm fine with that, as long as your breath's good. If you've got bad breath, I stop right there, in the middle of everything, even if I'm stark naked, and announce to the cameras that your breath's so bad I could puke."

So there would be tongues. Well, okay, there had already been tongues. Samantha had seen a few of them, captured right there on film. Evan was nothing if not daring on film, and that included sex scenes.

Samantha rotated her head from side to side, then did a few shoulder rolls. Once everything was in place for the next part of the scene, she sat back down and got her tools together. When Gary called action, she clicked her stopwatch and focused on the actors and filming in front of her. Just another part of the job, she reminded herself, watching as Evan, a sheet draped around him and Tracy, smiled down at her, and lowered his head to kiss her.

There was definite tongue.

Samantha bit the inside of her cheek. She tried to take a deep breath, but felt her lungs constrict, and gave up.

Tracy moaned and slid her knees up Evan's sides while she smoothed her hands down his back. "Oh, Jack," she murmured. "Jack..." She pressed his face between her palms and made him look at her. "I need you. Prove you're here, and you're alive. Prove that I'm alive," she demanded. "I want you in me."

Samantha's throat tightened. Hadn't she said that to Evan just the other night?

She gripped her pencil so tight she thought it might snap.

Maybe she hadn't actually said it out loud. Maybe she'd just thought it. Really loud.

As she watched Evan and Tracy writhing on the bed, Evan moving forward and back as if giving Mattie her wish, as if he was inside her, loving her the way she wanted to be loved, proving they were alive, some of the faces of the cameramen—who surely had seen it all—grew a little pink around the edges, and she herself felt like fanning her face with her script pages.

Wasn't Gary going to call cut?

Oh, right, this was a master shot.

Oh, goody, that meant they'd be doing cover shots and close-ups next. Actually—she risked a glance at her watch—they'd probably be doing those tomorrow.

No. She looked at Gary's face this time. He wouldn't want to lose this magic. He'd be looking to get as many close-ups done today as possible to capture it.

She clicked her stopwatch off with relief, as Gary finally called cut.

This was going to be a long day.

CHAPTER THIRTY-ONE

Intense day?" Liz asked, collapsing on the couch at home next to Samantha.

"Mmm." Samantha couldn't gather the energy to speak. It was after midnight.

"I had to sit in meetings all day with studio execs since you guys had a closed set." Liz propped her feet on the coffee table. "Was it weird for you?"

"Hmm."

"I figured." Liz waved a hand at the opposite wall, where they'd hung Evan's painting next to the Batman cape. "I'm starting to associate Evan with Batman. Do you think that's a good thing or a bad one?"

"Depends on how you feel about Batman."

Liz snorted, then studied Samantha. "This is where you ask me if it's the Michael Keaton version, the George Clooney one, or Val Kilmer. Or..."

"Is there any chocolate in the house?" Samantha asked.

"Clearly you're not a good Gary substitute."

"I already know you'd say it's Christian Bale. That kid from *Gotham* is too young."

Liz made a half-hearted reach for her bag. "I need to call Gary. You miss the point of the game completely. This is really depressing."

"So it's Val Kilmer, then?" Samantha said, then laughed as Liz fell back, groaning. After they'd both sat and contemplated the painting and cape for a while, Samantha said, "It was pretty weird."

"I know. Val Kilmer has the looks for it, but—"

"Watching Evan have sex," Samantha said. "I mean…You know what I mean."

"Not really, but I can imagine."

"I know better," Samantha continued. "I've been on plenty of sets for sex scenes. They get tedious. Move an arm here, tilt your head there, now move back and forth and look like you like it."

"Sounds titillating."

"It will be on screen. You wrote a damn hot sex scene."

"I know." Liz beamed.

"But I started feeling really possessive, watching Evan with Tracy J. He was so…intense."

Liz held up a hand. "Please don't tell me he was more intense with her than with you."

Samantha turned to her. "I'd give you a withering stare, but I'm too tired."

"Now that's more like Gary," Liz said, patting her on the arm.

"I was thinking…" Samantha began.

"Uh oh."

"Do you think it could work? Me and Evan? After…"

"After the great reveal?"

"Something like that."

"Honey, you know I can't answer that. You'd know better than I would." Liz looked at her again, and Samantha turned to meet her gaze. "Do you want something after?"

Samantha nodded. "More than chocolate."

"Shit."

"Yeah."

They both stared at the painting again.

"I wasn't sure if I could, maybe, break it to him gently, like you suggested," Samantha said. "Tell him everything, but in a way that stresses how good things are with us right now. Do you think there's any way to prep him for it?"

"You've sort of done that, haven't you? You blathered something to him that first day of filming, you told him you did something evil—" She pulled away, laughing, as Samantha tried to pinch her. "You told him you'd divulge your little secret eventually. Now it's, I don't know, sitting him down, reminding him of all of those things, then telling him about the missing pieces, and making sure you're wearing something slinky you can take off fast, so you can ease the tension with sex. Of course, sex is good for that anyway," she said, tapping a fingernail against her front tooth and looking up at the Batman cape.

"I am not going to use sex as a distraction," Samantha said. She wondered if they could make a relationship work after he knew everything. She'd like to think they could, and Liz made it sound fairly straightforward, but that was probably just wishful thinking.

CHAPTER THIRTY-TWO

As soon as Evan opened the door to Sound Stage 37 on Wednesday morning, Oliver charged around crew members and over cables to stand in front of Samantha, who stood next to her chair with a clipboard in her hand.

"Did you get Rocket Raider Six yet?"

As Evan trotted over to catch up to them, he saw Samantha pull out her stopwatch. "Until they can get it on one of these, I'm saving my pennies. I hear Keesha got an advance copy of version Seven, though."

Oliver's eyes got wide and he scanned the crowded room. "Keesha!" he shouted, barreling toward her.

Evan closed his eyes and pressed his fingertips to his forehead. "We went over the rules about ten times before I let him come here today." He raised his head to give apologetic looks to the nearby crew, then looked at Samantha. "He's forgotten them all."

"That's because you didn't present them in *Star Wars* lingo." She set the clipboard down and reached for a binder bulging with multicolored paper before settling herself into a director's chair.

"Must be where I went wrong," he said with a smile. He wanted to brush the hair back from her face, but there were too many people around. "We haven't had time to talk recently. How are you?"

"Fine. Exhausted. I can't believe we only have three more days left and we're done."

"It's going fast," he said, not sure how to read the expression on her face. It looked both sad and hopeful at the same time.

"I'll be glad when it's done and…things can move forward."

Evan nodded. He felt the same way, and he'd been trying to figure out just how to present a scenario for that to her. But first, he had to actually find time to be alone with her. Sneaking kisses behind the sets was one thing, but what would they do when the film ended, the real world intruded, and they moved on to other jobs? "Me, too," he said. "Maybe we can talk about that soon. After we wrap."

She smiled at him, and was about to respond when Oliver came rushing back.

"Keesha's gonna get me a copy of version Seven. Isn't that cool?"

"Ultra," Evan said. "Do I need to remind you of the rules while you're on set, young Padawan?"

Oliver hung his head, but he was smiling. "No, sir." He patted the empty chair next to Samantha. "Can I sit here?"

"Yes, you may," she told him.

Evan said, "His babysitter should be here any minute."

Oliver made a face, and Samantha said, "He's fine for now. We're all early and Marcus and his crew are having some trouble with the set, so we're a little behind, anyway."

"Do you mind if I join you, too, then?" Evan set up another folding chair next to Oliver, who was moving his head around, trying to take everything in. "So what do you think of the sound stage?" he asked his son.

"Pretty cool," Oliver said. "It looked kinda boring outside, like my school. But this is way better."

Samantha leaned over and said, "At least this one isn't haunted, like Studio 28 at Warner Brothers."

Oliver gaped at her. "There's a haunted studio?"

Samantha rested her elbows on the opened binder in her lap and said, "You ever hear of the Phantom of the Opera?" When Oliver nodded, she said, "Well, the 1925 version of that movie was filmed on Stage 28, which was the opera house, and it's one of the oldest movie sets in the world. But they've had a lot of mysterious occurrences there, like lights going on and off and doors shutting by themselves." She pointed up to the wooden railing above them. "See the catwalk up there? Some people have reported seeing someone in a cape running along the catwalk. Spooky, huh?"

"Is it the Phantom?"

Samantha shrugged. "No one knows. But don't worry. We're only in boring old Stage 37 at Underwood, and I don't think they have any haunted studios."

Oliver took a long time to look around the room, and Samantha smiled at Evan before asking Oliver, "So are you excited about the new *Star Wars* DVD?"

He saw Oliver's eyes go wide before he turned to Samantha. "You like *Star Wars*?"

"Yep. I've seen all of them. In the *theater*."

"Do you remember, in Episode Two? When Jango Fett's head got cut off?"

Samantha glanced at Evan. "Should I worry about this?"

"It's questionable," he told her.

She eyed Oliver for a moment before saying, "I remember."

"It was sad," Oliver said with a nod.

She nodded. "It was."

"Do you remember, in Episode Two? When Jango Fett's on the platform? And he's escaping?" When Samantha had verified that she did, indeed, remember, Oliver spent the next seven minutes and twenty-three seconds giving her a complete recounting of the events of that moment. Samantha timed him, in between listening, making notes, and taking script changes Keesha handed to her, then showed the watch to Evan with a smile and a raised eyebrow.

"So is this your job?" Oliver asked.

"It is," Samantha told him.

"So how come we're sitting down and they're all moving around and doing things?"

Before Evan could reprimand his son again, Samantha answered. "Well, when you make a movie, there ends up being two…teams, I guess. One team gets everything set up, and the other team acts and films, but both teams can't work at the same time. I get really busy when we start filming, so I sit down and do all of my catch up work until then."

"Oh." Oliver watched the carpenters raise a fake wall, then said, "I have a therapist."

"Oliver," Evan warned, ready to get up and take him outside.

"I have issues," Oliver added brightly.

"Don't we all, honey," said Keesha, as she walked by. She shared a high five with Oliver and he grinned at her until she'd gone out of sight.

Oliver turned back to Samantha. Kicking his legs against the chair, he asked, "Do you have a therapist?"

"Not at present," she said, "but I sometimes think I should."

"I'll share mine with you, if you'd like." Both Evan and Samantha had opened their mouths to speak when Oliver said, "Do you like my Dad?"

"*Oliver*." Evan gave Samantha what he hoped was an apologetic look. "That's a personal question, and you've just overstayed you're welcome."

She smiled. "It's okay." She turned to Oliver and said, "Yes, I do. He's a very nice man."

Oliver smiled too, then turned to Evan. "Are you two going on a real date?"

Evan jumped up, pinching at the bridge of his nose. "Okay, that's enough…" He stared at his son, who gave him a genuinely innocent look, then glanced at Samantha, who looked slightly puzzled, but was smiling, too. "I'm sorry," he said to her. "Maybe bringing him was a bad idea."

"He's very bright," she said.

"Too," he agreed. He turned to his son. "When Bettina gets here, I'm going to have her take you home."

"But I like it here. I'll be good, I promise. It's just you said you like Samantha, but you're going to the premiere with that south girl, but it's not a real date."

"Right." Evan had told Samantha about having to escort Tiffany Lynn Stearling from Georgia to a movie premiere, but he didn't need his son bringing it up again in front of her. He began turning in a circle, looking down.

"Are you waiting for it to open up and swallow you?" Samantha asked, gesturing toward the floor.

He laughed. "Too late for that to save me. One," he said, pointing at Oliver, "it's not polite to talk about other people's personal lives in public. Two, you know it's part of my job to go to movie premieres. And three, apologize to Samantha for being rude."

Oliver hung his head, and now looked up at his father through his long bangs. He turned to Samantha and mumbled, "I'm sorry I was rude."

"It's okay," she said. "And if it's all right with your father, I'd like to say that being curious is a good thing. You just need to pick your timing."

Oliver straightened up and grinned at her. "Yeah. Hey, Samantha, what's red and green and goes a million miles an hour?"

Evan threw up his hands. "You want him for awhile?" he asked, and sat down again.

Laughing, Samantha said to Oliver, "I don't know. What's red and green and goes a million miles an hour?"

Oliver giggled. "A frog in a blender!" he squealed triumphantly.

Watching Samantha laugh with his son, Evan felt riveted, amused. Hopeful.

"Okay." She leaned toward Oliver. "I've got one. You ready? What goes 'ha, ha, ha, ha—bonk!'?"

"Ohh," Oliver said. "What?"

"A man laughing his head off."

Giggling, Oliver turned to Evan. "That was a good one, wasn't it, Dad? We'll have to tell Bettina when she gets here."

"We will, indeed." He reached out and ruffled Oliver's hair, smiling at Samantha over his son's head. She smiled back and shrugged, then turned to Oliver again.

"So, Oliver," she said, "do you know what happens when your dad goes out there and Keesha calls for quiet on the set, and Gary calls, 'Action'?"

Oliver nodded, then ran a forefinger across his mouth. "Dad does his acting. And I. Zip. My. Lips."

"He got something right, at least," Evan said.

Samantha smiled at him. "He's like his dad," she said. "He gets a lot of things right."

Evan decided right there that no matter what it took, he'd get Samantha alone to re-negotiate their terms.

CHAPTER THIRTY-THREE

Evan kept an eye on Samantha as Gary gave the cast some last minute instruction for the next day, which would be their final day of filming. He wanted to talk to her, and hoped she wouldn't leave before he had finished here. He wiped his palms along his pants as Gary talked about how proud he was of this production, how well he thought everything had gone so far, and that he believed they would complete the shooting on schedule.

Samantha chatted with Keesha while she gathered her papers and other items. Keesha's phone rang and they gave each other a wave as Keesha wandered off.

"Evan, you're going to be on set a lot tomorrow, so we'll need..."

Evan leaned toward where Samantha stood nearby, searching for something in her bag, hoping he was nodding in all of the right places as Gary talked. She pulled out her sunglasses and popped them on her head.

Evan bobbed up and down on the balls of his feet.

"Now, Keesha will be gathering you all first thing in the morning. We think there may be some script changes," Gary said. "Nothing major, just..."

Samantha had gotten everything together and stood looking around the set. He thought she looked like someone who didn't want to be caught looking, and he smiled at her when their eyes met. She smiled back, ducking her head, then grinned at him and shrugged her shoulders. He figured she was giving him a little sympathy for being stuck with the pep talk.

He shook his head, wanting to let her know it was fine, they were almost done. But how to convey that he wanted to talk to her, too see her again, even if just to walk her to her car? He tried gesturing with his head toward the door, but that only succeeded in causing Samantha to nod, hitch up her shoulder bag, and give him a wave goodbye.

He clenched his hands, and turned to Gary, hoping to head him off at the pass.

Gary held a clipboard to his chest and was no longer looking at any of them. Evan noticed Tracy Jennifer had left without a word, and wished he could do the same.

"I'm just so proud of all of you. This has been a great first shoot for me…"

Evan looked a little closer at Gary, who appeared a bit misty-eyed. He gave Gary a hearty clap on the shoulder, making the other man trip a little and fumble with his clipboard. He looked up at Evan, blinking, as if not sure where he was. Evan squeezed his shoulder and said, "It's been a great shoot for us, too." Another clap on the shoulder, Evan told everyone he'd see them tomorrow, and then he turned and jogged out of the sound stage, pausing long enough outside to look left and right. When he caught sight of Samantha, he moved toward her, calling out as he got closer.

She stopped walking, and he grinned in response to her face lighting up when he came to stand in front of her, to her cheeks flushing slightly pink. He wanted to touch her, brush her hair back from her face, but thought he should wait. He really needed to talk to her and didn't want to be distracted.

"Hi," she said, leaning toward him. "I thought you'd be stuck with Gary for another emotional hour or two."

Oh, hell, he couldn't resist. He reached out and ran a hand down her hair. "I managed to head him off before he started practicing his Oscar speech."

She laughed and stepped closer. "I'm glad you escaped."

"So am I. We haven't seen each other for awhile." Really seen each other, he thought, not just on set.

"I know. Silly filmmaking has gotten in the way."

She was now so close, the only thing separating them was her binder. He wanted to grab it and fling it away. He knew her well enough at this point to know she'd kill him for that, and he couldn't help smiling at the realization.

"What are you smiling at?"

"Your binder."

She raised an eyebrow at him.

"It's in my way."

The eyebrow dropped and her mouth formed a little "O." "Right here on the studio lot?" she whispered. "Naughty."

"It's made for fantasy."

With elaborate gestures, he took the binder from her arms, set it on the ground next to her, and took her into his arms. He held her for a moment, not caring if anything else happened, because she felt so good there. He sighed into her hair, feeling her pressed against him, her head against his shoulder, arms snugged around his waist, and her hands pressed into the small of his back. This moment confirmed the decision he'd made earlier.

"I want to re-negotiate our terms," he said into her hair.

She stepped back and stared at him. "Re-what?"

"Re-negotiate," he repeated, wishing he'd handled this overture a little better. "Sex without strings."

"You mean you want strings?" She stared up at him.

"I want…" How often had he finished that sentence in the last five years, putting himself before anything or anyone else?

Once. On a porch in Walterville.

"I would like to get to know you better." He had found out that intimacy took on a whole new meaning when one person held something back. Samantha admitted she was holding something back—and he had a feeling it was another relationship, maybe something she'd ended or was ending, but that hadn't been completely resolved.

He could understand her hesitation, but he didn't want to be with a woman who had a wall up. He'd spent too much time with limitations or lies around him, and he didn't want that anymore.

He wanted Samantha. But he wanted all of her.

"Hard to believe I'm going to say this, but I can't get to know you better if all we do is have sex."

He saw the smile flicker across her face, only to be replaced by a more serious expression. "You want to know me better?"

He shoved his hands in the front pockets of his jeans and rocked back on his heels. "Well, I know you're good in bed, so I don't have to worry about that anymore, so what the hell. Might as well get to know your mind."

He had been hoping for a laugh, a bigger smile at least, but when she didn't say anything, he wondered if he'd gone too far. "Better say right now if you want more, too, Samantha, or if you want out. Because it's not working for me this way. I like you, but I won't push if all you really wanted was the sex and nothing else."

"But you won't stay, either."

He shook his head. "I won't stay." He knew they should revoke his testosterone card for this, but he said it anyway. "I have just enough self respect left to not stay with a woman who only wants me for my body."

She lowered her head, shaking it, but he thought he caught a little smile. When she looked at him, she was serious again. "One more day of shooting."

"I don't see any delays," he said, wondering what she was getting at.

She picked up her binder, reached for his hand and he let her lead him to a bench under a fake weeping willow just around the corner from the cafeteria. "There's something I'd like to tell you," she said. "And then you'll be in a better position to decide if you want to be with me or not."

So this was it, he thought. Finally. "Wait." He held up a hand. "It would help me to know if *you* want to be with *me*."

She stared at him. "More than anything," she finally said.

His heart stopped, and when it started again, it beat a little harder and a little faster than before.

Samantha looked away, pressing her lips together. "Please remember that."

He heard the catch in her voice, saw her blinking furiously. Instead of sitting on the bench, he crouched in front of her and rested a hand on her knee, but she wouldn't look at him.

"Hey, now," he said. "Whatever it is, you can tell me."

She swiped at her cheeks with both hands. "Oh, you're so goddamn nice."

"Not always," he said. "But I don't like playing the villain."

She finally looked at him, her face slightly tear-stained. "I don't either."

"I don't understand."

She rested her hand over his. "I know. Have a seat, and it'll be clearer soon."

He sat next to her, taking her hand. He felt her pull away a little bit, then let their hands rest on his thigh. When she started talking, she was looking in the distance again.

"I lived in L.A. a few years ago," she said. "Before I started working on *Honor Bound*." She licked her lips, pursed them, dropped her head. "I worked on this show…" When she raised her hand to push a section of hair behind her ear, he noticed her hand was shaking.

What in hell could be so bad? he thought.

"It was one of those tabloid type shows."

He made a noise and her head shot up and she looked at him. "I left it," she stated. "It was dishonest and immoral…" She looked away again, shaking her head. "I got caught up in it for awhile, but I finally realized…what an effect that kind of show had…could have…" She bit her lower lip.

"I know," he said. "They do more damage than anything else. And the viewing public has no idea. They're spoon fed these lies…" He had to stop or else he'd start ranting about tabloids, and how their reporting had damaged his own life. He didn't want to focus on that, but he could understand her reluctance in telling him this. Having worked for one of those shows, she must've been exposed to the kind of thing he'd experienced. Just as he didn't want to focus on his past with her, she must not have wanted him to focus on her own past.

"On this show…" she began.

He looked up at the sound of a voice calling his name. Christopher jogged toward them, waving his arms. "Glad I found you." He glanced down at their clasped hands, but Evan held tight.

Christopher bent over his knees, gasping. "Phone call. Wife." He took a deep breath and straightened. "Something about your son."

Evan stood up close to Christopher, wanting to shake him for not immediately saying it was about his son. Then he swore under his breath, realizing he'd forgotten to get his cell phone back from Keesha today in his haste to get off the set. "Is he all right?"

"I don't know. Your wife's on the phone in the production office."

"She's not my wife." He grasped Samantha's shoulder. "I have to go."

"Go," she said. "I hope he's okay."

He ran around the building, and down between two others to the office, opening the door so hard it hit the wall behind it, and grabbed the receiver from the desk. "Zoey? Is he okay?"

"He's fine. Little spill from his scooter. Just cuts and scrapes."

Evan slumped against the desk, letting out a breath and pressed his hand to his forehead He closed his eyes, feeling his heart beating hard against his chest. "Where are you?"

"Home. My home. He wants to spend the night at your house. I got a meeting with our booking agent anyway." She sounded petulant, but he held back from yelling at her, which is what he wanted to do. *Who cares where he wants to sleep?* he thought. *As long as he's all right. And where the hell were you when my son fell from that damn scooter you insisted he have?* He took a few more breaths. "Fine. I'll pick him up on my way home."

He hung up and went outside to see if he could find Samantha, but she was no longer at the bench, and her car was gone from the lot.

So the girl he was dating had worked for a tabloid television show. What an irony. But they both had pasts they wanted to leave behind, and he was willing to work on doing that with her if it meant they could have a future together.

He whistled as he hopped into the Jeep, relieved at her confession. He wanted to find out more about her job, but he figured he could handle her past involvement in that business.

SAMANTHA WENT HOME and put her boots on, hoping for a little of their magic, or at the very least hoping to avoid the heart attack that kept threatening.

She'd told him.

Well. Sort of. She'd told him in a vague sort of way, told him some real basic things, and had been about to tell him more when Christopher had barged up with the emergency.

Evan had left a message for her on Liz's voicemail that Zoey had been exaggerating in her usual fashion and that Oliver had just taken a spill on his scooter, but was fine. The boy was spending the night with him, but he hoped to see her soon, and he was glad they'd talked today.

She was glad, too, but she would be even happier if she'd been able to get the entire story out.

Well, happier wasn't quite the right word. Relieved was more like it. Still, it was a start, and confirmed that her idea of telling him in stages might be the best method. Hadn't she been telling him in bits and pieces all along as it was?

She was standing in the middle of the room, contemplating all of this, and how best to tell him the rest of the story, when the door flew open and Gary and Liz came in. They both froze in the entryway when they caught sight of Samantha. She'd become so accustomed to either or both of them storming in without warning and she'd been so preoccupied with her thoughts, it took her a moment to register their presence.

And a moment was all Gary and Liz ever needed to start their routine.

"It's the girl with the boots," Gary said.

"Is there a famous movie character with boots we can reference from now on?" Liz asked. She and Gary still stood in the entryway with the door wide open.

"Nancy Sinatra comes to mind."

"Puss in Boots. Boots the Wonder Dog," Liz added. "No, those are all animals. Not very flattering. Damn, now I've got that song in my head."

"*These Boots Are Made for Walkin'* is a great song."

"Yeah, the Sinatra version. But I've got the Megadeth one in my head."

Gary cringed. "Ooh, ouch. I'd forgotten your heavy metal days. Quick, think of another song." He snapped his fingers. "Something catchy. Something—"

Samantha knew of only one way to stop this. "I told Evan," she blurted.

Gary and Liz froze, then turned to Samantha at the same time. Gary, who'd been snapping his fingers, gestured toward her with the same hand. "You…"

"Told Evan," she repeated. "Well, sort of."

Without looking behind her, Liz reached for the door and shut it. She and Gary went to the couch, plopped on it at the same time, and stared up at Samantha with expectant looks on their faces.

Samantha sat in an armchair and said, "First I have to tell Gary something." She took a deep breath, reminding herself she needed some practice at breaking difficult news. "I've sort of been sleeping with Evan."

Gary raised an eyebrow at her. "Sort of?"

"Okay. Not sort of. Definitely."

"And?"

Samantha stared at him. "Why aren't you surprised? Outraged? Something."

Gary leaned back and flipped a hand at her. "Honey, everyone knows you're sleeping with him."

Samantha gawked at him. She turned to Liz, who shook her head.

"Don't look at me," Liz told her. "I didn't say a thing. And Keesha did warn you about the gossip."

"Smam," Gary said, "you of all people should know there are no secrets on a movie set. No one talks outside the set during production, but they sure as hell talk to each other. Besides, you two were all over each other." While Samantha continued to gawk, Gary went on. "For the record, I was surprised and shocked at first. And outraged. For various reasons. For one, I wish you'd told me."

Finding her voice, Samantha said, "I was afraid to. To distract you, to mess anything up for the film."

Gary nodded. "And for another, really now, this situation has *Dynasty*, *Dallas* and *Scandal* written all over it." He turned to Liz with his hands clasped together against his chest. "I think our girl is back."

Liz beamed. "Looks like it."

Samantha gaped at them. "What are you talking about?"

"You," Gary said, grabbing her knee and rocking it back and forth. "Our capricious girl. The one who laughs and wears bright colors and dives right into things without thinking."

Samantha looked down at her red boots, jeans skirt and purple top, thinking how much she'd laughed the other day just sitting with Oliver and exchanging jokes. She'd done a lot of pondering lately, but she'd also dived in way too many times without thinking. As Liz would say, that way lies madness.

Gary shook her knee again. "Honey, we know you've got an anal retentive streak a mile wide, and we love that part of you, too. But you'd let that side take over for a while, and *really*. That side doesn't know how to dress *or* live." He sat back, studying her. "So what'd Evan say when you told him?"

"Well, I only got so far as telling him I'd worked on a tabloid show."

"And?"

"And he berated tabloids for awhile, and I was going to tell him the rest when we got interrupted and he had to leave."

"So close," said Liz.

"So what are you going to do now?" Gary asked.

"Find a way to tell him the rest. Soon." She looked at each of her friends in turn. "Without screwing it up or breaking my heart," she added, her eyes filling with tears.

"Oh no no no," Gary said. "Oh, honey, no. Don't tell me you're in love with him."

Samantha put her hands over her face and cried, releasing some of the tension that had built up over the last six weeks.

"Of course she's in love with him, you relationship dodger," Liz said as she went to Samantha and perched on the side of the chair. "Some people actually get attached to the people they have sex with."

"Then maybe some people shouldn't have sex with inappropriate men."

Samantha felt Liz lean away from her and heard Gary squeak in protest. "Ow!" She raised her head in time to see Gary rubbing at his arm.

"How you can be so understanding, and in the next minute so callous, I'll never understand," Liz told him.

"I could say the same of you, Stanley Kowalski."

"Wait." Liz held up a hand. "The Brando version, Treat Williams or Alec Baldwin?"

"Brando, darling, always Brando."

"Just checking. But you know, Diane Lane in the Alec Baldwin one?" Liz slid from the edge of Samantha's chair to the arm of the couch next to Gary.

"Luminous as always. But overshadowed by a cast that—"

"Hello," Samantha called to them. "My drama now."

Gary and Liz turned to look at her, blinking as if they'd forgotten she was there. "Sorry," they said together.

"What do I do?" Samantha asked them.

Gary looked at Liz. "I'm tempted to go into a routine about how certain people never listen to other people and go ahead and do what they want anyway, but my thoughts are currently filled with Brando falling to his knees bellowing, and, well…it's hard to think past that." He turned to Samantha. "Okay, first I need to know something."

"What's that?"

"Is Evan any good?"

Samantha rolled her eyes.

"Transcendent, I hear," said Liz.

"That's good, that's good." Gary nodded. "I was thinking more lusty, primal—"

"Okay, Caligula," Liz told him.

"Ooh, la, la, like you ladies always want it clean and pretty."

"You're still stuck on Brando, is the problem."

Gary nodded again. "True. Okay. Seriously now. Are you really in love with him?" he asked Samantha.

She nodded.

"Do you want to continue a relationship with him?"

"Yes, but once I tell him everything, it's going to squash what we have."

"But you think you actually have something? And do you think he thinks you have something?"

Samantha nodded again. "He told me today he wanted to renegotiate our terms." At Gary's blank look, she gave him a quick rundown on the "no commitment" situation.

"Fascinating." He turned to Liz. "Again, you knew about this already." He waved a hand before Liz could reply, and continued. "Okay, so we agree you're going to tell him. The whole enchilada. You've wanted to do this for a while, but you didn't for various reasons. You got involved with him on the set of a very demanding movie. You need a break." He held his hands out and shrugged, as if this were obvious. "Give yourself a little time to let things settle, figure out how best to present it. Going in there feeling this emotional won't do either of you any good."

"You know," Liz said, "that makes sense."

"I can be sensible when necessary. Are you coming with us to the OC party tomorrow?" Gary asked Samantha.

Samantha wiped at her eyes. "The what?"

"The Oppose Cynicism party," Liz said. "Remember that e-mail that went around? The girl from Nebraska getting a receptionist job at Star Casting and sending an e-mail out to everyone on their distribution list about her job there? And I mean, *everyone*. Talent, executives, even their competition. How excited she was to be in L.A., and she named more than a few names of celebrities who came through the doors, but don't have representation at Star Casting."

Samantha nodded. She'd gotten a copy of it herself. The poor girl had meant to send the e-mail to a group of her friends, but it had ended up everywhere. People in the business were forwarding it to their co-workers and a few had commented on how refreshing the girl's enthusiasm was, and had wondered when they'd all gotten so cynical. In light of that, one of the e-mail recipients had invited the girl—and anyone else—to a party to oppose cynicism. They also wanted to sympathize with her, since she probably no longer had a job.

Gary said, "All of our crew got the e-mail, and a few of them are going. I know Evan isn't because he's got that premiere. So it would be a chance for you to take a break, have some fun, and get some perspective on this thing with Evan. You want to do it right, don't you?"

"Of course." And maybe it would be a good idea to go to this party. At the least, it would keep her mind off thoughts of Evan with a beautiful girl on his arm at a premiere.

CHAPTER THIRTY-FOUR

So this isn't a real date, right?" Oliver asked.

"Right." Evan lifted his chin higher as his son pulled the bow tie tight around his neck. He sat on a chair in the living room in his tux, feet bare, leaning forward, watching Oliver's determined expression as he attempted to fix the tie as he'd been shown. "Sometimes actors go to movie premieres with other actors, like we talked about," Evan continued. "A little looser there, son." He resisted the urge to run a finger under the collar of his shirt. "But the actors are just friends," he finished.

"But you like Samantha more than friends?"

"Right."

"But it's important to get to know her real good first, right?"

Sometimes his son astounded him. "Right."

"Otherwise, it might not work. Like Mom and Dan." Oliver squinted at the tie, pulling it tighter.

This was the first he'd heard anything about Zoey and Dan not working. "What happened…" he began, but stopped when the doorbell rang. Good timing for an interruption. He had no right to quiz his son for details on his ex-wife.

Oliver sprang up, releasing his grip on the tie. "I'll get it! I'll get it!" he announced, racing to the door with Walker barking after him.

Taking a deep breath, Evan pulled the tie away and draped it around his neck. He sat with his hands clasped between his knees, listening to Oliver greet his mother. Zoey would be taking him for the night so that Evan could escort Tiffany Lynn to the premiere of her new film, and then attend the after-party if he chose.

His publicist, Nancy, had put it that way—"It's always your choice, Evan"—but both of them knew better. It was a necessary step to move forward in his career, and he'd agreed to do this, no matter who he escorted. Unfortunately for Evan, Tom Hanks had gotten back in time, so Tom would have the honor of escorting his lady tonight. So, at Tiffany's side, Evan would smile through the flashbulbs and schmooze through the party, all in the name of positive press. Combined with *Broken*, he believed this would lead to more work. Paul already had some scripts he was going to send over next week.

He smiled to himself. Not a slasher flick among them. He could choose from another tortured hero, an action adventure film, or a period piece. His smile widened at that one. He wasn't sure he was ready for wigs and tight breeches, but it could be fun. One of the hardest parts—making sure Oliver was taken care of—was handled because he knew Zoey could take up the slack. But he also knew he would have to do more publicity, like this premiere and some tours before making movies could be a bigger part of his life again.

It wasn't fastened, but he still felt a little like the tie was strangling him as he headed out to greet his ex-wife.

She stood alone in the entryway, staring at the latest painting he'd hung by the door, wearing pegged black jeans, purple Doc Martens and a purple tank top. Gypsy hoop earrings peeked through her black dreadlocks.

She glanced at him over her shoulder, gestured toward the painting with her chin. "It's good."

"Thanks." He glanced at his watch and realized he'd have to get his tie on himself if he wanted to be ready in time. He looped it around his neck again and lined up the edges. "So where's Oliver?"

She turned to face him, slapping a rolled up magazine against her thigh. "Getting his stuff."

"You're okay with taking Walker, too?"

She shrugged. "Sure."

He glanced at her, his hands stopping a moment. "Thanks for doing this."

"You gotta do this…" She waved the hand around that held the magazine. "Movie star stuff."

She was goading him, and he knew it, but he wasn't sure why. He felt no desire to get into anything with her and turned slightly away, focusing on getting his tie just right.

"So, you seen the latest *People*?"

"No." Evan kept fussing with his tie, having turned for help in the hall mirror, too distracted to wonder where she might be going with her question. He took a step back. Still crooked.

"You're in it," she said.

Evan yanked so hard that the tie came undone again. "Damn it," he muttered, and turned to look at Zoey. She held the magazine up, open to the Star Tracks page.

"So what fascinating moment did they catch? Walking the dog? Picking up Oliver from school?" He glanced down the hallway, then leaned toward her, lowering his voice. "If they took another picture of him—"

Zoey thrust the magazine in front of him, and he felt the blood leave his face. It was a half page, him and Samantha in profile, behind a trailer. They had their arms around each other and were smiling, she with her head tilted to look up at him, while he bent his head toward her. As if he were about to kiss her. It was titled "Duncan Tanner's Next Adventure."

Zoey tapped a magenta fingernail against the picture of Samantha's face. "I've seen her before."

Evan turned away, fussing with his suit again, but not really paying attention to what he was doing. He remembered that moment. He really had been about to kiss Samantha, but someone had called her to the set, and they'd stepped away from each other with great reluctance, smiling the smiles of two people who have a secret the rest of the world couldn't possibly understand. The photographer could have gotten another ten grand for a picture of him locking lips with someone. Double that if the someone turned out to be famous.

Samantha wasn't famous, and she wasn't Zoey's concern, but he knew Zoey would push until she got what she wanted from him. Without looking at her, he said, "You met her at the gallery. She bought my painting."

In the mirror, Evan saw Zoey hold the magazine up to her face. "No. Somewhere else. Thought she was an actress or something, but I can't place her."

"She's the continuity supervisor on *Broken*."

"You doing her?"

Evan ripped the tie from around his neck and turned to Zoey.

"Very nice. And none of your business."

"It's my business if it affects Oliver. I'm his mom, and he comes first in my life and I should come first in…" She flicked her hair out of her eyes with a twitch of her head.

"And in what?" Evan asked, wondering if the conversation he'd been meaning to have with Zoey was going to happen now whether he was ready or not. "Zoey, you and I…" Her eyes narrowed for a moment, and he wondered if he'd misinterpreted her hints about them being a family again; he'd thought they'd both understood it was completely over between them.

"I got a right to know what's going on," she said before he could finish. "For Oliver."

Evan dropped his head, letting out a sigh. "You're right," he said, meeting her gaze. "Yes, Samantha and I are seeing each other. Oliver knows about it, but he also knows he comes first in my life, too. End of what you need to know."

"Samantha," she mused. "Is it serious?"

"I hope so," he said. "Eventually."

"Nice for you," she said, all softness gone from her demeanor. "I'll make sure he brushes his teeth," she added, then turned away to get Oliver.

After he'd seen them out, Evan sat back on the couch again, his tie still undone, shoes and socks still waiting to be put on. He scrunched his toes in the carpet, looking down at them, and wished this were the end of the evening instead of just the beginning. He couldn't fathom Zoey these days, and he already missed Oliver—he'd seen so little of him in the past couple of weeks—and felt that it should be Samantha with him tonight, not a young girl he'd never met before.

He wished he and Samantha had had a chance to finish their conversation the other day so he could hear more about what had happened to her on that show; he knew if they talked about it and worked together, they could put it behind them. They'd wrapped filming on *Broken* yesterday, but it'd been a long day, and Samantha had immediately sequestered herself with Cooper to go over the final editing notes.

She seemed so skittish he wasn't sure which would be trickier, convincing her that her past could be dealt with or that giving a relationship with him a try would be worthwhile. One could follow the other, and all he had to do was ride out tonight, and then he could be with her again. He realized Nancy had the right idea with looking to the future, not the past. He wanted to move his relationship with Samantha to the next level.

He had finally gotten his tie done and was finishing putting on his shoes when he heard a car come up the drive. He knew he'd be acting just as hard tonight as he ever did on film. He waited until the chauffer rang the doorbell before heading down the long hallway to the front entry.

He'd play the game, but that didn't mean he had to pretend this was normal.

He greeted the driver with a firm handshake and opened the limo door himself. He slid onto the plush leather seat to be greeted by a mile of bare leg, tasteful cleavage and a million dollar smile.

Tiffany Lynn Stearling held out a perfectly manicured hand, the wrist draped in about $20,000 worth of diamonds, and said in a soft, southern accent, "Mistah Gallaghah. Aren't you a deah to escort me to this event."

He'd expected the accent, but he'd also expected an outfit that would show up on the top ten worst dressed list, with an attitude to match. He hadn't expected grace and manners, and realized that his own attitude had been geared toward hating all of this, when he knew from experience that premieres could be fun. Maybe this evening wouldn't be so horrible after all.

He held Tiffany Lynn's hand to his lips and smiled back at her. "My pleasure."

She tilted her head at him, still smiling, then rapped on the glass. "Drivah. Pro-ceed."

She turned to Evan and pulled her hand back, not so discreetly wiping it against a handkerchief she pulled from her beaded purse, then gave him another dazzling smile. "It's very kind of you to agree to be my escort," she repeated. She snapped her purse shut and he pulled back a little. "Would you be a deah and pour me a soda water?"

As he reached for the mini fridge and a glass, she said, "I'm appreciative of your situation, Mr. Gallagher."

"Evan," he said, handing her the glass.

She smiled at him with her lips closed, then set the glass down in a holder beside her without drinking from it. "Now, Mr. Gallagher, did my people advise your people of the rules?"

"Rules?"

She tilted her head to the side, a move he'd seen her do in her last film. "No touching," she told him. "The dress and the hair cost as much as my daddy's acreage in Savannah, and took all day to perfect." She gestured down her front, like an appliance model pointing toward the latest brand. "You may place a hand lightly on my elbow to give the impression of being a true gentleman and helping me out of the car, but you must stand far enough away that you don't brush into me by accident and risk disarray of the hair or makeup."

She reached up as if to brush her hands along her hair, but held them a few inches away, moving them back and forth to emphasize that great care and space needed to be given such sacred things.

"You may also place a hand on the small of my back, again, lightly, as we're walking down the runway, but again…" She tapped a finger in the air at him. "You must stand a foot or so away, because the rumor mill will be pumping as it is. No frowning when the pictures are being taken. You can look at the crowd and at me, but that's all. No looking up, no looking at your feet, and no expressions that indicate anything other than total pleasure at being there with me. As my escort."

All of this was said with that perfectly cultured, sticky sweet accent, as if she were sitting on the verandah with a mint julep and discussing the weather.

"If you want sex," she began, and he started. So, he couldn't touch her, but he could have sex with her?

"Pardon me?"

"If you would like sex," she repeated, more slowly this time, as if he were stupid, "it has to be after the event and not in the limo. It will be at the place of my choosing, and you will have to wear a condom. No drugs, either, unless I make the arrangements to get them. No taping the sex and if you talk about it later to anyone, I'll make certain your comeback fails, and *that* downfall will make the first one look like a ride at Disneyland."

She tilted her head, watching him. "Would that all be understood, Mr. Gallagher?"

He tilted his head in the same way, and pressed a fingertip to one of the beads on the skirt of her dress. "Could you repeat the

Disneyland part? I missed that."

She stared down at his hand, then up to his face when he didn't move his finger from the bead. Then she laughed, throwing her head back just enough to expose her throat, her laughter that practiced, tinkling kind that you wouldn't know had been perfected unless you'd worked on a laugh or two yourself. The laughter stopped abruptly and she took his hand with her thumb and forefinger and lowered it until it rested on the seat.

"My people told me you were a charmer." She dabbed at the corner of her mouth with the edge of a pinky, and looked out the tinted window. "I had no idea…"

CHAPTER THIRTY-FIVE

Don't tell me, don't tell me." The man standing in front of Samantha looked her up and down, one hand holding a gin and cranberry—with a maraschino cherry, of all things—the other rubbing his chin as if this were very serious business. He held that hand out and she shook it automatically. "I'm a producer." He pointed at her. "I'm good at this."

She wore high heels and a little black dress borrowed from Liz that showed more cleavage than she was used to. He barely came up to her chest. Hollywood was filled with irony. "Good at what?" she asked, taking a step back from him.

"Occupations," he said, prowling forward. He nodded toward her. "Possibly an actress. Casting agent. Someone with power, but still mid range on the totem pole." He began circling her, still with the drink in his hand and the fingers back on his chin. He looked her up and down as he went, appraising, not lascivious, but it made her feel nasty. She turned with him, to see if it would confuse him. It didn't work.

"A lot of drive in you," he said. "Not a director, but you could if you wanted to. Not a writer or production assistant." He wrinkled his nose, as if these were the lowest of the low.

Samantha had had enough. She turned to face him, bending low, as he was now studying her sandals. "I'm a writer," she told him, thinking of her new job as co-author of Liz's script.

He straightened up, sucking in his cheeks a moment. "You have excellent taste in clothing for a writer."

Samantha lifted an eyebrow at him. "For a producer, you have terrible taste in drinks," she said, and walked away.

She wandered through the living room where conversations competed with Maroon 5's latest single on the stereo and a flat screen TV on one wall turned to the *Celebrity Live!* weekend edition. Quickening her pace, Samantha turned away from that, the last thing she wanted to see, then went through the sliding glass door onto the deck and headed to an empty corner, catching bits of discussions from small groups of people huddled together as she went.

"He said I could be the next Brad Pitt..."

"It's in her contract that all of her clothes be size zero? But the girl's a six, so we have to make everything bigger and put these little homemade labels in that say zero..."

"...best screenplay since *Chinatown*, and everyone knows that's a structurally perfect script..."

"...it's just so terribly important in film these days."

"...they're calling it *Godfather* meets *Goonies*..."

Samantha had to stop at that one. The man who was talking paced back and forth, smoking obsessively, running a hand through his hair, then waving it around as he spoke, and the man who was listening, in a trim goatee, hand to chin, in a tailored charcoal suit and cream shirt, nodded in concentration at the smoker as if he were outlining the cure for cancer.

Samantha smiled to herself, shaking her head as she moved away and leaned her elbows on the railing to look out at the view. Three stories tall, the house behind her consisted of a series of metallic rectangles stacked like a child's blocks, and set into the side of the hill, seeming to defy gravity. It was architecturally gorgeous, and had been featured in *Sunset, Architectural Digest* and *Pacific Homes*, but it seemed cold and sterile to her. The view from the deck was much better: those amazing hills, shooting up from Sunset Boulevard, surrounding the myth that was Hollywood.

Samantha propped her chin in her hands and looked down, trying to pick out Hollywood Boulevard, where people would be lining up behind velvet ropes at Grauman's Theatre in the hope of catching a glimpse of one of their favorite stars, maybe even snapping a photograph, or more: getting an autograph, a handshake, a peck on the cheek that would be cherished and remembered even as the celebrities went on to the next event in their lives.

She tried not to think about it, tried to turn her thoughts away, but she couldn't help wondering what Evan was doing—*how* he was doing—waving to the crowd, joking around with Tom and Rita, Brad and Angelina, Goldie and Kurt, a beauty on his arm. Would they pose for the cameras, their arms about each other's waists, heads tilted toward each other, and murmur, "We're just friends," to reporters?

She took a deep breath, still looking down the hills. Filming had wrapped on *Broken*, she'd completed her clean up script for Cooper's final edit, and they would go into post-production on Monday. She'd take the rest of this weekend to figure out how to tell Evan everything. The direct approach seemed best. But maybe Liz had the right idea. A little sexy underwear might not hurt.

Smiling to herself, she went back inside.

She found Liz and Gary sitting on a black leather couch facing the front door and rating the girls who came in, trying to figure out which one might be the e-mail girl. Samantha stood in front of them, hands on her hips and ready to reprimand, but found she was too tired. She flopped down between them, leaned her head back and closed her eyes as Liz called out the most recent person who had walked in the door.

"No, no," Gary replied. "She's Paramount's new big thing."

"The studios don't own the actors anymore, Goldwyn," Liz reminded him.

Samantha gave up trying to relax and opened her eyes.

Gary slumped down. "I know. I miss those days. The razzle dazzle, the musicals." He straightened up. "Musicals! We should do a musical."

Liz clapped her hands together. "C'mon, kids, I've got my father's barn, let's put on a show."

They both held their hands up, as if doing a ragtime bit, and started singing, "All That Jazz."

Samantha got up to search for the guy who was good at guessing occupations.

EVAN PAID THE cab driver, tipped him well, then went inside and collapsed on the sofa, shiny black shoes, strangling tie and all.

He'd smiled so much tonight his face hurt. He'd touched and not touched just as Tiffany had directed, and he'd posed while flashbulbs burst incessantly, turning into one big flash so he couldn't see the photographers or crowd beyond them. As their publicists moved them along the red carpet, and paparazzi asked for pictures of Tiffany Lynn alone, he'd been able to break away a little to wave to the crowd, and even managed to shake some hands and sign a few autographs.

He could've happily ended the night at the theater doors when a woman pushed her young son to the front of the crowd and the boy held out a pen and piece of paper and said, "I'm gonna be Duncan Tanner when I grow up."

Evan had crouched down, the red velvet rope the only thing between them, and everything else had receded into the background. All he saw was the boy's big, dark eyes and bright smile, the innocence and the joy. He'd signed his name and wrote, "To the next Duncan Tanner." He'd wanted to ask the boy his name, sit down right there on the carpet and ask him what he liked to do for fun, how did he like school, did he have any brothers or sisters, but the publicist put a hand on his arm, and when he looked up, the noise and lights came back with a thump, and he staggered a little as he straightened up.

He managed to hand the paper back to the boy and rest a hand on his head before he was ushered ahead again, through the lobby with its intricate murals and red and gold columns, and into the auditorium just behind Tiffany, who continued to wave and smile at the crowd until the doors shut behind them. Then her expression switched from appreciative ingénue to interested party guest. She leaned toward the film's director and began pointing to different areas of the theater, from the red carpeting and seats, to the stone columns along the sides of the auditorium and the massive chandelier hanging above. Evan wondered how someone her age could be so poised, could have mastered the perfect mannerism for any given moment, when he felt like an open book to anyone who happened to be looking close enough.

He'd been so distracted in the theater; he couldn't even remember now what the movie had been about.

Tiffany had still been pressed against the director when the lights went up, so Evan paid an usher to call him a cab, and while he waited, he thanked everyone around him, including Tiffany, who gave him an unreadable look, then waved him on. He snuck out the back door and collapsed gratefully into the cab, sitting unmoving with his eyes closed until the car pulled up to his house.

He knew, eventually, he'd laugh about this night. It would be a good story to tell.

In about twenty years.

He let his forearm drop over his face, realizing he wanted to tell the story now, to Samantha. She'd listen, laughing along with him, being understanding without condescending, and then she'd help him erase the memory of Tiffany Lynn and The Rules. He wanted Samantha there with him, lying on the couch, undoing his tie, resting her head on his chest and looking at him so he felt like the most important thing in her life.

But she was at some party tonight, mingling with other Hollywood jaded types, probably taking everything in as she chatted and ate hors d'oeuvre, observing and filing it away. And he wanted to hear all of her thoughts on it.

He pressed a palm against his eyes, then dropped his arm and sat up. Enough sulking. That never got anyone anywhere. He ran a finger along the inside of his collar, then headed for his office, intent on taking charge. He rarely used his computer, but it occasionally came in handy, and he thought he could put it to great use tonight. He had a certain e-mail and address to look up.

CHAPTER THIRTY-SIX

Samantha finally had had enough when a casting agent cornered her and promised he'd find a part for her in the next Tom Cruise movie—all the while trying to put his hand up her skirt. It propelled her to find her purse, call a cab, and tell Gary and Liz she was leaving. Still keeping watch on the couch, they interrupted their show tunes to protest.

"No, don't go," Gary said. "This is so much fun. And we've earned this party."

"We made a movie," Liz added in a conspiratorial tone.

"Yes, we did," Samantha said to them, eyeing the row of empty martini glasses on the table in front of them. "And it was brilliant. And I'm tired."

"Sa-man-tha," Liz said, drawing out each syllable. She held out a hand and Sam took hold of it. Liz shook it harder than she seemed capable of at the moment. "We love you, we do. You know that, don't you? We love you for coming out here, putting up with so much, for the helping of us." With her free hand, she gestured between herself and Gary, smacking him on the shoulder with each pass. "For that dumb aud…audshon. No, not that."

"Reading," Gary said, pointing at Samantha.

"Yes! The reading. Furking brilliant." Blinking, she stared up at Samantha. "What'd I say?"

Samantha shook Liz's hand. "I love you too, sweetie. Both of you. And, ironically," she said, more to herself than to them, "I'm glad I came here. But I really have to go. I'm exhausted."

"Noo," they said in unison. "Stay," Gary added.

She held up a hand. "You two stay, have fun. Sing some more show tunes. I already called a cab. And promise me you'll call a cab, too."

Gary waved a hand around. "Or Brian said we can stay here." He leaned over, one eye partly closed, the other looking blearily at her. "Ten bedrooms this place has." He held up both hands, fingers spread out. "Ten."

Samantha nodded at them both, knowing they wouldn't remember any clever reply on her part. "I'll talk to you both in the morning," she said, turning away.

"After noon, I tink," Liz called after. "Tink," she repeated, and even though Samantha didn't turn around, she could picture Liz leaning toward Gary. "Did I say tink?"

Samantha's smile was fleeting as she headed out the front door and down the stairs. She held onto the metal railing with one hand and clutched her bag with the other, not used to steep staircases in party dresses and high heels. She concentrated on her feet, one step at a time, feeling as if she'd had many drinks instead of the one glass of champagne when she'd first gotten to the party, only there was no sweet tickle in her head, no gentle fizz, just a heavy feeling in her chest, worry over screwing everything up. Halfway down, she stopped, lifting her head when she heard a noise below her.

As if manifested from her thoughts Evan stood at the foot of the stairs, only he looked better than her imaginings. Her dreams had him dressed in jeans and a t-shirt, and Armani had done her one better. He stood with one hand on the railing, one foot on the bottom step, his hair slightly mussed, looking up at her.

She took three more steps down, but her legs had begun to shake, and she had to stop, gripping the rail to keep her balance but never taking her eyes from his. His hand stayed on the railing as well—just a few more steps and she could slide down and brush her fingers against his. The light from the Chinese lanterns nearby glowed warm against his skin, and he stood poised for a moment, but then went up the remaining steps until he stood one below her.

"Hi," he said, giving her a little smile.

She couldn't help but smile back. "Hi," she said, amazed she could manage even that one small word, with her heart knocking so hard in her chest and the air squeezed out of her lungs. She was unable to breathe without squeaking, so decided just holding her breath and watching him, freezing this moment in time, would work out just fine.

"How was your party?" he asked.

"Wretched," she said, surprising herself, then laughed.

His smile widened and she leaned forward, sliding her fingers down until they touched his.

"How was…the screening?" she asked, not really wanting to hear but suddenly needing to break the tension between them.

"Wretched."

Even as she laughed, his fingers tightened around hers, and he slipped his other hand around her neck, drawing her head down to his, and then he was kissing her and she lost her balance and slipped down until they stood on the same step, her legs between his, his arms tight around her, keeping her from stumbling again, his lips firm but tender.

When they pulled back, she gestured behind her. "Is this where we get the close-up, then you sweep me into your arms while the music soars and we fade to black?"

"No." He brushed a thumb across her bottom lip. "This is where I take you home and make love to you until you can't stand up."

"Oh," she squeaked.

He did sweep her into his arms then, a move that broke down the rest of her defenses, and headed toward his Jeep. She leaned her head against his shoulder, putting one arm around his neck, and heard his heart beating. She closed her eyes and breathed him in. He smelled like shampoo and warm skin after a day at the beach.

He managed to open the door with one hand while still holding onto her, and she did feel a little like she was in a movie. And that was the magic, wasn't it? What every filmmaker wanted to create and what every moviegoer wanted to fall into. The perfectly executed dream.

He caught her look just as he reached out to close the door. "What?"

She shook her head. "Nothing. I'm just really happy."

He smiled, then leaned in for a quick kiss. "So am I." He closed the door and headed around the front of the Jeep to the driver's side. Her eyes followed him, tall and lean in the tuxedo. She liked his other look, too, casual and a little unkempt, that said he didn't mind getting messy, digging into the realities of life, but it was something else altogether to see that scruff smoothed away and presented in a lovely, crisp package, bow tie and all.

She couldn't wait to get him out of it.

SHE THOUGHT SHE'D remember every moment of the drive to Evan's house, the warm breeze coming through the partly opened windows, the way the air smelled of warm concrete and pine after they'd put Bel Air behind them and reached Silver Lake, Evan's hand on the gearshift and the sound of his voice as he told her about the premiere.

She didn't think she'd want to hear, especially after he'd prefaced it by saying he didn't want to be indiscreet. But then he added he knew he could trust her with this and had been looking forward to sharing it with her. By the time he got to the part where Tiffany had advised him about not taping the sex, she was giggling so hard her side hurt and she found she couldn't wait to hear the rest.

"Don't disarray the hair?" She pressed a hand to her mouth. "God, I love this town. It's weirder than anything you can imagine. And then it tops itself."

He glanced at her with a grin. "You love it? You don't talk about it much, how you feel about the business."

She shook her head, surprised at the realization that she really did love it. "There was a time...I hated it. Especially the reporting. And there are certain things about it I still can't stand, but I love my job, and helping everyone else do a good job. I love the...the magic."

He took her hand and pressed it to his lips before laying it back into her lap. "You're magic," he said, and she shivered, remembering how she'd said that to him not so long ago.

"Is it tacky of me to want to get you out of that dress as soon as possible?"

She had to pull her tongue from the roof of her mouth. "I feel the same way about that tux. And you look amazing in it."

He pulled into the driveway, parking right in front of the door, and jogged around to the passenger side, but she was already out, had already closed the door, and was reaching for him. He pushed her against the car, kissing her hard, his hands in her hair, brushing over her body as if to memorize her. He spun them around toward the front walkway, still kissing her, barely taking the time to unlock the door and ease her inside, both of them stumbling down the hall, her skin hot wherever he touched her. She felt the backs of her knees bump against the bed and she slid down, pulling him with her, not wanting to be separated from him for a second, only wanting his hands on her, for him to be inside her, for this to never stop.

His lips trailed along her jaw line and down her neck, tickling, soothing, stirring. He hovered above her, pulling her arms out from her sides and over her head, their hands clasped and her back arched toward him. As if making a double snow angel, he lowered their arms back down in a wide arc, and eased her up into a sitting position. Leaning over, he ran his tongue from her collarbone to the edge of her shoulder and slipped it under the thin strap of her dress. He slid it off her shoulder with his mouth.

A shiver shimmied up her back from the sensation of his mouth and the silky material smoothing over the skin of her upper arm and she leaned toward him. "God, do that with the other one."

He did, this time trailing his tongue down the sensitive flesh on the inside of her arm and back up again, then reaching behind her to lower the zipper on her dress. She let out a sigh as he slid the dress down, then helped her to her feet so it could fall to the floor.

He stepped back then, and looked at her. She wore a black bra and matching silk panties and thigh high nylons—not because she thought this would happen tonight, but because she'd wanted to feel sexy—and she was very, very grateful she'd once again left the ratty panties at home.

"You are…" He shook his head. "I don't have the words."

"I do." She stepped out of the puddle of her dress and reached for his jacket, easing it off his shoulders. It fell to the floor, and she said, "You are…fascinating." She fiddled with the tie until she figured out how to loosen it, then tossed that behind her. "Charming." She stepped closer, and began undoing the buttons of his shirt. Slowly. "Intelligent." She pulled the shirt from his pants, and pressed her palm against his chest, then slid her hand down. "And so incredibly hot I'm surprised there isn't steam coming out of my ears."

He laughed, pulling her close. "Well, let's see if we can make that happen."

"I forgot funny, amazing and perfect."

He brushed his hands through her hair, tilting her head back. "I really lo—"

Her heart constricted. Had he been about to say what it sounded like he was going to say?

"I feel the same way about you," he finally said. "And then some."

She stared at him. Oh God, he *had* been about to say it. "I—"

Before she could say anything else, he bent down and kissed her. Hard.

She turned him around and pushed him onto the bed, the blood pounding in her ears, scared and happy at the same time—and wanting him more than ever. He grinned up at her, and she couldn't help grinning back.

Knowing she spoke more eloquently with her body right now than she could with words, she gave herself to him completely—and wore him out thoroughly. She wanted to know they had this between them, so when she told him she wanted more, he'd see that instead of what she'd done in the past.

She watched him for a long time after he fell asleep. She pressed a palm to his chest, just over his heart, feeling its strong, steady rhythm. She trailed her fingers through the hair on his chest, then let her hand rest on his stomach, warm and soothing. She hoped she could break it to him gently and that they'd be able to move forward from there, but she knew she'd also have to prepare herself for a different outcome. Either way, she would tell him everything else in the morning.

Everything, she promised herself, then leaned toward him and whispered, "I love you, too."

CHAPTER THIRTY-SEVEN

He couldn't sleep.

He wanted to sit up all night and watch Samantha. She lay on her side, one hand curled under her chin and a section of hair falling across her cheek toward her mouth. He brushed it back, caressing her face. He'd fallen asleep earlier, but had woken to find her curled against him.

He'd almost told her he loved her tonight, but wasn't sure what stopped him. Maybe he didn't want it to come out during sex. He wanted her to know he loved her because of her, not because she was sleeping with him.

He was just reaching for her, to caress her awake, when the doorbell rang. His hand jerked and he automatically looked at the clock. Two-thirty-eight. He grabbed his tuxedo pants and pulled them on, mentally reviewing a list of people who had the gate code: Oliver, Zoey, Paul, Bettina. None of them would ring the doorbell at this time of night.

Samantha stirred. "What is it?" she mumbled, looking up at him through a tumble of hair.

"Nothing. Go back to sleep."

He'd almost reached the front door when the bell rang again. The person on the other side held their finger to the buzzer to make it repeat. Evan swore when he recognized Zoey's outline through the glass.

He yanked the door open and she smirked up at him, pulling her hand away from the bell.

"Zoey, what the hell?" he hissed. "Where's Oliver?"

"Friend's house," she snapped. "Matt's house. He stayed over there."

"Are you drunk?" he asked. He gripped the doorjamb hard, angry with her, but relieved that Oliver was okay.

Zoey straightened, her eyes narrowing. "No, you asshole, but I wish I was. Sure would improve my life right now." She flapped her hand. "Doesn't matter. They canceled the tour. Not enough interest."

With his free hand, Evan rubbed at his forehead. "I'm sorry to hear that. But it's two in the damn morning. Go home."

"Saw you tonight," she said, as if she hadn't heard him. "On TV. You and that…girlfriend." She smiled now, but it looked spiteful, not happy.

So he and Tiffany Lynn had made it onto this evening's *Entertainment Tonight*. Nancy would be happy. In the meantime, Evan didn't know what to do with Zoey. "She's not my girlfriend." He leaned back, thinking he'd like to just slam the door in her face, but she'd probably lean on the bell again.

Zoey's eyes narrowed. "You," she said, staring behind him.

Evan turned and saw Samantha standing in the hallway. She'd put her party dress back on, but had taken an old cardigan from his closet and stood huddled in it now. Samantha glanced at him, then looked at Zoey.

"This is your fault, you bitch," Zoey said, and took a step as if she would charge at Samantha.

Evan caught her by the shoulders and gave her a shake. "Hey."

"We could've had something again," Zoey said to Evan. "She broke us up the first time, now she's between us again."

"What the hell are you talking about? There is no 'us' anymore, Zoey." Damn, he should've talked to her instead of putting off the inevitable. He bowed his head, running a hand through his hair. Now she was taking it out on Samantha.

"Could've been a family and she ruined it. Ruined it then, and ruined it now."

"What're you talking about? She didn't do anything."

Zoey smirked up at him. "No? Sending you to jail doesn't count?"

"What're you…Enough, Zoe. You've crossed too many lines. Go home and we'll talk later." With lawyers present, he thought, but didn't say that out loud. And he'd change the gate code in the morning.

Zoey gave him that smile again. "I knew I knew her from somewhere. Not an actress, though." She leaned around Evan, who still had her by the shoulders, and said to Samantha, "How'd you get him in bed? How'd you get Mr. High and Mighty to forgive you in the first place?"

Evan's head spun. Zoey was talking crazy. He needed to get her away from the house and away from Samantha.

"How's it feel to ruin people's lives, *Sami Scandal?*" Zoey said, still straining against him and talking to Samantha. "How'd it feel telling all those lies? Yeah, I figured it out tonight, you were on that show…"

That show. Evan looked at Samantha, but couldn't read the expression on her face. She'd said she'd worked on a tabloid type show, but hadn't specified her job. Zoey had called her Sami Scandal. That was the name of some trash reporter on…

It all clicked into place, and something slammed into his gut. Samantha just stood there, staring at him, her eyes big, clutching that cardigan tightly around her. "Jesus," he whispered, letting go of Zoey and pressing a hand to his forehead.

"Is it true?" he asked, raising his head to look at her.

"Yes," she whispered.

"Doesn't feel so hot, does it?" Zoey said. "Having your whole life ruined by little Miss Scandal and her lies."

Evan whirled on Zoey. "Get the hell out of my house. And don't come back."

CHAPTER THIRTY-EIGHT

Samantha didn't wait to see how Evan finally got rid of Zoey. She stumbled back to the bedroom, her mind reeling, found her purse, and collapsed on the bed. When Evan came back and stood in the doorway without saying anything, she was trying to fasten the straps on her sandals. She kept her head bowed, afraid to look up at him.

"You're Sami Scandal," he said, his voice cold.

"Was."

"That was your big mystery."

She nodded, her head still down, her hands wrapped around her ankle because they shook so badly. Was loving him and then losing him her punishment for all of this? That would be about right.

"You reported about Zoey, me, abandoning Oliver?"

"Yes," she whispered, finally straightening up to look at him. He still stood in the doorway, watching her, one hand clutching the frame. "I'm so sorry."

He looked away, then reached for his shirt from the floor. "I'll take you home." He took his keys from the bedside table and walked out of the room, putting the shirt on as he went.

Her knees wobbling, Samantha pushed herself up from the bed and followed him. Without speaking, they got into the Jeep and he drove through the gate, making sure it closed behind them.

"I'll need directions," he finally said, his voice flat.

She told him how to get to Liz's, then said, "I was going to tell you everything. There's an explanation."

He barely glanced at her before looking at the road again. "There is no explanation for this. No excuse."

"It's not an excuse," she said, trying to keep her voice level. "Just an explanation."

"Explanations won't restore my son's trust."

She flinched.

"You're right," she said. "Every time I try to rectify this situation, I screw it up more." She looked out the window, blinking back tears. She should have told him, should have told him right away. She couldn't remember now any of the reasons why she'd waited.

His voice broke through the haze of her grief, so cold it sliced into her. "Every time," he repeated. "How many times have you messed with my life behind the scenes?"

"Never," she finally said. "Not on purpose." She glanced at him. "I would never hurt you or your family. Please believe that."

Evan stared at the road, not looking at her. She leaned toward him a little and caught his eyes in the rearview mirror, bright with the glare of oncoming headlights. "But you did hurt them." He pointed at her, punctuating his words with the gesture. "You hurt my son."

"Not on purpose," she replied, hanging her head and looking at her hands tangled in her lap so she wouldn't have to see the accusation in his eyes. "And I would do anything to make up for it."

He made a noise in the back of his throat. "Would you get out now and walk home?"

"Yes."

He hit the brakes so hard she slammed against her seat belt. She sat back with a lurch and pressed her hands to her chest.

"Then get out."

She turned to look at him. He was watching her, but as soon as she caught his eye, he turned away. She looked down at the clasp of her seatbelt, hit the button to undo it and let it slide back into place. She opened the door, and leaned out, one hand on the handle, and one reaching for her bag on the floor. It looked like they were near Sunset Boulevard. Maybe she could call Liz.

"Fuck," he shouted. He slammed both hands against the wheel and repeated it a few times in a row.

Samantha froze, looking back at him. He'd dropped his forehead against the steering wheel and was clutching it with both hands. Before she could move one way or the other, or say anything, he'd straightened up, brushed his hair back from his face with both hands and swiped at his cheeks with his palms. "Close the door. I'll drive you."

Without a word, she closed the door and re-fastened her seat belt. Silence enveloped the car completely, broken only when it was necessary to give him further directions.

Evan pulled in front of Liz's house and left the car running.

She clutched her bag in her lap, looking down at it as if it might have some answers hidden inside it. "I'm sorry."

"So you said."

She felt tears pool in her eyes, and didn't want him to see them. She didn't want anything else between them now, anything that might change how he felt one way or the other. She didn't want him to hate her, certainly, but for too long she'd lived with all of this. For too long she'd avoided letting it out so she wouldn't have to deal with it. It was out now, and she needed to take responsibility for her part in it. And that meant accepting how Evan felt right now, without her tears affecting him in any way.

Still. She put a hand to her chest. God, it hurt. She looked at him, and despite her stern warnings to herself that they stay put, her tears slid down her cheeks to her chin and onto her hands. "And I meant it," she said. "I've been living with what I did for five years—"

"So have I," he said, staring hard at her.

She needn't have worried how her tears would affect him. His look remained icy. "And I'll live with the consequences," she continued, trying to speak past the hitch in her throat. She swallowed. "I've handled all of this badly," she said. "From the very beginning to now. I should have told you five years ago. I should have..." She wiped at her cheeks. "I should have done a lot of things differently. Then we wouldn't be having this conversation." She unhooked her seatbelt and reached for the door handle. "I know I can't saying anything to make it up to you—"

"No."

She flinched again. "Just know..." She almost said something dramatic like she'd regret it forever and spend her life trying to make up for it, but the drama, she knew, was cliché. "I feel like trying to explain to you I'm not a bad person." Another tear fell. Useless. Anything she might say would just be words to him right now.

She reached a hand up, as if to touch him, then dropped it and stepped out of the Jeep. "You deserve better," she said, not sure why, but knowing she needed to say it.

She closed the door and the Jeep stayed idling at the curb even as she let herself into the house. She allowed herself one glance before shutting the door, and just as she looked, he put the car into gear and drove away.

CHAPTER THIRTY-NINE

Samantha sat at the dining table the next morning, a cup of tea in front of her going cold, not moving, barely thinking, just staring out the window. What she saw out there, she wouldn't be able to say. But it didn't matter. It all looked gray and dreary to her anyway.

Liz clomped into the kitchen behind Samantha in her usual it's-too-early-to-lift-up-my-feet fashion, and stopped at her back. "Someone isn't wearing the same clothes they wore last night. Yet someone wasn't back by the time I went to sleep around three. Have ourselves a little coyote sex, did we?" she asked, coming around to face Samantha.

Samantha wished she could have a laugh over that one. She'd love to let Liz tease her about the producer who drank gin cranberries with maraschino cherries and were things so bad that he was the coyote sex? That would be preferable to the real reason she'd come home so late.

She looked at Liz. She tried to say something witty, or even prepare Liz for what had happened, but instead her lip trembled and she said, "He knows," before bursting into tears and dropping her head to the table.

"What?" Liz rushed over, patting her on the shoulder, then drew up a chair and sat next to her so she could drape an arm over her shoulders. "What? Who knows what? What happened? What happened to make you cry in my house?"

"Evan," Samantha said through her tears and running nose and the hands she'd pressed to her face. It came out sounding like "Bn," but Liz got it.

262

She hugged Samantha tighter. "Oh, honey, what happened?"

Samantha straightened up, reaching for a paper towel to wipe at her face. "What didn't happen?"

Liz patted her a couple times. "Well, that makes for a long list, doesn't it? Can we narrow it down a little? He knows? That means you told him?"

"I wasn't officially the first one."

"What? Who? No one else knows." Her eyes widened and she started to get out of the chair. "Gary? He wouldn't. Oh, no." She pushed back her sleeves. "I'll kill him," she said, looking around the kitchen as if searching for a proper weapon.

Samantha grabbed at her arm. "No. Not Gary. You're right. He wouldn't. But Zoey Highlander would."

"Zoey?" Liz sat back down, watching her. "I don't get it." She pulled a pack of tissues from her bag and set them on the table as Samantha's tears continued to flow. "Maybe you should start at the beginning?"

Samantha sniffled. "Okay." She blinked at Liz. "Do you want to hear about the sex first or last?"

Liz gave a whoop and came out of her chair again. She sat down abruptly. "Oh God, but where does Zoey come in?" She wrinkled her nose. "Do I really want to hear this?"

Samantha gave a little laugh, and reached for another tissue. "I guess I'd better start at the beginning after all."

She told Liz everything, starting with finding Evan at the bottom of the stairs at the party, to him literally sweeping her off her feet, their time together, Zoey's appearance and recognition of Samantha, and then her ride home with Evan.

"He dropped me off, I told him he deserved better than me, then he left." She waved the tissue around. "Why did I say that? It was so stupid. Actually…" She brushed her hair behind her ears. "He waited until I got inside before he drove away. He really does deserve better."

"No." Liz smacked the table, making Samantha jump. "Don't say that. There's no one better than you."

Samantha shook her head. "For him there is." She tried to give Liz a brave smile, but knew she'd failed.

Liz looked at her a moment, then asked softly, "Is there for you?"

"Not so far." She reached for another tissue, and gave a little shrug. "But it doesn't matter, does it?"

"Of course it does."

"How can you say that? He hates me. I destroyed things right and left, knew about it when I saw him again, and didn't say anything to him."

"You think he doesn't understand how hard it is to say something difficult? You had reasons, you know, good reasons. Well, mostly good reasons. But we've been over that and maybe it's not a good time to review all of it, but I stand by what I said. You're great for him, did you ever see him on the set, a little before and after, Mr. Serious at first, and then he'd catch sight of you and he glowed. The man *glowed*. And that's hard to do."

Samantha shook her head, but she was smiling a little. "Thanks. But he has every right to hold this against me and never forgive."

Liz shook her head back at her. "Do you even know the man?"

"What do you mean?"

"He doesn't hold grudges as far as I can tell. He speaks his mind, but takes the other person's thoughts into consideration. He's a gentleman—" She slapped a hand over her mouth. "I'm not making it better, am I?"

"Pretty much not," Samantha said.

"My point was, he's capable of forgiveness."

"For small things, maybe, for things the rest of us might grumble over for five minutes longer than he does." She shook her head. "But not for something like this. Not this."

"So maybe he'll take ten minutes." Liz leaned forward. "So how long is it going to take you to forgive yourself?"

"Why are you so wise this morning?"

Liz threw her arms out from her sides. "We're wrapped. I'm actually getting my movie made. I feel like the queen of everything, my friend, like I've got all the answers. And to top it off, even though the e-mail girl never showed up, I had a great time at the party, I don't have a hangover, it's Sunday, and I've given myself the morning off."

"Really?"

"I'm meeting with Gary this afternoon to go over some things, but I'm free until five o'clock." She cocked her head. "Want to do some retail therapy?"

"Oh, I don't know…"

Liz gasped. "You can't be that bad off. No one is so bad off they couldn't do with a new blouse or a pair of shoes. Some earrings, maybe?" She waved her fingers at Samantha. "Nail polish? Lipstick? A new belt? A bag?" She sat back when Samantha shook her head at all of them. "There's only one thing for it, then."

"What?"

"Costoso on Melrose." She pulled her purse toward her and began rummaging through it until she found her phone. "They give you mimosas and chocolate while you browse."

Suddenly the door burst open and Gary stood on the stoop, shoulders slumped, hair kinked out, eyes bloodshot.

"You look like grim death, Sophia," Liz said.

Gary came in and set his phone on the table between Samantha and Liz. "I have something to show you."

"Your latest escapades?" Liz asked.

"Noo. Not *my* escapades, anyway. Someone else broke the Internet overnight."

Samantha looked at him, even in her misery noticing that while he was volleying as usual with Liz, he'd completely ignored the *Walking Dead* reference, and the tone of his voice was different. Unlike Liz, he looked very hung over.

"Who, then? Kanye and Kim?" Liz asked. When no one laughed, Liz went on. "Listen, this isn't the greatest time. Samantha just…" She looked at Samantha, and when Sam nodded, she went on. "Evan knows about Samantha. Everything."

Gary's eyes bugged and he looked like he'd been goosed. "He saw this, too?" He picked up the phone and waved it around.

Samantha's heart dropped. "Saw what?"

"So, you don't…" Gary pulled at his hair. "Someone e-mailed me a YouTube link last night. From an anonymous Yahoo account." He blinked down at the phone. "I think you should watch it."

"I'm not going to like this, am I?" Samantha said.

"No," Gary said, tapping a couple times on his phone. "But if Evan already knows…But you didn't…" He slid the phone back between them on the table. "How'd he find out?"

Samantha peered suspiciously at the small screen. "It's a long story," she said weakly, as the theme music for *Celebrity Live!* played. "Gary, what is this?"

He gave her a look she couldn't quite read, something expressing both sadness and anger, and said, "Just watch."

The two co-hosts sat grinning their perfect white smiles behind the desk, looking happily at each other, as if they didn't hate each other and actually pulled each other's hair out between takes. Samantha shook her head at the memory, and crossed her arms tightly over her chest.

Julian and Lettie cheerfully introduced themselves, and then the camera panned toward Lettie for a close up of her face. Samantha noticed she wore her hair exactly the way Jennifer Aniston had hers now. "There was some excitement on the red carpet last night for the premiere of *In My Name*. There's a lot of Oscar buzz going around tinsel town for this movie—"

Samantha snorted. She couldn't believe they still called it "tinsel town." She looked back at the phone in time to see Evan on the screen. "I'm doing well," he said. "Making a new film, *Broken*, which should be out later in the year, and enjoying time with my son."

Back to Lettie, who leaned conspiratorially toward Julian and said, "Evan Gallagher escorted It girl Tiffany Lynn Stearling to that premiere, Julian. When asked, Evan said they were 'just friends,' of course. And for once, we believe an actor when they say that." She and Julian laughed as if this were the funniest thing ever said by any human being.

Samantha rolled her eyes. "This is still disgusting and inane. Why are we—" A picture flashed on the screen and she barely heard Lettie say, "...our very own *Celebrity Live!* alum, Sami Scandal, who was the one to break the story about Oliver Gallagher's abandonment, now seems to be creating a little scandal of her own with Evan..." before her ears started ringing and she pushed hard away from the table, but couldn't look away from the video, hands pressed to her mouth. The picture of Samantha as she had appeared on the show faded, and was replaced by one of her and Evan leaning up against a trailer, hugging and looking for all the world as if they were about to kiss.

"No..." she whispered into her hands. "Ohh, no." She shook her head. "No, no, no." She leaned over and pressed her head between her knees.

Vaguely, from somewhere very far away, she heard the phone skitter across the table and the sound stopped. She felt like her chest would burst. Like she'd drop right into the floor. Like she'd never be able to breathe again.

Like her world had just ended.

Gary, still sounding far away, said, "Smam?"

She shook her head, still pressing it between her knees. Someone put a hand on her shoulder and she heard Liz say, "He knows already, Sam. He heard about it before he could have seen this, right?"

Samantha lifted her head and looked at her, feeling as if she were hung over and people were telling her, "Hey, it's not that bad. You only took your top off in front of the President, not the Pope." She shook her head again. Tears threatened and she blinked them back. "So that's how Zoey knew. She said she saw Evan and his girlfriend on TV. The show was on at the party last night and I didn't even realize...Everyone's going to know who I am now," she whispered, looking from Liz to Gary, who sat on either side of her. "What I've done."

"Well, but—"

"No." Samantha held a hand up. "There's no good side to any of this." She stared at Gary, as another realization hit her. "This is going to kill your movie."

"Are you kidding?" Gary crowed. "Evan mentioned it. Publicity. Everyone's going to want to see it."

"Gary," Liz reprimanded.

Samantha jumped up from the chair and turned to face them. "You mean I tortured myself for two months, not telling Evan, to save your movie, when I could have told him right away, gotten it all out, and gotten you some free publicity from the start?" She threw her arms out from her sides, turned in a full circle, and slapped her hands against her thighs.

"Well, it's actually all in the timing," Gary said.

Liz socked him in the arm.

Samantha glared at him, then turned to stomp away. "Great. Just consider your free publicity machine shut down from this point on."

"Smam."

Liz jumped up to block her. "Wait a minute."

"Is my work on your movie done?" Samantha demanded.

"Well, yeah, technically, but—"

"Fine. I'll be on my way." Samantha veered around Liz and headed for the bedroom.

"That's just great," Liz called after her. "So you're going to quit this like you quit everything else."

Samantha turned to look at her. "Excuse me?"

"Quit. You're quitting."

"Like I quit everything else?"

"You ran away from *Celebrity Live!* and the situation with Evan, and us. You quit some job for *Honor Bound*. Then you ran away after the audition. Now you're quitting us again, and running away from Evan again. And yourself."

"I'm not quitting," Samantha said evenly, even though her heart was pounding so hard she felt like it would rocket her across the room. "I'm leaving to spare you any more embarrassment."

"Oh, please." Liz rolled her eyes. "Spare me *that*. You're deserting me, Gary and Evan."

"No, I'm not," Samantha barely squeaked out, her throat tight. "I don't have Evan to leave in the first place," she added, but didn't know how to defend herself against the accusation that she was deserting her friends.

Liz crossed her arms over her chest. "You're delusional." She glanced at Gary, sitting on the couch behind her and watching them. He raised an eyebrow, but said nothing.

Liz looked back at Samantha and threw her arms wide. "Delusional," she repeated. "The man is flat-out, drop-his-pants, spend-the-rest-of-his-life-with-you in love with you, and you're going to take off because you can't face it when things get tough."

Samantha took a step back. "He's not in love with me," she whispered.

"Okay. He's not in love with you. You're not going to break his heart if you sneak away in the night. But he is. And you are. So if you won't think about him, think about us." She gestured toward Gary and when she spoke again, her voice was soft. "You're going to break *our* hearts."

Gary spoke up from behind Liz. "Can I point out that while I'm not 'drop my pants' in love with you, I've been in love with you since the second we met, Smam."

Liz glared at him.

"You, too, of course, you delicate flower," he added to Liz, shrinking against the back of the couch.

Samantha snorted and put a hand over her mouth, not sure

whether to laugh or cry. So she did a little of both, then sat right down in the hallway entrance and looked at her friends.

"It's all too much," she finally said.

Liz sat down in front of her and Gary joined them a moment later.

"It's always too much," he said. "You have to pick your battles."

Samantha nodded. "You're right, you know," she said to Liz. "I run away from…well, everything."

"I know."

"Why didn't you tell me this before?"

"Couldn't catch up to you. And I assumed you'd figure it out yourself."

"I can't believe everyone's going to know. They're going to *know*," she repeated. "Who I am." She hit her thigh with a fist. "Who I was." She shook her head, looking down at her clenched hands. "I hate Sami. I hate her. I wanted her dead and buried. I can't believe they did that. They got rid of Sami when she embarrassed them, then they brought her back when it suited their purposes. I just can't believe it."

She pushed herself up and stood looking at the floor, but a noise and movement outside caught her attention. "Oh, no," she said, as a white van pulled into view, the familiar bright pink logo of her old employer clear through the window. "Oh, no," she repeated, then stared at Liz and Gary. "Reporters."

CHAPTER FORTY

T his is a little too *Days of Our Lives* here," Paul said as he pulled down a glass for Evan's beer.

Evan grabbed the bottle from him. "Don't bother," he said, waving away the glass. He drank half the bottle in one pull, then collapsed onto the stool behind Paul's bar. Paul's rec room took up one wing of his Malibu house and could have sheltered a small country. Evan liked coming here to get away from things—to hang out with Paul, play pool or just sit and watch the waves—but right now, he barely even registered where he was.

Paul studied him a moment, then said, "So Samantha is actually Sami Scandal who is the reporter who—"

"Tabloid reporter," Evan corrected, staring at his beer.

"Right." Paul waited a moment. "She's the one who broke the story about…"

"Yeah." Evan began to peel the label off the bottle.

"And *Celebrity Live!* had the gall to bring it up while you did press at a premiere."

"Yeah." Nancy had called with that news, but he'd refused to watch a copy of the segment. He was sure it was all over the gossip blogs by now, too.

"And you fell in love with this girl while you made *Broken*."

Evan jumped up as if he'd been pinched. "I'm not in love with her."

"Okay." Paul held up a hand. "You slept with her."

Evan settled back down. "I slept with the enemy, and she fucked me. Nice, huh?"

Paul winced. "Ouch."

"You don't know the half of it. I had to hear about it from *Zoey*."

Paul pulled a stool over and sat down across from Evan. "So it's more like Tim Burton does *Days of Our Lives*."

Evan gave him a little smile. "I think you might be developing a sense of humor there, Paulie." He took another swallow of beer and told Paul what had happened last night after he'd gone to find Samantha at the party. He skimmed over the sex, partly because it hurt too much to think about, but also because—despite the hurt—it was too private. Last night, he would have called it special. Not today.

Paul shook his head. "Amazing."

"That about says it."

"So what are you going to do?"

Evan stared at him for a moment. "About what?"

"The situation in Bosnia. What do you think?"

Evan grabbed his beer and stood up, then paced the burgundy rug in a tight circle. "There's nothing to do, man. Nothing."

"I thought you liked this girl."

Evan stopped pacing. "Did you miss the part where I told you she fucked up my life?"

"Did you miss the part where you fell in love with her?"

"It's not that simple. This isn't a movie, you know."

Paul held his hands out. "Never said it was."

Evan lowered his beer, then sat down again. "Right."

"So am I wrong?"

Evan stared down at the counter for a long time, not thinking anything specific, just feeling, the ache in his gut, the wrenching in his chest, the pain in his jaw from grinding his teeth for the past twelve hours. Finally he let out a breath he didn't even know he'd been holding. "No," he said. "You're not wrong." He swore a few more times, then dropped his head in his hands.

He was still reeling from everything. Whenever he thought about it, nothing matched up. It was like someone had slipped a mismatched piece into the puzzle box, and he couldn't make it fit no matter how many ways he turned it around. The problem was, everything else fit together. It was just that one rogue piece that threw everything off.

And that piece was a killer.

Take it away, and he loved Samantha and knew he wanted to be with her. Put it back into the mix, and it broke his heart. But no matter what, he couldn't get rid of that piece. And once again, he couldn't get rid of the damn paparazzi.

"It doesn't matter anyway," he told Paul now, raising his head.

"Why?"

Evan's frustration was so intense it felt close to rage. "Are you kidding? She blew my family apart. She blew my career apart. Oliver's life will never be the same since that story broke."

When Paul didn't say anything, Evan looked up at him. "What?"

"Not sure if I want you to hit me or not."

Evan squinted at him. "Just say it. You're going to, anyway."

Paul gave him a hint of a smile, finally saying, "Did you ever do something incredibly stupid when you were about twenty years old that you're thankful didn't get caught on camera?"

"Are you saying I should just chalk this up to a youthful indiscretion on her part?"

Paul shook his head. "Of course not. But it was stupid. And she was young. And did you wait around to find out why she did it? What she did about it later?"

Evan stared at him, gripping the beer bottle. "I didn't want to hear her excuses."

"Excuses? Or explanations."

Evan brought his bottle up, slammed it hard on the counter, then got up from the stool. "Whose side are you on?"

"It's not a contest, Evan," Paul said, holding his hands out again. "Don't walk out like this."

"Like what? Pissed off at the world because I got screwed over again?"

"That's pity talk."

"I've earned a little," Evan said, but he heard the petulance in his voice, and sat down again, not looking at Paul. The brush-off didn't stop his best friend, but Evan could've guessed it wouldn't. Deep down somewhere, he knew there was a reason he'd come to see Paul, and he knew also there was a reason he was still sitting here.

"Evan, this is the one thing you've held onto in your life. You don't wallow in pity. You take a bad situation and manage it. And if that doesn't work, you dig in, protect Oliver and wait for an opportunity to change it." Paul shifted on his stool, then continued.

"You've been through hell, man, I know that. What this girl did was stupid, but do you think she'd do it now?"

Evan flashed back to their first day of filming, when he helped her gather her dropped papers. *What I did*, she'd said. *It was disrespectful. I wish I could take it back.* He hadn't known then what she'd been talking about. Now he did. *You didn't deserve it, and I'm really sorry.* Then the night of the red carpet disaster, waking to find her curled up next to him. How he'd almost told her he loved her. Evan shook his head.

Paul waited a beat before adding, "You told me before any of this happened you knew your marriage wasn't going to last."

Evan started peeling the beer bottle label again.

"And you finally realized that in your career you'd been on a downhill slide of your own making."

Evan let out a breath, but didn't say anything.

"Do you want retribution?"

Evan shook his head again. "We did that already."

"Sued them and won," Paul said.

Evan knew Paul was still happy about that win. He hadn't wanted any part of it himself—he'd still been recovering from the situation, and knew suing a tabloid wouldn't put things into order again. His portion of the winnings had gone straight to a college account for Oliver.

"So what do you want to happen?"

"I just want to put this behind me and move forward."

"With or without the girl?"

And that was the question, wasn't it.

CHAPTER FORTY-ONE

Samantha stood on the doorstep of Evan's house, gathering her courage to ring his doorbell. She hitched her bag up on one shoulder, switched it to the other shoulder, let it slide down her arm to hold it by the handles, clutched it to her chest, then finally set it at her feet with a sigh.

He knew she was there; he had a security camera at the gate and without a sound from the intercom, the gate had rolled open when she drove up.

Thirty-seven days had passed since the night Evan found out her secret, and during that time, she'd sat down and done calculations whenever she felt herself going crazy. It was fifty-three thousand two hundred eighty minutes where she'd forced herself to stay in L.A. and not run away, and three million, one hundred ninety six thousand, eight hundred seconds where she'd had countless phone calls from reporters, friends and co-workers, both old and new, wanting her to confirm that she was, indeed, the infamous Sami Scandal. Her name and picture had already shown up on the tabloids and blogs, side by side with Evan's. Liz started calling her a living piece of irony.

She was still talking herself into ringing the bell, when Evan opened the front door, wearing faded jeans and a frayed paint-splattered dress shirt with the sleeves rolled up. She'd worn her red boots for courage.

"Hi." When he didn't reply, just stood there with a grim expression, she added, "Thank you for letting me in."

He crossed his arms over his chest and leaned against the jamb, not opening the door any wider, letting her know she could come up the driveway, but she wasn't welcome in his home.

"I did a terrible thing," she said without preamble, her words an echo of the ones she'd spoken that night he invited her to dinner, and she'd begun to explain everything then.

"Indeed." He stepped back and began to close the door.

"No," she said sharply. "Don't make me do that thing where I have to put my foot in the door. That only works in the movies. In real life, it just hurts." He paused, barely, not looking at her. "Please," she added, her voice breaking just a little on the word. "I have to stop running, and start facing things, and you deserve the whole story."

He raised his head to her, and she thought she saw something softer in his eyes, something to suggest he might actually listen to her—not enough to forgive her and keep falling in love with her, but enough to let each of them go on in peace after everything that had happened. That softness was gone in an instant, though, and she questioned whether she'd actually seen it.

Holding to the possibility, she kept going with her mission, giving him a condensed, but complete, version of the events surrounding her report to *Celebrity Live!* that night five years earlier. He didn't move as she spoke, didn't speak, barely seemed to blink, and she stuttered and stumbled a few times in the telling, but managed to get through it from beginning to end as straightforward as she could.

"So they fired me and I ran to North Carolina, started up a career there. When I heard *Honor Bound* would be ending, I got so depressed, I didn't look for another job, and even thought about quitting the business. Then Liz called and asked me to help with her movie. So I came. You pretty much know the rest."

She swallowed. He kept watching her, leaning there in the doorway, one hand on the doorknob, the other in his front pocket, his expression unreadable. She supposed it was a victory that he'd waited around this long. She figured she'd better not push it, but she sure wished he'd say something.

"Two more things. I'd been planning to tell you everything after the filming, and I'd tried plenty of times, but I never got it all out. I was so confused when I saw you that day in the gallery, so turned around when we started working together, and then...Walterville. Liz and Gary are my best friends and I was afraid if I told you, you'd quit the film, or make things impossible for them. Then, later, I was afraid you'd quit me.

"I never wanted to hurt you," she whispered. "Then or now. Especially not now, though, because…" Yes. She had to tell him, and damn the consequences. "I fell in love with you. Do with that what you will, but there it is."

She figured she should go now. She'd had her say. Beyond that one word, he'd been remarkably civil. But she couldn't leave things like this, without knowing how he felt.

"Please say something."

"You know what you did?" He stepped onto the front porch so fast she took a step back and would have stumbled if he hadn't caught her by the arm.

She shook her head, not sure what he was asking.

He grasped both of her shoulders, and glared down at her. "You got me to love someone when I didn't think I could do it again. You got me to trust and then you broke that trust. Why? Why'd you get involved with me?"

"You love me?" she asked, barely hearing the rest of it.

"Didn't I just say that," he growled. "I understand what happened. I don't like it, but I understand it. Everyone tells me I was self-destructing anyway, and I guess I knew that, just didn't want to admit it. I don't blame you for that damn tabloid report, but I do blame you for getting involved with me, knowing what you knew. Why?" he asked again. "Why did you do it?"

"I think I wanted to make it up to you," she told him as tears threatened. "Because I didn't know how to tell you, couldn't bring myself to tell you, although I tried. But then it was too late. I'd fallen in love with you, too. And I was scared."

"Damn it," he said, letting her go and flinging his arms out from his sides.

She wiped at her cheeks with the palms of her hands, not wanting to cry anymore. She also didn't want to keep going in a circle with him about what happened; they needed to finish this. "What's it going to take, Evan? What's it going to take for you to forgive me?" She straightened up, folding her arms over her chest, trying to be brave. "I won't ask you to keep loving me, but I need to make this right. In fact, I'm not leaving here until you tell me what it will take."

Mirroring her pose, he studied her. "You're not leaving until you get an answer?"

"That's right," she said, her voice breaking a little. Her heart beat so hard in her chest, she thought it would burst, but she held her ground.

He pulled her to him so fast she squeaked, kissed her until her knees went weak, then let her go just as abruptly. "Just bring me back my damn shirt."

"Are you kidding me?" she asked, reaching into the bag she'd set at her feet, and pulling out his old blue flannel. "Do you see what you'd be missing out on? I remember everything, I can translate days into minutes in my head, and I love you so damn much I take your shirt with me wherever I go."

He pressed his lips together and rubbed a finger across his upper lip. Not exactly a smile, but something.

Encouraged, she asked, "Who were you five years ago?"

"An idiot," he said, without hesitation. She wondered if he'd been pondering his past as much as she had hers lately. "But I'm not that person anymore."

"I'm not, either," she told him. "I thought because I wanted something badly enough, that excused my actions. The woman you got to know this time around is better than that. And she deserves a second chance."

"Hollywood loves a comeback."

"Didn't your publicist say that to you?" When he nodded, she asked, "Is she letting you go on a date in public yet?"

"No." He reached up, brushed a fingertip along her jaw, then pushed a lock of hair behind her ear. "But we'll have to face the tabloids together at some point, won't we?"

"Together?" she asked.

"If you'll have me."

It was her turn to nod, because she couldn't quite speak.

"I have a couple requests, though. No more secrets," he said. "And we need to take our time. Not only for us, but for Oliver."

She let out a breath. "Of course. Anything."

"No," he said, smiling at her. "Everything."

"Everything," she agreed as he took her in his arms.